Praise for the Cupcake Lovers series

Fool for Love

"Rich with emotional complexity and a cast of wonderfully rich characters, *Fool for Love* is an absolute treat."
—Kristan Higgins, *New York Times* bestselling author

"Ciotta writes with style, wit and heart. Can't wait for the next one!"
—Susan Andersen, *New York Times* bestselling author

"Ciotta is a master of the fun-to-read romance, and this outing is no exception."
—*RT Book Reviews* (Hot! 4 stars)

The Trouble With Love

"A great storyline with lots of twists and turns that include heartache, happiness, sadness, love, romance, quite a few secrets, laughter, tears, the small town of Sugar Creek . . . some mystery and darkness and then wonderful closure."   —*Romance Junkie Reviews*

"Hot romance, a little suspense, and a whole lot of charm."   —*RT Book Reviews* (Hot! 4 stars)

Anything But Love

"The core group of ladies that form the Cupcake Lovers Club all have a story to [tell and . . .] one of the best so far . . . Ciotta's books to be sexy

St. Martin's Paperbacks titles
by Beth Ciotta

Fool for Love

The Trouble with Love

Anything But Love

In the Mood for Love

in the mood for love

a cupcake lovers novel

BETH CIOTTA

St. Martin's Paperbacks

This is a work of fiction. All of the characters, organizations, and events portrayed in this novel are either products of the author's imagination or are used fictitiously.

IN THE MOOD FOR LOVE

Copyright © 2014 by Beth Ciotta.

For information address St. Martin's Press, 175 Fifth Avenue, New York, NY 10010.

ISBN: 978-1-250-00135-1

Printed in the United States of America

St. Martin's Paperbacks edition / July 2014

St. Martin's Paperbacks are published by St. Martin's Press, 175 Fifth Avenue, New York, NY 10010.

10 9 8 7 6 5 4 3 2 1

To my husband and real-life hero—Steve.
My rock, my love, my friend.

ACKNOWLEDGMENTS

Creating, getting to know, and writing about the Cupcake Lovers has been a unique challenge and sincere joy. Their romantic and quirky adventures are forever branded on my heart. A special thank you to my editor, Monique Patterson, for providing me with the opportunity to bring Sugar Creek to life.

I'd also like to acknowledge everyone at St. Martin's Paperbacks for their support. Most especially, this time around, Alexandra Sehulster and my publicist, Amy Goppert. Your kindness and enthusiasm is endearing and much appreciated.

My undying gratitude to my agent, Amy Moore-Benson— my champion and friend. A huge hug to Cynthia Valero for the most awesome brainstorming session ever, and to Elle J Rossi for critiquing every chapter as I wrote it and for keeping me sane and on track.

I'm blessed with amazing family and friends and I thank you all for your constant support! I'm forever grateful for the support from readers, booksellers, librarians, bloggers, and the wonderful people I've met in cyber-land. Thank you for everything! Cheers and Cupcakes!

AUTHOR'S NOTE

Though inspired by a northern region of Vermont, please note that Sugar Creek and the surrounding locations mentioned in this book are fictional. Escape and enjoy!

As an added bonus, in the ongoing celebration of cupcakes and camaraderie, we've included a few scrumptious recipes from Honorary Cupcake Lovers. My heartfelt appreciation to the amazing Gina Husta, JoAnn Schailey, Mary Stella, and Dawn Jones for sharing their cupcake-a-licious delights!

ONE

Marriage is a dinner that begins with dessert.
—Toulouse-Lautrec

The Kelly twins.

Double your pleasure, double your fun.

The lyrics of a gum commercial ran through Sam Mc-Cloud's head alongside several racy thoughts.

Two women at once.

Every man's dream.

Sam could live out that fantasy. All he had to do was take Krissy up on the offer she'd whispered in his ear. Or was it Katie? He'd never been able to tell them apart. They were in their mid-twenties. Blond, spray-tanned Barbies who dressed alike, talked alike, and even wore their hair and makeup exactly the same. Which struck Sam as odd. Just one of the reasons he'd declined their tempting offer. They also giggled too much and were intellectual pinheads. Not that that had bothered Sam's cousin Nash Bentley—who walked up to the bar just as Sam sent the girls away.

"You don't know what you're missing," Krissy (or Katie) said to Sam.

"Tell him, Nash," Katie (or Krissy) said with a wink and a giggle.

"Never kiss and tell," Nash said as he perched on the

stool next to Sam. But he did smile—the smile of a man who'd had the ride of his life. Considering Nash, a charter pilot and hot-air-balloon operator, drank thrills with his morning coffee, a tumble with the Kellys must've been a mind-bending rush.

Sam focused on his beer, not wanting to give the twins a reason to double back and double their efforts. If they were seriously on the prowl then pickings were slim. The Sugar Shack, owned by another cousin, Luke Monroe, was sparsely occupied. Not unusual given it was a weeknight and shoulder season for their small tourist town, but unlucky for Sam who wanted to be left alone. "Are they gone?"

"Slipped into the john." Nash motioned to the new hire, Joelle Jenner—a personable, crackerjack bartender, who didn't mind the late shift since Luke had mostly switched to days. Joey (as her nametag read) nodded and nabbed a chilled beer while sliding another customer a bowl of mixed nuts. Her counterpart, Decker, who pulled double duty as bouncer, hovered at the opposite end of the bar manning the TV remote and surfing stations. "Swear to God, the dude's got ADD," Nash said.

Sam was still thinking about the Kellys. "Don't you think it's strange that the twins do everything together?"

"Chicks always go to the head in packs."

"Not that."

"Oh."

"It didn't bother you?"

Nash grinned. "Oh, I was bothered."

"I mean that they're sisters."

"Twins."

"Which is—"

"Hot?"

"Inappropriate."

"Like you've never fantasized."

Sam didn't answer.

Nash took a pull off his longneck then laughed when he

caught Sam glancing toward the ladies' facility. "Having second thoughts?"

"Smutty thoughts."

"So much for being a monk."

"Who said—"

"Laura Payne. Two dates and you didn't kiss her once."

"That makes me chaste?"

"You didn't make a move on Alana Foster or Kady Bridges, either."

Sam glanced at Joey who was mixing a drink and suppressing a smile while stealing looks over the thick black frames of her glasses. The twenty-something heartland transplant was also the newest member of the Cupcake Lovers, the town's longtime social and baking club. A club devoted to supporting soldiers and various charities. Sam, who enjoyed baking as well as the camaraderie, was also a member of that club. He didn't know Joey well enough to know if she was a gossip, but he wasn't keen on this convo getting back to the CLs . . . or anyone else for that matter. He nabbed his mug then nudged Nash. "I see an empty table."

There were lots of empty tables. Sam chose one by the cobblestone hearth, far from the action of pool sharks or barflies or bartending eavesdroppers. Sugar Creek, Vermont, thrived on gossip. As a widowed father of two young children, Sam flew under the radar as best he could. Another reason he'd turned down a dose of double delight. Like he needed that kind of news getting back to his kids. Explaining the meaning of *threesome* or *ménage à trois* to Ben and Mina was not on his agenda anytime soon. *Never* suited even better.

Toting three cold ones, Nash set a bottle in front of Sam then settled in with the other two. "Women talk, cuz."

As someone who juggled female friends the way Sam juggled playdates for his daughter, Nash had no doubt gotten an earful from the eligible women Sam had crossed off his "wife" list. "What are they saying?"

"You don't want to know."

Sam countered with one of his death stares. Most people crumbled after five seconds. Nash broke after one sip.

"There's a pool," he said, while picking at the bottle's label.

"A betting pool?" There'd been a lot of those lately. The biggest being based on the gender and birthdate of another cousin's first baby.

Nash nodded.

"Go on."

"When you ask a woman out she assumes you're attracted. Sexually," Nash emphasized as if Sam needed clarification. "Touching. Kissing. Trying to get in her pants. Granted, not every woman's going to tweak your pole, but you've been out with how many women in the past month and a half?"

Thanks to Sam's matchmaking family and friends, and especially the Cupcake Lovers, *a lot*.

"And how many have you seduced?" Nash asked even though Sam hadn't answered his first question. His Casanova cousin curled his fingers in the shape of a *zero*. "At first Laura blamed herself, questioning her weight, but then she got talking to Kady, who'd already spoken to Alana, who'd overheard, well, you get the picture. I heard it from Viv Underwood."

Sam's most disastrous date.

"So now the general consensus is, it's not them, it's you."

Sam couldn't argue. He'd said as much when any of his mismatched dates had noted his distant manner.

"There's speculation," Nash said.

"Hence the betting pool." Sam glanced at his watch. "Speed it up, flyboy. Only booked the sitter till eleven."

Looking uncomfortable now, Nash leaned forward and lowered his voice. "For what it's worth, no one thinks you're gay. Given your history, the kids . . ." He cleared his throat. "Some of the girls are betting you can't get it up. A war injury."

Sam arched a brow.

"Others think you're crippled emotionally because of Paula."

Not long ago, that conjecture would have been dead on. Sam's heart had iced over after losing his beloved wife to cancer, but then last year he'd met Rae, who was now Luke's wife. Though Rae had never returned Sam's tender regard, she had sparked his numb spirit back to life. A few months after, he'd met Harper Day, a self-absorbed celebrity publicist who'd torched his senses with a sporadic, kinky affair. No one knew about that affair, so of course everyone assumed Sam hadn't been laid in close to three years. All Sam had to do was tell Nash about Harper and all bets would be off—his reputation as a sane, virile man intact.

But Sam didn't screw and tell, either.

"You asked," Nash said, mistaking Sam's silence for anger.

Sam wasn't pissed. He was restless.

Just then the Brody brothers—Adam and Kane— strolled in. Adam was a freelance sports instructor. Kane, a local logger. Both single. Both fixtures at the Shack. Instead of taking their usual seats at the bar, they joined Sam and Nash.

"Nothing against Joey and Decker," Adam said as he dropped into a chair, "but they're not Luke."

"*Luke*'s not Luke," Kane said. "Not as we knew him. Not that I'm jealous of the time he spends with his wife—"

"Yes you are," Adam said. "Rae gained a husband and the Shack lost its greatest host. Even when Luke's here his mind is somewhere else."

Adam and Kane, especially Adam, went way back with Luke. Sam didn't take offense to their comments. But he did feel compelled to defend his younger cousin. Something he might not have done six months ago when they'd been at war regarding Rae. "Luke didn't desert the Shack. He stepped up his game. New wife. Soon-to-be dad. Coaching the kids at Rae's school."

"As for the slump," Nash put in, "business is down everywhere."

"Luke's late-night presence wouldn't ensure bigger crowds," Sam said.

"Yeah. But *we'd* have more fun," Kane said. "Decker messes with our feng shui."

"Don't ask," Adam said.

"Speaking of *out of place*," Kane said. "Surprised to see you hanging at the Shack on a weeknight, McCloud."

"Hanging" at any bar hadn't meshed with Sam's lifestyle in years. He spent most of his nights at home with the kids. That's not to say he was a hermit. His carpentry work kept him out and about, and he spent plenty of time with the Cupcake Lovers. The club gathered every Thursday and participated in several annual events. They'd recently published a recipe book that had led to even more activity. Sam was tired of the growing attention and they had Harper to thank for the budding media frenzy. Not that Sam had seen the bicoastal publicist in weeks.

"Wait a minute," Nash said. "Why *are* you here?" He angled his head, frowned. "Tell me you had a date tonight and blew her off."

Sam shrugged. "We had dinner."

"Who was the girl?" Kane asked.

Sam polished off his beer, bracing for the men's reaction. After all, tonight's match-up had been with one of Sugar Creek's hottest and smartest women. "Jane Dunlap."

Adam whistled low. "And you're here drinking suds with Bentley instead of playing doctor with Nurse Dunlap?"

"If you think that's something," Nash said, "guess who else he shot down tonight? The Kelly twins."

"Oh, man." Adam dragged a hand down his face, stifling a laugh.

"Damn, McCloud," Kane said, looking half shocked, half amused. "You do know they're selective, right? And you passed? No wonder there's a bet—"

Adam nudged his brother.

"Sam knows about the pool," Nash said.

"Not that we're part of it," Kane said. "Although maybe the twins are."

Adam shifted. "If you want my advice—"

"Pass." Sam straightened as Willa, the only waitress on duty tonight, approached their table. She smiled. He tensed. He knew that look and he wasn't interested. She was pretty and sweet, but he didn't feel a flicker of heat. Instead, he had a vision of Harper, posing in a red silk bra and panties, seductively sucking cupcake icing from her thumb.

Damn.

Quick on the uptake, Willa flushed and turned her attention to Adam and Kane. "The usual?"

"As usual," Adam said, returning the smile Sam had withheld.

"Do you miss Luke?" Kane asked, stealing Willa's attention.

"I do. Then again, I mostly work nights and he mostly works days. He comes in awfully early," she said, "and he pores over the books and inventory, plus tending bar and hosting happy hour. Luke may have cut back on his overall hours but he works even harder than before. All for his wife and baby." Willa hugged her order pad to her chest and heaved a dreamy sigh. "Oh, to be in love."

Everyone at the table liked Willa so they bit their tongues. Everyone at the table liked Rae and had been friends with Luke forever. Wisecracks were definitely out. Luke, the town's former number one Romeo, was a lucky son of a bitch and they all knew it.

"Could we get an order of Nachos Grande with those beers?" Kane asked.

"Sure thing," Willa said with a bright smile. "Four plates?"

"Not for me," Sam said.

Nash flashed three fingers.

Willa peeled away and Kane leaned in. "What is it with this town lately? It's like everyone's been shot by cupid and bitten by the baby bug."

Nash nodded. "Dev and Chloe, Luke and Rae, Jayce and Rocky . . . although Rocky isn't pregnant. Yet."

"Yeah, but Monica and Leo are having twins," Kane said. "All I can say is, I'll be doubling up on condoms."

"That's if you ever get laid again," Adam said with a ribbing glance toward Sam. "Now that he's back in the game, all the women have their sights set on McCloud."

"And he's casting them off like flies," Kane said. "All I need to do is stick close and pick up the broken pieces of their pretty shattered hearts."

Sam gave him the finger.

Nash laughed.

Adam glanced at the plasmas hanging over the bar. "If Luke were here, we'd be watching ESPN."

"At least it's not a shopping network," Kane said. "Although what is it?"

"The Travel Channel. No, wait. He's switching. The weather." Nash finished one beer and started on the other. "We need to find a new hang. Not all the time, just once in a while. Something to shake up the monotony."

"Have you checked out the new bowling alley?" Adam asked.

"Rock 'n' Roll Lanes," Kane said. "How cheesy can you get?"

"I don't know," Nash said. "Music, bowling, and beer. What's not to like?"

"Took Ben and Mina on opening day," Sam said, happy to talk about anything other than his train-wreck dating spree. "They're especially kid friendly Saturday and Sunday afternoon. Nice atmosphere. Decent staff. Heard they cater mostly to adults after eight."

"Come summer," Adam said, "that place will be jammed with tourists."

"So maybe we should feel it out now," Nash said. "During slow season. Bowling night. Once a week. A couple of hours of sports and beer."

"What the hell," Kane said. "I'm in."

"I'll bite," Adam said. "What about you, Sam?"

"At the rate you're going," Nash teased, "it's not like you're going to hook up with Mrs. Right any time soon."

"We'll try not to corrupt you," Kane ribbed.

Someone beat you to it, Sam thought. If they only knew about his racy fling with Harper. But he wouldn't tell. Hell, he was trying to forget. Maybe he needed to shake things up, hang with the guys. Between his five-year-old daughter's obsession with tiaras, boas, and Miss Kitty, coupled with all the recent baby talk, matchmaking efforts, and additional baking tasks within the Cupcakes Lovers, Sam was OD'ing on women. And not in a good way. "Yeah, sure. Pick a night."

"Any night but Thursday," Nash said as Willa served up spicy nachos and cold brews. "That's Sam's night with the Cupcake Lovers."

Whereas Sam used to take solace in the camaraderie of the club, lately he'd been feeling like a fifth wheel. Not to mention, even though Harper didn't live in Sugar Creek full-time, she'd become the Cupcake Lovers' official publicist. Even though they'd cooled their secret affair, Sam still burned for that irritating woman. Which had pretty much crippled his efforts to find new love and the best mother for his kids.

"Actually," Sam said, suddenly desperate to escape all things cupcake, "Thursdays are perfect."

TWO

Harper Day greeted the morning with an obstinate smile and an optimistic attitude. Wednesday had sucked, almost as bad as Tuesday and twice as bad as Monday. She didn't even want to think about Sunday. But today, Thursday, would be the flip side of suckville.

This morning, she would conquer her anxiety enough to walk across her massive backyard to the edge of the small pond. She'd sit on the pier and dangle her toes in the water. She'd breathe in the fresh mountain air. Later, she'd venture to her rented car and drive to the end of the lane. Surely she could make it that far without freaking. She'd idle and breathe and think good thoughts. Maybe she'd conduct business via texts and e-mail. A phone call or two. Anything to detour morbid thoughts.

If that went well (and it would), she'd drive a little farther. She'd think happy thoughts, tune in to a sugary pop station and crank the volume. She would *not* obsess on the numerous possibilities of a horrible violent end while driving her car into town. Chances of being rammed by a suicidal driver or blown to bits by some terrorist missile were slim to none. She would *not* obsess on that "slim" percentage.

Harper stared up at the ceiling of her almost-but not-quite-wholly-renovated getaway, garnering the courage to roll out of bed and seize the day, still smiling even though her optimism had slipped a notch. She wasn't alone in her misery.

Local legend Mary Rothwell, a long-ago previous owner of this house and an original Cupcake Lover, had stared up at this ceiling hundreds of times. Granted, that had been back in the 1940s, but this was the same ceiling and this had been Mary's bedroom. Even though Harper had never seen the ghost of the woman who supposedly haunted this house, she definitely *felt* Mary. Or at least, commiserated with her restless soul. That's why Harper had specifically bought this farm. To fill a void in Mary's life, to connect with a kindred spirit. Harper had a lot in common with Mary. She would not, however, meet the same end. Harper was made of sterner stuff. She'd get through this rough patch and get on with life.

Today.

Motivated, Harper shot out of bed. She grabbed a remote and turned on the wall-mounted plasma screen while padding to her desk to fire up her laptop. She'd had a wall knocked out in order to create a combo bedroom/office—a comfortable, functional living space while the rest of the rooms were under renovation. Multitasking as always, she used one hand to tune in VH1 while the other keyed up CNN. She nabbed her phone and quickly checked for texts, e-mails, and PMs on her Twitter and Facebook accounts. No urgent pleas from any of her clients. No fires to put out. *That* was disappointing. Harper thrived on snuffing fiascoes and solving problems. Then again, kudos to her tribe for staying out of trouble for at least one night.

On the other hand, there was also the chance that they'd taken their crisis to someone else. Harper hadn't been the most hands-on publicist these last few weeks. Although she'd worked hard to meet her clients' needs via telecommunications, she'd bailed on several premieres and luncheons. Crowds weren't her thing just now. Wide-open spaces, public places weren't her thing just now. A liability given her line of work. A glitch she was striving to overcome. As a last resort, she'd flown from her home base in Los Angeles to the home she'd created in Sugar Creek. Her retreat. Her safe haven. A relatively isolated nonworking farm on the fringes of a small town in northern Vermont. Far away from her needy clients and demanding PR firm. Yes, they could still contact her, and she was counting on it, but they weren't likely to show up on her doorstep or insist they meet at a trendy restaurant or popular bar to discuss business. She needed private time to pull it together. A week or two. Maybe three, depending. Not that she didn't deserve a holiday. Harper had a reputation for working 24/7. No matter what time of day someone needed her, she was there.

Until recently.

Satisfied none of her clients were presently drowning in scandal, Harper peeled off her satin cami and boxers and pulled on a sports bra and capris. A health-and-fitness junkie, she worked out religiously. Exercise also helped to reduce stress. On any normal day, Harper was wound tight. She couldn't forget the tragedy and the threats that had inspired her to flee Canada three years back, but she could stem the guilt and worry by keeping insanely busy and spinning other people's lives for the better. In her case, that meant saving reckless or screwed-up celebrities from countless missteps and fiascoes. Taking control of their crises helped her to manage her own sense of helplessness. She'd been episode-free for almost a year. Partly because the man who'd sworn to "never let her forget" had finally given up. Or at least Harper had finally managed to block him from every aspect of her life.

Until last month.

Until the spa shooting.

Soon after, he'd crawled out of his hole long enough to hack his way into her work e-mail.

"Not going there."

Heart thudding, Harper stonewalled the memory of the recent senseless crime and the subsequent cruel taunt issued by the father of her former fiancé. Edward Wilson hadn't given up on making Harper's life hell. He'd just allowed her a false sense of hope.

"Bastard."

She hadn't heard from Edward again since that one e-mail three weeks ago, and she couldn't help hoping—again—that that had been his final jab. She understood his grief, but how would he ever heal if he clutched so tightly to the past? She'd asked herself that same question a million times and that's why she worked so hard to press on. Rather than wallow, she'd kicked into high gear. She'd donned invisible armor and a virtual cape. Harper Day to save the day.

Shoving Edward Wilson from her mind, she focused on a VH1 news bite featuring the celebrity troubled kid of the month. *Not* Rae Monroe, formerly Rae Deveraux. Thank God. Harper had worked magic to free the young heiress from the Hollywood gossip mill. Not an easy feat when the girl had a wacko, self-absorbed, attention-hungry former starlet for a mother. Tabloid sensation Olivia Deveraux. Just *one* thorn in Harper's side.

No longer smiling but channeling zippety-do-dah positivity, she twisted her long, thick hair into a high ponytail, snagged the water bottle off her nightstand and hydrated. She'd prefer a mug of java, but she'd nixed caffeine from her daily routine until her debilitating anxiety was more manageable. Alcohol was out, too. In her present mental state, a glass of wine induced melancholy instead of a mellow buzz.

No caffeine. No alcohol. Plenty of exercise and sleep.

She was beginning to feel like a freaking nun in addition to a freaked-out shut-in.

Sex would take off the edge.

Sex with Sam McCloud, the first man she'd slept with since Andrew, would be the ultimate.

Sex with Sam would obliterate every thought in Harper's head. She couldn't stress if she couldn't think. Too bad she'd sworn off the hunky carpenter along with caffeine. She'd kill for a dose of his electrifying heart-melting machismo. A Boy Scout and a bad boy rolled into one. The bad came out in bed. The best kind of bad. The kind of bad that whipped Harper into an orgasmic frenzy.

VH1 news segued into a music video, a sexy grind of a song that made her think about the way Sam rocked her body . . . in bed . . . against the wall . . . on the counter . . .

Desperate for distraction, Harper skimmed channels, landing on *Good Morning America,* hoping for a cooking or health segment and instead catching an interview with actor Dylan McDermott—who looked a lot like Sam McCloud. Only Sam was broader. Definitely more ripped. His eyes were a deeper blue and his hair, the same dark brown in need of a trim or taming. Ruggedly handsome, not pretty handsome. Mark Wahlberg/Jason Statham charismatic. Action-star hot. And he wondered why she called him "Rambo."

So much for distraction.

Harper climbed on her indoor bike, wishing she were mounting Sam instead.

"Great."

Why wouldn't that man stay out of her brain, her blood? She'd been in town for a few days and she hadn't texted him once. Texting—their only comfortable mode of communication. The strong silent type, Sam doled out casual conversation like a miser whereas Harper talked incessantly to keep from thinking too deeply. Dark things lurked in the depths of her mind. Shallow was safer.

She glanced at her phone, thought about Sam, then *nixed* the thought of Sam. "Not going there."

She stepped up the pace, looked back to the screen. McDermott, who still reminded her of McCloud (except Dylan was laughing and Sam never laughed), was talking about his latest project. She'd never handled a big star like Dylan, but she'd handled Sam. Her fingers burned in memory. The faster she pedaled the more she craved the irritating man who'd worked wonders refurbishing her house. The more her heart raced, the greater her lust. The man was screaming alpha. Former military. Confident. Competent. A master carpenter and furniture maker who also painted and baked.

Baked!

He was also a widower with two little kids.

Harper had minimal experience with children and she didn't want children—or rather the responsibility of children. The thought of failing them or losing them to some horrid end iced her blood. Which is why she'd ultimately cut off her secret affair with Sam. Even though it was just sex. Even though they only saw each other whenever she visited Sugar Creek which was hardly ever. They'd never work long term. Not that she wanted long term. Not that he wanted long term with her. Via gossip among the Cupcake Lovers, her newest clients, Sam wanted a mother for his children. Harper was *not* mother material.

So, yeah. No. She would not text Sam. There would be no racy exchanges. No amazing sex. No Sam.

No. Sam.

Heart pounding, sweat trickling, Harper pumped her stationary bike and stared out the same window Mary Rothwell had dogged for two long years. Mary had had blinding faith that her husband, a soldier gone missing in World War Two, would return. To her. She'd never lost faith in her beloved.

That's where Harper and Mary differed.

"Not. Going. *There*."

No dwelling on how she'd failed Andrew. Or how he'd wigged out. A public meltdown. A violent display. So like the spa shooting, although not really. Only in Harper's wounded mind.

Chest hurting, she pedaled past the pain. She would make it to the lake. She'd make it to the end of the lane. She'd make it into Sugar Creek. She'd disappointed a lot of people recently, but she would not disappoint the Cupcake Lovers. And while she was there, maybe she'd say hi to Sam just to be sociable. It's not that she didn't like him. It's that she liked him too much.

THREE

*This isn't easy for me . . . I've been thinking . . . Life's
funny . . .*
   Damn.
   None of the opening lines Sam rehearsed felt right. Bottom line, he was bailing on an important organization. On
the women who'd freely accepted him as the first male
member of the Cupcake Lovers. They'd welcomed him
into their world and now he was leaving at a crucial time.
He wasn't arrogant but he was savvy. He didn't need Harper,
a professional publicist, to tell him he was a valuable asset
to the club when it came to generating additional attention.
He was former military. A marine who'd served multiple
tours overseas. And now he was baking cupcakes for other
marines and every other branch of the military.
   He got why he was a perk to the club and he'd rolled with
it. He was all about the cause although, granted, he'd joined
the Cupcake Lovers as a way to shake up his morbid mind-
set after Paula's death. A selfish reason, but he'd honestly
enjoyed the company of his fellow bakers. Then he'd fallen
for Rae and there'd been that mess. He'd fooled around with
Harper and now she was involved in the club. Another potential mess. In the last months, a few of the members had
gotten engaged or married and three were expecting babies.

The dynamics of the club were changing. The discussions more out of Sam's realm. The "fame" factor was the tipping point. If he shared his reasoning, no one would blame him for quitting. Except Sam wasn't one for baring his soul. *I've lost my cupcake mojo* was the best he could do. Hopefully they'd read into that and let him go without a fight.

"Would you mind lending me a hand, Sam?"

He'd been deep in thought. So deep that Rae's soft voice startled him. Sam glanced at the woman he'd been enamored with for a good year, a woman he'd hoped to make his wife, a woman whose sweet disposition resembled that of his late wife. Like Paula, Rae would have been the perfect mother for Ben and Mina. Trouble was, she'd fallen for and married Luke. The match had been quick and seemingly written in the stars. Sam was happy for his cousin and for Rae, but damn, he was envious of their easy bliss.

"You okay?" Rae asked, and Sam realized he was probably staring like a moonstruck teen. Uncomfortable, since he'd put that infatuation to rest. Like his cousin Rocky had pointed out, Sam hadn't been in love with Rae as much as the *idea* of Rae. Unfortunately, it had taken him a while to get that, involving some pretty ass-wipe behavior on his part. Thankfully, all had been forgiven, all friendships intact. Still, there were times when Sam thought it best to walk on eggshells.

"I'm good." Pushing off the doorjamb, Sam smiled down at the mild-tempered philanthropist. Transforming the town's defunct day-care center into a thriving preschool with latchkey educational and sports programs for children up to ten was just one of Rae's good deeds. "What do you need?"

"Help in the kitchen."

Every member of the club took turns hosting the weekly meeting. Tonight they'd gathered at Rae and Luke's home, a charming single-family house that sat on several acres of land. Rae was worth a fortune. She could afford a mansion. She preferred a simple life with Luke. A grounded life for their soon-to-be child. Sam's heart jerked with affection. Or maybe it was simple respect. Man, he was off his game tonight.

The animated chatter of the Cupcake Lovers faded as Sam followed Rae from the living room to the kitchen. Along the way he noted the changes she'd made since the last time he'd been here. Rae had Paula's flair for whimsical warmth. He ignored the pang of melancholy. Paula was in the past. Rae was Luke's. Sam had to fricking move on.

"What's going on with you?" Rae asked as they breached the kitchen, a cheerful room recently painted in shades of lemon and lime.

"What do you mean?"

"Everyone else is bouncing off the wall thrilled about the exposure and sales thus far for *Cupcake Lover's Delectable Delights*. Instead of joining in the excitement, you were holding up the wall in a brooding funk."

"I don't brood."

"Could have fooled me."

"I was thinking."

"Broody thoughts."

Sam's lip twitched. "Why am I here?"

"To help me with the teakettle."

Yeah, boy, *that* was fishy. Rae was one of the most capable and self-reliant women he knew. "You can't carry a teakettle?"

"If you ask Luke, I shouldn't even carry a cup of sugar. I'm only five and a half months pregnant and he treats me like an invalid."

"He loves you. He worries."

"I know. And that makes me the luckiest and happiest woman in the world. It's just . . ." She smiled and shrugged as she dialed down the burner. "He's driving me crazy. I think we're spending too much time together. Every couple should have breathing space, individual hobbies, right? I feel awful saying it, but I'm glad he quit the Cupcake Lovers."

"Luke was never a natural fit. His baking sucked."

She shot him a chastising look. "Not for lack of trying."

When it came to friends, family, and worthy causes, the usually demure redhead was quick to rile. "Don't get bent," Sam said kindly. "Just stating facts. Ask Daisy or Rocky or—"

"I'm not bent. I'm . . ." She narrowed her eyes. "How did the spotlight turn to me? I hate that."

He knew that. He loved that. Harper, on the other hand, glommed onto anything that put her in the forefront of a celebration or crisis.

Rae set the kettle on a heating pad and reached for a canister of tea bags. "Seriously, what's troubling you, Sam?"

He preferred to break it to the club as a whole—a surprise attack. He knew, one-on-one, Rae would do her best to talk him out of quitting the CLs. "Nothing."

"I know Ben's been taking some heat from his classmates—"

"Ben's fine."

"There's been talk among some of the single women regarding your recent dates."

"I know."

"Luke says—"

"There's a betting pool. I know."

"I think it's awful."

Sam hadn't given it a second thought but he was touched that Rae cared. Then again, Rae cared about everyone.

"You can't force love," she said.

"I know." Sam tucked his hands in his jeans instead of touching her arm. He didn't want her to misconstrue his attentions. Months back, before he'd known about the attraction between Luke and Rae and even *after* he'd known, Sam had told Rae he was okay with being just friends. He'd lied. And then he'd pushed. He'd been unfair to her and a bastard to Luke. But he'd been desperate to move beyond Paula. The wonder of Paula. The grief of Paula. Why couldn't he be attracted to Jane Dunlap or Laura Payne? Interesting, *hot* women with stable, meaningful careers. Desperate to change the subject, Sam gestured to the stocked three-tiered cupcake holder standing on the opposite counter. The featured cupcake of the evening. All part of the weekly meeting tradition. "What's on the agenda?"

"A new recipe I've been dying to share with everyone." Rae grinned. "I call them Kick-in-the-Pants Kupcakes. *Cupcakes* spelled with a *k*."

Intrigued, Sam folded his arms, angled his head. "What's the kick?"

"Cinnamon and cayenne pepper in *both* the dark chocolate cupcake and the cream cheese icing."

"Feeling adventurous, huh?"

"I admit to some recent odd cravings, but I swear, Sam, these are the shiz."

"The what?"

"The *shiz*. The shit. The coolest."

"Got it." Sam, who was not the coolest, filed *shiz* away with all the other jargon he'd been hearing lately from his nine-year-old son. Harper was another one who tossed around the latest slang and acronyms. Sam couldn't decide if he was an old fart or just old-fashioned. His fortieth was around the corner. Hell, maybe he was both. He gestured to the tea bags. "And the beverage to counter the kick? Chamomile? Green tea?"

"Raspberry Zinger. Although I'll be adding hazelnut creamer to mine."

Sam laughed. "How's Luke holding up with your cravings?"

"He's particularly fond of anything having to do with ice cream and cookies. Pickles and radishes, not so much. I'll come back for the cupcakes. Mugs are already out there. Let's serve tea."

Sam had hoped to resign and leave before tea, but, with two kids, he was also used to adjusting his plans on the fly.

"I'll take the kettle. You tote the bags. I assume my cousin won't have a gripe about one lightweight jar," he teased.

She rolled her eyes. "You've met Luke, right?"

Yeah. A man who, although in his past had been a major skirt-chaser, was always, and above all, devoted to family. "He'll get over it."

"Just know that you can confide in me or Luke or both of us anytime, Sam. We're here for you. Just tell us—"

"You're a good woman, Rae."

"There are lots of good women, Sam, but, like great cupcakes, not all of them are sugary sweet. *Your* perfect cupcake could be the one with kick. And if you sink in deep enough, long enough, maybe you'll taste the sweet among the spice. My advice? Get adventurous."

Armed with the canister and a stack of napkins, Rae breezed out of the kitchen leaving Sam to ponder her words.

Then it hit. *With the force of a fricking sledgehammer.*

In that moment, Sam realized the reason none of the women he'd dated over the last weeks had won his interest was because they'd failed to match up to his first wife in the first ten minutes. Just as he'd done with Rae, he'd been looking for a clone of Paula. And then, yeah, if he was being totally honest, Harper, who wasn't anything like Paula, had him twisted up—sexually, if not emotionally.

Head spinning, Sam hurried after Rae, catching up just as she entered the crowded living room.

"Tea's ready," she announced in a gleeful voice.

"Perfect timing," Rocky called over the excited chatter. "Take a seat, everyone. Let's get down to business."

Rocky was one of Sam's many cousins and, lately, one of his closest friends. President of the Cupcake Lovers. Sister to Luke and Dev Monroe. Granddaughter of Daisy Monroe, a senior Cupcake Lover (and a bit of a wack job). Rocky was the glue that held the club together as they encountered more attention and responsibility.

"What's the beverage of the evening?" she asked as everyone vied for a seat and Sam and Rae served.

"Raspberry Zinger," Rae said.

"Spiked with vodka?" Daisy asked.

Rocky snorted. "It's not cocktail hour, Gram."

"It's five o'clock somewhere!"

The other senior members, all in their seventies, and still kicking cupcake ass, snickered.

Sam smiled, scanning every face as he set aside the kettle and sat on the vacant leather ottoman. His sweeping gaze stuttered on Joey. She looked out of place. Mostly because this was only her second meeting and Sam wasn't used to her presence. Partly because she favored what Chloe called "cyberpunk" fashion. She also sported combat boots and a diamond stud in her nose. Not exactly how he envisioned a girl from Nebraska.

Every other woman in the room, aside from Daisy, had a more conventional look. Ethel, Helen, Judy, Monica, Chloe, Rae, Rocky, Casey . . . Every member involved in the Cupcake Lover recipe/memoir book, except for their past president, Tasha Pain-in-the-Ass Burke, who had since moved to Arizona—thank God.

Sam cracked his neck, gathered his thoughts. He wanted to break the news before they broke out the cupcakes. He hadn't anticipated feeling this awkward. Former military or not, deserting his colleagues wasn't his style. Then again neither was being in the spotlight and, thanks to Harper, several interviews and book signings were in the club's immediate future.

"So much going on," Rocky said, while sipping tea. "I don't know where to begin."

"I'll start," Sam said.

"Where's Harper?" Daisy asked. "We texted earlier and she told me she was definitely coming."

"She must be running late," Casey said.

"I vote to delay any important discussions until she

shows," Daisy said. "As our publicist she needs to know what's what."

"The Cupcake Lovers have been thriving since the forties," Ethel, another senior member, said. "We've never needed a publicist to monitor meetings."

"That was then, this is now." Daisy sniffed and pushed her neon-green bifocals up her nose. "Get with the times, Ethel."

"Come down to earth, Daisy."

"Ladies," Rocky cautioned.

Daisy waved off her granddaughter and pulled her phone from her rainbow-colored purse. "I'll send Harper a quick text, ask for an estimated time of arrival."

"Just type *EST* with a question mark," Sam said. Daisy, who'd been addicted to texting ever since Chloe had exposed her to the process, insisted on typing out every word, which made for some long-ass texts. They'd all been subjected to them, all except Ethel who didn't own a smartphone.

"I spoke to Harper on the phone yesterday. Briefly," Rae said as she passed around plates and napkins. "She doesn't seem like herself."

"She's been back at the farm for almost a week," Rocky said. "We've spoken on the phone, too, texted about décor, but I haven't seen her once. I meant to stop by, but I've been jammed with another job."

"She hasn't responded yet," Daisy said while staring at her phone. "That's just wonky."

"Maybe she's driving," Joey said.

"So?" Daisy said.

Right, Sam thought. Like that had stopped Harper before. In fact, their first encounter had been via an accident caused by Harper's reckless texting while driving.

"I'll be back with the cupcakes," Rae said as she zipped toward the kitchen. "Carry on!"

"I'll help," Joey said. Even though she looked out of

place, she was doing her damnedest to fit in. To the club's credit, no one commented on her radical goth girl vibe when she disappeared into the kitchen behind the sweetly sophisticated heiress.

Sam shifted on his stool, anxious to blurt out his news. Once those Kick-in-the-Pants Kupcakes were served, he'd be forced to stay. He wasn't about to add *rude* to *quitter.*

"Harper usually drops by Moose-a-lotta for cupcakes and bean juice," Chloe said, "but so far she's a no-show."

"I'm sure Harper's fine," Sam said. "Listen—"

"Not that I'm prone to gossip," Ethel said, "but I heard Harper's had everything from laundry to food delivered to her house daily. Who does that?"

"People who are used to being catered to," Sam said. "Probably a West Coast thing. Listen—"

"I don't think so," Chloe said. "I think something's wrong."

"I agree," Rae said, back in the room and already doling out cupcakes alongside Joey.

"Nothing's wrong," Sam said. Even so, he texted Harper. A racy text. A text she wouldn't be able to resist. He waited a beat. Two beats.

"Maybe she's finally falling prey to the Rothwell curse," Helen said.

"A curse?" Joey grinned. "Cool."

"Not an actual curse," Monica said for the record. "More like an urban legend connected to a home once owned by one of the first Cupcake Lovers, Mary Rothwell."

"Mary's husband went missing in World War II," Daisy said, "but she was certain he'd return."

"She became a recluse," Ethel said, "determined to be at home when he walked through the door."

"Only he never did," Daisy said. "Mary died of a broken heart."

"According to residents over the years," Monica said,

"the longer you live in that house, the deeper your anxiety and depression."

"Maybe Harper's too depressed to leave," Ethel said, "and that's why she's ordering everything in."

"Have you met Harper?" Sam asked, unable to keep the sarcasm from his tone. "She's a control freak. Focused and determined."

"That doesn't make her impervious to depression," Chloe said.

In Sam's mind it did. If depression welled, Harper would pound it into the ground. She didn't have time for anything that would take away from her bulldog mentality and needy clients.

"Speaking of anxious," Casey broke in, "I can't believe you're here, Chloe. You're due to give birth any day."

"I know. But the baby hasn't dropped and . . . never mind." She glanced at Sam who'd made it clear in the past, simply by holding silent, that he wasn't comfortable discussing the intimate details of pregnancy. A subject that had become more prevalent over the last several meetings. Natural since Chloe, Monica, and Rae were expecting, but awkward for Sam. In the coming months, techniques for breast-feeding and issues with postnatal care would crop up. He'd been through it all with Paula, twice. He had his own brand of wisdom in these matters. But she'd been his wife. These were his friends. Time to swap cupcakes for bowling.

"I have an announcement," Sam blurted just as his cell phone pinged. He glanced at the incoming text. A response from Harper.

NEED U. NOW.

Typical Harper—bossy—and a tantalizing response to his racy proposition.

But then she followed with: PLEASE

"I have to go." Sam pushed to his feet and rushed to the door. Chloe was right. Something was wrong.

FOUR

The Rothwell Farm was located in a woodsy area northwest of Sugar Creek. Highway 105 to 236, then a ten-minute streak down Swamp Road. A right onto Fox Lane and three minutes later the renovated Victorian with its federal-blue exterior and snow-white trim would come into view.

Sam had been hooked on the late nineteenth-century house ever since he'd been a boy. Owners came and went, claiming—as noted by the Cupcake Lovers—the longer they resided there, the more they experienced periods of irrational depression. Hence, the supposedly haunted house was frequently deserted. As a kid, Sam and his cousins had snuck in dozens of times hoping to catch a glimpse of the ghost of Mary Rothwell.

They never did.

Harper had been living in that house on and off for several months. She didn't believe in ghosts, or so she'd said, but she *was* obsessed with the legend of Mary Rothwell. So much so, she'd instructed Rocky to decorate the master bedroom/office in the colors and style reminiscent of the 1940s—the decade in which Mary had lived here. Rocky thought it was creepy. Sam thought it was odd. Although, once he'd joined the renovation project, the changes that had felt most right to both Sam and Harper had been those that turned back the clock. Returning the home to its World War II-era glory was just about the only subject Sam and Harper agreed on.

NEED U. NOW.

PLEASE

Harper's troubling text was burned on Sam's retinas. He called, but she didn't answer. He texted. No response. What the hell? Had she fallen down the stairway? Been attacked by a burglar?

Sam pictured Harper broken and bleeding, and punched the gas.

Up ahead, the sun dipped below the horizon. Come nightfall, this rural area would turn pitch-black. Sam could find the Rothwell Farm blindfolded. He'd grown up in Sugar Creek. He knew every highway and back road, every mountain trail and logging road. He'd made this particular trek a hundred times over the last few months. Mostly to work on Harper's house. Sometimes for a text-prompted quickie. With Harper it was always a quickie. They had an agreement. Sex, just sex. And she had rules. No sleeping over. No talking after. Not that Sam was a wind-bag, but, considering they were well past a one-nighter, banging and running without a shade of intimacy was this side of smarmy. Not that it had prompted him to end their affair. That had been Harper.

A right onto Fox Lane. Two minutes later—because he was fricking *flying*—Sam wheeled his truck into Harper's long drive and skidded to a stop. He jogged to the porch, snagged the spare key tucked behind the backplate of the wall sconce, and pushed through the door without knocking. "Harper!"

She didn't answer, but he heard the TV . . . and a whimper. And *wheezing*.

Chest tight, he ducked around the corner, into the living room. The monster plasma screen was alive with the sights and sounds of war. A newscast on CNN. Harper was hunkered on the large vintage sofa Rocky had had delivered last month. She was doubled over, head between her knees, gasping for air.

Asthma attack?

Relief torpedoed his dread. He'd imagined far worse.

Tempering his galloping pulse, he nabbed the remote from the table, muted the volume then crouched in front of Harper. Laying a calming hand to her convulsing back, he asked, "What's happening, hon?"

"Can't. Breathe."

"Asthma? Allergy?"

"Anxiety."

"What?" Sam reached through the thickness of her long, dark hair, cupped her face and bade her meet his gaze.

The first time he'd laid eyes on Harper he'd pegged her as *Sports Illustrated* model gorgeous. He thought no less now. Even though her face was flushed and sweaty. Even though her sky-blue eyes were dazed.

She was gasping for air, massaging her chest. "Can't feel my fingers. Can't. Breathe. Heart racing. Too fast. Too. Much."

So, what? A heart attack? How was that possible? She was a healthy young woman, for crissake. "Harper. Listen. Focus. Do you have a condition I don't know about? Is there medicine I should get?"

She shook her head, rocked, and gasped.

Her distress was unsettling. "I'll call 911."

"No." She grabbed his hands as he went for his phone. "Talk to me."

Sam gawked. *Talk?* On top of everything else, she was delirious.

"Talk . . . talk me down."

Then he got it. *Anxiety.* As in panic attack. *What the hell?*

"Feels . . . feels like I'm . . . dying."

He squeezed her hands. "You're not dying. You're hyperventilating. Adrenaline's spiking." He'd seen this before in the field. Trained soldiers freezing in the midst of an assault or when faced with an atrocity their mind couldn't process. Sam had always muscled through similar crises himself. He considered himself lucky and he hadn't thought twice when a fellow soldier had panicked. He'd simply offered aid—part of the buddy system, solider helping soldier.

"Focus on my voice, Harper. Breathe deep. Slow. Count with me."

"What?"

"One. Two. Three. Come on."

"Four. Five."

Sam nodded for her to continue, watched as she fought to slow her breathing. She had a death grip on his hands. He stroked her white knuckles then gave her something to focus on aside from her distress. "Mina asked about you the other day. More accurately, she babbled about you for fifteen minutes. Something about purple being the new pink. I'm guessing that's why she insists on wearing her purple snow boots every day even though it's almost June."

In between ten and eleven and a deep breath, Harper smiled. The barest crook of those lush lips, but at least it wasn't a grimace.

"The other night," Sam went on while holding her troubled gaze, "Ben brought home a note from his teacher regarding a missing homework assignment. Know what he said to me? *'Don't worry, Dad. I know how to spin it.'*" Sam raised one brow. "My son spent random afternoons on this property, a few hours around you while I stained cabinets and grouted tile."

"I . . . never . . . thirteen . . . fourteen . . . claimed to be . . . fifteen . . . a good influence."

"An influence nonetheless."

Her expression relaxed, her shoulders slumped. She fell

back against the cushions with a ragged sigh. Her brow was damp, but her breathing had evened.

"Better?" Sam asked as she pulled her fingers from his.

She massaged her chest, nodded. "Thanks."

"Sure."

Her cheeks burned red and she averted her gaze.

Sam rose and sat beside her, his thoughts whirling. He'd never known Harper to be embarrassed. He'd never seen her panic. Last winter she'd flipped her car on icy roads and seconds later she'd been texting a client, blasting Sam when he'd chucked her phone before pulling her out of the overturned car. She was always in control, always controlling. Seeing her in a tailspin had shaken Sam in a new and perplexing way.

Looking wiped, Harper pushed her bountiful hair off her flushed face—gorgeous, even when distressed—and twisted the wavy mass into a messy knot. "Sorry I bothered you," she said, staring at the television and massaging her chest.

"Glad to help." Sam pulled his phone from a hip holster. "I should call the CLs. Let them know you're okay. They were worried when you didn't show and then I ran out."

She slid him a look. "I don't suppose you could lie—"

"How's a plumbing emergency sound?"

She smiled then—a grateful, albeit shaky smile.

Sam's heart kicked. Yeah, boy, that was—in Daisy's words—wonky. He focused on his cell, dialed Rocky. "Yeah. Sorry to interrupt. Harper's fine. Plumbing emergency."

"Was anything ruined?" Rocky asked.

His cousin ran an interior decorating business. While Sam had been tackling various carpentry and electrical challenges on this old house, Rocky had been purchasing retro furnishings and redecorating every room. She'd been at it for months. Not because she was slow or inept, but because Harper was so damned finicky. "Minimal flooding in the kitchen," Sam lied. "Nothing that a mop and a new coupler won't fix."

"Guess you two won't be making the meeting."

He glanced at Harper who was doing her best to look composed. And failing. "No."

"We'll fill you in later then," Rocky said with a secret smile in her voice. "Have a good night, Sam."

Sam disconnected, cursing the day he'd let it slip to Rocky that he had the hots for Harper. Knowing Sam had been struggling since Paula's death, his cousin had encouraged him to pursue a no-strings-attached fling. He'd begged off, saying Harper wasn't mother material and he couldn't afford a casual affair. He'd yet to confess to Rocky that he'd folded, but he suspected she knew. After tonight's Kick-in-the-Pants analogy, he suspected Rae also had a clue. Or at least thought Harper and Sam would make a good match, although God knew why.

"Thanks for keeping this quiet," Harper said as she pushed to her feet. "I'd be even more grateful if you'd forget this ever happened."

Sam knew that tone. He knew that cocky stance. He was being dismissed.

Like hell.

She'd cited anxiety as the source of her problem, so she must've had a panic attack before. She knew enough to recognize the symptoms. Sam was seeing another side of Harper, a vulnerable, fragile side that caused him to dig in. He was curious. He was also intrigued that she'd tuned in to CNN—hard news—when her news of choice was fluff. *Entertainment Tonight. Hollywood Access.* Yet her gaze kept gravitating to the graphic content on the screen. It shouldn't have bothered him, but it did. Had she seen something that had triggered a personal panic button?

Sam nabbed the remote, thumbed off, then relaxed against the cushions of the vintage daybed sofa—just one of the treasures Rocky had snagged in her 1940s antiquing spree. "What prompted the attack?"

Harper turned to face him, crossing her arms, and narrowing her eyes. "Don't you need to be somewhere? Like home? With Ben and Mina?"

"Hired a sitter till nine. Cupcake Lover meeting, remember?"

"Then you should be *there*."

"How can I fix your plumbing emergency if I'm *there*?"

"You're a pain in my ass, McCloud."

"Ditto. What prompted the attack? Something on the news?"

"What? No."

"Did you see Mary?"

"I've told you before, I don't believe in apparitions. I believe in restless spirits."

"The term you used before was *kindred spirits*."

"That, too."

"You intimated you and Mary Rothwell are kindred spirits," Sam said. "Meaning you have something in common. Like what?" In the past, he'd steered clear of the subject, half convinced Harper was a New Age flake, the kind who put stock in ghost hunters and psychics. He'd assumed she was enamored with the romantic slant of the Rothwell legend—most women were.

"I didn't panic because of anything having to do with Mary," Harper said by way of an answer.

Instead of working that bone, he explored elsewhere. "Someone try to break in?" It wasn't the first time Sam had had reservations about a woman living alone in this secluded patch of woods. Not to mention, Harper owned a tempting collection of electronics. Although her decorating taste leaned toward vintage, she'd stocked several rooms with state-of-the-art audio/visual components. She'd even had her bedroom enlarged and augmented so that it doubled as a high-tech office.

"Nothing like that," she said.

"Then what?"

Harper hugged herself, worked her jaw. Her right eye ticked, and Sam warned himself to tread lightly. The last thing he wanted was to incite another attack. His death glare never worked on Harper so he utilized patience—his secret weapon.

Five seconds and one annoyed huff later, she broke. "I was getting ready for the CL meeting," she said. "Then I got a text, backed up by an e-mail."

"From?"

"My firm. I called but I was routed to a freaking assistant who recited some scripted bull." She glanced away, rocked back and forth on her three-inch pumps.

Sam had a thing for Harper's vast collection of sexy footwear. He wouldn't call it a fetish, but close. Nads tightening, he tore his gaze from her stylish heels and shapely calves. Locking on her face didn't ease his untimely arousal, but it did help him focus.

"I've been dismissed," she blurted. "Fired! Services no longer required! Two fricking weeks' notice. Severance. Then *poof*! Gone!"

There are worse things, Sam thought. Although maybe not for Harper. The woman was an overzealous workaholic. Always on the phone. Always plugged in to one or another media outlet via her phone, laptop, television . . .

"Do you know what this means?"

Was that a trick question? "You're out of work."

"I'll be deported!"

Well, hell. Sam shifted, bothered by the notion as well as Harper's distress.

"I'm a Canadian citizen. For the last few years I've been in this country, living and working compliments of an L visa. A three-year visa that expires in two weeks!"

Instead of rocking, she was pacing now. Sam kept his

tone even, his posture relaxed, hoping to offset Harper's intensifying agitation. "What's an L visa?"

"It's when a U.S. employer transfers a manager or an executive from an affiliated Canadian office to one of its U.S. offices. Spin Twin Cities PR is based in Toronto *and* L.A. I've been with the firm for years. I never thought . . . I always assumed . . ." She palmed her chest and rubbed. "I can't go back . . . I can't . . ." She dropped into a chair and massaged her chest. "Damn."

Christ.

Sam leaned forward, braced his elbows on his knees. "There must be another way. Another work visa—"

"There's not. Oh, God." Harper flopped forward, head between her knees. "Give me a minute," she said in a tight voice. "I've got this. One. Two . . ."

Sam pushed off the sofa, confused as to the crux of her anxiety. He'd thought it was because she'd lost her job. But she seemed more upset about being deported. Why? With a shark reputation like hers, surely she could secure work at another top Canadian firm.

He gripped her arms and pulled her to her feet, chest tight when he noticed her shimmering eyes. What the hell had reduced hard-ass, badass Harper Day to tears?

Instead of breaking into sobs, she blindsided him with a kiss. A punishing kiss. A frenzied clashing of lips and tongue. One hand tangled in his hair while the other wrestled with the buttons of his fly. She palmed the bulge in his boxers.

Jesus.

It was always like this. Down and dirty. Fast and furious. Sex, just sex. Usually Sam was game, but this time emotions factored in. Harper was a knotted mess and Sam was barely coherent. Her kisses alone fried his logic.

She tugged at his waistband and his conscience kicked. Sam took control, shifting her hand to his neck, holding her close, deepening the kiss, and tempering the frenzy. His heart pounded against his chest. His blood cooled to a simmer as he had a mental man-to-man with the dude down south.

Nuns and puppies. Miss Kitty and Astro Boy.

Harper trembled in his arms, melted into the kiss, and Sam felt a shift in his universe.

A heartbeat later, she broke away, resting her head on his shoulder. "Was that a no?"

Sam struggled to right his world. "We're not going to muddy this with sex. We're going to talk."

She tensed and pushed away.

Sam caught her hand, held her gaze. "Why can't you go back to Canada, Harper?"

Whatever calm she'd gleaned from his kiss threatened to snap. But the words flowed. "Because I'd never have a moment's peace. He . . . I . . ." She trailed off, switched gears. "I'm needed here," she rushed on in a brittle voice. "My work is here. People are counting on me. Fifteen celebrity clients in L.A. The Cupcake Lovers and associated charities. I promised Daisy I'd orchestrate a televised special to raise awareness. And Rae . . . I promised I'd keep the paparazzi off her ass. I gave my word. I refuse to bail."

Which is exactly what he'd been in the midst of doing with the CLs. It was the first time the typically self-absorbed publicist had trumped Sam in decency. Pole-axed, he pulled Harper against his body, stroking her back as she battled for composure. Since she was opposed to any nonsexual type of embrace, this was another "intimate" first.

What the frick?

They'd never been emotionally close. Harper had made sure of it. She'd even ended their affair. Yet tonight they'd connected on a new level. He couldn't fathom the reason or catalyst, unless . . . "You mentioned a man."

She tensed.

" 'I'd never know a moment's peace. He . . .' He, who? An abusive ex? A stalker?" Given her beauty and preference for kink, he could easily imagine Harper falling prey to a dangerous man.

"No. Nothing like that. I just . . . I let down a lot of people back home. Including myself. There's nothing there for me anymore. My work is here. People depend on me. I can't fix things if I can't fix things."

He had no idea what that meant. She'd been rambling against his shoulder, avoiding eye contact. But he felt her tension and sensed she wasn't being entirely truthful. Quick on her publicist feet, she kept spinning the conversation away from what Sam sensed was a deeply troubling issue. She was proud or stubborn or scared. Maybe all three. One thing was certain, she was adamant about not abandoning those she deemed in need.

"There are lots of good women, Sam, but, like great cupcakes, not all of them are sugary sweet."

He looked past his own narrow mind and put himself in Harper's clients' shoes. Knowing you could count on someone to save your bacon was a bona fide blessing. He remembered how Harper had sent cupcakes home for his kids, how she'd drawn Ben out of his shell by telling him about the superheroes she'd represented at Comic Con, the way she'd soothed Mina's ruffled boa feathers when the kids had made fun of her obsession with tiaras. He flashed on the time she'd taken control when the paparazzi had swarmed Rae. Harper was bossy and arrogant, always in control.

But somehow always saving the day.

"Your perfect cupcake could be the one with kick. And if you sink in deep enough, long enough, maybe you'll taste the sweet among the spice."

Sam sorted through scattered thoughts as Harper vented against his shoulder, cursing her former employer for putting her clients at risk. He didn't ask how she planned on helping the celebrities on her client list when she'd been canned. He didn't mention that her devotion to a bunch of narcissistic, kamikaze B-listers and reality stars struck him as over-the-top. Questioning her judgment wouldn't quell her misery. Offering a possible solution might.

"Marry a U.S. citizen and your spouse can petition for permanent residency."

"Brilliant, Rambo. With a slight glitch." She pushed off him now, a trace of her normal snark seeping through the anxiety. "I don't do relationships. There is no steady someone. No single male friend who would give up his freedom solely as a favor to me. Where do you suggest I find a husband? Match.com? Craigslist?"

"Sugar Creek."

Harper blinked. "Who—"

"Me."

She looked at him as if he was crazy, and maybe he was. Hard to grab hold of a sane thought when your head's spinning. Finding Harper in panic mode, experiencing her vulnerable side—Christ, he hadn't been aware she *had* a vulnerable side—had messed with Sam in a major way. That kiss confirmed their intense sexual connection and hinted of something deeper. This moment, he knew four things.

He was sick of waking alone every morning.

Weary of being a single parent.

Done with searching for Paula's clone.

Most importantly, Ben and Mina liked Harper.

She wasn't his ideal choice in a wife or mother, but she damn well stirred his blood. She wasn't perfect but neither was he and how many couples had perfect? Sensing she needed to be saved from someone or something provided a second incentive. Sam was hardwired to rescue and protect—an adrenaline high chased with a shot of contentment.

"By the way," he added, knowing how her mind worked. "That wasn't a declaration of love."

"Thank God." She was gawking at him, but she'd tempered her breathing. Her mind was racing. He could see that. No secret, they mixed like oil and water. She narrowed her eyes. "What do you get out of it?"

"Aside from hot sex on a regular basis?" *Aside from a companion to fill the void in my life?* "A mother for Ben and Mina."

"I don't want to be a mom."

"Then go back to Canada or purchase a husband on Craigslist." Okay. That was harsh. But Harper pushed his buttons. Nothing was ever easy with this woman. Marrying the first time had been a breeze. So perfect. Then again, he and Paula had been head over heels in love.

Harper snatched her phone from the leather-topped, black lacquered coffee table—another Rocky score. She scanned her texts, probably hoping her firm had sent a retraction, but not seeing one. "Bastards." She massaged her chest, breathed slow and deep.

"Don't overthink it, Harper. Bottom line, we'll both benefit. Think of it as a business deal. We can work out details and guidelines later." He glanced at his watch. As much as he wanted to stay, he needed to go. "The kids—"

"Are waiting."

"You okay?"

"Hunky-dory."

They engaged in a stare-down that rocked Sam to his core, amplified by a dose of déjà vu. As if they'd gone this marriage route before—together—which they hadn't.

The air crackled. *That* was familiar ground. Intense sexual sparks that often prompted sex. Only this time there was something more. That nagging hint of something deeper.

She didn't move. Maybe she was waiting for him to take back the marriage offer.

He didn't.

"Think it over," Sam said as he turned toward the door. "Let me know."

He walked out into the night, breathed the fresh country air. His whirling thoughts settled the farther he got from the house. His pulse rate doubled. Holy shit. He'd just proposed marriage to the most vexing woman he'd ever met—a woman with *kick*. Two steps from his pickup truck, his phone pinged—an incoming text from Harper.

YES.

FIVE

Sun streaked through the lacy mint-green curtains of Harper's bedroom. Those same curtains fluttered a ghostly dance, compliments of the morning breeze blowing through the partially opened panes.

Groggy from a restless night, she kicked aside her rumpled blankets and hugged a pillow while gazing across the room at the two windows facing Fox Lane. According to legend, Mary Rothwell had sat in front of those windows every day, for hours on end, waiting for a glimpse of her husband, Captain Joseph Rothwell. Even though she'd been told he'd gone missing in action, she believed with all her heart he'd find his way home. To her. She'd died. Waiting.

Harper remembered the first time she'd heard that story. A native of Toronto, Canada, she used to pop into the U.S. on breaks from the university. Sometimes she and her schoolmates would drive down to New York City—a weekend of shopping and theater in the Big Apple. Sometimes just over the border to Vermont for a spontaneous ski trip. A few of those trips had landed her in Sugar Creek. She'd heard about the haunted Rothwell Farm from the proprietor of a bed-and-breakfast on her initial visit. The sad, romantic tale had seeped into Harper's being, and years later when she'd been looking for a vacation home, a place to retreat and rejuvenate far from the chaos of L.A., she'd thought of Sugar Creek. She'd never dreamed the Rothwell Farm would be available, but it was. And—bonus—it had been a steal. She hadn't cared that it was rundown or that there was a dogged depression associated with the house. This house had history and surely some of the residents' emotions had seeped into the walls and floorboards over the decades. Maybe the house had never recovered from Mary's sad tale because no one stayed long enough to imbue the walls and floorboards with happier vibes.

Even though Harper had only been in residence sporadically, she'd filled this house with life. With upbeat music, endless television, and lots of chatty phone calls. She'd baked dozens of cupcakes—something Mary used to do. She'd had several long consultations with Rocky regarding furnishings and decorations. Rocky was always a positive, vibrant force. Sam's kids had only visited the house a few times, but they'd added an infectious dose of innocence and laughter. Even though she'd felt awkward when interacting with them, she'd appreciated their presence. And Sam . . .

Every time Sam was in this house with Harper, the atmosphere snapped and sparked. Whether they were immersed in their own work—her spinning crises, him focused on carpentry—or banding to discuss blueprints and paint samples . . . the air was charged.

Of course, most of that was due to their sexual chemistry.

Jumping his bones last night had been rash, but instinctual. *Medicinal.* In the midst of her meltdown, her complicated thought process had narrowed to a one-lane highway. Destination: distraction and salvation. Mode of transport: sex. Specifically sex with Sam.

She'd been stunned when he'd waylaid her efforts. Even more stunned when he'd tempered her desperation with a kiss that had hummed through her body like a siren song. Hypnotic and tender. That kiss had soothed and seduced her soul, even as she'd blasted her former employer, no doubt confounding Sam with her convoluted ramble. That kiss had prompted her to text him without fully contemplating the ramifications of marriage to a widowed father of two, a man who was rooted in Sugar Creek, a confident, capable man who challenged her in every way.

YES.

Even now . . . even though her brain said no, her soul cried *yes.*

It was frightening . . . and encouraging. A sign that there was life beyond Andrew. Although that in itself felt like a betrayal.

One step forward, two steps back.

Harper pitched the pillow and stretched. Her neck hurt. Her back ached. She blamed a night of restlessness. Between being fired, the panic attack, Sam's proposal, and her shocking acceptance, her mind had refused to shut down. One worry led to another.

Had Edward learned of her dismissal? Could he feel her sweating deportation? Was he anxiously awaiting her return? Plotting his ultimate revenge? What if . . . What if . . . What if . . .

Sleeping with her phone in hand, she'd obsessively checked her e-mail through the night as well as her multiple social media accounts. Edward had hacked his way in before, he could do so again. He could also post anonymously or under an assumed name. But there'd been no taunting message. Maybe the taunt was in the anticipation.

If only I hadn't lost my job.

Unemployment. Another dilemma that had fueled her insomnia. She'd been tempted to zip off e-mails to a couple of associates, trying to get a better handle on her dismissal, but she'd resisted. What if they didn't write her back? Or what if they did? What if they made her feel worse by sharing specific complaints about her past behavior and recent failures? Like she needed something new to obsess on? She wasn't the most popular person at Spin Twin Cities. She knew her coworkers considered her an enigma. Publicists were supposed to be personable. And she was . . . in a guarded and calculated way. What she wasn't was chummy. Harper hadn't had any true friends in a long time. She hadn't had a "boyfriend" since Andrew. Her libido had been comatose long before his death and hadn't sparked back to life until Sam. Even then she'd done everything in her power to ensure a purely physical, *meaningless* relationship. After the debacle with Andrew, she'd sworn off intimacy in order to shield her tender heart and fragile composure.

Yet I've agreed to marry Sam.

She couldn't explain her bizarre decision beyond that hypnotic kiss and the obvious. He'd thrown her a lifeline. A way to stay in America. A way to avoid Edward. A chance to reconnect and continue with her old clients.

That's if they'd have her.

If not, she'd reach out to others. Plenty of people needed the kind of help she could provide. She'd build a new client list. Since she wouldn't be relying on the L visa, she could freelance. Which, given her independent streak, wasn't a bad thing. She wondered if Sam would be willing to relocate to L.A., not that she was ready to return.

Yesterday, she'd braved the distance between her house and the pond. She'd sat on the end of the pier. She'd dangled her toes in the water. All exactly as planned. Except she only lasted ten minutes before anxiety reared its butt-ugly head.

What if some crazed murderer was lurking underwater? What if they pulled me in and held me under? A terrifying watery demise?

What if someone was hunting in the woods and a bullet went astray, striking me instead?

What if, what if, what if?

Once her mind latched on to a fear, it was hard to let go.

She'd scrambled back to the house in a sweat. She'd run on her treadmill until she'd outrun the panic. She'd showered and focused on good things, brainstormed several promotional ideas regarding the Cupcake Lover recipe book. She was determined to succeed with her second attempt to leave the grounds. A trip into town. A meeting with the CLs.

She'd dressed for confidence—a bold blue dress and a pair of spiky Mary Janes. She'd been jazzed about discussing business with the club. But then she'd gotten that damned "pink slip" text. The top guns hadn't had the decency to call her. Although, to be fair, most business these days was conducted via texts and e-mails. Less personal. More efficient. Still. She'd been with the firm for seven years. The cold dismissal was hard on the pride and disruptive on every level—professionally, financially, personally. The thought of returning to Canada—for good—had tripped all sorts of panic buttons. She barely remembered texting Sam. She should've texted Rocky. The Sugar Creek native was easily as grounded and responsible as Sam. Compassionate, too. Plus their association was purely business. Whereas with Sam . . .

Harper looked away from the billowing curtains, suffered another painful neck twinge. As if that wasn't bad enough her muscles ached and her head throbbed. Compliments of an anxiety hangover. She glanced at her alarm clock.

It was 7:05.

Sam would be getting the kids ready for school. Once they were married, would that task fall to her? Through the night, she'd wondered about a lot of things regarding her role as wife and mom. She couldn't wrap her brain around the domestic role. She could, however, imagine spending more time with Sam. Even though he irked her more often than not. Even though they had little to nothing in common beyond housing renovations. She admired his grounded sensibilities. He was unflappable. Strong and reliable. She knew now why she'd reached out to Sam and not Rocky. Harper breathed easier when Sam was around, even when she was composed.

Her cell phone chimed. An incoming text. She nabbed the smartphone from her nightstand.

Daisy.

GOOD MORNING, SLICK. SORRY I DIDN'T ACKNOWLEDGE YOUR LATE-NIGHT TEXT. GLAD YOU'RE OKAY. I FELL ASLEEP WATCHING A JERRY LEWIS MOVIE WHICH MADE ME THINK OF THE JERRY LEWIS TELETHON AND THE RAT PACK. MAYBE WE SHOULD HAVE A CUPCAKE LOVERS TELETHON. DO YOU HAVE ANY CONNECTIONS WITH JERRY LEWIS OR FRANK SINATRA JUNIOR? CAN WE MEET TODAY? I'LL FILL YOU IN ON THE CUPCAKE LOVERS MEETING AND THE LATEST GOSSIP. I'M WORKING AT MOOSEALOTTA TODAY. DO YOU WANT TO DROP BY FOR LUNCH OR SHOULD I VISIT YOU LATER AT THE FARM?

Harper rubbed her eyes, the screaming-long text aggravating her already pounding temples. Daisy texted a lot and she spelled everything out. Harper itched to print out a list of acronyms for the woman. Or to download a hands-free texting app to her phone so she could simply talk and send texts sans typing. Although, come to think of it, that could lead to even longer messages. Gathering her thoughts, Harper texted back, reminding herself not to use acronyms because Daisy always asked for an explanation, which, made their exchanges twice as long.

NO RAT PACK CONNECTIONS. JUST WAKING. NEED TO CHECK MY AGENDA. CAN I GET BACK TO YOU LATER ON PLACE AND TIME?

Harper's brain cramped as she spelled out each and every word. Maybe she could turn Daisy on to Skype or FaceTime. She hoped the woman didn't press because

Harper needed to mentally prepare before she committed to leaving the house. She also wanted to get her thoughts together regarding the loss of her job and her impending marriage to a man she barely knew. One of Sugar Creek's own. A Cupcake Lover, no less. Relation to Daisy, Rocky, Luke, and by extension of marriage, Rae and Chloe. Harper realized suddenly that by saying yes to Sam she'd signed on with the entire Monroe clan.

"Good Lord."

She groaned when her phone chimed with Daisy's response.

VINCENT'S GRANDAUGHTER WAS IN LAS VEGAS LAST MONTH. SHE MET DON RICKLES. MAYBE HE CAN HELP US.

Don Rickles? Wasn't he like a hundred and five by now?

JUST LET ME KNOW WHEN YOU CAN SQUEEZE ME IN. I'M FLEXIBLE. HOW'S YOUR PLUMBING TODAY? SAM'S A WONDER, ISN'T HE?

Harper blinked. She knew Daisy was referring to her fake flood in the kitchen, but her wording sent Harper's thoughts down another road. Her face heated as she wrote . . . SAM'S GR8. TTYL.

A second later, Daisy texted: WHAT'S THAT MEAN?

Gah. Harper had no sooner typed out every word of her previous message, signing off with Daisy, than her phone chimed again. This time it was Sam. Even though he couldn't see her, she smoothed her mussed hair as she read his text.

U OK?

Harper's pulse tripped. No polite greeting, but a show of concern. She typed: FINE. U?

GOOD.

KIDS?

KICKING MY ASS.

She wasn't sure what that meant exactly. Although she knew his son, Ben, was shy and nerdy and often sulky.

Little Mina was the opposite—an animated, demanding chatterbox who had Sam wrapped around her little finger.

ABT THE PROPOSAL . . . Sam continued.

Harper tensed. CHANGE YR MIND?

NO. U?

NO.

Harper frowned when her phone actually rang. Apparently Sam felt the need to *speak*. She pushed up and leaned back against her mountain of pillows. She cleared her froggy throat. "Yes?"

"Let's keep this private until we discuss specifics," Sam said.

The sound of his voice sent a sizzle through her being. He could probably give her an orgasm by reading a grocery list. She knew she had it bad for the man—sexually—but this was ridiculous. Assuming the kids were within hearing distance, Harper kept her response clean and short. "Okay."

"Are you free for lunch?"

She blinked. "What? Like a date?"

"It would help pave the way if we established a relationship. Lunch for starters."

Harper saw the logic. Marrying out of the blue would cause community gossip and maybe tweak the suspicions of the USCIS field office. Wedding an American simply to attain a green card was highly discouraged. "I'll whip up something for us here," she said.

"The point is to be seen, Harper. Together. In public."

A restaurant. With employees and customers. People she didn't know. Where anyone could go postal.

"You still there?" he asked.

"Yeah."

"I'll pick you up at noon."

"One would be better," she said. More time to mentally prepare.

"One it is."

Harper stonewalled a nagging what if. "Okay."

They disconnected and she swung out of bed with a "can do" attitude.

Yesterday, Spin Twin Cities had served her a pink slip and lemons.

Last night, Sam had provided a recipe for lemonade.

He was right. They could both benefit from this business arrangement, the hot sex being a perk. She knew she was hard to take sometimes. She could be manic and bossy. But her heart was in the right place. Did Sam sense that somehow? Did he see beyond the walls she'd worked so hard to erect? He *must* have. Why else would he offer to share his life with her? Why trust her with the children he so obviously adored?

The fact that Sam was willing to take a chance on Harper filled her with mixed emotions. If nothing else, it was a rousing kick in the ass.

Embracing the future, Harper swigged water then traded her teddy for workout gear. She switched on CNN, switched it off, switched it on. Better to be aware. She skimmed TMZ then pulled up a contact list of her clients. She had a lot of work to do before Sam got here and . . . right.

Daisy.

Harper hopped on her exercise bike, phone in hand. Her multitasking abilities were excellent if she did say so herself. She pedaled and texted: AGENDA FULL THROUGH LUNCH. MEET ME HERE AT SIX?

Five seconds later Daisy replied: COCKTAIL HOUR! WOO-HOO!

Harper smiled. Not for the first time, she imagined the eccentric geriatric as the star of her own quirky reality show. She texted back: PINK COSMOS FOR TWO. Because even though she'd been avoiding alcohol, Harper figured she'd have reason to celebrate by six o'clock.

Today she was going to make it into Sugar Creek and back without a meltdown.

Today she had a lifeline.

SIX

Daisy Monroe shuffled into the kitchen rocking (as the kids said) plush moose slippers and a hot-pink robe embroidered with a purple crown and the word PRINCESS. She didn't care that her morning ensemble was more suited to a teen. She cared that it made her smile.

Last year she'd invested in her own business, a trendy café called Moose-a-lotta. She not only worked behind the counter, she sometimes dressed in a moose costume, appearing at special functions as Millie Moose, the mascot of Moose-a-lotta. Her partner, Chloe, nine months pregnant with Daisy's first great-grandbaby, had had an encounter with a bull moose resulting in a life epiphany. Born and raised in the Green Mountain State, Daisy had a lifelong appreciation of the antlered creature and it had been a hoot decorating their café with eclectic moose-a-bilia. Clocks, pillows, salt and pepper shakers, mugs. They even had their own logo—a cartoonish moose wearing cat-eye glasses and chef's hat—a reflection of the owners' personalities. Daisy owned an assortment of metallic and blingy bifocals and Chloe had graduated with honors from a culinary arts institute. Which is why they'd met in the first place, but that was another story.

As for the princess robe, it had been a gift from Daisy's honey, a man who appreciated her whimsical side. A man who treated her like royalty. Which is why she had decided this very morning not to operate behind Vincent's back, but instead, to include him in her scheme.

As always, the owner of Oslow's General Store, Sugar Creek's go-to grocery since 1888, had beaten her to the kitchen and had breakfast waiting on the table. Daisy told herself it wasn't because he didn't trust her not to burn down his house (her concentration wasn't what it used to be—or so her family told her), but because he liked doting on her. Which felt significantly different than being made to feel like you were no longer able to care for yourself.

Vincent turned to face her, toasting her with a percolator and a wide smile. "Morning, Petunia."

She found it amusing that he'd nicknamed her after a flower when she'd been legally named for another flower. She thought it was cute. Like Vincent. (Or Speedy, as she sometimes called him.)

"Morning." She smiled as he pulled out her chair and poured her a cup of coffee, treating her—as always—like royalty. Princess Petunia. *Hee.* "I got a text from Chloe," she said as he took his seat, "asking if I could work the afternoon shift instead of the morning. A last-minute scheduling snafu."

"Not a problem," Vincent said, while slathering his toast with apple butter. "I'll take a break from the store and drive back to give you a lift. Marvin can handle Oslow's for a half hour solo."

"Your son could handle the store all day, every day. Something he's told you time and again, but you're too set in your ways to retire."

"I'm too young to retire."

"You're seventy-three."

"You're seventy-six and you're still working."

"Yes, but this is my first job. You've been working your whole life. You deserve a break. At least cut down to half days like me and we could have some fun together."

He glanced over. "I thought we *were* having fun."

He looked a little stricken and Daisy was reminded of how sensitive Vincent was compared to her deceased husband. Just one of the things she loved about him. Smiling, she reached over and brushed crumbs from his snowy beard. "Of course, we're having fun, Speedy. I meant *more* fun."

Vincent was a grounded man with a gentle soul. Which was nice, but kind of boring. She'd been pleased as punch when she'd learned he occasionally indulged in nocturnal joyrides, racing the back roads and tipping the needle past seventy. *Yes*! Hence, his pet name—Speedy—which no one else understood because Vincent Redding plodded along in everyday life. Slow and easy. Steady and sure. A chubby, white-bearded, Santa-like man who favored baggy-seated denims, plaid shirts, and red suspenders.

The ever cautious man narrowed his eyes. "What did you have in mind?"

Over the last few years, Daisy had developed a reputation for being reckless. She preferred to think of herself as a thrill-seeker. So what if she incurred a few bumps and bruises as a result of the random adventure? Life was short and, after losing Jessup (a man who'd expected Daisy to behave like a prim and proper wife) to cancer, she'd vowed to make up for lost time, grabbing the gusto, the brass ring, and whatever else snagged her attention along the way.

"I'm compiling a family bucket list," she said while drenching her French toast with a local maple syrup.

"What's a bucket list?"

Daisy gaped at her other half, her significant other, the man she was living with in sin—unless you counted the vows they'd taken at Rocky's wedding as legal, which they weren't. "Haven't you ever seen that movie?"

"What movie?"

"The one with that actor, the one with the crazy eyebrows and dark sunglasses. You know, the one who starred in the 'cuckoo nest' movie. And that other actor, the handsome black geezer from *Driving Miss Daisy*."

Vincent munched on his toast and considered. "Jack Nicholson and Morgan Freeman?"

"If you say so," Daisy said.

"What movie?"

"The Bucket List!"

"Never seen it."

"We'll have to remedy that," Daisy said. "Just know they lived life to the fullest even if it meant breaking the rules."

"Knowing you," Vincent said, "I understand bucket list. But what's family bucket list?"

"A bucket list involving family."

Vincent sipped coffee then smiled, his kind eyes twinkling with interest. "Could you expand on that explanation?"

Daisy nodded. Her old heart fluttered and it had nothing to do with her ongoing medical issues. Her first husband, Jessup Monroe, her wedded husband of fifty years, wouldn't have asked her to *expand* on her thoughts. Jessup, God rest his soul, had been too wrapped up in his own business to care diddly about her personal aspirations.

Focusing on the here and now, Daisy plucked a folded paper from her pocket and passed it across the table. "I'm blessed to have a large family—including extended family beyond the immediate Monroes. Some of them are floundering in the romance department. Before I kick the bucket I'd like to make sure they're as hooked up and happy as I am right now. With you."

Vincent flushed as he slipped on his reading glasses. "I

appreciate the sentiment, but if you're asking me to play matchmaker—"

"I'll do most of the work, but I'd appreciate a partner in crime." She wasn't supposed to drive anymore, not that she didn't sneak now and then, but she had lots of places to go. Every one of her grandkids and nieces and nephews had offered to give her a ride anytime, anywhere, but she'd prefer to keep these matchmaking missions private.

"Your heart acting up?" Vincent asked.

She'd had a mild attack over a year ago—something she'd managed to keep from the family until Vincent had spilled the beans, darn him. Now everyone hounded her all the more about her health. "No," she said. "Why?"

"You mentioned kicking the bucket."

"No one lasts forever and this matchmaking thing could take a while. Take Sam for instance."

"I see he's at the top of your list," Vincent said while squinting at her writing. "Chicken scrawl," he called it.

"He's a tough nut," Daisy said, while cleaning her plate. "The Cupcake Lovers have all but given up on fixing him up. But not me. I know another tough nut, and I think I can crack them both."

"I know this nut?"

"Harper Day." No sense holding back when Daisy had planted the seed to move forward earlier this morning.

Vincent wrinkled his nose. "The snooty publicist?"

"Not snooty. *Aloof.*"

"Same difference. She's shopped at Oslow's, though not in a while. Organic produce only."

"She's health conscious."

"I've tried talking to her, friendly conversation. She has a way of answering your questions and ignoring you at the same time. Always on her phone—talking, texting."

"Multitasking," Daisy said.

"It's rude," Vincent said.

"I told her that once," Daisy said. "I don't think she can

help herself. Her brain's always running. She comes to Sugar Creek to wind down, but I've never seen her in slow mode. Never seen her relax. She doesn't have any interests outside of work. Except maybe Sam." Daisy leaned forward and waggled her eyebrows. "I've seen her sneak looks at Sam and vice versa. I think they'd be good together."

"Never mind that her primary residence is across the country," Vincent said. "Sam likes sweet-natured women. Harper's self-absorbed and, like you said, kind of manic."

Daisy had thought the same thing, but then she'd started picking up on little things. Things maybe other people didn't notice. Harper wasn't self-absorbed at all. She was obsessed with keeping self-destructive people on track. A Hollywood soul-saver who was also obsessed with lost-soul Mary Rothwell. A gifted publicist who had a soft spot for the Cupcake Lovers and their devotion to spreading sugary sunshine to soldiers.

Daisy would bet her Millie Moose costume that Harper stuffed down her own needs and dreams because she felt other people's needs and dreams were more important. Daisy knew a kindred spirit when she saw one.

"Remember how I used to be?" she asked Vincent. "Reserved. Prim and proper. *Aloof.* There was more to me than met the eye, but I kept it locked away, kept my true self to myself, and pretended to be the person Jessup wanted me to be. Sensible and serene."

Vincent slid his glasses to the end of his nose and peered over the rims at Daisy. The sympathy in his direct gaze made her legs all noodly. "I always sensed you were holding back. I like that you're comfortable enough with me not to put on pretenses."

"Comfortable enough and safe enough," Daisy said. "Harper needs to learn that it's okay to kick back and enjoy life. To focus on her own happiness."

"And you're going to help her with that."

"I'm going to point her in the right direction."

"Sam."

"He needs a challenge. Someone to spice up his life."

"Harper."

"See! We're on the same wavelength."

"Mmm."

"I have an appointment with Harper later tonight. Out at the Rothwell Farm. I don't suppose—"

"Sure."

"Maybe after, we can take a joyride through the state park."

His lip twitched. "Maybe." He turned his attention back to the list. "Hey. My granddaughter Peppy is listed."

Peppy Redding would be another tough nut. Mostly because she was such an odd bird. A songwriting guitar player who'd flitted all over the country trying to hitch her wagon to a star. Struggling financially, she'd returned to the home roost, temporarily living with her dad, Vincent's son Marvin, and taking up with a local band. All Daisy really knew was that Peppy was a disappointment to her father and a source of concern for Vincent.

"Why is my granddaughter on your family bucket list?" he asked.

Now it was Daisy's turn to frown. "I guess I assumed, given our . . . situation, well, I thought . . . Don't you think of my family as your own?"

"I'm fond of everyone, of course. But I guarantee they don't think of *me* as family."

"Sure they do."

Vincent tossed her a skeptical look.

"Okay. Maybe not my son. And maybe not Devlin." Her eldest grandson was practically a chip off his old man's block, both of them being overprotective stick-in-the-muds.

"It would be easier if we made our *situation* legal."

"Why ruin a good thing?"

Vincent sighed. "More coffee?"

She'd hurt his feelings. *Again*. But darn it all, she'd already been that route with Jessup. It's not that he'd abused her, but he'd strangled her spirit, manipulated her behavior, narrowed her scope. Daisy didn't believe in divorce. And she'd feel bad about kicking a man out. If things turned sour with Vincent, she needed to be able to walk away. Just one of the reasons she'd moved out of her home and into his. It gave her the freedom to leave. Life was short and freedom was priceless.

"I'll do it," Vincent said as he stood to clear the table.

Daisy snapped out of her reverie. "You'll cut back on work to help me with my family bucket list?"

"Yup."

"Just like that?"

"Nope."

Daisy shot to her moose-slippered feet, snatched up her dishes, and shuffled to his side. "What's that mean?" she asked as he filled the basin with hot water and a squirt of Palmolive.

"Means you owe me."

Daisy slid their dishes into the sudsy water. "What are we talking?"

His fleshy lips twitched into an ornery smile that sort of scared and excited Daisy at the same time. "When I know, Princess Petunia, you'll know."

SEVEN

Sam steered his truck along Swamp Road at a leisurely pace. Unlike last night, he wasn't racing to Harper's rescue. He was picking her up for a date. Their first date. Considering he'd already proposed marriage, they were going at this bassackward. Then again their short association had an overall slam-bam theme. From their adrenaline-surged initial meeting to their subsequent erotic liaisons. Sam had caressed, sampled, and admired every inch of Harper Day's delectable body, yet he didn't know anything about her beyond the obvious. That wouldn't go well with immigration and it didn't sit right with Sam. Today they'd take it slow. Today they'd talk. As in a meaningful two-sided conversation.

"This should be good."

It would definitely be a first.

Sam flexed his fingers as he turned onto Fox Lane. *Sweaty palms?* He angled the rearview mirror and glanced at his reflection. He'd nicked his jaw trying for a closer shave than usual and the creases fanning from the corners of his eyes were pronounced due to a sleepless night. He swore he spied a gray hair and that it had sprouted just this morning compliments of a war raging between Ben and Mina.

In truth, aside from the shaving injury, Sam looked like he did every day. He'd never been leading-man handsome. Not even ten years and two kids ago. He'd always been rough around the edges. Solidly built with rugged features. Although some women—like Paula—went for the unconventional. Other women—like the several he'd speed-dated last month—seemed enamored by his single-dad status. They praised his devotion to his children, thought it was admirable and sexy. He should have been charmed or at least intrigued. They'd expressed motherly tendencies as well as interest in Sam's hobbies and goals. They'd probed to find his softer side, attempted to connect emotionally.

Unlike Harper who'd only wanted Sam for kinky sex and his mad (as she called them) carpentry skills. Their relationship was this side of warped and yet he'd suggested marriage without a second thought. Without discussing it with the kids first. Typically, he was more grounded, more cautious, more sensitive to the long term.

Fact: Harper wasn't keen on being a mom.

Fact: Harper had no interest in, or was incapable of, an emotionally intimate relationship.

Hello, train wreck.

Or maybe not.

Sam couldn't shake his discussion with Rae. She'd suggested breaking with convention, being adventurous. Considering future bliss with cayenne pepper as opposed to maple syrup. The military had trained him to rely on his gut and his gut screamed Harper.

There was also the sense that she was running from someone or something. Yeah. There was that.

Sam focused back on the road, tensing as the Rothwell Farm came into view. It's not like he had to impress, seduce, or court the enigmatic publicist. She wasn't marrying him for his looks, wit, or charm. She was marrying him for a green card. Still, he'd changed clothes three times before deciding on a white open-collar shirt and his go-to-teacher-conference jeans. He hadn't second-guessed his appearance on any one of a dozen dates he'd been on in the last month. Why he was sweating a sure thing was a mystery.

Or maybe he was sweating because this *was* a sure thing.

Even though he'd spent the night wrestling with a hundred reasons not to marry Harper Day, he had no intention of backing out. He was haunted by that kiss, by the hint of a deeper connection, by the glimpse of a woman with heart. Try as he might, he couldn't block the image of her fighting back tears and struggling to breathe. That vulnerability had snaked through his blood as sure as her signature perfume.

It was the image he had in his head as he parked the truck then scaled the porch. An image that shattered as soon as she opened the front door. She was talking on the phone and she held up a finger signaling Sam to give her a minute or ten. Something she'd done a million times before. Just one of her irritating habits.

"I know I missed the premiere. Yes, of course I know it was a big deal. Sapphire, I . . ." Harper rolled her eyes and fell back, motioning Sam to step inside.

Instead of moving into the living room and taking a seat while she finished her business, he hovered in the foyer, making it clear he was waiting. Even so, background chatter prompted him to look into the next room over. The chatter came from the TV—a journalist and a cop.

Once again *Hollywood Access* had lost out to CNN.

Huh.

Harper continued to pacify her client.

Sam glanced at his watch. One o'clock. He signaled Harper to wrap the call.

She turned her back while trying to state her case. Only Sapphire—whoever she was—wouldn't allow Harper a word in edgewise. The woman—a celebrity client, he assumed—was ripping Harper a new one. Sapphire's voice was so shrill and loud, Sam heard about every third word, most of them foul. And here he thought only marines utilized *fuck* as a verb, adjective, and noun.

"Have I not been there every other time you needed me?" Harper interjected. "What about that glitch with paparazzi? I . . ."

Sam stuffed his hands in his pockets, rocked back on his heels, and admired the curvy publicist's backside. Overall, Harper had a body to die for. Although Sam appreciated her stylish wardrobe, he liked her best in the raw. Call him a dog, but he liked Harper naked. Naked now would be good. He had a major case of blue balls.

She turned and caught his gaze.

He knew, without a doubt, if he chucked her phone under the sofa and hauled her into his arms, she'd be hot and ready for a go against the wall. Tempting. But also distracting.

Sam glanced at his watch and mouthed, "One-oh-five."

"I'm sorry you feel that way, Sapphire," she said calmly to the woman while glaring at Sam. "Maybe we could revisit . . . I'm sure I can spin that . . ."

Ah, yes. Harper doing what she did best. Smoothing ruffled feathers. Fixing someone's problems. Taking control. No trace of the panicked woman who'd lost it the night before. Harper in full Harper mode. He knew her well enough to know this could go on forever. But he also sensed a new element of desperation that rubbed him the wrong way. Why was Harper, a woman who bent over backward for clients, essentially begging mean-spirited, foulmouthed Sapphire to give her a second chance?

Sam turned on his heel. If Harper wouldn't end the verbal abuse, he would.

"Wait," Harper said. "Hold on . . . Sam!"

He looked over his shoulder, saw her holding the phone to her chest.

"Where are you going?"

"We had a date."

"I know. I'm coming. Just—"

He opened the door then walked out.

"Dammit," she blurted. Then . . . "I'll get back to you, Sapphire."

Sam didn't know how Sapphire felt about being cut off. He didn't care. One thing he'd learned during the time he'd spent in Harper's company was that most of her clients were has-beens, one-time-wonders, or reality stars. Most of them were self-absorbed and reckless. All of them were needy. He'd never understood why Harper wasted her time putting their train-wreck lives back on track. Maybe he'd ask her today. Burning question number ninety-five.

That's if this date ever got off the ground.

Just as he reached the truck, he heard the front door slam. He turned and saw Harper eating up the stone path in her shiny yellow heels. She was wearing a short, flowery dress and a snug yellow sweater. Her long dark hair bounced around her perfectly made-up face. She was gorgeous. And angry.

"What the hell, McCloud? You'd break our date just because I'm running late?"

"I suggested noon. You said one would be better. It's one-ten."

"What are you, the Time Nazi?"

Sam opened the passenger door and helped her up into the truck. His gaze lingered on her long legs as she set aside her massive pocketbook and buckled in. "Why did you let her talk to you like that?"

"Like what?"

"She was screaming at you, Harper. Berating you. I'd have to be deaf not to overhear."

"Sapphire's high-strung to begin with and I let her down." She frowned. "I've let a lot of people down lately."

"Doesn't sound like you."

"Haven't been myself for the last month."

"Why's that?"

She broke his gaze, stared at the dashboard. He'd never known her to be at a loss for words, but she was struggling now. She clasped the silver bracelet around her wrist. Twirled it once, twice. "You'll think I'm crazy."

"Try me."

Sam stood rooted, his body positioned between the open door and Harper's wired body. He was keen to her every twitch. Saw the moment anxiety reared. Now she was staring out the window, mind spinning. Along with that bracelet. *Twirl. Twirl.* "You look pretty," he said.

An unexpected compliment that snatched her out of her daze. Exactly what he wanted.

"I like your dress," he added when she looked at him quizzically. Which sounded lame and awkward, even though he meant it.

She arched a brow and smirked. "No offense, Rambo. But no wonder your recent string of dates bombed. You suck at casual flirtation."

He skated over the teasing insult. Besides, it was true. "Who told you about my recent dates?"

"Daisy. She keeps me apprised of all Cupcake Lover issues."

"My social life has no bearing on the Cupcake Lovers."

"You're kidding, right? You're in the limelight alongside every CL involved in the recipe book."

"About that—"

"I'm sure any one of those prospects would have made a better wife and mother than me," she said, getting back to his dates.

"Maybe." If Harper was jealous or resentful, she didn't show it. But Sam detected a hint of annoyance. Interesting, since she'd been the one to end their affair. "But you've got something they don't."

"Kinky urges?"

"My attention."

Harper held it together as Sam drove them into Sugar Creek. A twenty-minute jaunt that felt like eternity. She alternated between checking her phone for texts and fingering her Serenity bracelet. She helped herself to his radio, dialing in cheery pop music to offset her darkening mood. She asked Sam to play tour guide, even though she was familiar with the area. Anything to distract her from morbid thoughts. Turned out he knew far more than she did about Sugar Creek and the surrounding land. Then again he'd lived here his entire life. She wondered what it felt like to love a place so much, you never wanted to leave. Harper had never felt rooted in that way, although she'd always had an affinity with the Rothwell Farm. Which prompted the question: *After they married, where would they live?* The farm was her safe haven and she had unfinished business with Mary. She didn't want to move out. She'd just moved in!

Harper fingered her bracelet, tempered her breathing. "How is this going to work exactly?"

"The marriage?"

"No, *lunch.*" Okay. That was snarky. But it had also been reflex. She'd learned to protect her heart by pushing people away.

Sam shot her one of his wicked death stares. "Why don't you shelve the sarcasm and tell me what's twisting you up?"

Harper stiffened her spine. "I'm not fond of sharing my . . . personal misgivings."

"Welcome to the club. What's with the bracelet?"

Self-conscious now, Harper stopped twirling the bangle. "You know how some people stroke rosary beads as a way of meditation? Same concept."

"Are you Catholic?"

"No."

"Religious?"

"Not particularly." Although the underside of her bracelet was inscribed with the Serenity prayer. "You?"

"I take the kids to church."

"That doesn't answer my question."

Sam rolled back his shoulders. "My faith has been tested over the years, so I'm a little shaky on my exact belief."

Same as her.

The awkward confession pulled Harper out of her self-absorbed misery. While decorating the farmhouse, Rocky had shared stories about her family, including bits about Sam. Harper knew he'd lost his first wife to ovarian cancer. That it had been an intrusive, lengthy battle and that Sam had been devastated when Paula had died. Harper assumed that crisis had shaken his faith. She'd gone through a similar shock with Andrew.

Although Andrew's fate, along with another, could have been avoided.

If only Harper had intervened.

Pulse racing, she shook off the memories, the guilt. That was Edward talking.

Because she didn't want to mention Andrew, she didn't ask about Paula. Instead she turned up the music.

Sam shut it off.

She focused on her phone.

Sam took it away.

"Dammit, McCloud—"

"The CLs mentioned you haven't been in town since you've been back. That you've had your meals and supplies delivered to the farm. Why is that?" When she didn't answer, he pushed. "You mentioned letting a lot of people down. Your clients? Why did the firm let you go?"

Harper balled her fists in her lap. She wanted to massage her aching chest. She wanted to stroke her bracelet. She wanted to punch Sam. But none of that would soothe her brewing anxiety.

The small town of Sugar Creek, with its quaint buildings and cobbled streets, loomed just ahead. She spotted the steeple of the Methodist church, the red-brick façades of the two-and three-story shops. The numerous trees populating the manicured parks and lawns and the green mountains that served as a verdant backdrop helped to create an old-fashioned scene reminiscent of a folk art painting. While the vision as a whole was serene, Harper's pulse skittered with dread.

Though the local population was small, Sugar Creek attracted hordes of tourists. Mostly they took advantage of the outdoor recreation—biking, hiking, skiing, snowmobiling—depending on the season. But in between they explored the delightful shops and restaurants. They relaxed in the town square. Stocked up on groceries at Oslow's General Store. Bought necessities at J. T. Monroe's Department Store. Took advantage of the wireless Internet in Moose-a-lotta—just one of the draws of Chloe and Daisy's kitschy café. They dined and socialized at the Sugar Shack, a popular pub owned by Rae's husband, Luke.

The more Harper thought about the crowds and strangers, people who could have a gripe, or a death wish, or a mental problem . . . People who could act out in any way at any time, the greater her anxiety. She envisioned having a full-blown panic attack as Sam escorted her into a restaurant. The possibility served a brutal blow to her pride. She'd been so sure she had a grip on her phobia.

"Turn around," she said, adding, "Please," and cursing her strangled tone.

Sam cast her a glance. Not one of his stern glares, but a look of concern. It messed with her stubborn determination to fight her own battles. An unsettling first.

"I have a problem with crowds," she admitted. "With public places."

"Since when?"

"Since last month. There was an incident. That's what's twisting me up. That's what got me fired. Or at least contributed to my dismissal. It triggered this insane fear of random violence and mass killings."

"Is that why you've been glued to CNN? Are you looking for a pattern? Trying to find reason in senseless attacks?"

Harper crossed her arms so as not to stroke her bracelet. Her insides churned and her head thrummed. This subject was dangerously close to Andrew's tragic meltdown. She didn't want to go there. Hard enough dealing with the incident in L.A.

"We need to talk about this, Harper. I can't subject Ben and Mina to whatever crisis you're going through if I don't know the details."

She got that. And, seriously, part of her wanted to confide in Sam. She'd tried everything to get a grip on her intensifying agoraphobia short of weekly visits to a shrink. Spewing her guts to a professional psychiatrist was akin to undergoing brain surgery sans anesthesia. Thank you, but no. That said, she was desperate to regain control of her life.

"I won't think you're crazy," Sam said, speaking to her earlier concern.

Harper studied Sam as he slowed his truck at the last intersection before town. Her breathing eased as she soaked in his calm and grounded strength. She couldn't talk about Andrew, but she could talk about the spa shooting.

"Pull over, Rambo. Someplace private. And give me back my phone."

EIGHT

Grenville's Overlook.

Sam made a U-turn, backtracked a mile, turned left then crossed the historic covered bridge to get to the other side of Sugar Creek—the river, not the town. He parked his truck near a copse of trees at the slope's edge, affording them a prime view upriver. The water sparkled and rippled, a gentle current conducive to canoeing, kayaking, and inner-tubing. As a boy Sam used to cannonball off the covered bridge with his cousins. He doubted Ben would be so adventurous. Mina was another story. Sam dreaded that day. For now his kids were happy with an occasional rafting expedition.

"Let me guess," Harper said as he keyed off the ignition. "You used to bring girlfriends here to make out."

Sam's lip twitched. "That was a long time ago."

"Your wife?"

"Paula was fond of moonlit picnics."

"That doesn't sound like your cup of tea."

"It's not."

"But you did it. For her."

Sam didn't answer, but he did look Harper's way. She was studying him as though puzzling through a riddle. He felt the same way about her. "You mentioned someplace private and Grenville's was close." Anxious to know the details behind her sudden and peculiar fear of crowds, Sam unbuckled his safety belt. "Want to walk and talk?"

She leaned forward, peered out and around the wooded river as if searching for a lurking ax murderer or sniper—a psychopath in a hockey mask looking for a random kill. She pressed back against the seat, hunkered in. "I'm good." She typed something into her phone, swiped the screen then passed him the android.

FIVE DEAD IN FIVE STAR LUXURY SPA SHOOTING

The article was dated a month and three days ago. The crime had taken place in Los Angeles, a chic fitness club near Rodeo Drive. Sam read for details, noting a man had strolled into an exercise class, pulled two guns, and started firing. Five dead, including the shooter. Seven wounded. Sam read every name. No mention of Harper.

"I was there," she said. "With a client. We were in another room, indulging in pedicures and mimosas. We never saw him. But we heard the gunfire, the screams. Everyone in our portion of the salon scrambled for cover or an exit. Except me. I bolted toward the chaos. A male attendant tackled me."

Thank God, Sam thought.

"I hit my head and blacked out."

"Better than getting riddled by bullets." He pictured Harper barefoot with newly painted toenails, half tipsy on a champagne cocktail. "What were you thinking?"

"I wanted to help."

"By putting yourself in harm's way?" Sam couldn't fathom her rationale. It wasn't like she was trained in offensive tactics. Or was she? Another reminder of how little he knew about the woman he'd offered his name and protection.

"He could have been firing into the ceiling for all I knew," she said. "A scare tactic. A warning. A threat. I thought if I could reason with him, talk him down . . ."

Spoken like the publicist who solved clients' melt-downs on an hourly basis, a woman who got off on spin-ning disasters into moments of redemption or convoluted misunderstandings. Sam dragged both hands down his face. "Are you that confident? Or that naïve?"

"If you're going to judge me—"

"Not judging. Trying to understand."

"Never mind why I did what I did," she said. "The last thing I want is to be psychoanalyzed. Just let me explain my present dilemma so you know what you're dealing with for the sake of Ben and Mina. Not that it's cause for concern, because I'm going to kick this problem's ass."

"Worried I'm going to retract the marriage offer?"

"Yes."

Blunt and honest. "Go on." Sam shifted, giving Harper his avid attention. In doing so, he was once again struck by her stunning features. Her shapely figure. Her stylish wardrobe. He tried imagining her going head to head with a crazed shooter, but couldn't.

"I'm grateful to be alive, of course," Harper said. "But I could have just as easily been in that fitness room. After I'd regained consciousness, my first thought was, *Why not me?* Survivor's guilt, right? Totally natural, yes? But then that thought manifested into, *It could still be me.* Anytime. Anywhere. Mass shootings. Acts of terror. They happen all the time. In schools. Malls. Movie theaters. Work spaces. Military bases. You can't predict when someone's going to snap. You can't avoid the possibility of being maimed or killed in a surprise attack unless you avoid all public places. Unless you hide out in a safe place."

"And for you that's the farmhouse," Sam interjected.

"I told the firm I needed a short break to get my act to-gether. I had plenty of holiday time. Plus I can work from anywhere. Yes, I teed off a few clients by dodging public meetings these last few weeks, but I'd promised to make amends. Firing me was bogus and I'm convinced they only used this momentary lapse as an excuse. Certain people in the firm have it out for me. As if being talented and motivated is a sin. I won't apologize for being good at what I do. I won't apologize for being detached. It keeps me sane and focused. I have to . . ."

She trailed off and Sam raised a brow. "Have to what?"

"Never mind. I'm babbling. I do that sometimes when I get fired up. I just—" She broke off and shook her head. "I'm haunted by the random senselessness of that shooting. I worry that something horrible could happen at any time. And I'm embarrassed to admit that I'm battling an intensifying case of agoraphobia. I'm petrified of venturing into Sugar Creek, a town that has a nonexistent crime rate."

Sam absorbed her fear, her concerns and compassion. He marveled that, though they'd been involved sexually on several occasions, he'd never once sensed Harper's softer side. She was sensitive. How had he missed that?

She took back her phone and tapped the screen. "I never realized how lax the gun control laws are in the state until I researched the other day. Lax as in *no* state gun control laws."

She passed Sam the phone, pointing out a list of statistics. Statistics he knew well. Stats that didn't faze him. Many were steeped in tradition, like the right to hunt, which was written into the Vermont Constitution.

"Vermont is one of four states that allows you to carry concealed without *any* permit," Harper went on. "People as young as sixteen can buy a gun and carry concealed without parental permission! Any hormonal teen could have a bad day, get drunk, and go on a shooting spree."

"My dad taught me how to hunt when I was ten," Sam interjected. "He gifted me with a twelve-gauge shotgun when I was fifteen. I had plenty of bad days, got soused a few times with friends. I never went on a shooting spree."

"You're one person," Harper said. Again she tapped

her phone's screen. "Close to fifty percent of Vermont households contain firearms."

"A liberal, gun-friendly state," Sam said, "with an impressively low homicide rate. Vermonters own guns to manage our natural resources, to maintain hunting traditions, to protect our homes and loved ones. The intent is not to maim or kill innocent people."

"But it *does* happen!"

Sam didn't argue. Yeah, it happened. Once in a blue moon. He dragged a hand through his hair. *Unbelievable.* His first real discussion with Harper and they were arguing gun control.

"Obviously you're progun." Harper took back her phone. "So naturally you think my fears are ungrounded and unreasonable. You may not think I'm crazy, but I'm sure you're leaning toward hypersensitive or overdramatic."

"You know I served in the marines, right?"

She glanced over, expression intense. Body rigid. "Your point?"

If he touched her right now, Sam was pretty sure she'd shatter. She was wound that tight. "Several years of combat," he continued. "Several years of spontaneous and unexpected ugly." He wasn't fond of talking about his time in the field, but he sensed it was important for her to know that he understood her fear. "There were weeks when I spent every minute bracing for a violent assault. Ambushes. Land mines. Air strikes."

She held quiet a long moment, as if envisioning those assaults, as if imagining the horror. "That must have been exhausting." Her eyes sparked with something new. *Sadness? Compassion? Respect?* "Relentless terror. I think I'd crack. Some do, you know. Crack, that is. Some later than sooner."

PTSS. Post-traumatic stress syndrome. Sam had never suffered that particular ill effect of war. But he knew soldiers who had. Did she? He thought about the spa shooting. An angry husband on a rampage. Former military, perhaps?

"How did you manage?" she asked.

"Mental toughness and cool confidence. Extensive training in defense helps. Living in constant fear is paralyzing, Harper. Instead of worrying about what *could* happen, learn to defend yourself in case something *does* happen."

"Take control. Narrow the odds."

"Increase the odds of securing your safety and the safety of others." Again he envisioned her in that spa conflict. "Rushing into a hostile situation, unarmed and blind to the specifics, was—"

"Stupid?"

"Unwise."

"Are you suggesting I enroll in a karate or kickboxing class? I'm not fond of group activities. That's why I exercise alone."

"I can give you some pointers. Teach you some techniques."

"I refuse to handle a firearm."

"The best defense is to avoid confrontation in the first place. It's about being observant and aware," Sam said. "When all else fails it's about neutralizing an attack. I can teach you to do that with an umbrella."

Her lip twitched. "Seriously?"

"Seriously."

"You're that good?"

"I'm that good. And you're that capable." He reached over and grasped her hand. He meant it as show of faith, but his heart tripped over itself as something warm flowed through his blood. Something akin to affection, which was crazy because, aside from sex, he wasn't exactly *fond* of Harper. Or at least the Harper he'd been subjected to in the past. Last night he'd gotten a glimpse of her vulnerability. Today, she'd peeled away another layer, revealing a courageous though reckless streak. Sharing her fears and talking about something real, something more serious than a soap opera star with weight issues being crucified in a tabloid.

They'd had a lengthy discussion and even though they had opposing viewpoints on gun control, they'd never been more in tune. Sam felt it. And he knew Harper felt it because she didn't pull away or make a sarcastic crack. She studied their hands then blew out a breath.

"Where do we start?" she asked.

Sam smiled. "With lunch."

NINE

Harper wasn't surprised that Sam had made lunch reservations at the Sugar Shack. Aside from it being Sugar Creek's most popular restaurant and pub, the Shack was owned by Sam's cousin Luke, and frequented by several other family members and friends. If Sam wanted word to spread fast about their "date," setting the scene for their impulsive marriage, this was the perfect venue. One she would have chosen herself if she were vying for attention for a client.

Sure enough, Harper spied Luke tending bar just as a hostess escorted her and Sam to a cozy booth. Luke who was married to Rae, Harper's client and Sam's ex-flame. As Harper understood it, there'd never been anything intimate between Sam and Rae, but Sam had been attracted to the tenderhearted woman and that had caused a rift between Sam and Luke. That had been months ago, around the same time Harper had purchased the Rothwell Farm. Now Rae was married to Luke and pregnant with his child and all was forgiven and forgotten regarding the rift. Not that Harper had ever asked Sam, but she'd gotten the lowdown from Daisy who seemed to know everything about everyone. It occurred to Harper that Daisy would be the perfect resource if she wanted to get the skivvy on the dynamics of all the Monroes.

Or . . . she could ask Sam.

Something had shifted between them. She'd felt it last night when he'd talked her down and most keenly when they'd kissed. Then today when she'd spilled her fears and he'd commiserated. They'd talked, really *talked*. And though she didn't agree with his stand on gun control, she respected his opinion based on his personal experience. Mostly she appreciated that he didn't attack her own views and, instead of mocking her fears, offered to help her overcome them. For the first time in ages, Harper hadn't felt alone and that sensation had bolstered her spirits as well as tempering her irrational anxiety.

"Why are you smiling?" Sam asked from across the table.

She glanced up from her menu. She'd been smiling? "I don't know. I . . . I guess I'm happy. Happy that I made it into town. Happy I'm not stressing about an attack. I mean, nothing's changed. The possibility still lurks, but I'm not obsessing on it. Instead I'm obsessing on you. Us."

He arched a brow.

"I don't get us."

"That's because we don't make sense. Not yet anyway."

The waitress approached and Harper immediately noted her penchant for goth. She wore black pants and a white top—the standard colors of the Shack's informal uniform—but the pants were massively baggy with lots of buckles and the white tee was adorned with an embroidered skull and roses. Raven-black hair with deep purple streaks pulled into a high ponytail. Short blunt bangs. A small silver hoop in her nose. Big black-framed glasses that overwhelmed her small heart-shaped face. Her nametag read JOEY and she looked like she belonged in a sci-fi flick as opposed to a small-town pub.

"Hey, Sam," she said.

"Let me guess," he said. "Luke was short a waitress and you volunteered."

"It's not like he can't handle the bar himself," Joey said.

"Joey is Luke's newest hire," Sam said to Harper. "Although she typically tends bar. Joey, this is Harper Day. The Cupcake Lovers' publicist."

"The lady who lives in the haunted house." Joey rocked back on her army boots and smiled. "Cool. Heard about you at the meeting last night."

Then it clicked. "You're the newest Cupcake Lover?" Daisy had mentioned a new girl, Joelle—*Joey*—saying she was a snazzy dresser. Only Daisy would consider gothic snazzy.

"I have a cousin and a couple of friends in the military," she said. "When Luke told me about the Cupcake Lovers, I had to join. I mean, it's a great cause, right? Plus I've been picking up some rad baking tips. I'm totally into broadening my horizons and keeping busy. Speaking of . . . What'll you have?"

Harper envisioned a publicity photo featuring the all-American Cupcake Lovers, with the addition of cyberpunk Joey, and cringed. How was she going to spin this oddball member? Something to ponder later. Right now her mind was fixed on Sam and their impending marriage.

He ordered a cheeseburger and fries.

Harper ordered a salad—mesclun greens topped with dried cranberries, dried apricots, and toasted walnuts, served with maple vinaigrette. That pretty much summed up their relationship. Hell-raiser burger versus health-nut salad.

"Anything to drink?" Joey asked.

"Sparkling water, please," Harper said.

"I'll have a beer," Sam said. "Something light on tap."

Joey took their menus and left.

Sam eyed Harper. "No wine?"

She shifted, thinking about the last time they'd shared a bottle of merlot. A precursor to their last hot and sweaty tumble more than a month and a half ago. "I feel punch-drunk as is."

Sam studied her with an enigmatic expression. "Feeling a little dazed myself."

Not for the first time this afternoon, she noticed Sam wasn't quite himself. Or at least the Sam she'd known up until now. She was used to seeing him with a five o'clock shadow, but today he had a close shave. Too close, considering the nick on his jaw. He typically sported faded, paint-splattered jeans and baggy T-shirts. Today's wrinkle-free oxford shirt and stain-free jeans hadn't escaped her notice. On any given day, Sam McCloud revved her pulse. Today he'd stopped her heart. The man had dressed to impress and that was both flattering and frightening. "You can still back out."

"But I won't. In fact, I found a way to speed things up."

Harper's pulse kicked and so did her ego. Typically she was the problem solver. The one who brainstormed solutions and set plans into motion. Sam had offered marriage less than twenty-four hours ago and, in addition to caring for his children and shifting the hours of his workload, he'd researched the intricacies of a Canadian/American marriage? She should have researched the details herself, but instead she'd jumped on the phone trying to mend bridges with various clients, her deportation shoved to the back burner.

"Now you're frowning."

"Just thinking."

"Overthinking. Here's the deal. Since you've already been living in the United States under another visa, we can circumvent the tedious interviews, marry in Vegas, and address the necessary paperwork for permanent residency later."

Harper blinked. "It can't be that easy."

"I can expedite matters further by completing an on-line marriage preapplication for the marriage license."

"Eloping to Las Vegas."

"Before your L visa expires. Which gives us two weeks."

So . . . in less than fourteen days she'd be Mrs. Sam McCloud, a wife and a mother.

"Now you look faint," Sam said, his lips twitching into a teasing smile.

Harper toyed with her fork rather than squirm in her seat. He'd never teased her before. He'd never looked at her with such kindness. She didn't know how to respond. Not without being snarky, and she didn't want to fall back on that defense. Not now. The most guarded part of her ached for what she feared most—an intimate, emotional connection with a good and caring man. Even so, she couldn't risk it. "I'm having a hard time wrapping my head around this business arrangement." She raised a saucy brow. *That* she could manage. "With the exception of the hot sex."

Sam reached across the table and covered her hand with his own. She thought it was to still her nervous fork action, but instead he curled his fingers around hers and brushed his thumb over her skin. A definite show of affection. She had no idea if it was for real or for the benefit of anyone and everyone watching. Either way her mouth went dry.

"About the sex," he said.

But then Luke was there, two drinks in hand. "Whoa. Okay. Bad timing."

"Don't be silly," Harper said, donning her publicist hat. "We were talking about a movie." She casually slid her hand from Sam's. Thankfully he didn't stop her, nor did he refute her lie. Not that Luke looked convinced.

"Sure. Okay." Sugar Creek's former number one play-boy set a foamy beer in front of his cousin and served Harper a glass of sparkling water. "Just wanted to say hello. Thank you in person for keeping my wife in the good graces of the press."

"Rae makes it easy," Harper said with a professional smile. "Her humanitarian efforts are impressive and her level of modesty almost unheard of. She has the respect of the media."

"Unlike her mother," Luke said with a scowl.

"Don't go there," Sam said. "That woman's not worth an ulcer."

Harper agreed. Olivia Devereaux and her husband of the moment, an arrogant, powerful businessman—filthy rich in his own right—had tried to manipulate and ruin Rae in order to gain control of her fortune. Seedy business. A tabloid reporter's dream. Spinning the debacle for the better had been one of Harper's finest efforts. Finest because Rae was a privileged soul with a pure heart. A rarity in Harper's specific line of work. "I'm sorry I haven't been over to visit," Harper said, "but I did advise Rae on that matter she asked me about."

"She told me," Luke said. "Thanks. I'm going to break it to the family on Sunday."

"Break what to the family?" Sam asked.

Harper flushed knowing she, an outsider, was privy to a Monroe secret. After suffering from dyslexia for years—a condition he'd successfully covered up—Luke had made the choice to conquer his reading disability. Rae had been tutoring him for months and now he wanted to come clean, serving as a spokesperson in order to inspire kids and adults battling similar challenges. Harper couldn't wait to promote his cause, but she was on hold until Luke came clean with his family.

"You'll find out with everyone else at Sunday dinner," Luke said to Sam. "Speaking of . . ." His expression turned downright ornery. "Why don't you bring Harper along?"

Harper tensed. She'd heard about the traditional Monroe Sunday dinners. An ever-changing menagerie of family and close friends connecting over massive home-cooked meals. "I don't think—"

"Good idea," Sam said.

"But—"

"Great." Luke smiled. "I could use the extra support," he said directly to Harper, leaving her no gracious way to refuse.

Harper had to give Luke credit. Though she didn't know his exact intent, he'd manipulated her big-time. "Absolutely," she said with a perfected fake smile. "See you there."

"I should get back to work," he said. "Enjoy lunch."

He left and Harper frowned at Sam. "Sunday dinner?"

"The perfect venue to cement our unexpected but amorous attraction. Luke just presented us with a gift, Harper. He picked up on the attraction and gave us his blessing."

"This is wacky. Three months ago, you and Luke were at war."

"Now we're not. We're family. Family trumps all else."

Harper wouldn't know. She was an only child. Her parents were divorced and estranged and more interested in their own lives than the life of the child they'd brought into the world.

Joey served their food with the speed and grace of a top-notch waitress.

Sam thanked her and Harper fought to temper her wayward emotions. "On second thought," she said as Joey loaded the table with fresh condiments, "I'll have a glass of your house chardonnay."

"You got it." Tray tucked under her arm, Joey zipped toward the bar, ponytail swinging.

Harper's phone pinged with an incoming text. "Sorry," she said to Sam. "It's from Daisy."

He doused his fries with ketchup while she read the text.

SOMETHING CAME UP. NEED TO RESCHEDULE FOR TOMORROW. MORNING AND MIMOSAS OKAY?

Damn. Although, on second thought, maybe tomorrow was better. Closer to Sunday. Harper planned on picking Daisy's brain regarding her extended family. No way was she going into that Sunday dinner unarmed.

MORNING AND MIMOSAS . . . SPIFFY.

Harper tucked away her phone, stabbed her healthy greens, and blurted a flurry of concerns. "How are you going to break it to the kids, and when? Where are we going to live? I need to tell the Cupcake Lovers I was dismissed from the firm. Rae, too. Maybe they won't want me to represent them anymore. I hope that's not the case, but I owe them the choice. Are we supposed to pretend we're in love or are we going to own up to a marriage of convenience? Although, if the truth got back to immigration, I'd be screwed. On the other hand, pretending, that doesn't seem fair to the kids. And what if we're not compatible? You and me? How long do we have to stay married in order for me to obtain U.S. citizenship? What if we can't make it that long? Jesus, Sam. This has disaster written all over it."

Harper abandoned her fork and massaged a throbbing temple.

Sam bit off a fry, raised a brow. "Are you done?"

"For the moment." She hated and loved that he was so calm. She hated and loved the way he made her heart race with a single tender look. Joey showed with a glass of chardonnay and it was all Harper could do not to hug her. She cautioned herself to sip, not gulp. She handled complicated problems for a living, why couldn't she methodically sort through her own mess?

Sam wiped his face and hands with a napkin, surprising Harper when he stood and rounded the table, sliding into the booth beside her. Her breath stalled as he casually draped his arm over the top of the cushion, behind her, around her, and angled in. He searched her face, her eyes. "We're compatible."

"How do you know?"

He leaned closer, enveloping her in his masculine scent, his heady charisma. He brushed his mouth over hers, a brief, chaste kiss that sizzled through her blood.

She blinked up at his handsome face. Yeah. There was that. The intense physical attraction. A definite perk to the business arrangement. If she could put up with contrary clients like Sapphire, surely she could handle one headstrong man and two little kids. Except the kids would put a damper on the kind of sex she'd experienced thus far with Sam, putting a serious kink in the kinky. "About the sex," she said, picking up on the subject Luke had walked in on.

"It's on hold until after we're married."

He had to be kidding. Yet he didn't flinch. Harper frowned, still vibrating from that barely there kiss. "Surely you're not that old-fashioned."

"You're right."

"But—"

"We played by your rules first time around. Now it's my turn."

She narrowed her eyes. "Why do I get the feeling you're getting off on taking charge?"

To her libido's distress, he just smiled.

TEN

Adam Brody strolled into Rock 'n' Roll Lanes wishing he had better things to do than checking out a new hang for a bunch of single guy friends. But he didn't. So here he was.

The establishment itself was pretty large. A fifteen-lane bowling center with a separate game room, featuring various arcade games. Two separate areas that offered billiards and darts. A snack bar, a café, and a sports bar offering live entertainment. Rock posters picturing bands from the fifties to eighties lined the walls along with vintage guitars and costumes and assorted neon signs.

At least three employees welcomed him within the first five minutes.

McCloud was right. Friendly staff. Fun atmosphere. The bowling alley was buzzing with a mostly adult Friday-night crowd.

Adam bypassed the counter that rented balls and shoes and went directly for the sports bar. He knew the bartender, Clive, from the ski slopes. They nodded in greeting and Adam ordered a beer while eyeing the nearby stage where five musicians—all women—quipped while plugging in various cords and amplifiers. "Who's the band?"

"Mountain Fever."

"Never heard of them."

"You and me both. Easy on the eyes, though."

Adam sipped his beer, watched the stage.

The woman front and center, bent over and intent on freeing a knotted microphone cable, straightened.

Adam perked up, too.

Hello, gorgeous.

"Who's the chick?" he asked.

"Which one?" Clive asked.

Adam only had eyes for one. "The stunner blonde with the two long braids."

"Ivy Vine," Clive said. "How'd you like to have that climbing up your body?"

Adam didn't answer but he imagined.

"What are you grinning at?" Nash asked as he moved in beside Adam and ordered a beer. "Sorry I'm late," he added. "Where's Kane?"

"Last minute hookup."

"With who?"

"He didn't say." Adam sipped his beer, eyes glued to the stage or rather Ivy's ass, as the woman turned to the drummer and set the tempo of the song with the pounding heel of her boot. "Know anything about her?" Adam asked over the blaring music.

"Which one?"

"The lead singer. Ivy Vine."

"Nope. But I know the guitar player." He pointed to the short-haired sprite in the flowery dress and cowboy boots. "Peppy Redding. Marvin Redding's daughter. Vince's granddaughter."

"Sugar Creek native," Adam said. "Why don't I know her?" he asked, even as his gaze gravitated back to Ivy.

"She was a few years behind us in school, plus she bounced back and forth between her mom and dad. Split custody. Her mom transplanted to Nashville. Peppy's been bouncing around the country the last couple of years, chasing fame. Heard she fell on hard times and now she's back and staying with her dad. According to Vince, that's not going so well. Speaking of, I'll be damned. Check it out."

Adam looked to where Nash pointed. Vince Redding and Daisy Monroe sat at a table, close to the stage. Too close for Vince if the napkins he'd just jammed in his ears were any indication. Daisy, on the other hand, bopped back and forth to "Goodbye Earl," an old hit by the Dixie Chicks. Not in time exactly, but bopping nonetheless. "Your grandma's a riot, Nash."

"She's something all right." Nash drank more beer then gestured back to the stage. "Ivy sort of looks like Rocky."

What? Adam did a double take. Oh, hell, no. She did. Tall and curvy. Tight jeans, fitted T-shirt. *Blond braids*. Once upon a time Adam had had a secret friends-with-benefits affair with Rocky. She was married to someone else now and Adam had put whatever affection he'd felt for Rocky to bed, so to speak. Still, his heart had taken a beating. It wasn't the first time. Aside from a short fling he'd had with a gorgeous brunette over Christmas, his apparent heartbreaker of choice was the stereotypical Hollywood blonde.

Nash nudged him. "Introduce yourself when they go on break."

"She looks like trouble."

"With a capital *T*. If you're taking a pass, let me know. Ivy's hot. Actually, they're all hot. Except maybe Peppy. Don't get me wrong. She's cute. But subdued. You know, it might help her career if she showed some cleavage or curves or both. She's in show biz, after all." Nash polished off his beer then nodded toward the lanes. "Come on. Let's knock back a few pins. Get a feel for this place." He ordered two more beers then took the lead.

Adam followed although his mind lingered with Ivy. Maybe she was different. Maybe she was down-to-earth and looking for a long-term relationship. Something Adam had been craving for a long while. No harm in introducing himself. Near as he could tell she was single. No ring. Maybe she'd be up for a late-night breakfast.

An hour and a few games later, Adam drifted back to the Rockin' R stage while Nash hit the john. The band was on break. He didn't see Ivy, but he spied Peppy getting up from Vince and Daisy's table and moving toward the bar. Trying to look nonchalant, he ordered two Buds just as Peppy stepped up and ordered three drinks, one being a Fuzzy Navel that had to be for Daisy. Nash's grandma's taste for wacky cocktails was town renowned.

"Great music," Adam said.

Peppy glanced his way. She looked like she wanted to argue, but instead said, "Thanks."

"Not a local band."

"No," she said. "The group's based in Pixley. We're booked here for the next four Fridays, though."

She turned her attention back to Clive who slid her the first of three drinks. Nash was right. Peppy was cute. Petite in height and build. Impish features. Dark brown hair cut in short wispy layers. Kind of a boyish cut but on her it looked . . . cute. If she had curves, he couldn't tell, but her bone structure was slight and from what he could see she had nice legs.

"Take a picture, it'll last longer," she said.

Busted. Adam met her amber gaze, saw a flicker of amusement and a slight flush of red to her freckled cheeks. At least she wasn't pissed. He smiled. "Let me buy your drinks."

"Thanks, but I'm good." She slid Clive some cash.

"So your lead singer," Adam said.

"What about her?"

"Is she single?"

Peppy's expression turned from amused to annoyed. "What are you, in fifth grade?" She managed the three drinks like a pro, smirked at Adam. "Ask her yourself."

"Smooth," Clive said to Adam after Peppy hustled away.

Adam closed his eyes and cursed. He hadn't meant to hurt Peppy's feelings. In fact, he'd meant to go against type and to flirt with her instead, but then he'd gotten flustered. *That* was a first.

Ivy drifted into view, beer bottle in hand, laughing and flirting with the three men surrounding her. Peppy was sipping cola through a straw and entertaining two seniors. If Daisy and her granddad weren't there, would she be sitting alone in a corner, biding her time until the next set while her hot bandmates enjoyed all the attention?

Nash breezed in and nodded toward Ivy. "Looks like Bill Tully and friends beat you to the punch."

Adam dragged a hand through his hair, wondering if he was ever going to meet the girl of his dreams. "I'm outta here for the night."

"Something I said?"

"No." Adam gave Peppy a parting glance then waved to Nash. "Something I said."

ELEVEN

Saturday morning dawned and Sam couldn't decide if it was a new day or a continuation of the day before. He blinked into the hazy morning, senses fuzzy. He'd drifted off at some point during the night, but he was fairly certain he'd never reached REM. No dreaming. Just a barrage of memories and projections. Life before with Paula. Life ahead with Harper. A tornado of emotions, but mostly a sense of anticipation.

Worry had contributed to his insomnia, as well. Braced for an emergency text, he'd checked his phone several times throughout the night. Even though Harper had seemed calm and stable when he'd driven her home, that didn't mean she wouldn't suffer a bout of panic at any given moment. That spa shooting preyed on her heart and mind and no doubt haunted her dreams. Sam was perplexed by the severity of her reaction to the attack since she hadn't actually *witnessed* the horror. Although she had heard the shots, the screams. Her imagination had probably taken it from there, painting a bloody picture and cranking the terror up a notch. Plus there'd been the news reports, the graphic descriptions, and a leaked crime-scene photo. Sam had easily researched the incident on the Internet. A definite dose of ugly.

Regardless, Harper had made it through the night without reaching out to Sam. He was glad and, also, oddly disappointed. It was nice to be needed.

He glanced at his bedside clock. Seven A.M. Was she awake? Showering? Exercising? Surfing the Net or the television? He'd asked her to lay off the hard news, specifically bad news. Being informed was one thing. Obsessing another. She'd noted his logic, but was she following his advice?

Sam stared up at the ceiling, obsessing in his own right, aching for a bedmate. Specifically Harper. They'd never slept together through the night. He looked forward to that as much as their next round of lovemaking. Although he'd put the kibosh on sex until after they'd married. Part of his strategic plan—one that focused on emotional rather than physical intimacy. At least it sounded good in theory.

Sporting morning wood and a dull headache, Sam forced his thoughts away from his future wife and focused on how he was going to make that future happen. Time was of the essence and he'd yet to broach the subject of marriage with the kids. He was still waging the best campaign. Since Ben and Mina spent every other weekend with their maternal grandparents, Sam would have these next two days to get his act together. Two days to sort through details of his alliance with Harper. Two days to strengthen their bond and to lay groundwork with his family. Two days to figure out the best way to break the news to Ben and Mina.

Suddenly a tour of duty sounded like a cakewalk compared to tackling this next phase of his life.

"Pull it together, McCloud."

He swung his legs over the side of the bed just as his bedroom door flew open and a little girl skidded into his room.

"Da-*deeeee*!"

Mina's high-pitched screech would have tweaked his concern, except she didn't look scared or hurt or upset.

She looked pissed. Sam regarded his tangle-haired, red-faced daughter with a raised brow and strained patience. She'd been at war with her brother for more than two weeks. "What did Ben do now?"

"He won't let me flip the pancakes."

"What pancakes?"

"The pancakes we're making for breakfast."

Sam blinked. What the . . .

Adrenaline spiking, he stabbed his legs into his sweat-pants. Since Paula had died, he'd taken to sleeping in box-ers and a tee, always at the ready should the kids cry out in the middle of the night, always decent should they burst into his room without knocking which they almost always did. He nabbed his phone with one hand then scooped up Mina—ratty teddy bear and all. "You're not supposed to use the stove without me being there."

Two weeks before, there'd been an incident when Mina had taken it upon herself to roast a marshmallow over the gas burner, and not long before that she'd fritzed the microwave by nuking soup in the fricking can. Ben had more kitchen sense, but his mind often wandered. "Dam-mit, honey."

"You said a bad word."

"I know. I'm sorry. But I wish you would have asked me first."

She scrunched up her impish face. "We wanted to sur-prise you."

They'd surprised him all right. They'd somehow gotten past his room and down the stairs without rousing his at-tention. Even when sleeping Sam was attuned to every creak in the floorboards, every footfall on the steps. Whis-pers, murmurs, sighs, coughs, sneezes, cries . . .

Sam descended the carpeted stairway with his young daughter on his hip. His pulse settled as he hit the first floor—no sight or smell of smoke or fire. Concern gave way to curiosity as he cleared the kitchen and spied his son expertly shifting a fat golden-brown pancake from skillet to platter.

Short and slight for his age, Ben peered over his scrawny shoulder and glared at his sister. "You're such a baby, Mina. We were supposed to spring the surprise together."

"I'm not a baby," Mina blasted, clutching her teddy bear tighter.

"Are so."

"Am not."

"You tattled to Dad just cuz I wouldn't let you cook. You're not allowed to cook."

"Neither are you," Sam reminded his son. "Not unsupervised."

Ben turned back to the skillet, turned off the burner. "I was careful," he said in a quiet voice.

Since Ben typically played by the rules, Sam was doubly intrigued. *We wanted to surprise you.* Setting Mina to the floor, Sam marveled that he'd been oblivious to the early-morning activity. How could he have been so distracted, so immersed in his own thoughts? Either Ben and Mina had been quiet as mice or Sam was really off his game. The counter was a cluttered mess of bowls, measuring cups, a quart of milk, and a box of Bisquick. In contrast the kitchen table was neat as a pin, three places set with a small vase of wildflowers in the center. His nose twitched and he glanced to the coffee maker. Sludge-black java dripped into the glass carafe.

"Can I flip a pancake *now*?" Mina asked.

"All done," Ben said as he set the spatula aside. "You get the juice."

"And the syrup!" Looking excited now, Mina hustled to the fridge.

Head spinning, Sam eyed his son as he set the heaping platter on the table then doubled back for a small basket of toast. The pancakes looked fluffy and delicious. Ben had never had a head for sports or mechanics, but he remembered everything Sam had ever taught him in the kitchen and devoured any game, show, or book in the fantasy realm. The boy, God love him, had inherited Paula's domestic and whimsical qualities. He was also painfully shy.

Mina, who wasn't the least bit timid, set a carton of orange juice on the table then raided the pantry for the maple syrup. They'd cooked . . . on their own. Set the table . . . on their own. Working as a team to prove . . . what? Suspicious, Sam helped himself to a mug of what looked like espresso. "Who taught you to make coffee?" he asked his son.

"Bridgett."

One of the three sitters Sam relied on. Especially in the summer when the kids were out of school and Sam was up to his eyeballs in carpentry work. Bridgett had been the sitter-on-duty while Sam had attended the Cupcake Lover meeting.

Sam sipped his coffee and smothered a grimace. Yup. *Sludge.* Either Ben had added too little water or too many grounds or Bridgett couldn't make coffee worth jack. Sam kept that speculation to himself. He also squelched the scolding crowding his tongue regarding the stove. Something about the way Ben's shoulders were squared. A determination and confidence that Sam rarely saw in his boy. "What's the occasion?" he asked as they all three took a seat.

"We're grown-up now," Mina said.

"Self-sufficient," Ben said.

Sam raised a brow.

"We even packed our bags for the weekend," Ben added. "And don't worry about this mess. We'll clean it up." He narrowed his eyes on his little sister. "Right, Mina?"

"Yup."

"The word is *yes,*" Sam corrected, then, "You're willing to help your brother with the dishes?"

"Yup. I mean, yes. *Sir.*"

Sam eyed them both. "You two in cahoots? What's going on?"

"What's cahoots?" Mina asked.

"Bridgett said you won't get married, because you don't trust anyone to take care of us," Ben blurted, eyes glued on his plate.

Sam fumbled his fork. "She told you that?"

"No. She told Rudy."

Bridgett's boyfriend. "Rudy was here?"

"They were talking on the phone," Mina said as she chewed.

"Don't talk with your mouth full, honey." Sam didn't appreciate knowing he'd been the subject of gossip in his own home. Especially given what Ben and Mina had overheard. Regardless, he strove for casual as he nabbed a piece of toast. "It's not polite to listen in on people's conversations," he told them both.

"We weren't listening on purpose," Mina said. "She was talking really loud."

"Rudy was mad because she spends so much time babysitting," Ben said. "She's going to quit, but you don't have to find someone new. I can take care of Mina."

Mina nodded. "And I'll make sure Ben does his homework. We don't want you to be a lonely old man, Daddy."

Oh, hell, no. What else had Bridgett said? "Mina, honey, I'm not—"

"We were talking. Mina and me," Ben interrupted, "and we decided we're too old for sitters."

"You don't have to trust someone to take care of us," Mina said. "We can take care of ourselves." She poured more syrup over her already soggy pancakes. "Now you can marry any ol' person."

"We vote for Harper," Ben said.

Talk about being blindsided. Sam sipped sludge, giving his stunned brain a fortifying jolt. *Of all the women in Sugar Creek.* "Why Harper?"

Mina beamed. "She likes purple."

"She's kind of cool."

"She makes good cupcakes."

"We could live in that rad house."

"She knows Cinderella."

Sam assumed his daughter was referring to an actress. One of Harper's clients or a celebrity acquaintance. He eyed his son who still looked uncharacteristically driven. "Anything else?"

Ben's shy gaze skipped to Sam and then back to his pancakes. "She's lonely, too."

The oven timer dinged in tandem with Harper's phone. She glanced back and forth from the vintage chrome and porcelain stove to her ultramodern android then decided to multitask. She snatched her phone from the counter while opening the oven door, poking a toothpick in one of the aromatic cupcakes—*done!*—then glancing at the text. *What?*

MINA WANTS THE BUTTERFLY ROOM.

Sam's text shocked Harper to her sneakered toes. She assumed two things. He'd told the kids about their impending marriage and he'd decided they'd move in here at the farm. Rocky had decorated the third bedroom with a butterfly theme. Mina was claiming that whimsical room as her own.

"Holy . . ."

Heart thudding, Harper donned oven mitts then transferred two muffin pans from the heated oven to a cooling rack on the counter. Although she'd spent last night and this morning readjusting her mind-set and rethinking her career plan, Sam was in full action mode. Researching legalities, prebooking a Vegas marriage license, breaking the news to his kids, deciding where they would live. Alleviating stress and handling complications with speed and apparent ease. Harper felt grateful and resentful at the same time. Taking control and solving problems was her drug of choice. An addiction that kept her soaring above the dark waters of her past. An addiction that enabled her to disconnect from her true self, a person who preferred rose-colored glasses to battle gear. A woman who'd unwittingly contributed to two deaths and multiple heartbreaks because she'd given in, given up, and given over.

No one was going to die if she botched this marriage, but hearts were definitely at stake, especially where Ben and Mina were concerned.

Harper was so flustered that she texted while wearing the mitts which resulted in gibberish that garnered a Daisy-like response from Sam.

????

Blood roaring in her ears, Harper connected verbally. "You told the kids?"

"They told me."

"What does *that* mean?"

"They don't want me to be a 'lonely old man.' Declared themselves self-sufficient then gave me permission to marry 'any ol' person,' although they voted for you."

Harper palmed her forehead. "Why me?"

"You know superheroes and Cinderella."

"Oh. Well, I do. Sort of."

"Hard to deny them when they plied me with pancakes," Sam went on, sounding amused. "But I did slow their horses."

"Meaning?"

"I fessed up to thinking you're *cool,* too, and said you were definitely a contender."

Harper rolled her eyes. "Gee, thanks."

"Just planting more seeds so the actual marriage doesn't come out of the blue."

She flashed on their lunch at the Shack. The way Sam had cozied up. The things Luke had overheard. Surely Luke had said something to Rae, who probably said something to Rocky or Chloe. That particular seed was no doubt growing like a weed. Now the kids would say something to a cousin or an aunt or an uncle or a friend. Within twenty-four hours everyone in Sugar Creek would be whispering about the town's most unlikely couple. "I guess that makes sense." Harper smiled a little, knowing she'd been preapproved by Sam's kids. They thought she was *cool*?

"Are we still on for this afternoon?"

Sam had promised a lesson in self-defense. Though she knew his intentions were good, once again it put him in the position of authority. She hated feeling ineffectual and clueless. Maybe she'd search YouTube for an instructional video and bone up on some self-defense tips before Sam arrived.

"Harper?"

"What? I mean, yes. Sorry. Distracted." She tested the cupcakes for coolness. "Are you bringing Ben and Mina?"

"Just dropped them at their grandparents for the weekend."

"That's right. You told me. Right. Great. So you're free for the night." Frustrated, Harper jumped on an opportunity to take charge. "Bring a bag. You're staying over."

"You're inviting me to spend the night? All night?"

"We might as well get our feet wet."

"No sex."

"Right. Whatever. We'll"—*ugh*—"talk. I have a say in this relationship, too, you know."

"Of course you do. I'll sleep in a guest room."

"Are we going to sleep together once we're married?"

"Yes."

One word loaded with a world of innuendo. Harper fought his machismo charisma for all she was worth. "Then we'll sleep together tonight," she said, vying for control.

"Think you can lie next to me and keep your hands to yourself?"

His teasing tone stroked her libido and chafed her nerves all at once. A confounding sensation. "Get over yourself, Rambo."

He didn't answer, but she sensed his smile, damn him.

"I have to go," she said. "Daisy's on her way over. She wants to talk to me about future engagements for the Cupcake Lovers." *And I want to pick her brain about your family.*

"About that," Sam said, "I'm thinking about resigning."

"From the Cupcake Lovers? That's crazy. Forget it. They need you. I need you."

"Yeah?"

"Professionally."

"Mmm."

His suggestive tone knotted her already nervous stomach.

"What are you wearing?"

"Seriously? Real sex is out but phone sex is in?"

"Get over yourself, Harper. I just want to make sure you're dressed in something conducive to your first lesson in self-defense."

She fell back on snark to combat a case of butterflies. "Should I dig out an umbrella?"

"Not today," he drawled, making her weak in the knees. "Today's hands-on."

TWELVE

"Here's the plan, Speedy."

"You mean it's changed?"

"Strategically, I'm thinking it might be better if you didn't come inside."

Vincent slowed the vintage Caddy to a stop, just behind Harper's rented wheels. He shifted the column gear stick into park and sighed. "So much for being your partner in crime."

Daisy's conscience kicked. Especially since, unbeknownst to Vincent, she'd already acted solo. Late last night. An impromptu opportunity with Peppy. Daisy had acted on a whim, but not without strong intuition and "a sign." Still, it had been a bold call and Daisy had thought it best to see how phase one played out, if at all, before filling Vincent in on that particular matchmaking endeavor.

Now here she was, yet again, ditching her wingman.

Chagrined, Daisy started to soothe her beau's feelings then realized they weren't really hurt. His mouth was pursed in a crooked grin. Sometimes it was hard to tell if he was smiling or frowning behind that big bushy beard. Sometimes, like now, it was obvious.

Vincent squinted at the renovated farmhouse then

looked to Daisy. "You're thinking this matchmaking scheme might work better if it's just you girls."

Daisy stifled a snort. She hadn't thought of herself as a "girl" in a long, long time, although last year she *had* traded her fuddy-duddy Jackie O wardrobe for bohemian hippie duds. She'd grown particularly fond of gypsy skirts and tie-dyed peasant blouses. She'd also adopted the habit of dyeing her hair various vibrant shades. Why should the kids have all the fun? In fact, early this morning she'd tinted her springy curls electric blue in honor of the forthcoming summer's blue skies. Between her free-spirited fashion sense and her determination to live life to the fullest, she supposed she *was* sort of girlish. Or at least young at heart.

"Just give me a half hour to plant the romantic seeds," Daisy said, "then swing back to help me fertilize the love grove."

"I have no idea what that means."

She smiled. "It'll be fun."

"Unless it's a disaster."

"According to Rocky who heard it from Luke, Sam invited Harper to Sunday dinner," Daisy said. "Those dinners are for close friends and family. Rocky said Luke said those two were pretty chummy yesterday over lunch. I didn't imagine the attraction. It's *real*."

"Then let nature take its course."

"Nature, smature. According to my horoscope—"

"You don't really believe that mumbo-hooey, do you?"

"Only when my stars are aligned." Daisy didn't know the ins and outs of astrology and she wasn't what she'd call a staunch believer, but she did put stock in positive thinking and she was positive she was right about Harper and Sam. All they needed was a hearty nudge. "According to my horoscope, I should trust my instincts in matters of the heart."

"I believe whoever concocted the hooey is referring to

your heart," Vincent said. "Not the hearts of friends and family."

"If you ask Harper, a professional publicist, it's all in the interpretation."

Vincent narrowed his eyes, his pursed lips flattened, and Daisy sensed his good humor was suddenly taxed. "I know you like Harper," he said. "And I know you think she runs deeper than the shallow flatlander she's shown herself to be. But, bottom line, Petunia. That woman makes a living by twisting words and painting illusions. Are you sure she's right for Sam and the kids?"

Even though Daisy was hopped up on horoscope, intuition, and good intentions, Vincent's earnest concern and honest observation was hard to ignore. She thought about her family bucket list, about all the names listed, the names of people she loved or, as in the case of Peppy, cared about because that girl was loved by Vincent. Life was short and even shorter for Daisy since she was already three quarters of a century old. Not to mention she'd already lost one husband and several other assorted kin to illnesses and accidents over the years. Her son Jerome had barely escaped the clutches of the Grim Reaper during a recent battle with cancer and her daughter Kelly might as well be dead since she lived all the way out in Nevada and rarely communicated with family. Daisy just wanted everyone to be happy. And in her mind, life was all the more joyful if you had someone to share it with. Although, granted, it had to be the *right* someone.

Reassessing her plan, Daisy sniffed and nodded. "Instead of planting the seeds, I'll dig deep and get to the point."

Vincent raised a brow. "No stealth matchmaking?"

"Nope. Either she's interested in Sam or she's not. I'll ask straight out. If she is, I'll ask if she'd be willing to move to Sugar Creek for good because if she's not, what's the point, right?"

"Right."

"But if she *is* interested and *if* she is willing—"

"You'll fertilize the love grove."

The gleam in Vincent's eyes and the slight upward tilt of his mouth was as good as a thumbs-up. Smiling, Daisy hooked her patchwork handbag over her shoulder, ignoring the arthritic ache in her bones and an irritating bout of heartburn. What were a few physical maladies when you were blessed with a loving partner? Because she knew it would bring him joy, Daisy gave Vincent a cheeky salute. "I'll be in touch, Speedy."

"Hold up," he said on a chuckle. "Let me get your car door."

Daisy saw Harper open the front door of the house. She stepped onto the porch and waved at Vincent as he rounded the hood of the Caddy. He waved back then helped Daisy out. "See there," Daisy whispered to her beau. "That was friendly of her."

"She's talking on her phone."

Daisy patted his chest and smiled. "There's something to be said for multitasking."

"Not in my book." But then he smiled and kissed Daisy's forehead. "Good luck, Petunia."

If it weren't for her stiff hip, she would've kicked up her metallic sneakered heels. "Who needs luck when my stars are aligned and you're on my side?"

By the time Daisy Monroe arrived at the Rothwell Farm, the gingerbread cupcakes were cooled and frosted, mimosas were made, and Harper had decided to approach the woman point-blank. No fancy wordplay or dancing around the bush. By the time Sam arrived, Harper wanted a firm grip on the dynamics of his family as well as a friend in the field. Daisy was eccentric, but she generally shot from the hip and she not only knew the dish on her own family, but on most everyone in town. A valuable ally, especially since Sugar Creek would be Harper's new home base. As of last night, she'd decided to bail on her efforts to reach the powers that be at Spin Twin Cities in an effort to reverse their decision. She still hoped to salvage her relationships with her former clients—even if only for the sake of her pride and reputation. If they were truly parting ways, she preferred to do so on good terms and not because they felt she'd failed them or because the firm had promised to hook them up with a better publicist. The more Harper thought about *that* betrayal, the easier it was to move on.

"I didn't realize you weren't driving," Harper said to the colorful senior as she scaled the front steps.

"My reflexes aren't what they used to be," Daisy said. "At least that's what my family tells me."

"You seem spry enough to me," Harper said then gestured to the boat of a car backing out of her driveway. "Vincent's more than welcome to join us."

"That's kind of you, Slick," Daisy said, "but he has some errands to run. He'll be back."

"You changed your hair," Harper said as she ushered Daisy into the house. Between living in a big city and being ensconced in the entertainment industry, Harper had seen it all. But for a small and conventional town like Sugar Creek, Daisy's penchant for neon hair color and bohemian fashion was pretty radical. As far as Harper could tell, the woman was fearless.

Daisy patted her bright blue curls. "You like?"

"Bold and dynamic," Harper said as she led her toward the kitchen. "Just like you."

"Once upon a time I was demure and conservative. Practically invisible."

"I can't imagine."

"Sometimes we stuff down our true nature in order to keep the peace, or to please others, or because we're intimidated or, heck, brainwashed. I came out of the closet four years ago."

Harper tripped over the kitchen threshold. "Excuse me?"

"I released the inner child. The real me. Spoke my mind. Took chances. Had fun. I'm sure my once beloved, dearly departed husband is spinning in his grave." Daisy hooked her handbag over a ladder-back chair, sniffed. "Gingerbread?"

Harper blinked. "Yes. I, um, baked a treat to go with our mimosas." Still absorbing Daisy's ramble, Harper revealed a platter of orange-frosted gingerbread cupcakes and the pitcher of orange juice spiked with champagne. The same beverage she'd been sipping prior to the spa shooting. She considered it a conquest that she'd been able to mix the cocktail this morning without flashing back and obsessing. Staying focused on the future had helped, part of a mind game Sam had taught her the day before in an effort to instill cool confidence.

"I'm sure they're as delicious as they look," Daisy said. "You impressed the club when we met here in February. You're a fine baker, Harper."

"Coming from a senior Cupcake Lover, that's an epic compliment. Thank you."

"If you lived here all the time, in addition to being our publicist, you could be a full-fledged member. Which, if you ask me, would be pretty spiffy since Mary Rothwell was a founding member and since you're living in her house. Although it's *your* house now and a fine house it is." She gestured to the refurbished cabinets and floor, the retro knickknacks and crockery. "You've worked magic on this place."

"I couldn't have done it without Rocky and Sam," Harper said, her heart tripping as Daisy led the conversation in the very direction Harper wanted to go. "Would you like to have our chat and refreshments on the back porch? It's a beautiful day."

"I'll grab the cupcakes and napkins," Daisy said, springing into action. "You pour the mimosas."

By the time Harper joined Daisy outside the woman had already dished out their cupcakes and was now resting comfortably in a bright red Adirondack chair. Harper set their flutes on the matching table. They held silent as Harper dropped into a second Adirondack, both gazing out at the vast lawn and the rippling pond beyond. Colorful wildflowers sprouted everywhere, their vibrant petals fluttering in the warm breeze. The temperature was mild, the sun bright, and the sky a vivid blue with scattered fluffy white clouds. If one looked beyond the fields and the surrounding woods, you could see a long stretch of rolling green mountains. Rothwell Farm, Harper's farm, was surrounded by nature. A far cry from the asphalt, glass, and steel surrounding her small apartment in a bustling section of Los Angeles. She didn't miss the crowd and chaos now, but in a week? A month? Once she'd conquered her phobia and the anxiety attacks, would this isolated property feel like a prison? Half a dozen pulse-tripping what ifs manifested, but Harper pushed them back by thinking ahead.

"About Sam—"

"Speaking of Sam—"

Harper smiled. "You go first."

Daisy cast a curious look over the purple rims of her rhinestone glasses. "I heard he invited you to Sunday dinner."

Harper passed her guest a mimosa. "I know how intimate those dinners are, Daisy. I feel like I'm intruding."

"Do you have eyes for Sam?"

So Harper wasn't the only one intent on being direct. "I, um, yes. That is, there's an attraction." Why lie? As Sam had said, it would make their hasty marriage less jarring.

Daisy gave a fist pump. "I knew it!" She clinked her glass to Harper's. "To *my* intuition."

They both sipped and Harper wondered how many other people had heard about the Sunday invite and

Harper and Sam's touchy-feely lunch at the Shack? TMZ had nothing on the Sugar Creek gossip vine.

"Next question," Daisy said after another sip. "Do you think you could be happy living in Sugar Creek full-time because I don't think Sam would do well with one of those long-distance relationships. He had enough of that when he was deployed overseas and separated from Paula. Plus you have to think about Ben and Mina. Sam and the kids are a package deal."

"I'm no longer working for Spin Twin Cities," Harper blurted. This conversation was moving along at break-neck speed, which was usually Harper's speed except she wasn't as quick on her feet with her own problems as she was with those of her clients.

Daisy's penciled eyebrows shot to her hairline. "You quit?"

"We parted ways. I'm going to freelance. I hope this won't have a negative bearing on my relationship with the Cupcake Lovers. I still have my contacts and my skills and the same, no, an even stronger determination to get things done. In fact, I called in a favor and I think I might be able to get the Cupcake Lovers a feature on *Brice and Kaylee—Live!*"

Daisy choked on her drink, massaged her chest.

Harper patted her back. "Are you okay?"

"*The* Brice and Kaylee?"

"I only know of one," Harper said with a smile. She understood Daisy's shock. Brice Kendall and Kaylee Davis had risen to fame on the talk show circuit somewhere near the height of popularity of *Regis and Kelly.* Then Regis had left and Kelly had scrambled to retain favor with a new cohost while Brice and Kaylee soared higher. Considering their nationwide viewership, landing a guest role on their show was a very big deal. "It might not happen until the fall," Harper said. "But I'm ninety-nine percent sure it *will* happen."

Daisy jabbed a scrawny finger in Harper's direction. "*You,* my dear, are a miracle worker. And you wonder why I call you *Slick!*"

"Not a miracle worker," Harper said. If she was she'd go back in time and handle things differently with Andrew.

"What's wrong?" Daisy asked. "A cloud just passed over your face."

Harper shook off dark thoughts. Ever since the spa shooting, ever since Edward's last taunt, she'd been bombarded with memories and regrets from the past. *Focus on the future.* "Just wishing I could make the talk show appearance happen sooner."

"Any time's a good time in my estimation. National exposure for the recipe book and our causes. We'll take it! So . . . since you're no longer with that L.A. firm, does that mean you're free of L.A.?"

Harper wouldn't say that exactly since she'd yet to shake the gloom of the spa incident, but she was absolutely free to relocate. And because Sam was marrying her, it meant she could stay in the States. "I'll be making Sugar Creek my main residence." *At least until I have my green card.* She couldn't think beyond that. She could look ahead a week, a month, but she couldn't think in terms of forever. Especially since it would be a loveless marriage. A marriage of convenience. Which screamed of a very rocky road if not a full-scale disaster. As a way of making the situation bearable for all concerned, Harper was committed to make the best of it. Learning about Sam's background and that of his family was the first step in smoothing the way.

"Hot diggety! One for two so far. I might as well attack the next name on my family bucket list since Vincent was right and nature got the jump on me with Sam."

Harper frowned. "Why are you working on a bucket list? Are you okay? I noticed you rubbing your chest."

"Heartburn," Daisy said. "Nothing a cupcake won't cure." She bit into one of Harper's creations and moaned.

"Heaven," she said after chewing. "Dark rum? Golden raisins?"

Harper nodded.

"Ginger syrup?"

"Crystallized ginger."

"You're a natural-born Cupcake Lover, Slick."

Harper wasn't sure why that statement made her so happy except it gave her a sense of belonging. For the first time in a long time, Harper reached out. "I need a friend, Daisy."

The woman's eyes widened as she licked cream cheese icing from her thin smiling lips. "I can be your friend."

Thinking back on all the coworkers and acquaintances who'd simply tolerated her, Harper swallowed an emotional lump. "I'm not an easy person to like."

"Sure you are," Daisy said, her old face shining with compassion. "You just have to look past the bluster to the nice person trapped inside."

THIRTEEN

Adam prided himself on a few things. First and foremost being a stand-up guy. Ask anyone in Sugar Creek, except maybe Jayce Bello, and they'd sing Adam's praises to the moon and back. Yet he'd gone to bed and woken up feeling like a world-class jerk.

He blamed Peppy Redding.

Or rather their awkward exchange.

He felt guilty for hurting her feelings which was crazy because it hadn't been that big of a deal. At least that's what he kept telling himself. She probably dealt with crap like that all the time. Part and parcel of performing in bars. Dealing with schmucks like him. Not that Adam was a genuine schmuck. Ask anyone. Except maybe Jayce and Peppy.

The more Adam thought about that doe-eyed spitfire, the harder he ran. He usually jogged in the morning, but he'd overslept. Then he'd had a business appointment. Even though he'd cinched yet another freelance gig at a regional resort, he couldn't shake his shitty mood. Craving solitude, he'd blown off a fishing trip with Kane and Nash, returned home and changed into running gear.

By the time he hit the trails snaking through the woods behind his house, the temperature had climbed to seventy.

Regardless Adam tacked on an additional two miles, craving an extra kick of endorphins. By the time his house came into view, he was drenched.

Chest tight, he blew out of the woods and sprinted across his back lawn. A lawn in need of mowing. He added that chore to his mental check list as he hit the back deck and pushed through the kitchen door. Shower, OJ, clean clothes, water. All needed pronto, but not in any particular order. He nabbed a bottle of chilled water from the fridge, swigging as he cut through his cramped living room. He had recently sold his place and moved into a small two-bedroom rental in order to save money. At one time he'd hoped to partner with Rocky, running a local bed-and-breakfast. That plan had fallen apart and Adam had set a dream goal that challenged his bank account. He'd been living on a shoestring and was in the process of yanking the straps even tighter. He'd been so motivated, so focused, he hadn't felt the stress of it all until today.

That's because your mind's not on the prize. It's on Peppy.

"Damn."

He peeled off his sweaty tee, tossed it in the hamper, and swiped back the shower curtain. Just as he reached for the nozzle, someone knocked on the door. He wasn't expecting anyone and most locals gave a shout before dropping over. It had to be Kane and Nash. Kane had given him a hard time on the phone about bailing on the fishing trip. He probably coaxed Nash into stopping by on their way out of town, a last-ditch effort to change Adam's mind. Kane had always been one to push.

Overheated and short on politeness, Adam wrenched opened his door. "A damned pain in my . . ." Oh, no. Oh, *shit*.

A waif girl with big brown eyes and windblown hair blinked at him through the warped screen door. She gaped. "No way."

That was pretty much his thought.

She glanced at a folded napkin in her hands. "Is this 187 Route 3?"

"Yeah."

"Adam Brody?"

"Yeah."

"No. Hell, no. Sorry. Bye."

She turned on her heel and Adam nearly knocked the screen door from its hinges. "Wait. Don't go. Don't . . . Peppy!"

She froze in her tracks. Her back was to him, not good, but at least she wasn't running away. Not yet anyway.

"You've come about the room?" He'd only placed the ad yesterday. Wasn't supposed to run until Monday. He'd told his brother and his best buds, Luke and Nash, that he was on the lookout for a roommate. They knew he was saving for a business venture. Other than that he'd kept the specifics of his dream goal to himself. "Peppy."

He stepped closer, noting the stubborn set of her shoulders, her slight height, and her cute butt. No shapeless dress today. A pair of 501 Levi's, a fitted black tee, and black-and-white hightops. He'd seen the front of her T-shirt through the screen door. Johnny Cash, a guitar, and a banner that read: I WALK THE LINE.

Peppy Redding: *rebel*.

"Are you looking for a room?" Adam asked. "I have a room. Rent includes access to the kitchen, bathroom, and living room—which is every room but my room."

Her fists clenched and he knew he'd said the wrong thing. *Again*. "Not that I wouldn't want you in my bed . . . room." *Damn*. "Just pointing out the house is small. Small, but comfortable."

She'd yet to face him, but she'd yet to walk away.

Feeling even more flustered than the night before, Adam jammed a hand through his damp hair, remembering suddenly that he was shirtless and sweaty. Is that why she wouldn't turn around? Because he was shirtless? Was she shy? A prude? Turned on? Not that he cared. Oh, hell. He cared. Mostly, he just didn't want her thinking he was a jerk. Nash had mentioned she had money problems. Adam wasn't strapped. Just focused. "Did I mention rent includes utilities? And . . ." He shrugged, scrambling. "Three months' access to a personal sports trainer?"

She whirled on her rubber soles, expression intense. "Why would I need a personal trainer? Because . . . what? I'm fat? I'm soft? I'm weak?" She advanced on him, dark eyes narrowed. "Why would I—"

"For the fun of it. The thrill of it." *Jesus.* When had he turned so inept with women? "Listen. I'm sorry. I was an ass last night."

She shifted her weight, cocked a brow. "Yeah, well. Ivy tends to turn men's brains to mush."

Except it had been Peppy who'd rattled his thoughts. "Come inside. I'll throw on a shirt and give you the nickel tour."

She glanced at her beat-up wheels then back to Adam, who felt just about as dinged as that Chevy. "Sure. Okay. But only because I'm desperate."

FOURTEEN

Sam knocked and Harper yelled, "Come in!"

For the—What if he was a burglar? A murderer? Although a criminal wouldn't knock. *Still*. For someone who was jumpy about surprise attacks, Harper's easy invitation seemed odd.

Sam tried the knob. *Locked*. Okay. So she wasn't inviting the random visitor into her home. She was inviting the man she was expecting. The man who knew the location of her hidden spare key. It implied a sense of trust that would have warmed Sam except he assumed it was more about her being engrossed in a phone call or text. Too busy to extend the courtesy of opening the door.

Duffel in tow, Sam snagged the hidden key and entered without a word. He didn't immediately see Harper but he did hear the TV.

He rounded the corner expecting CNN. Instead, animated contestants were whipping up exotic confections—cupcakes to be exact. So, she'd honored Sam's suggestion, bypassing troubling newscasts in favor of upbeat programming. Or maybe she'd switched channels when Sam had pulled into the drive. Given her stubborn and obsessive ways, he found it hard to believe she'd abandoned her morbid fascination with random violence purely based on his advice.

"Be there in a sec!" she called from another room. He imagined her chatting away, pleading with her past employer or a former client. Given her laptop was set up on the coffee table, he assumed she was in work mode. Curious, he glanced at the screen. Part of him expected to find a Web site listing crime statistics. Another part anticipated a Hollywood gossip site. In fact, she'd been shopping online for cleaning products.

"Why didn't you tell me Ben has skin allergies?"

Sam straightened and turned. Harper blew into the room, flushed and harried, carrying a basket stuffed with bed linens and towels. She hadn't been texting or talking on the phone. She'd been doing laundry. The sight of her dressed down and in full domestic mode stirred a part of him he'd thought long dead. He'd never expected Harper to fill Paula's shoes in that way. Yet here she stood, hair twisted in a messy knot, wearing faded jeans rolled to mid-calf and a pair of beat-up sneakers.

Sam relieved her of the overflowing basket, chest tight when he caught a whiff of gingerbread and soap instead of her normal seductive perfume.

"I always use scented dryer sheets," she said, motioning Sam to set the basket on the sofa while she muted the television. "Daisy told me about a time when the kids spent the night with her and Ben broke out in an itchy rash. You attributed it to her laundry detergent. I remember you mentioning Mina's peanut allergy when I sent you home with a batch of cupcakes, but you never said a word about Ben's sensitive skin. I know you're not moving in right away, but if the kids visit, if Ben dries off with one of my towels or, I don't know, builds a tent or fort using my sheets, I'd rather him not break out in a rash."

Sam's lip twitched even as his heart jerked. "Ben's not a tent-and-fort-building kind of boy."

"That's not the point. Why didn't you tell me?"

"It wasn't an issue before. Plus you've always kept our

conversations short and shallow or relegated to refurbishing this house."

"That was then and this is now. Now I'll be responsible for keeping Ben and Mina fit, healthy, and happy. I barely know them, and because you never . . . Because *I* never asked, I hardly know anything about them. Except whatever Daisy told me which, come to think of it, wasn't very much considering how long we talked. It's just that we had so much to cover."

She blew out a breath then took another, averting her gaze while handing Sam two corners of a light green sheet. "Do you mind helping me fold these? I ran them through a hot-water rinse. It'll have to do until my new cleaning supplies arrive. I ordered perfume-free detergent and fabric softening dryer sheets."

"Those products are available in Sugar Creek," Sam said as they folded the sheet in half.

"I ordered in bulk."

She didn't want to drive into town, to risk shopping in a store, thereby leaving herself open to a random attack. Even though they'd addressed her agoraphobia, even though she'd made progress, the fear lingered. Sam got that and he didn't press. Not now. There was too much going on here.

"Don't get me wrong," Harper railed on. "I'm thrilled they're willing to move into the farmhouse. This is where I want to be. But now I'm worried that it's too isolated or too drafty or too depressing. You know how the legend goes."

Sam listened as she prattled on with a string of *what ifs*. The woman was fixated on the happiness and safety of his children. Something shifted inside him with every voiced concern. Meanwhile they folded the sheet smaller and smaller until they were toe-to-toe with only a squared linen between them.

At last, she met his gaze. "I just . . . I've never been responsible for children, Sam. It's scary considering all that could go wrong."

"I know." He dealt with those fears every day. "But you won't be alone in this and, lucky you, I have years of experience."

She smirked. "You think I'm overreacting."

"In this case," Sam said as he molded his body to hers, "it's a turn-on."

She gazed into his eyes and his pulse and libido spiked. He pressed closer, testing his resolve, her restraint.

She arched a brow. "You're wrinkling my sheets."

"Not in the way I'd like."

"You said sex is off limits until after we're married."

"Making love. Not kissing."

"What if I don't want to be kissed?"

"Then step back."

She stayed where she was. Wrapped in his arms.

Hell, yeah. Sam took advantage. Hands tangled in her knotted hair, he angled in, brushing his lips over hers—a soft, sizzling tease before the main event. He felt as if he'd been waiting for this kiss his entire life. He savored, absorbing Harper's essence as their mouths fused in a sensual dance that kicked . . . his . . . ass.

There was far more to this woman than he'd ever imagined. The mystery, the possibilities, intrigued him on an intellectual level. Her complexity touched his heart and seduced his brain. If he could bottle the high he was on right now, he'd make a million.

Keeping his hands off her curves was a challenge but he was determined to push the envelope. To build anticipation, establish intimacy. Sam was on a mission, but he was by no means a saint. While deepening the kiss, in his mind, he slowly stripped Harper's tee and jeans from her trembling body. In his mind, she took control and pinned him against the wall. Something she'd done on more than one occasion, a role he'd always reversed. They both got off on taking control and as far as Sam was concerned this was by far the sexiest encounter in their racy history.

Because, right now, he'd never been in more danger of *losing* control.

Mind over instinct.

Will over desire.

Harper pressed her palm to his chest, just enough pressure to signal a time-out. They stared into each other's eyes a long moment before she cleared her throat and cleared the sensual fog.

"I haven't had sex since the last time we were together," she said. "I'm not sure why I blurted that but I thought you should know. I'm hot to trot."

"Same here. On both counts."

"Remind me why we're abstaining?"

He'd never given her specifics in the first place.

"A reason would be nice, Rambo. A reason would be fair."

"If I tell you—"

"You'll have to kill me?"

"It might scare you off."

"To where? Canada?" She eased back just enough to hug that now rumpled sheet to her chest. "We made a deal, Sam. You need a mother for your children. I need a green card. I'm not going anywhere."

She sounded defiant, determined. Yet through the veil of snark, Sam caught a whiff of fear. Canada spooked her. *Why?* Instead of pulling her back into his arms, he shoved his fingertips in the back pockets of his jeans, and stayed on topic. One challenge at a time. "The physical attraction, the sex . . . it's intense."

"That's a bad thing?"

"Only if it snuffs a deeper connection."

Her right eye ticked. "You mean an emotional connection." She shifted her gaze to her cherry-red Chucks. "When you made this offer you said you didn't love me."

"I didn't."

"But you do now?"

"There's potential."

She inched back another step but met his gaze. "I don't want you to love me, Sam."

"Why?"

"Because I can't love you back."

"Why?"

She hugged the sheet tighter. "I might fail you somehow."

"I'm willing to take the chance."

"I'm not. And don't ask why."

"Okay." He'd said enough. Pressed enough. Her anxiety was palpable.

"Are you going to retract the offer?"

"No." Sam sensed her immense relief and his curiosity regarding her issues with Canada spiked. There was more to Harper's inner war than that spa shooting and it was rooted in her past.

"I'd never know a moment's peace. He . . ."

He.

That one slip had burrowed deep in Sam's brain. Once again, he imagined an abusive ex. Or maybe a psychotic client. Someone she'd *failed.* Or . . . someone who'd cast blame. How was he going to get the details when she so clearly didn't want to talk about it?

There was an easy solution. Rocky's husband, Jayce, was a crack private detective with his own successful and lucrative cyberbusiness. Luke had hired Jayce to track down Rae when she'd disappeared. And he was pretty sure Dev had retained Jayce's services for a few personal agendas. But hiring someone to essentially spy on Harper was a slippery slope.

Sam fell back on his secret weapon. *Patience.* "Let's back up."

"To where?" Harper asked, sounding trapped between anxious and angry.

"To the part about the kids." He saw her tension ease as he focused on the future. "How'd you like to know more about Ben and Mina?"

FIFTEEN

Harper hadn't realized how curious she was about where and how Sam lived until he invited her to his house. Since the kids were staying with their grandparents, he'd suggested a tour of their living quarters as a low-stress introduction to their everyday lives. Harper saw the wisdom in that. She'd get a snapshot of Ben's and Mina's likes and dislikes, their hobbies and habits—good and bad. She'd have a better idea of what to expect once they moved into the farmhouse. She'd also get a bigger picture of Sam.

"I wish you would have let me change my clothes," Harper said as they tooled down Swamp Road.

"You look great."

"I look frumpy."

Sam cut her a glance that reignited the heat he'd conjured with that ten-alarm kiss. "Impossible."

The compliment only amped her already jumbled state. This man had smoked her senses with a kiss that seemed to last an eternity and yet ended far too soon.

Harper squeezed her thighs together, determined to ignore a deluge of lusty urges. Even though she was dressed in her frumpiest clothes, she'd never felt sexier. It had everything to do with Sam. "Thank you," she said, as she flipped down the mirrored sun visor then rooted in her purse for a tube of lipstick. "But I prefer to have a more polished appearance when I'm in public. I have an image and reputation to protect."

"Maybe in L.A.," Sam said. "You're in Sugar Creek now."

"I'm still a publicist. A professional."

"With a private life. You don't have to be on all the time, Harper. Especially with me."

Harper tensed as she applied her favorite cherry-red lipstick. "You think I put on pretenses?"

"I think you put up walls."

Daisy had made that same observation. Harper wondered how and why she'd suddenly become transparent. Granted, she'd been thrown off by the spa shooting and then with the shock of being fired. Her life was in upheaval, so naturally she was off balance. What surprised her was that she wasn't scrambling more to keep Daisy and Sam at arm's length. She'd even asked Daisy to be her friend. Harper wasn't ready for this, any of this, and yet she wanted it with all her heart. She wanted to belong to someone, somewhere. Sugar Creek had been calling long before the tragedy with Andrew and long before she'd bought the Rothwell Farm. Life had kept her moving in other directions. Fate, it would seem, had other ideas.

"Speaking of walls," Harper said, deftly changing the subject. "Why are you and the kids so willing to pick up and move? Is your house falling down around your ears?"

"The house is fine."

Of course it was fine. Sam was a top-notch carpenter. "Are you going to sell it?"

"Eventually."

"Maybe you should rent it out instead," Harper said. "What if things go bad between us?"

"I've got two years to avoid that scenario."

Two years for them to fall in love.

Although she'd be granted conditional residency and a

green card after they wedded, the USCIS required married couples to prove their marriage was still intact two years later in order to be eligible for permanent residency. If Harper wanted to become a U.S. citizen she'd have to keep up the pretense of a real marriage for at least two years.

She shifted her gaze to the passing landscape. Between the rolling fields and the verdant shrubs and trees, it was like sailing through a sea of green. Even the distant mountains—which, come autumn, would burst with yellow, orange, and red—stretched and peaked in endless shades of emerald and jade. Vibrant wildflowers and the occasional red barn added color to the sparsely populated countryside. Beautiful, but remote. By Harper's standards anyway. No malls or shopping strips or multiplex movie theaters. No superstores or deluxe fitness spas. With the exception of outdoor sports, the cultural scene in Sugar Creek extended to the Sugar Shack, Moose-a-lotta, the library, and the new bowling alley. A bit constricting for someone who'd lived in two metropolitan cities. Granted, Harper wasn't keen on frequenting crowded establishments just now, but what about when her fear from the shooting subsided?

"What if I'm not cut out for small-town living?" she blurted. "Or what if I build a new client list that requires me to live in L.A. or New York? Would you be willing to relocate? Or to maintain a long-distance relationship?"

"Why don't we take this a day at a time?"

Harper blinked over to the man behind the wheel. "Is that a maybe?" She hadn't expected that. "You and the kids are homegrown Sugar Creek."

"Is that your subtle way of saying we're hicks?"

"That's not what I meant. I just can't imagine you and the children moving away from friends and family. Not to mention the culture shock."

"You know that old saying 'Home is where the heart is'?" He waited a beat then added, "Time will tell."

Harper focused back on the road. She wondered if Sam

could hear the pounding of *her* heart. He flipping scared her . . . and excited and inspired her. She didn't respond because she didn't know what to say. For a business arrangement he was making this terribly personal. She wasn't sure how she felt about that. She hadn't had a single clear thought since that smoldering kiss.

Out of habit she checked her phone. She used to get a hundred voice mails, texts, e-mails, and PMs per day. It was already midday and she'd only gotten twelve. One had been Sam, one Daisy, nine had been junk mail, and the last—confirmation on her cleaning supply order. How had she fallen off the map so fast and so thoroughly? She knew for a fact that there were plenty of celebrities in need. People spinning out of control or people who'd crashed and burned. People desperate for someone to pick up the pieces and to put things right. Harper used to be that someone. She *needed* to be that someone.

"Here we are."

Harper blinked out of her thoughts. She'd lost track of time. Instead of speeding through the countryside they were entering a picturesque neighborhood. Each house occupied a large plot of land, far enough apart to allow for privacy, close enough to jog over in your jammies to borrow a cup of sugar. Sam steered his pickup into a gravel drive and Harper noted a beautiful two-story home—a snowy white saltbox with black-shuttered windows and a bright red front door. Cheery and family oriented right down to the white picket fence, the tire swing hanging from the branch of a large maple tree, and the little yellow bicycle (augmented by pink handlebar tassels and a matching basket) leaning haphazardly against a hedge.

As was his way, Sam helped Harper out of the cab and escorted her to his front stoop. Her stomach knotted. *Anticipation. Dread.* She noted the unusual "sign" decorating the door—an antique-stained turquoise picture frame with a pewter WELCOME plaque in the center, topped with a jade-green bow. A charming and unique contrast to the red door. "Did you make this?" Harper asked.

"I tried to interest Ben in woodworking. He picked this project out of a magazine but lost interest after choosing the colors." Sam shrugged as he slid his key from the lock. "I guess that makes it a joint venture."

It was the second time today Sam had noted Ben's lack of interest in building things. So the boy wasn't his father's son. *Hmm*.

Sam opened the front door, revealing a page in his life. Harper got a whiff of air freshener. Something flowery. Probably one of those plug-in things. She tried to imagine Sam skimming the grocery shelves for room fresheners, but it didn't compute. Her next surprise was the living room. She'd expected leather furnishings—something manly—or generic bargain furniture, something kidproof. Yet the sectional sofa and matching club chairs were plush and awash with vivid color. So were the walls. And the curtains. So much cheer and whimsy. So not Sam.

Paula.

Feeling like an intruder, Harper hugged herself against conflicting emotions as Sam led her into the dining room then through the kitchen. She hoped she looked more casual—arms crossed, posture lax—than intimidated. She wasn't merely getting a peek into Sam's life, but into Sam's life with Paula. Clearly his wife had influenced the colors and themes. Clearly, Sam hadn't changed so much as a throw pillow since her death. Or he'd added or replaced items in keeping with her taste. Harper realized that by moving out of their house, Sam was cutting ties with their past. By marrying Harper, he wasn't only gaining a mother for his children. He was creating a new life for himself. It made her feel better to think that they were both marrying as some means of escape. It made things less personal. It also gave her purpose. Sam needed her.

He needed her in order to move beyond Paula. Beyond his old life. If Harper could pave the way for Sam's future happiness, surely her soul, and his, would benefit.

Even as she brainstormed the future, she commented on the present. "Considering you have two young, active kids this place is unbelievably tidy."

"I picked up after they left. Trust me. It doesn't always look like this."

He led her upstairs and on the way Harper got a visual sense of Ben and Mina throughout the years. The stairway wall was cluttered with countless mismatched frames of the children at various stages of their lives. There were also pictures of Sam and Paula. Harper tried not to linger, but they made an impression. They'd been happy and they'd been in love. Both Daisy and Rocky had mentioned what a sweet soul Paula had been. That sweetness radiated from her pictures, from this house. It was . . . nice.

Harper tore her gaze from the last picture to Sam's broad back. She'd been anything *but* nice. She'd been snarky, shallow, bossy, and manipulative. Most recently she'd been a basket case. And *she* was his means of escape?

She cleared the landing and Sam motioned her through the first door on the right. "This is Mina's room. You want to know her? Look around."

Harper moved into the five-year-old's room and all gloomy thoughts disappeared. Who could be worried or stressed or depressed in the midst of sweet disarray and whimsy. The room exploded with stuffed animals, dolls, playhouses, and various other toys. Pink and purple bins overflowed with clothes and shoes. Mina's walls were painted purple—bright purple—and accentuated by fanciful illustrations—a castle, a princess, and a menagerie of mythical creatures. Entranced, Harper stepped closer and admired a doe-eyed unicorn. "Is this an appliqué?"

"Paint."

"Using a stencil?"

"Using a brush and my moderate skills."

Moderate? Harper's artistic skills extended to juvenile doodles. Ask her to draw a fairy princess and you'd get a stick person with a three-point crown. "Rocky mentioned you sometimes accent your custom-made furniture with detailed flourishes and patterns, but I assumed . . ." She shook her head, amazed. "You drew this freehand?"

When he didn't answer she turned and saw him leaning against the doorjamb, arms folded over his chest. He looked uncomfortable, like he was embarrassed about his artistic talents. Or maybe it was because he'd painted girly unicorns and castles instead of something more . . . Rambo-like.

And he'd painted all this for his little girl.

Shame washed over Harper when she thought about how she'd once considered Sam a monosyllabic tough guy of average intelligence. Then again, she'd never encouraged or allowed him to open up. Throughout their brief acquaintance and fling, she'd done her utmost to keep him at emotional arm's length. She'd indulged in the fierce physical attraction. She'd reveled in the hot sex. Because she didn't want intimate, she'd pushed for kinky, playing out some of her wildest fantasies. Just now, surrounded by castles and tiaras, Harper wanted something in between, something romantic. Instead of Rambo, she wanted a knight in shining armor. Her vision clouded and she swore she saw Sam in full body armor. Richard Gere as Sir Lancelot. No. Clive Owen as King Arthur. Wait. Worse. Sam Mc-Cloud as Harper Day's champion.

"You okay?" Sam asked as he pushed off the wall.

"Fine." Feeling ridiculous, Harper palmed her brow. "Just . . . reeling. I've never seen so much . . . stuff." She tore her gaze from Sam and focused on the twin bed over-run with more stuffed animals. Some pristine. Some terribly worn. All adorned with boas and tiaras. She noted a few scattered books. Disney tales. And a bookshelf crammed with Disney movies. Given the young girl's animated sunshine-and-lollipops persona, Harper wasn't surprised by her fairy tale fixation. She was, however, envious. Harper had long given up on true love and happily-ever-after.

"And Ben's room?" she prompted, feeling overwhelmed by Mina's youthful optimism.

Brow raised, Sam backed away from Mina's threshold and moved a room down. There was still a sense of the fantastic but coming from a darker side. Ben's walls were painted a deep blue—no illustrations—and crowded with posters of various superheroes. His shelves featured an extensive collection of action figures—all perfectly posed. His bookcase was packed but meticulous. Mostly manga and anima novels, from what Harper could see, and arranged in alphabetical or series order. No clutter on his floor or his bed. No overflowing bins of clothes. Just a favored hoodie hanging on a clothes hook. Unlike Mina, Ben was methodical. A neat freak. A brainiac geek who favored video games over live sports.

Harper drifted toward a small desk and smiled when she saw a sketch pad. Penciled drawings—far beyond her stick figures. Superheroes kicking villainous butt. "Ben inherited your talent for art."

"That's about all he inherited from me."

"You're disappointed because he isn't interested in carpentry."

"Or mechanics or sports or . . . I'm not disappointed. Just concerned. He'd rather flip pancakes than toss a ball. He'd rather read than Rollerblade. He can't remember a thing I've taught him about engines and yet he can recite the history of every manga and *Marvel* superhero. Several of his schoolmates, other boys, they're—"

"Picking on him?"

"Pretty sure Ben's being bullied," Sam said, "but he won't say."

"Proud. He got that from you." Harper moved about the room, noting the nuances of Ben McCloud's world. She'd met him three times and every time he'd been timid and sullen. Except when she'd talked about Comic Con. She remembered having the intense desire to fix his young life. Given her history and experience, she knew a brewing disaster when she saw one and that was Ben McCloud.

"Mina suffers from some sort of separation anxiety," Sam said as Harper studied Ben's bookshelves. "She acts all independent, but she's not. The first days I dropped her off for kindergarten she cried and begged me not to leave her behind. The teacher said it would pass. We're at the end of the year and it's worse than ever. I buy her things— boas and tiaras—to make her happy. That's part of the reason she has so much *stuff*."

"Only the bribes aren't working," Harper assumed.

"I've handled it wrong. I know. Now she'll expect a reward every time I want her to do something she's not crazy about. And then there's Ben. My son goes out of his way to please me even if he hates what I ask him to do, so I've started not to ask. I can't . . . I need help, Harper. He likes you. Mina likes you. I . . ."

"Tolerate me?" She turned and was surprised to find Sam looking at her with tender regard.

"I admit you push a lot of buttons," he said. "Although lately . . . different buttons." He moved in, brushed strands of hair from her heated cheeks. "I'm thinking I don't know you at all, Harper. I'm thinking I'd like you a lot if I did."

Her heart pounded in her ears. "It's not like I'm a closed book."

"Aren't you?"

"I could reveal a few chapters, although it wouldn't be very interesting."

"I'm betting different."

Every nerve in her body sparked as he pulled her against

his body. Her mind raced, wondering if *his* bedroom was nearby. She couldn't withstand the intensity of another drawn-out four-alarm kiss without having something more. Her mind exploded with racy scenarios just as he nipped her lower lip and music filled the air. No. Not music. Ring tones. Their phones were chiming in tandem. Incoming texts.

Easing apart, both frowning, they checked their screens.

"It's Daisy."

"It's Luke."

CHLOE'S IN LABOR.

SIXTEEN

"I feel like a party crasher."

"You got the text, too," Sam said as he raced the open road toward Pixley. "Means you're invited."

"But I'm not a close friend of the expecting couple," Harper said. "Or a family member."

"You're the Cupcake Lover's publicist and Chloe's a key member. Dev's the most influential man in town, and Dev and Chloe's child will be the first in the new generation of Monroes. The club's probably expecting you to spin the arrival of a future CL into positive promotion for the recipe book."

"You're part of the club. Does that include you?"

"I appreciate anything that inspires contributions toward our targeted causes. As far as anything that involves *us* being in the spotlight as opposed to the book or the soldiers and their families . . ." He shook his head. "I know a few of the ladies are getting a rush out of the exposure—the fan mail, the local radio interview, the book signing at Burlington's Book and Baubles, that short feature on *Good Morning Vermont*—"

"The tip of the iceberg," Harper interrupted. "I had a heavy client list before. Now I don't. I can do better for the Cupcake Lovers."

"I've seen what you can do. What you did, what you *do* for Rae. That's why I'll be resigning from the club. One of the reasons anyway."

The publicist in Harper freaked. Sam was her ace in the hole. Her sizzle. Yes, the history and the mission of the club intrigued more than a few media outlets. The fact that, after several decades, the Cupcake Lovers continued the simple kindness of shipping cupcakes to soldiers overseas earned interest and gratitude and plucked at many a heartstring. They were definitely a "happy news" story. But it was the club's one male member, former military, no less, and a phenomenal baker to boot, that generated the most traction. Especially with the visual venues. A ruggedly good-looking man who exuded the charisma of a Hollywood action star, Sam McCloud was any spin doctor's dream.

"Not comfortable in the spotlight," Harper said. "Got it. But surely if someone . . . say as big as Brice and Kaylee called . . . if they wanted to book the Cupcake Lovers for their talk show . . ."

"I don't care if David Letterman knocked on my door. I've never been one of those people who craved their fifteen minutes of fame."

"A phrase coined by Andy Warhol back in the late sixties," Harper said as she checked her phone for more messages. She was trying for nonchalant. Meanwhile she flashed on the time one of her top (and most arrogant) clients refused to sign for another season of a popular reality show, determined to move on to more highbrow entertainment. Like *that* had a chance of happening. Between Harper and the client's agent, they'd enticed Tatiana (Tah-Tah) Remington to re-up via a publicity campaign designed to stroke her monumental ego. *That* Harper could spin. Sam didn't care about recognition or adoration. It was almost beyond Harper's scope. "Warhol spoke of notoriety in the future, only he had no notion of social media. Today, most people would kill for *five* minutes of worldwide fame that could be achieved in a 140-character tweet if tweeted and retweeted by the right people." She glanced over at Sam who always seemed at a loss or annoyed when she was immersed in social networking—a necessity given her line of work. "Do you even *have* a Twitter account?"

"No."

"Facebook?"

He shook his head.

"Instagram? Tumblr? MySpace? I heard MySpace is making a comeback. Google Plus?"

"There's such a thing as sharing too much information," Sam said. "Especially personal information. What would I *tweet* about?"

Harper shifted in her seat, jazzed by the turn in conversation. Social media. Publicity. Her comfort zone. She saw a way to not only benefit the Cupcake Lovers, but Sam. "It doesn't have to be personal, although the personal touch helps. Your primary focus could be your work. Carpentry, furniture-making, renovation. You could post pictures of your designs, your creations."

"I do that on my Web site."

"I've seen your Web site. Your furniture is stunning but the site . . . It's static and boring and the Web design borderline amateur."

He raised a brow.

Oops. "Tell me you didn't design it yourself."

"I wasn't going for flashy."

Two or three snarky retorts came to mind; instead Harper said kindly, "If you don't have the time or desire to create an eye-catching, user-friendly site, you should hire a personal Web designer. Then choose one social media outlet. Just one, and start interacting—"

"Why?"

"Because you'd be building a platform and potential

future clients. It's a tool, like advertising. A way to get people talking about your furniture. It could increase business."

"Business is fine."

"It could be better," Harper said with confidence. "Not that I know your financial situation—"

"Also fine."

"But if you contacted more buyers for your custom-made furniture, you could concentrate more on your own projects rather than hiring out your services for renovation and roofing jobs, right? Work from home rather than away from home."

He slid his shades to the end of his nose and shot her an enigmatic look. "Since you do most of your work from home wouldn't that put an additional strain on our relationship? Twenty-four/seven under the same roof?"

"Except we wouldn't be under the same roof. You could convert the barn into a workshop and storage unit. I'll keep to the house. That way we'd both be there for Ben and Mina this summer instead of relying on a battalion of sitters."

"I don't have a battalion of sitters. I have, *had,* three. Pretty sure Bridgett is on her way out."

"I'm just saying, this marriage thing, it's going to be a big adjustment. Not just for us, but especially for Ben and Mina. If you thought they had issues before . . . What if they hate living at the farm? What if they grow to hate *me*? What if Ben crawls further into his shell and Mina clings even tighter? I'm thinking if we're both around as much as possible maybe we could head off any catastrophes or at least watch each other's backs. I just . . . I want to make this as easy on them as possible. It's not their fault that I'm facing deportation."

Harper fingered her bracelet—*twirl, twirl*—and cursed her recent penchant for "what-ifing" herself into a frenzy. Usually she used that quirk in a more positive way.

What if I pitch a story to TMZ and it goes viral? What if it gets so huge that it lands in a broadsheet? What if the massive hits garner my client a feature on The Today Show *or better yet, a guest appearance on* Late Night *with* Jimmy Fallon?

Except she wasn't spinning the career path of a jaded celebrity. She was overseeing the lives of two innocent children. Fanciful Mina and misfit Ben. If seeing their rooms had tugged at her heartstrings, what would happen when she interacted with them on a daily basis? Would she rise to the occasion or drop the ball? The potential for failure was massive. And all because Harper was desperate not to return to Canada.

She stared out the front window, her phone dead weight in her hands, her heart heavy in her chest. "I don't think I've ever felt so selfish."

"Funny," Sam said as they passed a slow-moving car. "I was admiring your sensitivity."

Harper flushed. He thought she was *sensitive*? Most people considered her self-absorbed. Coworkers at Spin Twin Cities, but first and foremost Edward Wilson.

"You cared more about yourself than my son."

Temples throbbing, Harper scrambled to change the subject, thumbed on her phone and pulled up her Twitter account. "That thing you said about spinning the birth of Chloe's baby into something positive for the CL's charities—I'm on it."

Sam reached across the seat and palmed her thigh.

Harper swore his touch burned through the fabric of her jeans, scorching a path to her constricted chest. She tweeted like a madwoman intent on blocking tender thoughts regarding the man who kept chipping away at her iced-over heart.

"That thing you said about my Web site and amping my business," Sam said. "Noted."

* * *

By the time they reached the hospital in Pixley—a thirty-minute drive east of Sugar Creek—Sam was a little in love with Harper Day. He'd been primed to lose his heart for months. He never guessed it would be to her. Her rabid concern regarding Ben and Mina were his undoing. Although Harper was inexperienced with children and even though she'd claimed she didn't want to be a mom, he knew she'd go out of her way to ensure they were cared for and, if she could *spin* it, happy.

She'd been silent for the last ten minutes of their drive, focused on her phone as she worked some sort of media magic via her social networks. Sam figured she'd fill him in once she had something to report. Meanwhile he'd stolen the occasional look, admiring her beautiful profile and aching to kiss that gorgeous mouth, a mouth that had commanded his attention since the moment they'd first met. A mouth that had skimmed and scorched almost every part of his body—most especially his favorite part. Yeah, boy, the woman was not shy.

By the time he parked the truck in the medical center's crowded lot, Sam had a full-fledged hard-on. Luckily his T-shirt was untucked and hanging low enough to conceal the bulge in his jeans. Nevertheless, he blocked their former racy liaisons from his mind as he rounded the hood and helped Harper out of the cab. The plan was to walk off this damnable boner by the time they entered Pixley General. Which gave him less than a minute.

Good luck with that.

"I texted Daisy who spoke to Chloe and Dev and then texted me back with a thumbs-up regarding my agenda," Harper blurted, still focused on her phone as Sam guided her through a maze of cars. "I didn't want them to feel exploited, so I waited for their permission. Which didn't take long, and since I'd already prepped a release, I'm already off and running. "

"I can see that."

"I'm doing a media blitz through my personal accounts as well as the Cupcake Lovers fan page."

"I didn't know we had a fan page."

"On Facebook."

"Oh, right. Rocky mentioned something about that a while back."

"I can't believe you've never been on it."

"Rocky and Chloe manage it."

"But as a CL member you should contribute." Harper waved him off. "We'll talk about it later. I'm busy hyping the fact that a new Cupcake Lover is on the way. Boy or Girl? Ideas for names? Stay tuned for a cybercupcake celebration. Every now and then I intersperse mention of the CL mission," she said, talking and texting at the same time. "And I've shared links to Operation Shoebox and Soldiers' Angels. Celebrate the arrival of our new little cupcake by supporting—"

"Toast."

"What?"

"Thought I could walk it off, but, yeah. No. I'm toast." Sam snaked his arm around Harper's waist, steering her away from the front entrance and down the west side, into the hedges, behind a sign and a tree. Not perfectly secluded, but secluded enough.

"What are you—"

"Hold that thought." He pulled her into his arms and kissed her with the randy passion of his youth. Instead of resisting or tempering his attention, Harper matched his fervor, wrapping her legs around his waist when he lifted and backed her against the brick wall. She clung, she kissed, she grinded against his erection. They vied for control and his adrenaline spiked. Sam was vaguely aware that they were making out in the bushes like a pair of horny teens. Mostly he was thinking about getting in her pants, moving inside her, and rocking both of their worlds. He'd been hot for this kiss for hours. Hell, he'd been hot for a kiss like *this* for a lifetime. In this moment, Harper was all he knew. All he wanted. The intensity of his need shocked some sense into his lust-crazed brain. He was *not* going to nail her in broad daylight, in public.

Harper must have sensed his hesitation. They pulled back at the same time, staring at each other in stunned silence. Sam noted her smeared lipstick, flushed face, and mussed hair, thinking she was the most passionate and beautiful woman on this planet. Wondering how he'd gotten so lucky a second time around.

"Don't look at me like that. Don't . . ." Looking panicked now, Harper scrambled out of Sam's arms. She dug in the purse strapped over her shoulder, passed him one of those individually wrapped towelettes. "You have lipstick on your face."

"You, too."

They both wiped at the smeared evidence of that mind-warping kiss. Sam tempered his breathing, sensitive to the tension in Harper's shoulders as she tamed her hair into a tidy ponytail and reapplied her lipstick. He could almost see her erecting more walls. Donning more armor.

"That thing about us not having sex until after we're married," Harper said in a rush. "I want to revise that. I don't think we should have sex at all. Before *or* after. We should probably nix the kissing, too. Yes, definitely. Kissing is out. Except maybe a peck. For appearance's sake. Since we'll have to sleep in the same room, maybe we should consider twin beds. Separate beds. Absolutely. Why tempt the devil? We agreed this was a business arrangement, right? We both have an agenda, a goal. So we should keep sex and feelings and stuff out of it. Keep it simple and civil and—"

"It won't work."

She blinked up at Sam with the dismayed gaze of a trapped animal.

"You can't shut me out, Harper. I'm already in."

She balled her fists at her sides. "I meant what I said about sex."

"I'm sure you did."

"I'm going inside."

"Right behind you."

She turned and pushed through the hedges. No graceful way about that but at least she managed not to take a header when her toe caught on a root.

Sam adjusted himself and followed, his heart pounding against his ribs. Harper was falling for him. They'd moved beyond *just sex*. They'd moved on to intimate. If she could, he was pretty sure she'd run. But then she'd have to return to Canada. Obviously, he was the lesser evil. His pride might have reared if he weren't feeling so damned smug. And, oh, yeah. *Happy.*

His phone pinged with an incoming text. From Harper. Who was literally three steps ahead of him.

SCREW YOU.

Sam's lips twitched as he thumbed his reply. ANYTIME.

SEVENTEEN

"Are you sure you're not overheated?"

"I'm sure. Just don't let me walk into any carts or gurneys. My vision is limited."

"Give me your paw."

"I need it to wave to people."

"Wave with your other paw."

"Technically they're hooves. Oh, never mind." Daisy reached out and Vincent grasped her . . . whatever. She appreciated his help even though she was feeling prickly. She *was* overheated and her glasses had fogged up. But she didn't want to take off her moose head in public and ruin the illusion. She'd just spent twenty minutes in the children's ward spreading cheer as Millie the Moose. It was a heck of a lot better than twiddling her thumbs in the waiting room worrying about Chloe and wondering when it was ever going to be her turn to visit. She'd been hugging a little boy suffering from a kidney ailment when Vincent had nudged her saying the text she'd been waiting for had finally come through.

Tickled pink that she was finally going to have her chance with Chloe, Daisy waved her good-byes, the children's giggly cheers ringing in her antlered ears as Vincent escorted her out of the ward and into the elevator. The only thing Daisy enjoyed more than working at Moose-a-lotta was her occasional jaunts as Millie Moose. Sometimes she felt like she'd missed her calling. Like she should've been a professional actress. Although Chloe (who'd lived in New York City and had dabbled in everything from acting to costume design) had assured Daisy the entertainment biz wasn't all it was cracked up to be. It was most definitely a high-stress field if Harper's hyper demeanor was any indication.

"'Birthing Center and Mother/Baby Unit,'" Vincent said, as the bell dinged and the doors opened.

"In my day they called it a maternity ward."

"Just reading the sign, Petunia. Watch your step now. Are you sure you don't want to take off that head?"

"Not until I'm behind closed doors. And don't call me Petunia. I'm in character." She waved at who she thought was a doctor although it could have been a janitor. Hard to see anything clearly at a distance through the grid eyes of the moose head, not to mention her own misty specs.

"Er, Millie," Vincent said. "This way." He tugged her to the left and she almost lost her balance as her furry hooves shuffled across the linoleum floor. Lordy, it was hot inside this furry costume. Air circulation was, as Chloe would say, the pits. Daisy was starting to feel light-headed, but then she saw her son and daughter-in-law coming out of a room, and her senses perked right up. Chloe, her business partner, her friend, and the almost mother of Daisy's first great-grandchild, was in that room. She could hardly wait to see her. But first Daisy had to get past her son. She knew the minute Jerome spotted her because he stiffened and frowned.

"For the love of . . . Mom?"

"No, Millie."

"She's in character," Vincent whispered.

"She's in a moose costume," Jerome said, looking stuck between exasperated and mortified. "How do you even breathe in that thing?"

"Through my nose."

Kaye, who'd always been a good egg in Daisy's book, squeezed her husband's arm. "Stop badgering your mother."

"Seriously," Jerome said. "Why are you in that thing?"

Daisy would have pushed her specs up her nose and sniffed if she could have. Instead she perched her plush (albeit raggedy) paws (hooves) on her padded hips. "I'll have you know the kids in the children's ward loved me."

"They did," Vincent said.

"No doubt," Kaye said with a lopsided smile.

"How's Chloe?" Daisy asked.

Kaye sighed. "A little anxious. The baby dropped but Chloe isn't nearly dilated enough. They may have to perform a C-section."

"Oh," Daisy mumbled, feeling a little rattled herself. Not a terrible thing, but not smooth sailing, either. Surgery of any kind typically involved some sort of risk. "When will we know?"

"Not for a while," Kaye said. "We could be looking at tomorrow morning."

"Exhausting and stressful for Chloe," Vincent said.

"Her father's a nervous wreck," Jerome said. "Dev took him down to the cafeteria for a cup of coffee."

"And what about Dev? How's he holding up?"

"He's a rock," Kaye said. "In front of Chloe anyway."

"Considering how overprotective he is," Daisy said, "I'm sure he's driving the hospital staff crazy."

Jerome scratched his jaw. "Pretty much."

"Naturally, he's worried about Chloe and the baby," Kaye said, "but I think it's escalated by his past experience—"

"Never mind about that," Jerome said.

"Everything will be fine," Daisy said, even as her heart squeezed. *Poor Devlin!*

"Absolutely," Kaye said.

"Chloe asked for you," Jerome said to Daisy. "Maybe you could . . ." He looked away, jammed a hand through bristly gray hair. "Do you have any idea what it's like trying to have a serious conversation with a moose?"

"No idea at all." Daisy looked to her beau, one of the only men in her life who, as Chloe would say, *got her.* She jerked her antlers toward the door. "Coming with?"

"Chloe asked for you," Vincent said softly, "not me."

"I'm sure you're welcome."

"I'll wait out here."

Daisy pushed into the room, sad that Vincent was always setting himself apart from her family. As if he didn't belong. Which was silly. She was also peeved at her son who had a perpetual stick-up-his-patooty—just like his father. Hadn't Jerome's near brush with death taught him to embrace the moment? To welcome the absurd? Apparently not. It was petty of her, but she suddenly wished she had wrenched off her head in the hall. One gander at her brilliant, newly dyed blue hair and Jerome would have rethought his gripe with her antlers.

"Daisy?"

She shook off her irritation and turned toward Chloe's sweet voice. In doing so she got a quick screening of the surprisingly cheerful décor. "Looks like my grandson scored you a deluxe room, kitten. Private, too."

"Not that I've had much privacy," Chloe said. "Between the doctor, the nurses, and family—"

"Would you like me to leave?"

"No, no. I didn't mean that. I'm glad you're here. But why are you in costume?"

"Oh, right." Daisy tugged off the moose head, welcoming the rush of cool, fresh air. She told Chloe about her stint in the children's ward as she shimmied out of the rest of the suffocating fur suit. Her capris and her peasant blouse were a little sticky and she smelled like stale Frebreze, but other than that she was no worse for wear. Fluffing her short curls, she moved to Chloe's side.

"You changed your hair color."

"In honor of summer-blue skies."

"I like."

"Then why are your eyes tearing up?" Daisy asked as she gripped Chloe's hand. "Are you in pain? Should I ask for drugs?"

"I had an epidural. I'm good. That is, I'm okay. I just . . ." Her brown eyes shimmered with unshed tears. "I'm a little scared. The baby's big," she said as she lovingly palmed her belly, "and I'm small. Too small. If I don't . . . they might . . ."

"Cesarean. I know. But that's okay, sweetie. You're healthy. The baby's healthy. Everything will be fine."

"But what if it isn't?"

"Why wouldn't it be?"

"Devlin already lost one baby."

"First wife. Miscarriage. Long time ago."

"I kept putting it off. Getting married. For real, I mean. I know we said the vows during Rocky's wedding. So did you and Vincent. But that wasn't real."

"Not in a legal sense," Daisy said while smoothing strands of hair from her clammy face. "But where the heart is concerned—"

"I want it to be real, Daisy. I want to be Mrs. Devlin Monroe when my baby comes into this world. I want him or her to have his or her daddy's name. I held off on marriage because I didn't want to jinx things, but now I think I jinxed things because I waited. And now it's too late."

"Too late for what?"

"To get married before the baby's born," Chloe squeaked as the first tear rolled. "Haven't you been listening?"

"Avidly," Daisy said while handing her a tissue. "Just having a hard time keeping up. Maybe it's the fumes from the fabric deodorizer. I sprayed the costume right before I pulled it on."

"You need to be careful about that."

"You know me," Daisy said while waggling her brows. "Evel Knievel of Sugar Creek."

Chloe smiled a little but not enough.

"Did you tell Dev about your change of heart?"

She shook her head. "He's been pushing me to set a wedding date for months. Seems a little unfair of me to say *now* in the zero hour."

"Fair, schmair, and it's not the zero hour. The doctor said you could be in labor throughout the night. " Daisy's mind whirled. "If only you had a marriage license."

"We do. Devlin—"

"Then it's not too late!" Bouncing on the heels of her metallic sneakers, Daisy grabbed a pen from the little nightstand and pulled her folded page from her pants pocket.

"What are you doing?" Chloe asked as she hugged her belly.

"Crossing you and my grandson off my family bucket list."

"What's a—"

"I'll be back with a preacher," Daisy said as she hurried toward the door. "Don't let anyone steal Millie."

"But—"

"My stars are aligned," Daisy called over her shoulder. "No worries, kitten!" Giddy as a kid on Christmas morning, Daisy sailed into the hall and snagged Vincent's arm. "Come on, Speedy. We're on a mission."

She waggled her fingers over her shoulder at her son and daughter-in-law, smiling when she heard Jerome say, "Good God. My mother looks like she dipped her head in Ty-D-Bol."

EIGHTEEN

Stepping into the crowded waiting room was like braving the sidelines of a star-studded red carpet. The excitement was palatable, the noise level intense. Harper half expected the paparazzi to swarm which was ridiculous. It's not like Chloe was giving birth to a prince, although maybe that's how it felt to these people.

Come to think of it, given all Harper had heard and experienced, the Monroes *were* as good as Sugar Creek royalty—Daisy being the grand, albeit eccentric, matriarch. Her son Jerome was the CEO of J. T. Monroe's Department Store, family owned and operated for generations. He also dabbled in local politics. *His* son, Devlin (Chloe's fiancé), served as CFO of the family business. A financial wiz, Dev (as Sam called him) also headed his own investment company. According to Daisy, her grandson had a bit of a Midas touch and his advice and astute financial planning had benefited several clients, including a few family members.

As for Chloe, although relatively new to Sugar Creek, she was held in high regard. Not only because she was Dev's lady, but because she'd partnered with Daisy to open Moose-a-lotta. A gifted baker, she was also one of the Cupcake Lovers' newest shining stars.

Harper had processed all that information as she'd gravitated toward the group of people she knew best—the Cupcake Lovers. Ethel, Helen, Judy, Rocky, Monica, Casey, Rae. They were all here, most all with a husband or partner. Joey was missing, but given her newbie status, that made sense. Daisy had shuffled off to visit the children's ward as Millie Moose and Sam was mingling with various family members—most of whom Harper didn't recognize.

Every once in a while Sam caught Harper's eye and she immediately looked away. No man had ever kissed her like Sam. Or maybe it was that no man had ever made her feel the way Sam made her feel. Not even Andrew. A man she'd professed to love. A man she'd agreed to marry. Maybe that's why she'd ultimately failed him. Maybe her affections hadn't been strong enough, real enough. Maybe she'd been more in love with the idea of being a bride than a wife. The possibility shamed Harper and pushed her thoughts into dark places. She didn't want to go there, so she kept to the light, informing the Cupcake Lovers of her media plan regarding the impending birth of the newest CL. Because everyone was happy for a distraction, they'd jumped on their phones to join in the cyberparty. The younger set were off and running. The seniors, bless their hearts, were following along if not contributing as quickly. Except for Helen who looked a little frazzled.

"I'm sorry," she said when Harper approached. "How do I get that . . . what did you call it?"

"App." She smiled at the older woman who'd only recently upgraded to a smartphone.

"We just learned how to use the texting option," her husband said. "Everything else is Greek."

"You can install Facebook via the Google Play Store," Harper said.

They both blinked.

Harper reached for Helen's phone. "Could I—"

"Please."

"Let me watch," Daniel said. "We need to get with the times. Can't always rely on a young person to be around."

"Gotcha." Harper purposely slowed her efforts. "Social media is the key word here." She walked Helen and Daniel through setting up a personal Facebook account enabling them to interact on the Cupcake Lovers Fan Page. She adjusted their privacy settings. "Then you go here and—"

"Comment," Daniel said. "Thank you, Harper. I think I have it."

"Me, too," Helen said with a thousand-watt smile.

"I'm sure you do." Harper's heart bumped against her ribs as she watched the senior couple post their first comment. She'd never known her own grandparents. Would they have embraced technology as eagerly as the Coles? What about her parents? Did either one of them visit Harper's social feeds in order to catch up on her life? It's not like they ever called. Her gaze skipped to Sam, who'd been circulating among his relatives and friends, mingling amiably in his subdued way. According to Daisy, although he'd lost both of his parents, he'd grown up surrounded by skads of aunts and uncles and cousins. He also had a brother presently serving in the military. Harper had grown up with her parents, period, although they'd never been what she'd call a family. Not like the Waltons or Bradys or the Monroes and their extended clan.

Feeling self-conscious now, she reached in her purse for her iPad, planning to find a corner where she could hide with her tablet and network with focused fury.

Rocky snagged her arm and attention. "Nice of you to help Helen and Dan like that."

Harper shrugged. "Sometimes I forget the entire world isn't as hooked up as me."

"Speaking of hooked up. You and Sam—"

"You're wondering why we arrived together."

"I'm thrilled that you're involved."

"Who said—"

"Hollywood has nothing on Sugar Creek when it comes to gossip," Rocky said.

"I'll keep that in mind."

"I'd ask how serious it is," Rocky said in a low voice, "except this is Sam, who doesn't do casual. Plus he invited you to Sunday dinner."

"Which is at your house," Harper said. "He should have checked with you first."

"We're not that formal. Speaking of . . ." Rocky, who was also dressed in jeans and a tee, motioned to Harper's casual attire. "I see you're finally relaxing into country living. I didn't even know you *owned* a pair of jeans."

Still gripping her iPad, Harper shifted her weight, anxious to check on the cybercelebration. Feeds like Twitter moved at lightning speed. "I didn't expect to be working today. Not in public, anyway."

"We really appreciate this," Rocky said while checking her own social apps. "Because of this cybercelebration, in the last ten minutes alone, I've seen a lift in sales for the recipe book. Not only that, people are sharing the links to our favorite charities and urging friends to match their pledges. You do so much for us, Harper, and we barely pay you a dime."

"You're a nonprofit organization."

"Still . . . Daisy told me you parted ways with Spin Twin Cities and now you'll be freelancing. I hope you have other clients lined up aside from us. Otherwise you'll starve."

"I'll be fine." She didn't want to get into her real motivation for supporting the Cupcake Lovers and was looking to redirect the conversation when Rae stepped in.

"Did you see some of these name suggestions?" the soft-spoken heiress asked while scrolling down her phone.

"Sugar or Maple if it's a girl. Jago or Oakley if a boy? I blame it on the celebrities who made it trendy by naming their children after fruit and months of the year. No offense, Harper."

"None taken. I didn't have a hand in naming those babies." Or any baby for that matter. None of her clients had had children under her watch. Drug issues, alcohol issues, extramarital issues, yes. Babies, no.

"Have you and Luke decided on a name yet?" Rocky asked.

Rae, who was close to six months pregnant and looking stylish as ever in a cute sundress and wedge-heeled sandals, smiled at her sister-in-law. "You asked me that last night. The answer is still no," she said with a teasing smile. "But we've narrowed it down. I can tell you it won't be Peaches or December."

Rocky laughed. "Well, at least with you, I know to shop for a girl. Do you know how frustrating it's been not being able to shop gender-specific for Dev and Chloe's baby?"

"They wanted to be surprised," Rae said. "I think it's sweet. Speaking of sweet . . ."

She trailed off and in the lingering silence Harper looked up from her iPad, mid-text. Rae and Rocky were both smiling at her. "What?"

"Luke told me Sam got awfully cozy with you during lunch. I thought maybe he was exaggerating. But I keep seeing Sam stealing peeks at you and . . ." She smiled even bigger. "He's totally smitten with you, Harper."

"Tough guys like Sam don't do smitten," Harper said.

"Okay," Rocky said. "He's hot for you."

"I think there's more to it than that," Rae said.

"It's a physical thing," Harper gritted out in a near whisper. "Just sex."

Rocky smiled.

Rae blinked. "*Really*? How long has *that* been going on?"

"A while. Here and there. Off and on." She didn't intend

to share details, but Harper was determined to squelch the illusion of love. Entirely for her own benefit. Love would muck up everything. "It's not a big deal."

"He invited you to Sunday dinner," said Rae.

"You left your job in L.A.," said Rocky.

"You did?" Rae asked.

"Booted out is more like it," Harper said, "but the result is the same."

"So you'll be staying on permanently in Sugar Creek?" Rae asked.

"That's the plan," Harper said, glancing at Sam who was now talking to Luke. She was starting to feel incredibly guilty about this marriage of convenience. She knew Sam's family and friends were anxious for him to find true happiness and new love and Harper was marrying him for a freaking green card. "Excuse me," she said, anxious to escape. "I need to catch up on some of these posts."

She spied a corner, but she also spied a television mounted close by. A senior couple was staring up at the screen, shaking their heads.

"What is it?" Harper asked as she moved closer.

"A young man opened fire in a terminal at O'Hare in Chicago," the man said.

"Apparently he had a bone to pick with TSA, but he shot at anyone in uniform," the woman said. "It's just awful."

"A few minutes ago, they mentioned a school shooting in Montana," the man said. "What's this world coming to?"

Harper stared at the screen. Aerial shots of the airport. B-roll of the terminal. Interview with a cop. Her mind filled in the blanks. Panicked innocents running for cover. Victims covered in blood.

"I'm Spike Martini," the man said. "This is my wife, Rose."

"I'm one of Daisy's sisters," she said. "Dev's great-aunt. And you are?"

Stunned spitless.

An airport shooting. A school shooting. Why not a hospital shooting? What if a grief-stricken man who'd lost his son or daughter or wife to a botched surgery burst through the doors of Pixley General, guns blazing? What if he took out the Cupcake Lovers and all of Sam's family and . . .

Sam.

Harper felt his calming presence, his hand on her shoulder. "Aunt Rose, Uncle Spike," he said. "I see you've met Harper."

"Not officially," Spike said.

She realized then that she'd neglected to answer their question. Her brain had latched on to the shooting. *Another* shooting. She couldn't tear her gaze from the screen. How many people had died? What were the shooter's motives? Did someone try to talk him down before he turned the gun on himself?

"Harper's the publicist for the Cupcake Lovers," Sam continued. "Mind if I borrow her for a moment?" He palmed the small of her back. "Come on, hon."

She was mortified. Because she'd frozen. Because she was trembling. She saw the look of concern on Spike's and Rose's faces. And when Sam guided her out of the room, she saw everyone watching. *Dammit.*

Once in the hall, Sam cupped the sides of her face and looked into her eyes. "Let it go."

She nodded, even though a dozen what ifs clogged her brain.

"How's the cybercelebration going?"

"What?"

He nodded to the iPad clutched tight against her chest. She blinked out of her daze, opened her Facebook page. She skimmed the happy posts, the smiley faces, the new pledges. "Good. It's good."

One arm around her waist, Sam angled in. "Show me how that works."

She swallowed hard, corralled her senses.

Luke stepped out of the waiting room. "Everything okay?"

"We're good," Sam said.

But then Dev, a renowned control freak, blew in out of nowhere, looking uncharacteristically harried. He stopped short of the waiting room, jammed a hand through his dark hair. "Exactly who I wanted to see. Thank you, Jesus. Now I don't have to go in and face everyone."

Harper's stomach knotted.

"What's wrong?" Luke asked.

"Chloe wants to get married. *Now.*"

"Whoa."

"It'll be short and sweet and extremely private. Hospital policy limits visitors and they're balking on raising quantity even by one person."

"No wonder you don't want to brave the waiting room," Luke said. "The only thing we've all been anticipating as much as your baby is your wedding."

"Sorry to disappoint," Dev said, "but right now I'm most concerned with making my girl happy."

"How can we help?" Sam asked.

"Gram and Vincent are grabbing the preacher," Dev said. "Luke, I need you to distract Chloe's dad. He's driving me nuts. You know Roger. He likes you. I left him in the café. Go do your thing, and when the preacher arrives, I'll give a shout. I can swing Roger and Mom and Dad in the room, but that's about it."

"Understood." Luke rapped his brother on the shoulder then took off.

Dev turned to Sam. "You know the armoire you made me? Master bedroom. Bottom left drawer. Marriage license. Rings."

"Even if I race the back roads, we're talking forty-five minutes, Dev."

"The longer you stand here—"

"Got it." Sam snagged the house key from Dev's hand then looked to Harper. "Ready?"

He didn't want to leave her. She could see it in his eyes. He was worried she'd have a meltdown. She wouldn't. She was past that now. As long as she stayed away from the TV and resisted Googling *airport shooting*.

"Hold on." Dev glanced from Harper to the waiting room then back. "Is that an iPad? It has a camera, right?"

Harper nodded. "Yes. Why?"

"You're coming with me." He turned to Sam. "Why are you still here?"

Against her better judgment, Harper planted a peck on Sam's cheek. "See you when you get back, Rambo."

Before she could step back, he palmed the back of her neck and kissed her full on the mouth. Then he was gone.

Dev grasped Harper's elbow and hurried her toward the elevator. "That was interesting."

"You have no idea."

NINETEEN

"Chloe have the baby?"

"Not yet," Luke said. "But I do have news."

Adam switched his android to speakerphone and balanced it on the sink's vanity. The last thing he needed was to drop it in the john. "All ears."

"Dev and Chloe got married."

"What, for real?"

"Like ten minutes ago. In her hospital room. Took all of four minutes. *If that.* Chloe had a contraction and Dev told the preacher to hurry. Mom and Dad and Chloe's dad witnessed. Dev sat on the bed next to Chloe and they both palmed her belly, as if holding their baby as they said the vows. It was freaking emotional. Crazy, considering the venue."

"Thought you weren't in the room," Adam said.

"I wasn't. But thanks to the Cupcake Lover's publicist, several family members got to watch on their androids via something called Skype."

"I know Skype," Adam said as he dropped to his knees and snapped on a pair of latex gloves. "Unlike you, I'm not a Luddite."

"I'm working past that," Luke said. "Anyway Rae and Rocky got all teary so they slipped into the bathroom to fix their faces. Jayce is speaking with Dev and I'm taking a breather, trying to get my head past this delivery thing. Chloe's been in labor for hours and it doesn't look like the baby's coming any time soon. They might have to schedule a Cesarean."

"Not necessarily a cause for worry, right?"

"No. So the doctors and everyone say. But how would you feel if it were your wife and baby?"

"Not sure," Adam said honestly as he doused the bowl in blue. At the rate he was going, he wasn't sure that day would ever come. "If you're worried about Chloe facing complications—"

"Of course I'm worried. And if *I'm* worried, imagine how my brother must feel. Just the thought of Rae—"

"Don't go there."

"Easier said than done."

"Rae's healthy, right? Baby's healthy? Everything's good?"

"Yeah."

"Then don't borrow trouble. Stay positive." Adam stepped off the pep talk he often gave to nervous students and suggested a break instead. "Maybe you should take Rae home. Make her dinner. Hang out until you get the call instead of waiting and stressing. Plenty of other relatives there, right?"

"Yeah. Although some are breaking and coming back later. Leo just pried Monica out of here. She's even further along than Rae and he's worried about her getting overly tired." Luke blew out a breath. "So what are you doing?"

"Scrubbing the toilet."

"What do you mean?"

"Blue stuff. Scrub brush."

"It's Saturday night, Adam."

"Yup." Since Adam was on speakerphone he was pretty sure Luke could hear the squirting, spraying, sloshing, and flushing as he endeavored to rid his toilet of any dried pee splashes and assorted gross stuff on the bowl and tank. It's not that Adam was a disgusting slob, but a girl was moving in.

Tonight.

"When I called Nash to tell him Chloe was in labor," Luke said, "he told me you bailed on the fishing trip with him and Kane. Tell me it wasn't to clean your house. I'm seriously starting to worry about you."

Luke was one of the few people who knew about Adam's long-ago broken affair with Rocky. Adam had brooded over several beers at the Shack for several long months. He was done with that now. But he had been preoccupied with his secret goal.

"You know how I was looking for a roommate?"

"Yeah."

"Found one."

"Who?"

"Peppy Redding. Know her?"

"Not well, but yeah. I know she's always been a pain in her dad's ass and that nothing's changed on that front. Not for anything, Adam, but that girl's notorious for having wanderlust. Vincent said she picked up some gigs with a regional band, but her bank account's bare. What if she sticks you for the rent?"

"She paid a month up front. I'll worry about July in July."

"If she's still in town then."

"Could you be any more cynical?"

"Just looking out for a friend. You've been working your ass off for months, socking away money for whatever this goal of yours is. You've been deliberate, focused, cautious. Taking on a roommate was a financial decision, yet you welcome the first applicant who knocks on your door? An unreliable musician with a restless soul and debt up to her eyeballs? A woman, no less? How's that going to work when you have a lady over for the evening? Oh, wait."

"What?"

"Are you hot for her?"

"No." Adam stashed the cleaning supplies under the sink then did a one-eighty. Clean and lemony. Good to go. "She's cute, but she's not my type. Plus she's aloof."

"Then what?"

"I feel sorry for her."

"Oh, hell, Adam."

"I appreciate you calling with the update on Dev and Chloe, but I need to go."

"Don't let her get under your skin. I know you and—"

"You're one to talk. You who hires a new waitress every time a girl's desperate for work even though you're always overstaffed."

"That's the Shack. This is your home."

"Hanging up."

"Toss anything moldy from the fridge and don't forget to vacuum between the sofa cushions. Clipped toenails and chip crumbs tend to gross girls out."

"Bye." Adam rolled his eyes, then on second thought checked the fridge one last time. He wasn't worried about the sofa. He chucked a questionable peach then snagged a bottle of apple juice. Halfway to the living room, he heard a loud bang. Sounded like a car backfiring, but way out here, who knew? Could've been someone taking a potshot at a gopher. He moved to the living room window and spied Peppy getting out of her car and kicking the tire. She looked mad as hell. Kind of like last night. And earlier today. Adam got the sinking feeling that Peppy Redding was perpetually bent out of shape. Like he needed that aggravation, but what was done, was done. Adam, unlike some people he'd known, always kept his word.

He pushed through his front door, properly dressed. Jeans, tee, sneaks. And for good measure, a baseball cap. Nothing sexy or inappropriate. No reason for her to avoid his gaze.

Yet she did.

"Need help?" he asked as he neared.

"No. Yes. Maybe. I don't know." She kicked the tire again. For good measure . . . or maybe she was just angry with the world and needed to kick something, anything. "I don't have much," she said as she pulled open the back door of her dinged-up car. "Couple of suitcases. Couple of guitars. An amp. Some recording gear. I travel light."

"Makes things easy," Adam said as he snagged both suitcases. But he was thinking, *How sad*. Peppy had to be in her mid-twenties and this was it?

"I should've gone straight to my gig and come here after. I would've been hanging out in the bar with nothing to do for a few hours but at least I would have been there. Instead, I let Dad get my goat and all I could think of was clearing out." She grabbed a black case and a backpack. "Let's get this stuff inside. The sooner I take off the better. I don't want to push Dingboy past sixty."

"Maybe I should give you a lift," Adam said as they approached the porch.

"What? And drive back four hours later to pick me up? Or worse, sit there and wait throughout my entire gig? Uh, no. Besides, I'm sure a hunk like you has better things to do on a Saturday night."

She thought he was a hunk?

"Not that I think you're all that, but some of the girls in the band took notice. And yes, Ivy was one of them. I'm sure that makes you deliriously happy."

It didn't make him sad. That was for sure. But the rush was dampened by the knowledge that Peppy was less than impressed. She didn't even know him! Yeah, okay. He was a little pissed at her pissy attitude. Peppy Redding was probably, no, *definitely* the rudest woman he'd ever had the misfortune of . . . inviting into his home.

Shit.

"Home sweet home," she said as she made a beeline for the second bedroom. "Just dump my suitcases . . . anywhere," she finished as Adam tossed them on the twin bed he'd taken the frickin' time to dress with clean sheets and a quilt handmade by his grandmother.

Peppy Redding had stretched his patience to the limits in less than five minutes. A record, especially since Adam was an extremely patient man. He glared, resenting her waif features and soft curves. Physical qualities that appealed to him on a surprising level. She wasn't his type. Yet she intrigued him. Beyond reason. Clearly his disastrous history with women had mangled his judgment. "You best hit the road. Wouldn't want you to be late for your gig."

"Aren't you the conscientious one," she said as she sauntered—yeah, freaking *sauntered*—out of the house. "Don't wait up."

As if.

Yet he knew he would.

TWENTY

Time blurred.

Relatives and friends came and went and dwindled to a lone few.

Midnight rolled around and Sam finally hit his own personal wall. Not because he was exhausted or bored or anxious, but because he was worried about Harper. Refusing to leave the hospital, she'd been operating on coffee and adrenaline for hours. He'd tried coaxing her into grabbing a decent meal at a nearby restaurant, but she didn't want to leave the grounds for fear Chloe would give sudden birth.

"Can't miss the big event," she'd said. "Constant and timely updates are crucial. Because of the enthusiastic posts from myself and several other CLs, we, the Cupcake Lovers, have picked up several new fans today. Sales are up on the recipe book and, according to my contacts at our targeted charities, donations are rolling in. All because we've raised interest and awareness by hyping this happy event. When Chloe delivers the baby, I need to deliver the news. Pronto. Pics, too."

"Dev could do that. Or Rocky. She's intent on spending the night."

"That burden shouldn't fall to either one of them,"

Harper said. "They should be enjoying the arrival of Baby Monroe, not worrying about posting to all the right places in the most advantageous way. That's my job."

Sam didn't argue. She was the Cupcake Lovers' publicist. And maybe the frenzy and hoopla soothed the wounded ego of a woman who'd just been fired from a high-profile firm. Also, there was no denying Harper's efforts had made a positive impact on donations. Sam had contacts within those military organizations, too. But, as she'd said earlier in the day, "That was then, this is now." He'd just checked in with Dev who'd urged everyone, including his parents, to go home.

Walking into the nearly deserted waiting room, Sam homed in on Harper. She was stationed in the same corner, typing on her iPad, checking her phone. She'd been at it for hours, yet her energy level was high, her focus intense. How long could she go on like this? He flashed on his days in the field, times when he'd been on duty and in the zone—energy level high, focus intense—and he instinctively knew . . . she could go all night.

"Pack it up, Slick."

Harper looked away from her iPad and frowned up at Sam. "That's what Daisy calls me."

"I know. I heard. It stuck. You've worked wonders today. Time to give it a rest."

"But—"

"Dev asked everyone to go home and to get some rest. The doctor scheduled a cesarean for ten A.M. tomorrow. If anything changes, Dev'll call."

"But what if—"

"Dev will call," Sam repeated, while urging Harper to her feet. "You can twit, tweet, whatever from home. *Just got the call . . . racing to hospital . . .* I'm sure you can spin it and build anticipation when we make our way back here. Meanwhile, as exciting as this is, I doubt even the most avid CL fans will be glued to the Internet throughout the night."

She blew out a breath, glanced at her tablet then back to Sam. "If you're sure—"

"I'm sure." Sam watched as she typed in a last post then powered down. He resisted the urge to check his phone to see what she'd written. He didn't want her to think he was spying. Although she had encouraged him to *plug in* and *interact*.

He'd asked Rocky to help him set up Twitter and Facebook accounts on his phone and to hook him up with the Cupcake Lovers page as well as Harper's and those belonging to a few pet organizations. When he wasn't speaking with family members or touching base with his kids, Sam had settled in close to Harper. She'd kept her head down, working and drinking coffee like a fiend. Sam had matched her java intake while following the action on those social sites via his phone. Twitter was a fast-moving blur. He did better with Facebook and, frankly, he was surprised by the content and frequency of Harper's posts and comments to other people's posts. She was entertaining, informative, and engaging. She didn't focus solely on the Cupcake Lovers, but on cupcakes in general and on soldiers and their families. He'd been stunned by her empathy. As if she'd experienced similar situations. He knew Harper was obsessed with the legend of Mary Rothwell and her MIA husband, but was she keyed in to the plight of military personnel on a more personal level?

It had taken all of Sam's restraint not to Google her name, not to call Jayce. He wanted to learn about Harper's past from Harper, not by poking around behind her back. When the time was right, he'd ask her straight-out. Maybe that time was now.

Her cell phone rang, beating him to the punch.

Harper shushed Sam by holding up a finger. Even

though he'd softened toward this woman overall, *that* particular habit was still damned annoying.

"Yes," she said. "I did and . . . Really?" She glanced at Sam then plopped back in her chair and fired up the tablet she'd just shut down. "You've been . . . Wow. I mean, naturally you'd be interested. They're a dream combination. Cupcakes and soldiers. Pure gold, but . . . That soon?" she asked while reading something on her screen. "Chloe wouldn't be able to make it for obvious reasons and two other members are expecting. Not sure if it's medically safe for them to fly. And . . . Sam? Yes, he is. No argument there, but . . ." She cast Sam a look, blushed. "I'll see what I can do and get back to you ASAP. Thank you for calling, Val."

Harper disconnected then tucked both phone and tablet in her massive purse. "That was my contact at the *Brice and Kaylee—Live! show*," she said without meeting Sam's gaze. "Valerie's been watching the growing hype and interest regarding Chloe's baby and the Cupcake Lovers and their overall mission. The show's filming live in Vegas this week and one of their scheduled guests fell out. They're inviting the Cupcake Lovers to join them . . . as featured guests."

She bounced out of her chair and paced. "This is gold, Sam! Network TV. National coverage. Do you have any idea how many people tune into Brice and Kaylee on a daily basis? Add to that those who catch up via DVR, YouTube, and Hulu. The exposure could catapult *Cupcake Lovers' Delectable Delights* to the bestseller lists. We're talking mega sales and that means mega income for your charities, which will generate even more attention for the club. It's everything Daisy hoped for and more. The Cupcake Lovers will become a household name, at least for a while. Long enough, for certain. Five minutes of fame can make a massive impact and . . ."

She faltered and stopped in her tracks. She squared her shoulders and balled her fists. Harper looked like a warrior, a woman on a mission, a woman who didn't intend to lose. Her determination was as good as an aphrodisiac in Sam's book.

"I know you're opposed to the limelight," she said, "but I need you on board, Sam. They want as many Cupcake Lovers as possible and it's incredibly short notice. We'd have to fly there day after tomorrow. Chloe's out. Monica and Rae are possibly out. And because it's a weekday, Casey might be out. She has a business to run. Not that you don't, but Val asked for you specifically. Which I totally get. She knows a rating boost when she sees one."

Sam raised a brow.

"A gorgeous former marine who bakes and is a loving father to boot?" She threw her arms wide. "Come on! You'll have women viewers drooling on their remotes. Although it would help if you smiled now and then. And if you could flirt up Kaylee . . . Never mind. You're not exactly a natural flirt. The strong, silent type. That's your angle. We can work that. It won't be that bad. I promise. Brice and Kaylee are gifted hosts. They'll do most of the work and no doubt Daisy will be a chatterbox so you just need to be your hunky Rambo self and . . ." Her face fell. "You won't do it."

He wasn't used to being thought of as a sex icon, wasn't comfortable working *that* angle. But it did please Sam that Harper considered him *hunky* and droolworthy. A stroke to the ego, especially given her sultry beauty. Plus, logic dictated other advantages. "I'll do it."

She moved in toe-to-toe, blue eyes wide. "You will?"

"For the cause," he said, smoothing renegade locks from her face. "And for us."

She looked a little stunned, backed up a step and twisted her hair into a new and tidier ponytail. "Us?"

"Don't panic."

"I'm not—"

"You are. Don't worry," Sam said as he scooped up her

oversized purse and looped it over her shoulder. "It wasn't a romantic sentiment." Palming the small of her back, he escorted her from the waiting room and outdoors. The air was fresh and cool, the moon hanging bright in a starry sky. Sort of romantic, but Sam didn't go there. Finessing her toward his truck, he took the logical route. "Your showbiz friend just graced us with a gift."

"I know."

"Not the Cupcake Lovers. *Us*." Sam helped Harper up into the cab. He lingered at the door, absorbing her exotic essence and vulnerability. She was by far the most complicated woman he'd ever known. "Now we have a solid, valid reason to travel to Las Vegas. *Business*. After the show wraps we'll go out to celebrate, and after too many drinks, we'll act impulsively and, in the spirit of Vegas, tie the knot in one of those themed chapels."

"That's so clichéd. But I do see your logic."

"Yeah?"

She nodded while buckling her seat belt. "Immigration will be less likely to question a quickie marriage under those circumstances."

"Exactly." Sam closed the door and rounded the cab. His brain raced with details. Arrangements for child care. For travel. For the ceremony. He needed to step up all his previous arrangements by six days. His heart pounded as he slid behind the wheel. In two days, he'd be married. Everything would change. His life. Harper's life. The kids' lives. Not that that was news to Sam, but now it felt real.

The air pulsed with urgency, anticipation, trepidation—his, hers—as he pulled onto the highway.

Harper whipped out her phone. "I need to tell the Cupcake Lovers about the talk show offer."

"Late to be making calls."

"It's three hours earlier on the West Coast and Val needs an answer ASAP. I'm sure she's put out other feelers given the time issue. If we don't grab the brass ring pronto we could lose it to showgirls or Elvis impersonators or hell, if I were Val, I'd go after those *Pawn Star* guys. Someone local instead . . ." She froze mid-dial. "Oh, no."

"What?"

"We'll have to fly."

"So?"

"That public shooting today. At an airport."

"A major airport," Sam said in a calm voice. "Burlington is relatively small."

"That doesn't matter. We'll still have to pass through security. Then there's baggage claim once we land. All those people, all the chaos. What if—"

"What if I book a private flight? Fly out of the local airfield? My cousin Nash pilots for a charter company. He's also got a weakness for poker. Won't be hard to lure him to Vegas."

She looked over at Sam with such relief that his heart jerked in his chest. "I bet I can get the show to cover the expense," she said. "Val was awfully keen on making this happen."

Sam reached over and squeezed her thigh. "Let's see who's up for the trip then take it from there." If Harper didn't get a grip on this phobia, he'd have to talk to her about seeking professional help. The thought of it snowballing and somehow affecting Ben and Mina was troubling. Also, he didn't want Harper living in fear. He wanted to vanquish her stress, her every worry and fear. He wanted normal and happy and, hell, maybe he was the one who needed a shrink. He was chasing a memory. Forcing a dream.

As he listened to Harper making call after call, working her magic with confidence and zeal, he acknowledged, deep down and for certain, her intense drive to finesse people's lives for the better. Once she had her green card, she could rebuild her former career as a spin doctor for troubled celebrities. Unless she redirected her passion. Could she be content solely promoting the Cupcake Lovers and Rae's charitable efforts? Was she capable of cutting back on her workload and devoting a portion of her energy and attention to Ben and Mina? To Sam? To herself?

Since he'd known her, she'd been a hyper, driven force. Even before the spa shooting. He'd never seen her dance or laugh or let her hair down—with the exception of their sexual trysts. What, he wondered as he sped toward Sugar Creek, would it take to make Harper *happy*?

By the time they reached the farm, Sam's mood had dipped and Harper had touched base with every member of the club. He'd known the results even before she'd rattled off her summary.

"Okay. Not as many as I'd hoped for," she said as they walked toward the house, "but pretty much what I'd anticipated. The only real surprise was Rocky. Since she's the president of the club, I thought she'd be a shoo-in, but she's adamant about sticking close in order to help Chloe after surgery. Monica and Rae begged off for the same reason although their situation is complicated by their own pregnancies. Plus, since Daisy is going, someone has to step in to cover a few hours at Moose-a-lotta. Casey said she can't afford to shut down her business for two days. Joey wasn't part of the recipe book and she hasn't been with the club long enough to contribute any connected stories. That leaves the senior members and you and I'm pretty sure you won't be all that talkative."

"Thought you just wanted me for eye candy."

She grinned while unlocking the door and moving inside. "Still," she said while flipping on a lamp, "it would be nice to have the perspective of another younger member to show that the Cupcake Lovers are multigenerational. A member who has stories to tell. Someone who's not camera shy."

"Tasha Burke." Sam couldn't believe he was suggesting

this, but Tasha had spearheaded the recipe book to begin with. Since she'd made her peace for past indiscretions, it only seemed fair to include her in this televised event. Unlike Sam, Tasha craved glory and attention like a drug. "Her mom and grandmother were longtime members. Tasha's a former president of the club and she contributed several recipes and stories to the book. I'd check with the other members first, but I'm fairly sure if you invited Tasha, she'd be on the first plane out of Phoenix."

"Brilliant! I guess she didn't enter my mind because she's no longer an active local member, but she's been commenting on the Cupcake Lover social networks all night. Knowledgeable, entertaining, and if she's as pretty in person as she is in the recipe book, bonus!" Harper texted as she spoke. "Checking with Daisy. Sam, seriously, thank you. I can't believe this is coming together. What a rush."

Sam attributed his funky mood to Harper's source of excitement. Any other soon-to-be bride would have been scoping out wedding chapels or obsessing over what she was going to wear. Harper's thoughts were consumed with a media coup. "I'll reach out to Nash," Sam said, palming his own phone. It pinged with a new text. Daisy? Luke? Dev?

Harper.

WANT YOU. NAKED. NOW.

TWENTY-ONE

In the past, Harper had never been shy about sending Sam a racy text. Then again, instinctually, she'd known he'd rise to the occasion—so to speak. There'd been a fierce physical attraction, a mutual attraction from the split second they'd met. Even though they'd clashed on several levels, she'd never doubted her ability to tempt Sam with sex.

Until now.

First he'd sworn off making love until after they were married. Then today, *she'd* said, no sex *ever*. Her juvenile, cowardly attempt to stave off emotional intimacy. But on the ride home she'd felt him shutting down and suddenly she wanted to get close. She was nervous about the wedding, nervous about the trip, but she didn't want to wallow or whine, so she'd focused on putting the wheels in motion. She was high on caffeine and adrenaline . . . and Sam.

Watching him interact with friends and family, seeing him choke up when he'd presented his cousin with the wedding rings and then hugged him for luck. Sam Mc-Cloud was a good man. She didn't want to screw up his life. She didn't want to hurt the children. She wanted to treat their marriage as he'd first suggested—a business arrangement. It was the only way she could fix all their lives so that they could all move on. Love would only compli-

cate matters. Still, witnessing the depth of affection between Chloe and Devlin as they'd said their vows, Harper
was suddenly and desperately keen on sampling even a
slice of that amorous pie.

She'd gone through the giddy infatuation stage of falling
in love with Andrew, but then he'd been deployed, and
during their long separation they'd fallen out of sync. She'd
assumed they'd rekindle the magic once he returned. They
were engaged, after all. But he'd changed and Harper had
been lost.

Connecting with Sam on several occasions today and
then feeling him pull back triggered old insecurities, making Harper twitchy. It was not something she felt comfortable discussing, so she'd fallen back on their old ways,
anything to lose herself in Sam's hypnotic kisses. She'd
sent him that sexy text on a whim and now she was afraid
to glance up for fear of rejection.

Her phone pinged.

COME HERE.

They were in the same room. Standing no more than a
foot apart. This was crazy. Eyes glued to her phone, she
typed . . . MY REWARD?

EYE CANDY.

Pulse skipping, she looked up and saw Sam peeling off
his shirt. Not in a Chippendale smarmy kind of way but in
a manner that affected Harper all the same. Sam wasn't
obnoxiously ripped, but he was extremely fit. A definite
six-pack and a chest to die for. What revved her most was
his arms. Strong arms that made her feel safe. And his
hands—gifted hands that caressed and thrilled.

He pocketed his phone.

She did the same.

"Come here."

She did as beckoned, expecting him to strip off her tee,
as well. Something swift and dirty, here and now. Over the
couch, on the floor, against the wall. Something familiar.

Instead he lifted her into his arms. "I'm taking you to bed."

"And then?"

"Fair warning."

Her senses buzzed.

"Nothing kinky. Not tonight."

"If you're not in the mood—"

"I'm in the mood. But for something I won't name."

Love.

It was so romantic. So un-Rambo-like. Harper's heart lurched and her stomach knotted. She tried not to read into it. He didn't love her, couldn't love her. She hadn't given him any reason. She told herself he'd been swept away by the emotions of the day, just like her. Still. "Sam—"

"Take it or leave it."

He breached the top landing and someone whispered, *"Take."* Harper's skin prickled. *Mary?* But it couldn't be. In all the time Harper had spent in this house, she'd never once seen or heard the ghost of Mary Rothwell. Sensing her presence, respecting her memory was one thing, hearing voices was another. Unless . . . was that Harper's own heart speaking?

Entranced, anxious, she palmed Sam's cheek. "Do your worst, Rambo." It was as close to romantic as Harper dared. Seconds later they were in her bedroom, in her bed. She tore at her clothing, but Sam slowed her efforts and took charge.

"There'll be no vying for control, Harper," Sam said as he peeled off her jeans. "For tonight, at least, I own you."

She didn't argue. Couldn't argue. She was too busy feeling. Sam's fingers skimmed and caressed. His lips sampled and savored. Harper knew his touch well, but she'd never relaxed enough to allow this kind of focused intensity. There was an added element, an elusive emotion that seduced her senses into an electrified stupor.

Rather than overthink it, Harper gave in and gave over.

She didn't grapple for control, which was scary and exhilarating at the same time. She stretched out on her bed, which would soon be their bed. It was almost too much to comprehend and yet it felt like the most natural thing in the world. Like they'd done this before, exactly like this, as if they were meant to be—like the Rothwells. The soldier and the Cupcake Lover. Only Sam was both and Harper was neither. But even as Sam murmured endearments, Daisy's voice echoed in Harper's ears, *"You're a natural born Cupcake Lover."*

As in reborn? An incarnation of an old soul?

Living in Mary's house. Baking in Mary's stove. Sleeping in Mary's room.

The thoughts welled then vanished as Sam drove Harper to erotic distraction.

Heart drumming, she sighed as his fingers skimmed over her stomach, her inner thighs and then . . . "Yes!" She bit back the habit of issuing orders. Sam didn't need or want direction. He knew her body, only this time he pleasured Harper on his own terms. This slow and tender domination trumped their wildest interludes, shaking and thrilling Harper to her core.

Desperate for release, she moaned and arched into his practiced touch, the walls around her heart crumbling when his mouth claimed hers in an achingly passionate kiss. Her body tensed and quivered, thoughts blurred. Stars shattered into iridescent sparkles as Harper peaked then rode the sensual wave.

Aching for more, she stared into Sam's eyes as he positioned his body over hers. She anticipated the first thrust like never before. And she knew this, too would feel different. That added element. She could name it now. *Affection.* She saw it in his eyes. Felt it skating around her own senses. It scared the hell out of Harper yet Sam tempted her down that road with every look, every touch. Trepidation melted away as he interlaced his fingers with hers, pinning her hands in the pillows and branding her lips with a possessive kiss. An amazing, cinematic kiss. More stars, a galaxy of stars. And rainbows. Freaking rainbows. The promise after the storm. A miracle as in—maybe, just maybe—a happily ever after.

Sam nudged her legs apart. "You're mine, Harper." He nipped her earlobe. "Say it."

"Take your pleasure, Sam."

He remained poised . . . teasing, tempting, demanding . . .

"Say it," that haunting voice urged.

Harper shivered, unnerved and needy. So needy. "I'm yours." *If only for tonight.*

Sam plunged and she was gone.

As she drifted into an orgasmic haze, Harper's senses exploded with euphoric sensations while Sam made slow and deliberate love. No kink, just old-fashioned, missionary-style coupling accentuated with soul-stirring kisses. He broke off, searching her face, her thoughts—so intense. "Let me in, Harper."

He didn't have to elaborate. She read it in his eyes, felt it in his touch. He wanted the key to her heart. Wanted the emotional intimacy she'd denied them from the start. This moment she was hard-pressed to deny him anything, yet she was too consumed to speak.

Oh, God. Oh, God, Oh, God. Tears pricked her eyes as Sam intensified their lovemaking. She wanted what he offered. Something beyond a business arrangement. She wanted what burned between Chloe and Dev, Rae and Luke, Monica and Leo, and yet she didn't trust herself, fate, the universe, whatever. Even so, Harper responded to Sam with every fiber of her body. The most exhilarating sex of her life, and when they climaxed together, as one, as a couple, Harper cried. She couldn't help it. Tears rolled down her temples, into her hair, her cheeks burning when Sam thumbed them away. "Before you ask," she said, "I'm fine. Just . . . overwhelmed."

"I'm thinking that's a good thing."

"Maybe."

Sam rolled onto his side, taking Harper with him. A tender embrace—protective and loving in nature. He finessed the covers, cocooning them both in her fresh sheets and quilted bedspread. They'd made love and now Sam was going to spend the night. All night. A first for them and a first for Harper since Andrew.

Twisted with conflicting emotions, she snuggled deeper into Sam's arms, taking comfort in his warmth, his strength. She wouldn't run from the affection welling inside her, but she didn't know what to do with it, either.

"It's okay," Sam said as if reading her thoughts. He kissed her forehead, held her close. "I'm a patient man."

TWENTY-TWO

Harper woke with a start—bolted upright in bed, heart pounding, brow sweating. Gunshots rang in her ears.

Andrew.

She'd fallen asleep thinking about Sam, but she'd dreamt about Andrew. She felt hollow and panicked. Something was off. Something was wrong. Guilt ravaged her gut. She couldn't do it. She couldn't marry Sam without telling him about Andrew.

But Sam was gone.

Moonlight blazed through the windows, illuminating the rumpled covers, confirming she was alone. Sam wasn't in bed and the bathroom door was wide open, light off. She glanced at the bedside clock. The digital numbers glowed 3:05. What the hell? Had she tossed and turned? Hogged the space, the blankets? Had he sought out the bed in the guest room? Had something upset him? News from Dev or the kids? Something that gave her insomnia or maybe caused him to leave in the middle of the night? He wouldn't leave without telling her, right? What if he'd gone downstairs for a drink of water and tripped and hit his head or . . . "This is crazy."

The nightmare had spooked her and now she was

having crazy thoughts. Obsessive thoughts. Sam was fine. She was fine.

Out of habit, she nabbed her cell from the nightstand. No emergency texts. No missed calls. Although there were several notifications from Facebook and Twitter, alerting her of activity on her personal account as well as the Cupcake Lovers'. Rocky would have texted her personally before posting an announcement if Chloe had given birth, right? Although maybe in the excitement . . .

Harper tapped the app, scrolled posts. Rocky had indeed commented on the Cupcake Lovers' sites, but only in response to other posts. Same with Tasha—an apparent night owl.

Harper skimmed. Nothing she had to address immediately. Same with her personal accounts. Except . . . Her gaze stalled on one post. A post on her personal Facebook page.

Why are you dragging your feet in Sugar Creek? Shouldn't you be packing? Time's ticking.

It was signed: *The Avenger*

She clicked on the avatar, an illustrated soldier brandishing a gun. There was nothing of value on his timeline. His privacy settings blocked her from prying. But she knew. She knew it was him.

Her response was automatic. She went back to her page and deleted the post without commenting. Without a second read or thought. It was Andrew's father. Reminding her he was waiting over the border. Waiting to torment her, to punish her for his son's death. He hadn't given up. He wasn't going to fade away.

Harper put her phone into sleep mode and shoved it in the nightstand drawer. Another first.

She stared into the moonlit room, braced for a panic attack. She was ready to beat it back, but instead all that welled was the urge to fight. She bolted out of bed and snagged her robe. Taking control was paramount. Control the situation. Control her life. She'd start with telling Sam about Andrew. She owed him that much. As for Edward . . . she'd handle him in her own way. She should have done it a long time ago. She wasn't ready before. Now, she was.

Sam couldn't get a grip on his insomnia. Making love to Harper had been exhilarating and exhausting. Emotionally exhausting because, in the back of his mind, he'd been managing past feelings for Paula and new feelings for Harper. Acknowledging and accepting that he could attain the same wonder, the same tender passion a second time without betraying the magic of the first. Sam was pretty sure he'd come to terms. His conscience was clear and his heart big enough to love two very different women in equal measure. A monumental realization. One that should have brought relief and a certain amount of contentment. Enough that he should have easily drifted to sleep holding his soon-to-be-wife in his arms.

Even though Harper hadn't said the words, he knew he'd touched her guarded heart. They'd connected on the intimate level he'd craved and he knew they could be good together. But something was off. Something he couldn't pinpoint. And that was what kept his brain churning.

Something about this house.

So he'd eased out of bed, careful not to wake Harper. He'd stolen downstairs, rooted sweats and a tee from his duffel and pulled them on. He'd checked all the doors and windows. Everything was locked. He'd peered outdoors from different vantage points. Nothing looked out of sorts. Yes, it was the middle of the night, but the moon bathed the yard and surrounding woods with a soft glow. A month back, he'd wired the front and back porches with motion-sensitive detectors. If anyone or any woodland creature approached they'd be greeted with floodlighting. Nothing had triggered the detectors. All was quiet. Yet Sam felt unsettled. As if they were being watched.

Mary?

It was a passing thought, one rooted in old ghost stories. But Sam had been in this house numerous times over the years and several times for extended periods over the last few months. He'd never seen an apparition or experienced a ghostly encounter such as cold spots, eerie sounds, or misplaced or reassigned objects. Hell, if he seriously thought this place was haunted he would've balked at making it Ben's and Mina's new home. Instead, he was contemplating his course of action regarding the move. Which spurred concerns overall pertaining to the next few days. If he put some of those tasks to bed, maybe he'd be able to sleep.

He sent a late-night text to Nash about the charter, then he powered on Harper's laptop, making sure he had everything in order regarding the marriage license. No blood tests required. No waiting period. As long as they provided proper identification, they were good to go. He looked into hotels and chapels. He'd narrowed the chapels down to two. Should he surprise her? Consult her? So far she hadn't voiced interest in details regarding the ceremony.

Sam pushed off the sofa and stretched, worked a kink from his neck while moving into the kitchen. It was his favorite room in the house. A room they'd renovated together. He'd designed and built cupboards reminiscent of those popular in the 1940s. She'd decorated the walls and counters with vintage cookware and art. The color theme was red and white. The stove, amazingly, was the same stove used by Mary Rothwell. Every owner had considered it unique and worth keeping. There'd been restorations and upgrades, but Mary had boiled tea kettles on those gas burners and baked cupcakes in the twin ovens. Sam didn't believe this place was haunted but, by damn, he *did* get the chills every time he looked at that stove.

Just now his gaze jerked left. He spied a cupcake holder, lifted the lid. No mistaking that pleasing scent. Gingerbread. The same scent he'd detected earlier today on Harper.

Sam smiled down at the freshly baked cupcakes. God, they smelled good. He knew Harper baked and baked well, according to the Cupcake Lovers and his kids. Everyone had sampled an array of her baked goods. Everyone but Sam. He'd always refrained. Which puzzled Harper. She'd said as much. Although she'd never intimated hurt feelings, she had to feel slighted. *He* would.

He hadn't dissected his unwillingness to taste her cupcakes until now. He knew if he sampled them and liked them he'd want to talk about them. Prior to her deportation threat, Harper hadn't been open to slow and easy, amiable conversation. Recipes were personal. She would have changed the subject or glossed over details. It would have pissed him off. So he'd begged off.

Things were different now, and he was curious.

Sam peeled away the foil-lined baking cup, licked the icing—cream cheese based with a hint of orange and sprinkled with crystalized ginger. The citrus zing pleased. He bit into the moist confection and smiled. "Damn," he said with his mouth full.

"That bad?"

"Jesus." Sam knocked crumbs from his chin as he turned. "You scared the hell out of me, Harper."

"It's not like I snuck up on you."

"Since I didn't hear you, yeah, it sort of is."

"You're eating one of my cupcakes."

"Busted."

"Why?"

"It looked good and smelled even better."

"But you object to the taste. Too much cinnamon? Not enough molasses? Too dense? Too light?"

She sounded pissed but Sam smiled. "You want to talk cupcakes?"

"I'm just saying, if there's something I could do to make these better . . . If you have a suggestion I'd . . . Why are you smiling?"

"Because you want to talk cupcakes." He traded one delight for another, setting aside the cupcake to pull Harper into his arms. "What are you doing up?"

"Things on my mind."

"Same here."

"Like?"

"Details. The charter plane, plans for the ceremony." He felt her tense, eased back and noted her frown. "Second thoughts?"

She held his gaze though, damn, hers was troubled. "I need to talk to you, Sam."

"Do I need a drink for this?"

"Probably not, but I might." She moved out of his arms, toward one of the custom-made cabinets he'd designed and installed. She nabbed a bottle of brandy and two snifters then set up shop at the kitchen table.

Sam finished off the cupcake, tossed the liner. He savored the wholesome sweetness while she poured two fingers of possible trouble. Settling into the chair across from her, Sam held silent, allowed her to pursue the conversation at her own pace. Whatever it was, she needed false courage before heading down that road.

After two sips of brandy, she rolled back her shoulders and began. "Something happened in Canada. Something bad. That's why I don't want to go back."

Now Sam sipped, bracing for her story, battling for calm. If someone had hurt her . . . *Dial it down, McCloud.*

Her gaze flicked to his. "I'm not sure where to start."

"Wherever's easiest." He kept his tone and manner light, even though his senses were on high alert. He wished she'd spit it out. The sooner he knew what they were dealing with, the better. But he wouldn't push. Not at the risk of her shutting down.

She pulled her robe tighter then leaned in and held on to the snifter like a lifeline. "I signed on with Spin Twin Cities, the branch in Toronto, as soon as I graduated from college. I was green, but motivated. I worked hard, mostly as an assistant to a senior publicist. A lot of hours, a lot of pressure, a lot of bullshit, but an invaluable learning ground."

"Media for Canadian celebrities?"

"That was part of it. But also corporate publicity. One company in particular championed a charity for military men and their families. My association with that company, that charity, was brief, but I met someone. A soldier." She paused and sipped. "Captain Andrew Wilson." Her voice sounded tight in spite of the brandy. "He was Regular Forces. Handsome and motivated—just twenty-eight."

"How old were you?"

"Twenty-six."

Five years ago.

"It happened so fast. We fell in love overnight and were engaged three weeks later. Andrew was charming and funny and, I admit, the whole man-in-uniform thing was sexy and exciting." She broke off and glanced around the kitchen. "Even back then, I knew about this house, had heard the tale of Mary. Sad, but romantic. I kept thinking, *This is how Mary must have felt about Joseph.* Smitten and proud. Enchanted by a man who protected his people, his country. And then of course, I was influenced by cinematic love stories, military romances, the ones with happy endings."

"Like *An Officer and a Gentleman*?" It had been one of Paula's favorites, too.

Harper blushed and nodded. "Sappy, I know. Anyway, it was a whirlwind romance—Andrew and me—and, at the time, I was all about fairy-tale weddings and happily-ever-afters. I got caught up in the planning—the dress, the shoes, the flowers—and Andrew fed my enthusiasm."

Sam held his tongue, sipped more brandy, and registered Harper's mounting anxiety.

"We'd been seeing each other for ten months when he got deployed overseas. I was shocked. Silly, right? I mean, he was on active duty. But he was in telecommunications, a computer specialist. I thought his work was here, in programming. He never talked about specifics. Said it was classified. Which was, oh, God, that was exciting, too."

Sam reached across the table and touched her hand. "I get it, hon. The allure of a soldier. Plus Andrew was an officer. If he was in telecommunications, he had to be damned smart. That's attractive, too."

"Yes, it is, and he was. Smart. Brainiac smart. So even after they shipped him overseas I thought he'd be holed up in a lab. On a base. Safe."

She fell silent and Sam continued to hold her hand. He'd dealt with information technicians. Split-second, high-intensity work in the battlefield. Keeping lines of communications open between the frontline and the back. Computers, operating radios, fiber optics, satellite communications. He'd seen technicians crawling through hostile territory to get to a regiment whose radio had gone out. Nothing safe about that.

"Andrew wasn't very good about corresponding with me. Odd considering he was in telecommunications, right?"

Her smile didn't reach her eyes and Sam noticed she'd used the word *was*. *Was* in telecommunications. Past tense.

"I missed him and I was worried—about him, us—but I kept telling myself he was focused on important work. Classified, he'd said. He couldn't talk about it. Still, I envisioned him toiling away in a tech lab on base." She broke off and looked away. "I was so naïve and he kept me that way. Even after he returned, he wouldn't talk about what he'd done or where he'd been."

"That's not uncommon," Sam said. He rarely talked about his own time in the field. What he'd done, what he'd seen. He'd especially shielded Paula. He didn't want her to worry and he damn well didn't want to expose her to the horrors of war. Sam got Captain Andrew Wilson loud and clear.

"Andrew was overseas for more than a year and when he came back," Harper said, "he was different. I'd thought the easy and exciting intimacy we'd once shared would return as soon as we reunited. But I was wrong. He was quiet, distant. Something was bothering him, but he wouldn't talk about it. The few times we slept together, he woke with nightmares. When I asked what they were about, he shut me down, and if I persisted, he got angry. He'd never been angry with me before. Not like that."

Sam could see where this was going so he didn't say a word when she finished off her brandy and poured a little more. He knew she wasn't going for drunk as much as numb. And he was here. He had her back. The hardest thing was not rounding the table and pulling her into his arms.

"Long story short, Andrew ended our engagement. He said he wasn't ready for marriage, that he loved me, but he needed space. I was hurt and confused. Not just by the broken engagement but by his erratic behavior. I didn't know what to say, how to be around him for fear I would set him off. I was young and fanciful then, sensitive," she said on a snort, "if you can believe it. I was intimidated by whatever Andrew was going through, and rather than tough it out, I gave him that space. I threw myself into my job and naïvely believed he'd work it out. He was so freaking smart. Of course he'd figure it out.

"Two weeks later," she went on in a barely there voice, "I got a phone call saying Andrew was in a standoff with military police. I thought it was a joke. A mistake. But I was assured by the newsman it was true.

"Andrew pulled a gun in a recruitment center. Railed against the military. Issued threats. I don't think he would have carried them out. He wouldn't harm innocent people. It wasn't in his makeup. I think he wanted to make a point and maybe, yeah, in hindsight, I think he wanted to die. He fired a shot, but not at a person, so I was told by that reporter. Unfortunately the bullet ricocheted and hit a civilian. The police opened fire as soon as Andrew pulled the trigger. Sometimes I think, if only I'd been there, maybe I could have talked him down."

"Is that why you tried to rush into the chaos of the spa shooting? To talk the shooter down?"

"Someone should have tried," was all she said.

"What happened to the civilian?" Sam asked. "The one Andrew unintentionally wounded?"

"Died on the way to the hospital. Andrew never even made it that far." Instead of throwing back her freshly poured brandy, Harper stood and carried the glass to the sink. Her hand trembled as she poured the liquor down the drain.

Sam moved in behind her, rested his hands on her shoulders. He wanted to catch her if her knees buckled. She looked that wrung out. "You blame yourself," Sam said. He'd seen it in her eyes, read it in her expression. "It wasn't your fault, Harper."

"There are those who disagree." She braced her hands on the counter, lowered her head. "Over the next few weeks I researched post-traumatic stress syndrome, I even spoke with a shrink. I know it wasn't directly my fault, but if I'd been a different person, a stronger person, I might have been able to convince Andrew to commit to professional help."

"Maybe. Maybe not. But, honey, if he hadn't snapped then, it could have happened another time. Maybe with you or maybe at even greater consequences. I'm not saying the loss of Andrew and that innocent bystander wasn't significant. I'm saying it wasn't your fault." He finessed her around, took her beautiful face in his hands. "I get you now, Harper. Really get you. I know this tragedy with Andrew is ugly and painful and I understand why you'd rather not talk about it, but I'm glad you told me."

She brushed away tears. "I just, I didn't want to marry you without explaining why I am how I am. I turned my back on Canada, on the past, on me. I left naïve, whimsical, pacifist Harper Day in the dust and became the obsessive, aggressive control freak that I am today. I couldn't work with troubled soldiers. I was too raw. But I could get in the trenches and save troubled celebrities from crashing and burning. I know it seems shallow."

"Noble. Celebrities need saviors, too." He hadn't thought so before but his perspective had shifted over the last few days. Certainly now. Even though she'd stopped talking, his mind raced, filling in blanks, piecing the puzzle. He better understood why she'd reacted so intensely to the L.A. spa shooting. How it tied into the recruitment shooting with Andrew. And why today's airport shooting had kicked those fears into hyper gear. He got her severe dislike of guns and lax laws. He even understood her manic mission to keep her clients' heads above water. She couldn't fix Andrew's problems so she was intent on saving every other tortured soul in her path.

He even got her obsession with this house and Mary Rothwell.

Sam got Harper Day to the core and he was equally in love with the person she pushed down and the person she fought to be. At this point, he imagined she was a combination of the two. Helping her find comfortable ground would be an honor. Soldier helping soldier, and by God, she was a warrior.

"I didn't realize how weary I was of being alone. I've never told anyone . . . I haven't talked about this in years."

When she melted against him, he held her close, stroked her back. "Running from the past isn't the answer, Harper, but I don't want you to go back to Canada. I want you here. With me. With the kids. We're going to Vegas and we're getting married. We'll take it from there. One step at a time. Together." He gave her a little squeeze, kissed the top of her bowed head. "Say it."

She smiled against his chest. "Together."

TWENTY-THREE

Adam was a fan of mornings. Especially Sunday mornings. So the fact that he woke with a dull headache and a bad attitude twisted his shorts even tighter.

He blamed Peppy.

He knew she was a musician. Musicians worked late hours. Her gig had been at Bluebells, a bar east of Pixley, so more than forty-five minutes away. If she owned a decent car he wouldn't have worried. But when four A.M. rolled around and she still wasn't home, Adam worried.

He called the bar and got an answering machine. They'd closed at two A.M. Even if Peppy had stopped for coffee at Carrie's All-Night Café, she should have been back by now.

Adam imagined that beat-up car broken down on a lone stretch of road. He imagined Peppy, a young woman—alone—in the middle of nowhere in the black of night. Dialing her cell phone had been smart and considerate, right?

"Peppy, it's Adam."

"Yeah?"

"Are you all right?"

"Don't I sound all right?"

"*Just checking. It's late.*"

"*What are you, my mother?*"

If he could've reached through the phone to shake her, he would have. Turned out she was with a guy, she had to go. She rushed Adam off and he tried to go back to sleep. Great. She was out getting laid on a Saturday night and he was home alone worrying. Did she know the guy? She didn't seem the one-nighter type, although what the hell did Adam know? Did she sleep around? Would she be inviting men over? Doing the nasty in the bedroom next to Adam's? Like he wanted to listen to that.

He tossed and turned for another half hour. A little after four-thirty, he heard tires crunching over gravel, heard a muffler backfire. He heard his front door open and shut, heard her bedroom door open and shut. And then, because the walls of this rental were so freaking thin, he heard Peppy punching her pillow and crying.

He would have preferred creaking bedsprings.

He told himself to mind his own business, fell asleep, woke up at eight . . . telling himself to mind his own business.

Now it was after nine. He'd completed his run, showered and dressed. He was starving, but Peppy was still sleeping. She'd probably sleep till noon. Did she sleep till noon every day? He was a freaking morning person!

Adam lingered in the hall, torn between his kitchen and the front door. Questioning his judgment or lack thereof. Their lifestyles were completely incompatible, yet he hadn't given that *huge* fact even a smidgen of thought before offering her the spare room in his teeny, tiny house!

"Bonehead," he said just as she opened her door, of course, because, hell, where Peppy was concerned Adam's timing was shit.

"You don't have to tiptoe around because of me," she said. "I'm a heavy sleeper."

"But you're up."

"Restless."

"Hungry?"

"Sure."

Adam turned his back on her, cursing the twitch in his pants. Turned on? Really? Seriously? Her short, layered hair was sticking up and out every which way. She had dark smudges under her bloodshot eyes. Mascara, he guessed. Those baggy lounging pants, featuring the heads of a cartoon monkey, and the matching tee weren't sexy by any stretch. But Peppy was. In a cute, sort of pathetic-looking way.

"Just slipping into the bathroom," she said. "Out in a sec."

"Take your time." Adam moved into the kitchen, nabbed a carton of eggs from the fridge. A green and a red pepper, mushrooms, onions. Multigrain bread. Spray butter. "Veggie omelets and toast," he announced when she walked in. "Sound good?"

"Sure."

He didn't look up from the stove, but he smelled soap and toothpaste. Not exactly Chanel No. 5 yet his dick perked all the same. "Shit."

"What's wrong?"

"What? Nothing. Wrong knife." It wasn't, but he traded for another anyway. Chopped the peppers, the mushrooms.

"Nice coffee maker," she said. "Filters?"

"Cabinet to the right of the sink. Top shelf." *Chop, chop, chop.* "See them?"

"Yep. Damn."

Adam turned. She was standing on her tiptoes, straining to reach the top shelf. Her tee had hiked up revealing two inches of bare skin between the hem and her waistband. The small of her back. Nothing racy. Still.

Adam bit back a groan, abandoned the knife. "You'll pull a muscle, reaching like that. Hold on." He moved fast, moved in behind her and reached up over her head. She tensed and froze and Adam realized that he had her pinned between his body and the counter, his front flush to her back, his groin pressed against her ass. The only thing between them . . . his erection.

Great.

Just. Freaking. Great.

He handed her the filters and stepped back.

"Thanks," she said.

"Sure," he said. He went back to chopping. Considered hacking off his most beloved personal part, because he was pretty sure "George," as Adam sometimes called him, was crazy. Peppy wasn't his type. She wasn't grounded. She wasn't even nice. Although today she was subdued. Not friendly exactly, but subdued. Then again she *had* cried herself to sleep. The guy she'd been with last night, had they argued? Or maybe they were a steady thing and they'd broken up?

Don't ask.

He made the omelets and toast.

She made coffee and set the table.

They worked in silence, until they finally sat down. Him in jeans and a tee. Her in monkey-face pj's.

"For the record," she said as she stirred way too much sugar into her coffee. "I'm not interested."

Oh, hell. "Me, neither."

She raised a brow.

"George has a mind of his own."

"You named your penis?"

"Every man names his penis."

"News to me, but okay. Tell George I'm not interested."

"Talking to my dick at the breakfast table would be weird."

"This whole conversation is weird."

"You brought it up."

"Actually George brought it up. Not that I'm not flattered."

"Are you?" Adam asked. "Flattered?"

"Yeah." She shrugged. "Sure. I mean look at you."

Now Adam's brow shot up.

"It's just. It wouldn't be smart. I mean we're room-mates. And I'm not looking for a serious relationship."

Adam was, but he held that thought. "So the guy last night. Not a steady boyfriend?"

"Who . . . Oh. No. That was Jerry. Cost me a fortune."

Adam choked on his coffee. "You paid him?"

"He jumped me and a bunch of other stuff, gave me a bill. What was I supposed to do, stiff him? A whole night's pay shot to hell."

"We can't be talking about the same thing."

"Jerry. From Triple A. My car stalled. My grandpa had given me his Triple A card for emergencies and . . . What did you think I was talking about?"

"Never mind. If you had a Triple A card, why did you have to pay? Wait. Because Vincent's name was on the card instead of yours?"

"Yep. Grandpa's card covers him not family, but don't tell him. I didn't want him to be upset or try to give me money. Hey, at least it got Jerry out there. Hard to find help at almost three in the morning."

"You could have called me."

"I don't know you."

"You didn't know Jerry."

"True, but . . . Listen. I'm sorry I was rude when you called last night. It was kind, actually. You just caught me at a bad time. I've been having a run of crummy luck. I'm frustrated and, okay, a little discouraged, but I'm not down. I'll bounce back and bounce back big. I have plans."

"Like what?"

"I'd rather not talk about them. I've got some irons in the fire. I'd rather not jinx them."

"I get that."

"You do?"

"Sure." He felt the same way about his dream goal. Talking about it might jinx it.

"You make a good omelet."

"You make good coffee."

"I live on coffee," she said.

Maybe that's why she was inhaling breakfast. Maybe she'd skipped dinner last night to save money. Probably got free coffee every club she played. Plus it would keep her alert for those late-night drives.

He offered her toast, watched her douse it with butter spray.

"I guess you don't use the real stuff, given you're a health nut and all."

"Who says I'm a health nut?"

She snorted and gestured as if to say, "Just look at you."

He was a sports instructor so, yeah, he was in great shape. Plus he enjoyed sports in his off time, enjoyed his morning runs. He ate healthy, lived healthy—mostly.

Peppy . . . She wasn't the athletic type. She was the creative type. Instead of a gym, she burned calories on stage. She was slim enough, but soft. Soft angles, soft curves. Not that that was a bad thing.

"I have an okay body, right?" she asked while stirring sugar into her second cup of joe. "At least *George* thinks so."

Adam's lips twitched. "George has good taste."

"But it could be better. My body."

It was one of those questions that made a man cringe. Like when a woman asked, *"Do these jeans make my ass look big?"* Phrasing the answer carefully was key. "If you're talking definition, healthier heart . . ."

"The definition thing, yeah. My heart's fine. So did you mean it?"

"Mean what?"

"What you said about rent including three months' access to a personal sports trainer—which I assume is you."

Huh. "The offer stands."

"Great. Let's do it." She wiped her face with a paper napkin. "I want a body like Ivy's."

"She's a lot taller than you, different build."

"Huge boobs. I know you can't help me in that department. But the toned-muscle part, the hard stomach that drives guys wild every time she wears a crop top."

"I can help with that."

"When can we start?"

One more sip of coffee and she'd be bouncing off the walls. "Later today. I need to drive to Pixley General this morning. A friend's wife's having a baby."

"Daisy's business partner. Chloe. I know. I was hoping to pay my respects, too. Even though I'm in and out of Sugar Creek a lot, I know the Monroes pretty well. And of course, Grandpa is awfully fond of Daisy. Mind if I catch a ride? Not trusting my car."

Adam marveled that this chatterbox was the same sulky brat who'd given him hell two days running. "Not a problem."

She bounced up. "You cooked. I'll wash the dishes."

"That's okay. I have my own way. You shower and dress."

"Right. Great. Thanks. I won't be long. Oh, and Adam," she said as she zipped toward the door with a big-ass smile, "When you see George, tell him I said thanks for the pick-me-up."

TWENTY-FOUR

"I can't believe how late we slept."

"That's the fifth time you've said that."

"And I still can't believe it."

Harper hurried out of the house ahead of Sam. She hitched her purse and laptop briefcase over her shoulder as he locked the front door. They'd showered and dressed in a hurry. His hair was still damp and he smelled strongly of soap. His shirt was clean, but wrinkled. She would have ironed it for him, but there hadn't been time. Even though he looked sort of rumpled, he looked damned good. She'd always had it bad for Sam physically, but since last night her desire for this man was off the scale.

"We'll be fine," Sam said as he escorted her down the steps—always the gentleman. "And you look great," he added as she fussed with the sash of her dress.

"I'll do," she said with a genuine smile. At least she looked professional today. She'd snagged a dress from her closet, a lightweight leopard-print pullover with an A-line skirt. The sash cinched her waist and the hem fell just above her knees. She stepped into a pair of black heels and pulled her long hair into a low ponytail. Just now she shoved on big trendy sunglasses. It was a beautiful sunny day. A beautiful day for the birth of Chloe's baby and a blitz on the Cupcake Lovers' social sites. Even though they'd be getting to the hospital later than Harper had wanted, Sam was right, they'd make it before the scheduled surgery. They were fine. It's just that she had so much to cover, including hotel accommodations for all of the Cupcake Lovers traveling to Vegas. Just as she'd hoped, production would cover expenses, but there were still a lot of details to handle.

"Did you just skip?"

Harper looked over her shoulder. "What? No."

"I know a skip when I see one. Mina skips all the time. It means you're happy."

Harper turned, heart in throat. "I am happy." She placed a hand to Sam's chest, fingered his collar. "Last night wasn't easy for me."

"I know."

"I don't like to think about it or talk about it, but I'm glad I did because, well, it helped. You helped. I feel a little better, definitely calmer."

He palmed her hand, squeezed. "I'm glad."

"I'm not running, but I'd like to put the past to rest."

"Understood."

"I'd like to move forward as quickly as possible. Together."

He held her gaze, stroked her knuckles, waited for her to explain. God, she loved his patience.

"Why wait until Tuesday night to seal the deal?" she asked. "Why not tomorrow? As soon as we land in Vegas? I'm sure we could find an excuse to steal away. I know you wanted to take advantage of the 'got-drunk-and-ended-up-married' cliché. A smoke screen for the real reason for our haste. And I still see the wisdom in that. We could follow through with that pretense Tuesday night, after the filming of the show, but let's do it for real tomorrow."

He didn't answer and Harper tensed. She was rushing

things, even more so than before, but Edward's post on her FB page had spooked her, along with the feeling of being watched. The sooner she and Sam were officially married, the sooner they'd secure her legal right to stay in this country. She considered telling Sam about Edward—he'd been so understanding about everything else—but her pride reared. She'd allowed herself to be bullied all these years by a lonely bitter man. The power he'd held over Harper shamed her. She'd handle Edward Wilson on her own. She just had to figure out how.

"Would it make you happy?"

Harper blinked back to the moment, to Sam. "Deliriously happy."

He smiled a little and her stomach flipped. "Then we'll get married tomorrow. Indoors or outdoors?"

She assumed he was talking about the ceremony. With Andrew she'd envisioned an elegant church wedding. Even though her parents weren't traditional (hell, neither one had taken real interest in Harper's engagement), she'd dreamed of an old-fashioned, fairy-tale wedding. Now that dream was tainted. "Something simple."

"Done."

Harper threw her arms around Sam and hugged tight. Yes, she was big on control, but when it came to their wedding, she didn't want any part of the planning. The venue, the dress, the flowers . . . none of that should matter. It had mattered far too much with Andrew. The possibility, no, the probability, that she'd been more in love with the idea of a wedding . . . more in love with the thought of marrying a brave soldier than with braniac Andrew Wilson himself, tore at Harper's soul and triggered more shame. "We should hurry," she whispered in Sam's ear. Hurry to the hospital, to Vegas, to us.

He hugged her back, kissed her forehead, her cheek, her mouth. "I need to do something," Sam said. "It'll take some time, not sure how much, but I need to do it now. You can come with me and wait or you can go ahead to the hospital and wait there."

"Can you give me a clue?"

"Paula's parents. I need to tell them about us. Not the deportation part. Not our business arrangement, no details. But I owe them the heads-up on our marriage. And the kids . . ."

"I understand." Harper's heart swelled. "I'll drive ahead. This is personal and—"

"Are you sure?"

She realized then that she hadn't driven off the property on her own in days. Because of her agoraphobia. Because of her fears. Sam was worried about her. She loved and hated that he was worried. "Of course I'm sure. I'll see you at the hospital. Later. Bring the kids. They'll get a kick out of seeing the baby. Everyone loves babies." She hugged Sam again then swung away before she lost her nerve. Harper strolled to her rented car (she'd have to purchase one soon) then tossed her purse and laptop into the passenger seat.

She gave her Serenity bracelet a couple of twirls then keyed the ignition.

She could do this.

Heart full, confidence high, she drove off the property, turned onto Swamp Lane, and made a beeline for Pixley. No sweat. No anxiety. She imagined Sam's smile and punched the gas.

Sam had sweated skirmishes with hostiles less than this confrontation with Paula's dad. No, not a confrontation, Sam told himself. Charlie wasn't like that. He'd voice understanding and he'd mean it. Still, Sam had come to this very house to ask Charlie Kessler for his only daughter's hand in marriage. Now Paula was gone and Sam was preparing to marry another woman. Surely the Kesslers would at least feel a sting.

Sam moved to knock on the door, noticed his palm was sweaty—*hell*—and wiped it down his thigh. He paused another second, gathering his thoughts, catching his breath. Sue had taken the kids to church, and since Sam had hoped to break the news to Charlie first, the timing was perfect. He told himself he was making a mountain out of a molehill. The Kesslers had encouraged Sam to get on with his life. They knew how much he loved Paula and they knew their daughter had wanted Sam to find happiness with another woman, a loving mother for their children. That had been her dying wish, although Sam had been certain he'd never be able to grant it. Paula would approve of Harper. Sam felt it in his heart. And he imagined her up in heaven just now, rolling her eyes at him for stalling on her dad's front porch.

It was as if she reached down and interceded. The door swung open and Charlie stood there, bushy gray brows raised in mild amusement. "Been hovering on the stoop for five minutes, son. Figured I better hurry this along before you lost your nerve completely."

"That obvious, huh?"

Charlie waved him inside. The house was neat as always, with the exception of a few of the kids' toys. Charlie motioned Sam to sit while muting the television. One eye on the Nascar race, he offered, "Coffee?"

"No, thanks."

His gaze shifted to Sam. "Snort of whiskey?"

"Look like I need one?"

"A little." With that Charlie settled into his worn recliner. "Figure you've come to talk to me about Harper Day. Whole town's buzzin' about the unlikely match." His eyes flickered with amusement. "Sounds interesting."

Sam dragged a hand through his hair. Leave it to Charlie to cut to the chase. "I should have said something sooner, but to tell you the truth, it sort of hit me out of nowhere."

"Happens like that sometimes."

"And, as Ben would say, escalated at hyperspeed."

"Uh-huh."

"It's not the same as it was with Paula, then again Harper isn't anything like Paula."

"Heard that through the grapevine, too. Plus Ben and Mina have mentioned Harper here and there. They like her."

"I know." Sam braced his forearms on his knees, leaned in and clasped his hands. "They told me if I wanted to marry Harper, they'd be okay with it. Said they don't want me to be a lonely old man."

Charlie's mouth crooked. "Sue and I don't want that, either. So . . . are you here for my advice or blessing?"

"You're making this awfully easy."

"No reason it should be hard." Charlie drummed his chunky fingers on the arm of his chair, cleared his throat. "Listen, Sam. Sue and I know how much you loved our daughter. We saw it, felt it. And we know you'll love Paula till your dying day. Making room in your heart for another woman doesn't diminish what you had before. Does Harper make you happy?"

Sam thought beyond the petty irritations. He thought about the way he'd felt this morning when she'd kissed him awake and hugged him good-bye. He thought about the tender heart buried within her bossy façade. "Yeah," Sam said, acknowledging a warm feeling. "She does."

"Is she accepting of Ben and Mina?"

"She'll do her damnedest to make them happy." He didn't doubt that for a second.

"Seems like a no-brainer then."

Sam smiled a little. "We don't want to wait and we don't want a fuss, Charlie. In fact, we're flying out to Vegas tomorrow on business for the Cupcake Lovers and while we're there we'll make it official."

"Eloping. Tomorrow." Charlie whistled low.

"I'm only sharing this with you and Sue. Given the whirlwind nature of Harper and my relationship, I don't want to give anyone time to try to talk us out of it."

"Didn't think *I'd* try?"

"No. You're one of the most nonjudgmental people I know, Charlie."

"When do you aim to break it to Ben and Mina?"

"Not sure."

"You could surprise them. Tell them after it's a done deal."

"They did preapprove the match." Sam nodded. "I could spin the surprise thing." Damn, he sounded like Harper in slick publicist mode.

"Tell them beforehand and they might let it slip to friends or family. You can count on me and Sue to keep your secret. Ben might hold strong, too. But Mina?"

Sam imagined his animated daughter and chuckled. "She'll want to tell the world." He blew out a breath, stood. "Right then. Surprise it is. I'll pick up the kids this evening as always, tell them about the business trip, drive them to school tomorrow morning. But could I impose on you and Sue to pick them up in the afternoon and look after them through Wednesday?"

"Be insulted if you didn't." When Charlie stood, Sam offered his hand, but the shorter man pulled him in for a swift hug. "You feel that? My baby's smiling down on you, son." He smacked Sam's shoulder as he walked him to the door. "Go be happy."

TWENTY-FIVE

"Step on it, Speedy!"

"We wouldn't be running late if you hadn't insisted on attending church and staying for the whole dang service."

"I never miss church," Daisy said. "Besides, I needed to say a special prayer today."

"I know you're worried about Chloe and the surgery—"

"Of course I'm worried. She's going under the knife!"

"Don't think of it that way."

"But that's the way it is. Maybe you should let me drive."

"Why?"

"You're going too slow."

"Going eight miles over the speed limit."

"Like I said."

Vincent edged to the side of the highway.

Daisy blinked as he unfastened his seat belt. "What are you doing?" she asked as he opened his door.

"Letting you drive."

Her eyes fairly bugged out of her head. "You are?" Her family had banned her from driving. Too many accidents. And the few times Vincent had let her behind the wheel it had been on deserted back roads. This was the highway to Pixley! With oncoming traffic and everything!

"If I let you drive," Vincent said as he stepped outside, "you'll feel in control. Which could help your fretting. Also, you'll be concentrating more on the road than Chloe."

Vibrating with excitement, Daisy scooted across the seat. When Vincent climbed into the passenger side they jerked the seat closer to the wheel. Then Vincent reached in the backseat, nabbed a small pillow and passed it to Daisy who slid it under her heinie for a higher view.

"Buckle up, Petunia. And don't forget you're carrying precious cargo."

"That you are, Vincent," she said as she accelerated and pulled onto the road. "That you are."

A half hour later, Daisy turned into the hospital's lot and parked the Caddy without incident. She even refrained from tapping the bumper of the car in front of her, which she often did given a slight problem with depth perception. She looked over at Vincent and smiled, her heart bouncing when he smiled back. "I love that you trust me," she said.

"I love that you're fearless."

Again her heart fluttered. Vincent Redding made Daisy feel like she was sixteen again. She didn't know about fearless, but she was impetuous . . . and head over heels in love. She started to say so, but the words stuck in her throat. Yes, she'd loosened up over the last couple of years, but she wasn't wholly comfortable sharing sappy sentiments. Besides, her man had already left the car, rounding the hood to help her out.

"Ten forty-five," he said as he waddled and she shuffled toward the hospital. "Not too early. Not too late."

Daisy gave a little *whoop*. "My first great-grandchild. What a thrill!"

"Speaking of grandchildren . . ."

Daisy followed Vincent's line of vision and saw two young people striding their way. His granddaughter Peppy and Daisy's grandson's friend Adam.

"I can't believe she moved in with one of the Brody boys," Vincent said close to Daisy's ear.

"The responsible, good-hearted Brody," Daisy reminded him. Not that Kane wasn't kind, but he wasn't ready to settle down. From everything that Luke had told Daisy, Adam was. "Peppy was driving Marvin crazy," Daisy went on in a whisper, "and vice versa. And Adam needed a roommate. I think they make a cute couple."

Adam was really tall and Peppy was really short. Adam looked like a sports star and Peppy looked like, well, like a sports star's little sister. Not quite the dynamic Daisy was going for. Still, her heart told her they were good for one another and, according to her horoscope she was supposed to trust her instincts.

"They're not a couple," Vincent said. "They're roommates."

"We're roommates and we're a couple."

"Yes, but we're mature adults."

Daisy snorted. "Speak for yourself."

The older couple and the younger couple reached the glass doors of the hospital at the same time. They exchanged pleasantries, although Daisy and Peppy did most of the talking. They talked and walked and got separated as soon as they entered the crowded waiting room. Even though they'd have to take turns visiting Chloe and meeting the baby, everyone had shown up at the same time. Daisy beamed, thinking that showed just how supportive and caring all her friends and family were. It made her feel warm and fuzzy as she made the rounds saying her how-do-you-dos and what-not. She turned downright teary when she got a dose of the happiness rolling off some of her grandchildren as they stood arm in arm with their spouses. Rocky and Jayce . . . Luke and Rae . . . And she could just imagine the way Dev was holding Chloe's hand right now. Even her stick-up-the-patooty son had his arm around his wife.

Daisy dug in her purse for a tissue, her fingers sweeping over her family bucket list. She'd crossed off Sam and Harper because she just knew that was a done deal. Any ninny could sense the sexual zing sizzling between them. She had high hopes for Peppy and Adam, too. She didn't know what the heck to do with Nash. Maybe he'd meet a nice girl when they were out in Vegas. Daisy was still sort of surprised he'd agreed to fly them to Sin City considering that's where his mom, Kelly (Daisy's only daughter), lived and they were pretty much on the outs. Daisy was miffed with Kelly, too, but she intended to seek her out all the same. Life was short.

Mind racing and turning to Vegas, Daisy made her way over to Harper who was juggling her phone and a laptop computer. "How's it going, Slick?"

"Great. Everything's great. As of ten minutes ago, the Cupcake Lovers are good to go in Vegas. Charter to Vegas, limo from airport to hotel, hotel rooms. I'll provide everyone with details and an itinerary after we board. Also," she said, while typing on her computer, "the social sites are buzzing about the TV show appearance as well as the CL mission. And of course everyone's dying to see a picture of Chloe's baby. Considering she's in surgery now, it won't be long." She glanced at Daisy, eyes dancing. "Are you bursting at the seams or what?"

Harper had no idea. "And how!"

Sam moved in, kissing Daisy on the head then settling in next to Harper and whispering in her ear. The way Harper smiled at him felt awfully personal so Daisy looked away.

She turned, heart skipping and racing and giving her a bit of a scare. Too much excitement maybe, but then she realized she was looking at Vincent who was looking at her and smiling one of his goofy, lovey-dovey smiles. She chalked her heart palpitations up to old-fashioned infatuation. Although she knew her feelings ran much deeper, being smitten was nice, too.

She serpentined through relatives and friends and tugged Vincent toward a quiet corner. "You should come with me to Vegas."

"What?"

"It'll be fun."

"That generally means trouble."

She waggled her brows.

Vincent grinned then stroked his beard. "I dunno. You're going on business. You'll be promoting the recipe book and celebrating with your friends. Plus I have the store to run."

"Marvin can run the store. And I don't have to stick with the pack the whole time. I could be a lone wolf . . . with you. *Ah-oooh*! We could do something wild and crazy."

He rolled his eyes. "Like what? I'm not a drinker or a gambler or—"

"Like elope."

Vincent blinked.

"They have all those wedding chapels. I'm thinking we should get hitched by one of those Elvis guys. He could sing 'All Shook Up.'"

"Or 'Love me Tender.'"

"Or 'Burning Love.'" Daisy snickered.

"Or 'Always on My Mind,'" Vincent said, because Vincent, bless his soul, was romantic. His smile slipped a little and she could tell he thought she was teasing. "Thought you were opposed to marriage."

More like she was opposed to the marriage she'd had the first time around with Jessup. It wouldn't be the same with Vincent. She'd been ignoring that glaring fact, because she'd been scared. Scared of losing her freedom and whatever time she had left in the world.

"You were right," she said, while fingering her rhinestone necklace. "While driving, I didn't obsess on Chloe's surgery. I focused on the road and where I was going. I thought about the future and I realized I don't want to miss out on a second chance at wedded bliss. We may not be young like Chloe and Devlin, but we've got that same zing, don't you think?"

"I certainly do."

"When I kick the bucket, I want my headstone to say 'Daisy Petunia Redding.'"

"That's the most romantic thing you've ever said to me."

"Is it?" She scrunched her brow. Maybe it was. Even though she spoke her mind a lot, she rarely spoke her heart. She'd never been a mushy person. Mostly because Jessup had always cooled her jets in that regard. "I can do better," Daisy said. She wanted to do better for Vincent. "I love you, Speedy."

He smiled and got all misty-eyed. "Guess that means I'm going to Vegas."

Just then a chorus of dings, pings, and chimes rent the air. Devlin had promised to text everyone when Chloe had given birth. Daisy beamed as she read and recited in unison with friends and family: IT'S A GIRL!

TWENTY-SIX

Sam couldn't remember the last time he'd smiled so much. The only thing that had trumped the sight of Chloe and Dev saying *I do* (albeit on his phone) had been the sight of Chloe and Dev posing for pictures with their new daughter, Lily. Lily Mae Monroe. Sweet name. Sweet baby. A tiny thing with a shock of dark hair and a button nose.

A sentimental lump welled in Sam's throat as Harper snapped a couple of publicity shots. Seeing Dev and Chloe cradling that tiny bundle of innocence . . . Sam had felt that overwhelming happiness with Paula. First with Ben. Then with Mina.

Twice blessed.

He waited for a pang of melancholy that never came.

"You're absolutely, one hundred percent sure you don't mind me posting this photo online?" Harper asked the radiant couple.

"On second thought," Dev said, "I'm wary of having Lily's picture floating around the Internet."

"But we already okayed it," Chloe said to Dev while smiling down at Lily. "Harper hyped it and people are waiting. It's for charity. Besides, I kind of want to show her off. She's so sweet. So perfect. So *beautiful*."

Dev smoothed Chloe's hair, kissed her brow. "Like her mommy."

"I should go," Harper said, looking uncomfortable now.

"Run with the picture," Dev said.

She smiled. "Okay. Great. Congratulations, you two." She sidled past Sam, brushing his hand with hers as she slid out the door.

Sam moved forward, touched the baby's cheek, smiled at Chloe then hugged his cousin. "You're in for the best part of your life, cuz."

"May need some advice," Dev said, clearing emotion from his throat.

Sam squeezed his shoulder. "Anytime," then moved in for a hug. He held tight a second longer, knowing Dev had suffered a loss years ago. He'd no doubt sweated bullets in surgery worrying about this baby, worrying about Chloe. On the outside, Dev was a rock, as always, but it didn't take much for Sam to imagine the inner turmoil his cousin had suffered in that operating room. Yup, an extra squeeze. Then another smile for Chloe. "I wish you could be with us for that talk show," Sam told her as he stepped back.

Her doe eyes glittered with sympathy. She knew he wasn't comfortable in the limelight. "You'll be fine, Sam. Tasha's flying in, right?"

"God help us."

She laughed. "Between Tasha and Daisy, you have nothing to worry about. They'll do all the posturing."

Dev's lips twitched. "Better you than me, cuz."

"Bastard," Sam quipped as he left the room. In the hall, he backed into Harper who was thumbing away on her phone.

"Gold, gold, gold," she said. "Sales up. Donations up."

Sam squeezed her arm. "Thank you for all you've done for the Cupcake Lovers."

"Just doing my job."

"Considering how little we pay you, you're going above and beyond."

"I don't mind. I believe in the cause. I wish . . ." She looked over her shoulder, lowered her voice. "I wish I would've turned my talents to helping soldiers and their families sooner."

"Meanwhile you've made a positive difference in a lot of troubled celebrities' lives."

"I suppose."

Sam noted her dip in mood and addressed something he'd wondered about. "I know Sapphire shot down your efforts to patch things up. Same reaction across the board?"

"After four clients, I gave up on reaching out. Figured if anyone valued my worth over the agency, they'd say so. I got a couple of well-wishes. Period. And not a peep out of any of my former coworkers. Doesn't say much about me."

"Or maybe it speaks to their shallow natures."

She arched a brow. "If you knew them, some of them, you wouldn't say that."

"You're right. I'm sorry." Ignorant to suggest everyone associated with Hollywood was a narcissistic piece of fluff. He knew better than to stereotype. He was better than that. But he knew Harper's feelings were hurt so he'd taken a cheap shot in her defense. "I don't know why you've been snubbed, Harper, but I'm certain your clients benefited from your kind heart and quick thinking."

She smiled then. Beamed, actually. "Thank you, Sam." She pressed her lips to his—soft and brief. Nevertheless the connection stirred his interest. As she pressed up against his body, her smile turned wicked. "I'm tempted to pull you into the janitor's closet for a quickie, but I should go. I need to pack for the trip, review final details. Plus we have dinner tonight at Rocky's and—"

"Glad I caught you." Rocky stepped in, along with Rae. "Sorry. Wasn't eavesdropping," she said. "Just rounding the corner and overheard about dinner. I hope you'll understand, but I'm canceling."

Sunday dinners at Daisy's house which was now Rocky's house were tradition. "Never been done," Sam said.

"First time for everything," Rocky said. "Between Lily's arrival and several of the Cupcake Lovers leaving for Vegas, everyone's got a full plate. Preparing, packing. Plus Gram said she wants the night free to dye her hair. Says blue's all wrong for the big event."

"Did you ask Daisy to tone it down for TV?" Rae asked Harper.

"I didn't. Although I have to admit something more sedate would be in keeping with the Cupcake Lovers' wholesome image."

"Don't know that I'd expect sedate," Sam said. "More like glitz. We're talking Vegas and national television."

"We could be talking sparkles," Rocky teased.

"I can spin sparkles," Harper quipped back, and Sam smiled, *again,* enjoying the budding camaraderie between Harper and his family.

"I wish you could be in two places at once," he said to Rocky and Rae.

Rocky swatted his shoulder. "You'll be fine."

"Chloe said the same thing."

"It's true," Rae said. "Brice and Kaylee will want to talk cupcakes and you're one of the best bakers in the club, Sam."

"I don't know about that."

"Spare me the false modesty," Rocky said with a grin.

"You're an incredibly talented baker," Rae said, "and a valuable liaison because of your military background."

"Agreed," Harper said, her bright blue eyes on Sam. "Why you'd want to quit the club is beyond me."

Rocky and Rae gaped. "What?"

Sam drilled Harper with one of his death glares, only she didn't cringe. She didn't even look contrite.

"Is this because of the baby talk?" Rae asked. "I feel awful."

"Don't. I'm not quitting." He shot Harper another pointed glare. "Happy?"

"Delirious." Smiling, she glanced at her phone, noted the time. "I should go. I've intruded enough on your family's time and there's so much to do in preparation for the trip. Although I understand why you begged off," she said to Rocky and Rae, "I'm with Sam. I wish you were coming. From what I've heard, Tasha Burke's a poor substitute."

"Tasha's no angel," Rocky said, "but she's earned this dance in the limelight."

Considering all Tasha had cost Rocky, all the strife she'd caused Dev, Sam marveled that he, too, felt it was only fair to include her. Then again, Tasha *had* owned up to her shit judgment and behavior, suggesting she'd changed for the better. *Maybe.*

"I don't know Tasha," Harper said, "but she can't be any harder to handle than some of my former clients. I'm sure it'll be fine." She pocketed her phone, winked at Sam. "Besides, we've got eye candy for the ladies."

Sam grunted as Harper zipped toward the elevator.

Rocky snorted in a pitiful attempt to smother a laugh.

Rae pressed her lips together.

"Not a word," Sam said to his cousin and friend as he watched Harper go. She'd busted his balls and all he felt was . . . happy.

Rocky cleared her throat. "Okay. Not about that, but—"

Sam turned. "What?"

"We weren't going to say anything," Rocky said.

"But maybe we should," Rae said.

"Spit it out," Sam said.

They tugged him farther down the hall, away from the hustle of staff, and lowered their voices.

"The Cupcake Lovers' social sites and Harper's personal

sites," Rocky said. "I followed them through the night. Chimed in here and there to keep a CL presence."

"Me, too," Rae said, palming her swelled belly. "Insomnia."

"There was a post," Rocky said. "A weird post."

Sam tensed. "What did it say?"

"Nothing overtly creepy," Rae said. "But there was a taunting tone."

"It was on Harper's personal page," Rocky said. "He, she, whoever, wanted to know why Harper was dragging her feet in Sugar Creek. It, he, she said—"

" 'Shouldn't you be packing? Time's ticking,' " Rae said.

"Time's ticking," Rocky echoed. "What's that supposed to mean?"

"I wouldn't have given it a second thought," Rae said. "Chalking it up to an impatient client. A nervous actor with an upcoming publicity tour. Someone who wanted her back in Hollywood pronto. I know how that rolls."

"But the attached profile pic was of an illustrated soldier with a rifle," Rocky said. "And he/she didn't use a name. He used a moniker. 'The Avenger.' It gave me chills. I told Jayce about it, but he pointed out the popularity of that superhero movie. Said it was probably something along the same lines as what Rae just mentioned."

"Which is why I wrote it off last night," Rae said. "But then I woke up thinking about the way Harper had holed up at the farm the first few days she was back in town. How she had everything delivered in. How she sounded distracted and tense when I spoke to her on the phone. And then Rocky mentioned that she'd seen that weird post and we got talking and thinking . . ."

"What if a disgruntled client or boyfriend's been hassling her?" Rocky asked. "What if that's what spurred her to leave L.A.?"

Sam knew Harper had left L.A. because of the spa

shooting. He knew she'd holed up due to agoraphobia. He didn't fill Rocky and Rae in because he knew Harper was embarrassed about her phobia. Nor did he tell them about the threat of deportation. That would spur talk of visas and green cards and/or questions about why she was reluctant to return to her native country.

"Shouldn't you be packing? Time's ticking."

Was that post referring to Harper's impending deportation? She'd led Sam to believe that her aversion to Canada was linked specifically to the bad memories associated with her former fiancé. He flashed back on Harper's initial anxiety attack and the moment when he, too, had wondered if she were being stalked or threatened. Was there more to her story?

Sam palmed his phone, cursing himself for not keeping up on those social sites. He'd peeked in for a while—intrigued but not hooked. Far from addicted. He'd spent the night submerged in Harper, in the flesh-and-blood woman. It hadn't crossed his mind to check the Internet in the middle of the freaking night.

"You won't find it," Rocky said. "I wanted to show Jayce this morning, but it's gone.

"Either Harper or the person who wrote it deleted the post," Rae said. "Which seems kind of fishy either way."

Sam skimmed Harper's page for more recent posts. No sign of the Avenger.

"Has Harper said anything to you about being hassled?" Rocky asked.

"No," Sam said.

"Maybe we've watched too many movies," Rae said. "It's probably nothing."

"But what if it's something?" Rocky asked

"She seemed fine today," Rae said. "Happy even."

"Maybe she never saw the post," Rocky said. "It was there and gone in the middle of the night."

Except Sam and Harper had been awake a good portion of the night, talking about Andrew. He thought back. He didn't recall seeing her phone, but she could have scrolled those sites before she'd come downstairs. If she *had* seen that post and deleted it, if she *was* being hassled, why was she keeping that news from Sam?

He thought about the feeling that had bugged him last night, the feeling of being watched. Suddenly, Sam wasn't so keen on Harper being alone at the house.

"Probably nothing," he said to the ladies in hopes of soothing their misgivings. "But thanks for the heads-up. By the way, where is Jayce?" he asked as he prepped for a getaway.

"Getting a cup of coffee with Luke," Rocky said. "Why? Are you going to ask him to do some cybersnooping?"

"If you don't," Rae said, "I might."

TWENTY-SEVEN

Harper couldn't remember the last time she'd been surrounded by such genuine, heartfelt joy. Friends and family who'd gathered to get the first peek at Chloe and Dev's little girl. Lily, they'd named her. After a flower, like Daisy. The core Monroes, as well as Chloe's father, had been especially emotional. Their tears and smiles as they'd fawned over baby Lily had been overwhelming for Harper. She'd missed out on family celebrations. She'd missed out on family.

As she drove toward Sugar Creek, she imagined a repeat performance, the same gathering of souls, the same jubilation when Rae and Luke welcomed their baby into the world. Birthdays and anniversaries within this large and tight circle of family were probably a big deal, a reason for large and chaotic celebrations. Did they know how lucky they were?

No one, aside from Harper and Sam and Paula's parents, knew but, as of tomorrow evening, *she'd* be a member of this large and tight circle. She'd be a wife and a mother and included in Sunday dinners and family barbecues and maybe the occasional lunch or shopping spree with Chloe and Rocky and Rae. Standing in the hospital hall, praising Sam's baking abilities and ribbing him just a little about his good looks, Harper had gotten a taste of what it would be like to truly bond with some of the Cupcake Lovers. Not just as their publicist, but as a friend, and in some instances, family. It was something she wanted to experience even if only for a while. Sometimes Harper felt as though she'd been born to robots, both parents missing the "caring" chip. She'd never been abused, but she'd always been ignored. What she couldn't get at home, she went after at school. *Attention.*

She'd gravitated toward clubs. Drama, journalism, media. She wanted to belong—to something, to someone. She'd made friends, lots of friends. Although looking back, they were more like friendly acquaintances. Too many to connect with too deeply. Too involved on too many levels. Always striving for acceptance and some form of adoration. Even after she'd signed on at Spin Twin Cities, she'd spread herself too thin.

And then she'd met Andrew and he'd been her hope, her promise of a family. Her own family. They'd have the perfect wedding and then three or four or maybe five children. She'd be a caring mom and he'd be a caring dad. But then Andrew had pushed her away, threatened her dreams, and challenged her spirit.

If only she'd been stronger, wiser, maybe she could have helped Andrew.

Or maybe not.

Harper couldn't change the past or predict the future, but she could live in the now. *Now* she had a shot at sampling her dream through Sam. Through his children and their extended family. What had started out as a business agreement was fast becoming a friendly alliance with potential. She was still scared of failing, but she wouldn't stand a chance if she didn't at least try.

Harper's mind spun faster than the wheels of her car.

What if, what if, what if? She turned onto Main Street, noted the stores. She thought about her butterfly room—Mina's—and the green room—Ben's. Mina would stuff her room with fairy tales and plush animals. Ben would organize his room with manga novels and superheroes. Harper wanted to contribute to the transformation. She wanted to buy them gifts. And for the first time in weeks, she didn't want to shop online.

Just as she parked in front of J. T. Monroe's Department Store, her phone pinged with a text.

Sam.

U OK?

She smiled as her heels hit the sidewalk. HUNKY DORY HEADING HOME.

YOURS OR MINE?

OURS.

Her heart skipped and so did Harper. SEE U SOON

Sam would have made it to the Rothwell Farm in record time if he hadn't been pulled over for speeding. Not a first, but the first in very long time. He was pissed about losing time. Pissed about the freaking high fine. But mostly he was anxious about Harper. He couldn't kick the feeling that there was more to her troubles than she'd confided and that that trouble had followed her to Sugar Creek.

Pulling up to the house and not seeing her car damn near stopped his heart.

He jogged up the steps, let himself in, called out her name. Silence smacked his ears, clouded perspective. She'd had a head start. She'd said, *"See you soon."*

Goddamn. What the hell?

He snagged his phone. No texting. *Voice.* He needed to hear her voice. And when he did, when she answered sounding perfect and calm, he dropped onto the sofa and pressed two fingers to his pounding left temple. "Where the hell are you?"

"Shopping."

"In a store?"

"Why do you sound so shocked? And angry?"

"Not angry." *Furious.* "Relieved." *Irrationally pissed.* "You didn't tell me you were stopping so I expected you to be here."

"And I wasn't. So you called because you were worried. And you're angry because I'm fine and shopping. Your mind traveled a darker path. What if I'd had a panic attack while driving? Or blown a tire? Or hit a deer? What if I was broken and bleeding in a ditch?"

"Something like that." He willed his pulse and temper in line.

"But it's nothing like that. I stopped on a whim. I'm fine, Sam. Better than fine. I shopped in a store, in public, and I didn't even twitch. No cataclysmic thoughts. No paralyzing fears. All I felt was joy, pure joy. If some tragic soul had come gunning in the toy section, I would have died with a smile on my face. Wait until you see what I got for Ben and Mina! I just checked out and I'm walking toward my car. I'll be home in fifteen minutes, give or take. And when I get there, I'll make it up to you. Sam?"

"Yeah?"

"Thank you for caring."

They signed off and he stared at his phone, gathering his calm, assessing her mood. She'd braved her debilitating fears to shop for his children. She sounded happy. Cheerful. But also a little manic. His heart scraped against his chest. He didn't love Harper a little. He loved her a lot. He felt a little, no, a lot coldcocked. He knew without a doubt that he was getting in deep with a woman who would never be easy. A woman with issues he'd only just begun to uncover. Harper Day was obsessive-compulsive. He'd bet on it. And that was just one of her quirks. Instead of scaring him away, it made him dig in. Even though she hid it from the world, Harper was a wounded soul. He wanted to help. He wanted her happy.

He imagined her walking through the front door, arms loaded with gifts. He imagined a smile to match the cheer he'd just heard in her voice. He wanted her to ride that wave of euphoria to Vegas and to own it throughout their wedding ceremony. He was thrilled that she'd conquered her fears enough to shop in public, but how would she fare in a bigger city, in the crowded casinos? He wanted her to obsess on the good what ifs, not the bad. Just long enough to get them to Vegas and back. Just long enough to ensure her wedding day was blissful, not stressful. Yes, they were marrying in haste and for practical purposes, but Sam wanted her to equate their alliance with hope, not fear.

In her mind, she'd failed Andrew, and she'd told Sam she didn't want him to love her, because she feared failing *him*. Why was she still wallowing in guilt after three years? Why hadn't she come to terms? Was someone fanning the flames? Casting blame? Holding a grudge? She feared random acts of violence. She feared Canada, returning to Canada. Was she running from bad memories . . . or maybe a bad person?

"Why are you dragging your feet in Sugar Creek? Shouldn't you be packing? Time's ticking."

The Avenger, whoever he was, knew Harper was in Sugar Creek. Even though Sam hadn't seen that post for himself, he couldn't get it out of his brain. He'd been set to ask Harper straight-out if she was being hassled, but in light of her cheerful state he didn't want to open that door. Either she was oblivious or in denial. Either way, something was off. Sam felt it in his gut and his gut was never wrong.

He wanted to know more about Harper's past. He wanted to know if she was being bullied and, if so, if the bastard was dangerous or simply an ass. Was he in Canada? Los Angeles? Was there a chance he'd show up on her freaking doorstep in Sugar Creek? Within the next week Ben and

Mina would be living in this house, too. And *that* was the thought that pushed Sam over and down the slippery slope.

He skimmed the contacts in his phone, telling himself he wasn't invading Harper's privacy, he was protecting her. Protecting the kids. He didn't feel an ounce of hesitation or regret when he connected with Jayce Bello. Rocky's husband. Sam's cousin by marriage. A former cop turned private detective who'd launched a successful Internet business that specialized in sniffing out cyberbullies.

"Need a favor," Sam said, explaining the situation, ensuring confidentiality, and voicing parameters.

Jayce listened, commented, and put Sam's mind at ease with two words. "On it."

Five minutes later, Harper blew into the house like a sonic burst of sunshine. She looked beautiful. She looked happy. Sam's heart took a massive hit as she made a beeline for him, slamming into his arms, shopping bags and all. She kissed him fast and hard, smiling, laughing. *Laughing,* for crissake.

"Do you know how much fun it is shopping for kids?" she asked, escaping his hold to dump her booty on the sofa. "I wanted to buy them each something for their new rooms. Just one thing. Something for them from me. Something to make them feel welcome in their new home. But one thing led to another and I couldn't decide, so I got them all."

Sam watched, entranced, as she emptied the bags and showcased her purchases. A sketch pad, colored pencils, two comic books, and an action figure of Ironman. A poster from one of the latest superhero flicks and a futuristic-looking reading lamp. For Mina she'd snagged a plush unicorn, a play fairy-tale castle, a wand that made tinkling noises, and a blinking tiara.

"I saw a beanbag chair that I loved, but they didn't have it in purple and . . ." Harper trailed off, wand in one hand, tiara in the other. "Did I go overboard? Step out of bounds?"

"You did great," was all he said. Any more and he'd be

gushing about how thoughtful she was and how much it meant to him that she wanted Ben and Mina to feel at home. That she didn't mind filling the rooms she'd had decorated in a specific retro style with whimsical and fantastical kid stuff. Sam pulled her back into his arms. "They aren't even here yet and you're already spoiling them."

"I couldn't help myself."

"I love that you couldn't help yourself."

She was on a shopping high and he was high on her. The air crackled as Sam angled for a kiss. His blood sizzled as their tongues dueled, as her hands roamed his shoulders, his back. When her deft fingers breezed up the hem of his tee, when she palmed his bare back—skin on skin—Sam wanted to feel her, too. All of her.

"What would you say if I said I want you naked?" he asked. "Here. Now."

"I'd say stop talking. Start stripping."

She already had his shirt shoved to his chest. He pulled it off then went to work on her dress—untying the sash and peeling the blousy fabric over her head. Now her ponytail was a little crooked and her beautiful face a lot flushed. Her blue eyes danced with mischief and hunger, tempting Sam to take her fast and hard. He knew her thoughts mirrored his. Once they married, once Ben and Mina moved into this house, there wouldn't be a lot of room for spontaneous sex, let alone kink. And even though Sam liked his sex slow and intimate, he couldn't deny the equal thrill of down and dirty with Harper.

Bending her over the sofa came to mind until he caught sight of the toys, which made him think of the kids.

"Upstairs," Harper said, working the buttons of his fly even as she tugged him in that direction.

He waylaid her hands, throwing her over his shoulder and whisking up the stairs. He wasn't sure how she'd managed it, but when he set her to her feet, she was braless. She backed into the bedroom wearing nothing but a black lace thong, shiny black heels, and a naughty smile. His mouth went as dry as dust but he managed, "You're beautiful."

"You're wearing too many clothes."

Sam shoved his jeans and shorts down his hips.

Harper swooped in and knocked him back on the bed before he got the chance to free his ankles.

Sam was entranced with her freaking hot body, her gorgeous face, and the raw lust sizzling between them. Lust laced with affection. "Leave the heels," he ground out as she peeled off her thong.

Her impossibly saucy smile turned wicked as she straddled his torso and shoved his arms over his head, his hands into the pillows, similar to what he'd done to her the night before. But then he felt a silky band around his wrist, craned his head and saw her lashing him to the bedpost with black stockings. He didn't know where she'd pulled them from. He didn't care. What he knew was she'd turned dominant and he'd let her have her fun because, he knew from experience, she was going to blow his mind among other things. And he knew when this was over he'd turn the tables and slow things down. There'd be that intimate connection, and she'd be a step closer to falling in love with Sam. Blood flowed south at the thought, making him granite hard.

For Harper.

She tightened the stockings, incapacitating his hands although he didn't need his hands to make her squirm.

"What are you grinning at?" she asked after nipping his earlobe. "I'm the one in charge."

"Enjoy it while you can, baby."

She cocked a challenging brow. "I'll have you begging for release."

He nipped her lush lower lip then suckled. Then smiled. "Looking forward to it."

TWENTY-EIGHT

"You sure about this?"

"Not sure if it's a great idea, but I think it's the right thing to do," Harper said. "Besides, you already spoke to the kids. We can't back out now."

"Yeah, well. Can't say I didn't work up an appetite." Sam winked at Harper then keyed the ignition.

She buckled in and tried to ignore the heat that wink inspired. They'd just spent two hours pleasuring one another first in bed then in the shower then—have mercy—midway between the bathroom and bedroom, up against the wall. She should be spent, every sexual desire sated, yet Sam stirred her juices with a damned wink.

How long could it burn like this between them? Surely things would cool at some point. Maybe even as soon as tomorrow. Maybe sex after marriage would sour because the marriage itself was a sham. Sam wanted a mother for his children. She needed a green card. They would mutually benefit from this alliance, but it was not a love match. She wondered if they could get the chaplain to refrain from using the word *love*, making their union less a lie. It shouldn't bother her, but it did. Just like it bothered her to elope to Vegas without having some sort of interaction with Ben and Mina beforehand. She hadn't seen them in over a month, and even though Sam had said they'd voted for her as his "wife," she'd feel better if she reconnected with them before she got on that plane. She'd suggested dinner. They had to eat anyway and since Rocky had canceled, Harper and Sam had no obligations and a couple of hours to burn. Afterward, Sam would drop her at the farm and then he and the kids would return to their house for the night. She understood that tomorrow was a school day and they had a routine. Sam would drive them to school then pick her up and, together, they'd drive to Starlight Airfield.

It seemed like a sound plan to Harper. All the same, the closer they got to the Kesslers', the more she twirled her bracelet.

"Whatever you're worrying about, stop."

Harper sighed. "What if I say something wrong?"

"Then you'll spin it around to something right."

"I just . . . I want the kids to like me."

"Then you can definitely stop worrying. They already do."

"The Kesslers. What if they don't like me?"

"They will."

"You're the most confident man I've ever met. Confident without being arrogant, that is."

Sam didn't respond, not that she expected him to. He focused on the road and Harper focused on her phone. She scrolled through several apps checking for e-mails, voice mails and texts, messages—public and private—on her social sites.

"Everything okay?" Sam asked.

She'd been checking periodically, partially out of habit, partially to make sure Edward hadn't issued a new taunt. "No crises."

"That's good."

Not hearing from Edward? Definitely good. Not hearing from previous clients? "I used to thrive on running to the rescue," Harper said honestly. "Calm seas are disconcerting."

"You want chaos?" Sam asked. "Brace yourself."

He pulled into a driveway and Harper tensed. She couldn't help herself. Four people poured onto the front porch before Harper and Sam even got out of the cab. Mina raced across the lawn. Ben followed, more slowly, dragging two backpacks. An older couple hovered on the porch side by side—*smiling*.

Harper registered their blinding kindness a split second before homing in on the kids.

"Daddy!" Mina rushed forward and jumped into Sam's arms. They hugged and then the little girl bounced over to Harper. "Hi, Harper! Like my shirt? It's purple!"

Harper stooped down to eye level with the five-year-old ball of energy. Mina twirled and Harper smiled. "I like the sparkles on the kitty."

"Hi, Harper," Ben said with less zeal. "Dad said we could pick where to eat tonight. We pick Rock 'n' Roll Lanes. Burgers and bowling. It's kind of fun."

Harper suppressed a cringe. *Bowling?* She hadn't planned on making a fool of herself this evening. *Crap.* At least she was dressed for the occasion. Jeans and a peasant blouse. Sandals, no heels. That was something anyway. She flashed one of her most polished smiles. "Okay."

He kicked at a nonexistent stone then chanced her gaze and lowered his voice. "It's okay if you stink at bowling. I stink, too."

Harper's heart cracked then swelled. She squeezed her own hands together instead of reaching for Ben's. "I stink worse."

He looked away. "Wanna bet?"

Harper stuck out her hand. "Sure."

"You'll just pretend to be worse," Ben said while eyeing her hand, "to make me feel better. Nice people do stuff like that."

Self-conscious now, Harper hugged herself. "You think I'm nice?"

"Sure. Don't you?"

Harper blinked. It wasn't often that someone struck her speechless. Crazy that a nine-year-old had just given her cause to search her soul. No. She didn't think of herself as nice. Rae was nice. Chloe was nice. Mrs. Kessler's aura screamed nice, and from everything Harper had heard, her daughter, Ben's mom, had been the epitome of nice.

"We should go." Sam touched Harper's shoulder, calling her back to the moment.

"Yeah, let's go! Let's go!" Mina chirped, clutching a ratty rabbit wearing a pink boa and jumping up and down like a crazed pogo stick.

"Get in the truck," Sam told the kids. "In the backseat and buckle up!" he called as they raced for the extended cab.

"Ready to meet the folks?" Sam asked as he helped Harper to her feet.

She rolled back her shoulders and squeezed his hand. *Ben thinks I'm nice*. "Ready."

Sam pushed through the evening battling a barrage of emotions. He noted a few key points throughout the heart-bending sequence of events.

Mina dialed it down a notch in Harper's presence. Typically, his animated, chatterbox daughter dominated the conversation. Typically, she demanded Sam's full attention, showing off or acting out. Typically she clung to him like a three-foot swatch of Velcro. But tonight she was on her best behavior. No tantrums, no clowning around, no clinging. She interacted and listened—mostly to Harper, but to Sam and Ben, too.

Ben was oddly protective of Harper, making sure she had the right-sized bowling shoes and weighted ball. Like with other live sports as well as anything mechanical,

Sam had thought Ben had turned a deaf ear to Sam's advice regarding the finer points of bowling. He'd been stunned to hear his specific instructions on technique flowing from his son to Harper. He'd also been stunned by a noted difference in Ben's attitude throughout the game. Ben wasn't particularly skilled at bowling, but instead of getting discouraged and sulky, he kept his cool and tried his best. He scored better than usual and Sam had fought to find the right tone and amount of praise. He didn't want to make too big a deal out of it as it would embarrass Ben, but he was damned proud of his son's efforts and improvement.

As for Harper . . . She didn't excel at bowling, but she didn't suck, either. At least that's what Ben told her. Honestly, she sucked, but like Ben, she tried. She even seemed to have fun. With the exception of scrolling through her phone apps every now and then, she'd participated full-out in the family event. She munched on a burger and fries with a smile, even though Sam knew she would've preferred a salad, and she'd answered all of Ben's and Mina's questions which, to Sam's disappointment, centered on her ties with Hollywood, rather than her everyday life—although Ben did ask if she liked pancakes.

At one point, Sam had tried to give Harper tips on form. It meant getting up close and personal—hands-on. He'd heard Mina giggle and he'd turned to see Ben giving him a shy thumbs-up. Sam knew in that moment that his kids had been on their best behavior as a way of impressing Harper. They wanted her to like them. They wanted her for a mom. *"We don't want you to be a lonely old man."* Sam had choked up for the second time in one day.

Two hours flew by in five minutes. Before Sam knew it, he was loading everyone in his truck and driving Harper home. The closer they got to the farm, the darker Sam's mood. He didn't want to leave her alone, not for the entire night. What if she got another taunting message? What if the bastard called? What if she decided to watch television while packing and saw some news report that set her off? What if . . . "Aw, hell."

"You cussed, Daddy!" Mina called from the backseat.

"I know, pumpkin. Forget you heard that."

"Anything wrong?" Harper asked in a soft voice.

"No." *Yeah. I'm thinking the worst and obsessing. I'm pulling a you.* He kept that thought to himself along with several others as he turned onto Swamp Road. He hadn't heard anything back yet from Jayce. Harper wasn't distracted or anxious. Sam had no immediate reason to worry and he sure as hell didn't want to set those wheels in motion for Harper.

"Are we there yet?" Mina asked.

"Almost," Sam said.

"Seen any ghosts yet?" Ben asked.

"No," Harper said. She shifted and turned. "You don't have to worry about those old stories, Ben."

"You don't think it's haunted?" He sounded disappointed.

"I think something sad happened there once and that sadness seeped into the walls. But I've been cheering things up, giving the walls and floors and every inch of every room a makeover with the help of your dad and Aunt Rocky. It's happy there now." She glanced at Sam, crooked a smile that hugged his heart. "And it's going to get happier."

Sam pulled into her driveway, scanning the property, the house. Nothing out of sorts. *Nothing to worry about.*

"Can we come in?" Mina asked.

"You're supposed to wait for an invitation, honey."

She poked Harper's shoulder. "Will you invite us inside . . . please?" she added.

Harper smiled. "I wish I could. I want to. But you have school tomorrow and it's getting late."

"You should walk her to the door, Dad," Ben said.

"You're absolutely right, son."

"And don't forget to kiss her good night!" Mina said as he swung out of the cab.

Sam rolled his eyes as he rounded the hood to help Harper out. He had no idea where Mina had gotten that from. Probably television or maybe one of the babysitters. Harper slid out of the cab into Sam's arms and it was all he could do not to kiss her then and there. She looked radiant in jeans and a loose-fitting, puffy-sleeved blouse, her thick hair twisted in a loose knot.

"Did you ask her yet, Daddy?" Mina called from the backseat.

"Ask her what?" Sam responded, transfixed by Harper's glittering blue eyes.

"To be our mom."

"That's private stuff," Ben said to his sister. "Stop being a Nosey Nate. You'll ruin it."

"I'm not a Nosey Nate!" Mina pouted.

So much for best behavior. "I'll be right back," Sam told the kids. "No fighting." He escorted Harper up the porch steps.

She lingered at the front door. "I'm really glad we did this, Sam."

"So am I."

"They're good kids."

"You're good with them."

"I'm good with people in general. Kids are just little, younger people, right? I was a kid once. I remember certain aspects. Insecurities. Needs. Mostly, they just want to know that they matter—what they say, what they do. I tried to be sensitive to that tonight. I wanted Ben and Mina to know that I was paying attention. That they matter." She glanced away suddenly, looking embarrassed. "Listen to me preaching to you. You could write a book on good parenting."

"I don't know about that, but thanks." Sam angled his head, studied her intense expression. "I'd like to know more about you as a kid. What you were like. What you said, what you did. Are your parents still around? Do you have siblings? You've never mentioned your family."

"That's because I don't have one." She groaned. "That sounded pathetic." She looked back to Sam. "I'm an only child. Parents divorced long ago. They're estranged. We're estranged. It's not a big deal. Just very different than what you have."

More than ever Sam wanted that report from Jayce. Details about Harper's past. He'd never been more intrigued with a person in his life.

Pulling her keys from her purse, Harper glanced at his truck, gave Ben and Mina a smile and a wave. "You should go," she said to Sam.

"They're okay," he said. "Trust me, they're riveted, hoping we'll change our minds and call them inside. They don't want this night to end and I don't blame them."

Harper leaned against the doorjamb, sighed. "I wish we could fast-forward to two days from now."

"Nervous about the flight? The show?" *Being alone?*

"Anxious to get on with life." She pressed a hand to Sam's chest, smiled. "If you don't kiss me good night there's a good chance you'll get an earful on the ride home."

"I'll get an earful anyway, but it doesn't have to be about that." Hand at the small of her back, Sam pulled Harper closer. "Unfortunately, their idea of a good-night kiss and mine are two different animals." He brushed his mouth over hers, sampled her lush lips briefly, just long enough to make him ache for more, then eased away. "Call me or text me if you need me. Otherwise I'll see you in the morning. Make sure to pack your identification."

She hesitated before moving inside. "You can still back out."

"But I won't."

"Because Ben and Mina want a mom and because I'm desperate for a green card."

"That's part of it."

"I'm not sure I can handle more."

"The question is, do you want more?"

Her gaze flicked to the truck, his children, and then back to Sam. "Yes."

"We'll take it slow. See what happens. No pressure, Harper. No expectations."

"Okay." She nodded. "Slow is good."

His heart hammered at the thousand things he read in her eyes—hope, regret, joy, fear. Sam smiled and brushed a thumb over her cheek. "See you in the morning, Slick. Sleep well."

Blushing, she moved inside and closed the door.

Sam waited until he heard the dead bolt lock then ambled toward his truck.

Slow. He could do slow. And when she was ready, he'd give her more.

One eye on the house, he slid into the driver's seat, jonesing to hear from Jayce, and gearing up for whatever grilling the kids had in store.

"That's not how they kiss in the movies," Mina said.

Sam glanced over his shoulder. "What movies have you been watching?"

"Bridgett likes those sappy, girly movies," Ben said. "You know. Like *Twilight*."

"That's the one where the vampires sparkle," Mina said. "You should watch it, Daddy. See how Edward kisses Bella." She hugged herself, closed her eyes and made kissy, mushy sounds.

Ben rolled his eyes and pulled his iPod out of his backpack.

Sam pulled out of the drive, wondering what other movies Bridgett had subjected a five-year-old to. A smile touched his lips as he realized he wouldn't have to fly solo when speaking to Mina about the kissing thing. He could scarcely wait to hear Harper's two cents.

TWENTY-NINE

Sunday had proven a full and interesting day for Adam. A morning of excitement at the hospital. The awkward greeting between Adam and Peppy's grandpa, the jubilant celebration of Dev and Chloe's little girl (a special whoop from those who'd won the betting pool), and the way Rocky had expressed subtle curiosity (or was it concern?) about Adam's choice in a roommate.

That afternoon, Adam had driven Peppy to Shady Oak, where he freelanced as a sports instructor, and introduced her to the resort's gym. She wasn't very athletic, but she was determined, and yeah boy, *George* had twitched every time Adam had laid hands on Peppy's soft skin in order to instruct her in technique.

They'd parted ways after—Adam to work out, Peppy to rehearse—and when he'd run into her again at home later that evening there'd been a sexual zing. Peppy didn't acknowledge it, but Adam sensed her interest, and *George*, damn him, wouldn't behave, so Adam had taken a cold shower, dressed, and gone back out. He'd met Kane and Nash at the Shack, intending to throw back brews to celebrate the birth of Lily—like they needed an excuse to drink. Only Nash had opted for soda, saying he had a long flight the next day, and Kane had bitched about the absence of Luke and Decker's annoying habit of flipping channels, surfing right over ESPN. Adam had bailed early, feeling restless and horny and, dammit, lonely. The latter two being crazy because Adam had plenty of friends and some of those friends were female and a couple would be up for a spontaneous tango. All Adam had to do was call. Instead he drove back to his teeny-tiny rental, hoping Peppy had gone out with a friend or maybe holed up in her room with her guitar. Just his luck, she'd kicked back on his couch with her acoustic, idly picking notes while watching a movie.

"Sorry," she'd said, leaping up as if her pants were on fire—those damned cute-as-hell monkey-face pants. "Thought you'd stay out later."

"So did I. What are you watching?"

"A Good Day to Die Hard."

An action flick. Huh. "I'll grab a beer and join you. Want one?"

"Sure."

So they'd shared the sofa, drinking suds, and watching Bruce Willis kick ass. There'd been that sexual pull, only Peppy had kept her distance and Adam had given George mental hell. They'd retreated to their rooms and Adam had fallen asleep hearing Peppy noodling (as she called it) on that guitar. The music wasn't loud, but the walls were thin so, later, he'd also heard her bed creaking as she tossed and turned.

Adam woke up at two twenty-five, four-oh-three, and five twenty-one. Whacking off would have solved his problem but he felt weird about that considering the object of his obsession was sleeping one room over. "To hell with it."

Adam rolled out of bed. Dawn was breaking. He'd head out early. Jogging would solve his problem, too. But first he needed to hydrate. His throat was froggy and dry. His brain fuzzy. Normally he would have padded to the kitchen buck naked since that's how he slept, but that didn't seem smart what with a woman in the house and George at full attention. So he pulled on a pair of boxers, eased out his door, crept down the hall. He froze on the kitchen threshold, mesmerized by the sight of bare legs and a cute ass clad only in those skimpy girly briefs— boyfriend shorts, he thought they were called. Peppy was bent over and peering into the lower shelves of his fridge. He considered retreating to his room without a word, but then she backed out with a piece of fruit, catching him staring, because . . . yeah. That shitty timing thing.

"Oh. Hey," she said, looking a little poleaxed herself.

"Hey."

She tugged down the hem of her tank top, which only caused the material to stretch tighter over her pert breasts. "I, um, I don't always walk around like this."

"Me, neither."

"I couldn't sleep."

"Same here."

"Thought I'd grab a snack."

"I see that."

"I really wanted a doughnut, but you don't have any of those. Plus I remembered what you said about a healthier diet so I . . ." She held up a fresh peach. "Hope you don't mind. It's the last one."

The whole time she'd been babbling, she'd been staring. At Adam. He felt the heat of her gaze sliding over his naked torso, knew the second she spied the tent in his boxers. Sexual zing, hell. More like *zap*! A freaking huge bolt of sexual lightning snapped between them. The air crackled with lust. Hers. His. He wanted to do something about that even though he knew he shouldn't. Even though there was a ninety-nine percent chance she'd shut him down, Adam moved in. "We could share."

"What? The peach? Seriously? You want it?"

He flicked his own gaze over the thin tank and brief

briefs that barely concealed her soft curves. He made it clear exactly what he wanted. Then he braced for her to bolt.

Or to slug him.

Instead, she leaned back against the counter, offered him the peach then shoved her shaggy hair out of her face. "You first," she said. "Your peach, after all."

Their fingers brushed and his pulse pounded. He bit into the juicy fruit, wanting to sink into feisty Peppy instead.

Staring up into his eyes, she stole back the fruit and took a big, messy bite.

George throbbed and Adam leaned down. "Juice." He licked the corner of Peppy's mouth, sampled her bottom lip—oh, yeah—then eased back with a slight grin. "Got it."

She narrowed her big brown eyes. "That work on most women?"

"Question is, did it work on you?"

Her gaze slid south. "You know how George has a mind of his own? Well, Lucy has a mind of her own, too."

Adam's lips twitched as his own gaze slid between Peppy's legs. "Lucy, huh?"

"Yeah. We're sort of at odds because I know that sleeping with you is a bad idea. It messes with the roomie dynamics. But Lucy . . . well, she hasn't seen any action in quite a while and George has her all jazzed. Because of her, I'm distracted. I don't like being distracted. I'm on a mission. So now I'm thinking if Lucy and George got it on and out of their system we, you and me, could knock out the, well, the distraction. I—"

"Peppy."

"Yeah?"

"You talk too much."

"Maybe you should shut me up."

"No maybe about it." Adam palmed her ass and hiked her up on the counter, stepping in so that she had to wrap her legs around his waist. He shoved his fingers through her crazy, messy hair and kissed her wild and deep. His heart hammered and George danced.

Peppy sort of froze, like she didn't know what to do with her hands, although her lips and tongue followed Adam's lead. When he eased back, she frowned. "Damn," she said. "I was sort of hoping you'd be a lousy kisser. You're probably great at all the other stuff, too."

"One way to find out."

Peppy shocked him by peeling her tank over her head, naked as a jaybird except for those cotton briefs. Those briefs did him in. "From here on out," she said, "it's just George and Lucy. You and me, we're out of the equation."

George wanted to meet Lucy here and now on the counter, but Adam still had one working brain cell and he wanted Peppy in bed where he could properly impress her with all the "other stuff." He snatched her off the counter, whisking her into his bedroom while she continued to make it clear that this was sex, just sex, and probably, no definitely, a one-time show.

"Peppy," he said as he playfully tossed her on his bed. "Shut the hell up." Before she could respond, he unleashed George.

Wide-eyed, Peppy yanked Adam onto the bed and rolled over on top of him. "From here on out," she said as she peeled off those tomboy panties, "Lucy does all my talking."

THIRTY

Monday morning took forever and a day to dawn. It didn't help that Sam had trouble sleeping. Rather than staring up at the ceiling—missing Harper, worrying about Harper—he'd spent a good portion of the night on his laptop, researching immigration laws, making sure he hadn't tripped up on legalities. He'd double-checked the marriage license and the plans for the ceremony. He spent time scoping other custom-furniture Web sites, looking for ideas on how to ramp up his own small-business site.

And he'd checked intermittently to make sure the Avenger hadn't issued a new taunt on Harper's or the Cupcake Lovers' social pages. All he'd seen were interesting or inspiring comments from cupcake fans and soldiers and their families. Still, when he'd finally crawled into bed, he'd slept with his phone in hand, braced for a panicked call or text from Harper.

Instead all was quiet.

Until Mina came bounding into his room at six A.M. "Dad-*deeee*!"

Getting the kids dressed and ready for school was a blur. Making breakfast, a blur. Driving them to school, a freaking blur. Mina, and even Ben, had talked nonstop—about Harper, about Sam and Harper's trip. How long would they be on the plane? (*"Several hours."*) How long would they be gone? (*"Two days."*) Could they stay home from school tomorrow to watch the Cupcake Lovers on TV? (*"No. But Grandpa will record it."*)

The entire time the kids had grilled Sam, he'd been processing thoughts of his own. Standing on the curb outside of the grade school, Sam hugged them both good-bye—even though Ben squirmed—knowing that when he returned it would be with a wife and mother. Life as they knew it, as a family, would be altered. Hopefully, no, definitely, for the better.

"Bring us back a surprise!" Mina said.

Sam smiled. "I will." Then he turned to Ben. "Take care of your little sister. I'll call later tonight."

Ben hiked his loaded backpack higher on his scrawny shoulders. "You don't have to worry about us Dad."

Sam nodded but he was certain he'd do exactly that until the day he died. Ben waved then took his sister's hand and led her toward the front doors. Sam waited for Mina to break free, to rush back to him with a tearful, *"I don't wanna go to school!"*

But she didn't.

"Huh."

Once the kids were safely inside, Sam climbed back into his cab, checked those social sites again for good measure. It occurred to him that he hadn't checked for messages on his own new page. Maybe Harper . . . "Oh, *shit.*"

Every muscle in Sam's body tensed as he read a message from the Avenger.

She'll wreck your life, soldier.

A picture was attached. A picture of Harper and a young man in uniform. Harper didn't look much younger, but she did look carefree. The fair-haired man looked like most soldiers Sam knew who'd yet to see battle. Confident. *Naïve.* Sam assumed the soldier she was hugging was

Andrew Wilson, her former fiancé. He didn't feel jealous, just alarmed and pissed as hell that some jerk wad was taking anonymous potshots at Harper. Sam had forty minutes before he had to pick her up for the airfield. He dialed Jayce. "You up? Dressed?" he asked when the man answered. "I'm coming over."

Approximately three minutes later, Sam pulled up to a house that he knew as well as his own. Until recently, Daisy had lived here. First with Jessup. Then alone. Aside from family Sunday dinners, there'd been hundreds of random parties, barbecues, and sleepovers with his cousins. A multitude of memories welled as Sam approached the three-story Colonial Revival. Rocky and Jayce lived here now and the same warm feeling greeted Sam as soon as the door swung open.

Unfortunately, his mood was dark and foul.

"Rocky here?" Sam asked Jayce as he pushed inside.

"Already on her way to the hospital to look in on Chloe. I've got business so—"

Keyed up to his social page, Sam shoved his phone in Jayce's face. "How the *fuck* does he know I'm involved with Harper? Who the hell is this guy?"

"I've got answers," Jayce said calmly while checking out the photo. "Want some coffee?"

"No."

"I need coffee."

Jayce passed Sam his phone then moved toward the kitchen.

Sam followed, deleting the post now that Jayce had seen it. Hoping to God it had escaped Harper's notice. While pocketing his phone, he heard a weird clicking and turned to see Brewster, a dopey-looking dog with one ear up, one down, following behind, his toenails clacking on the hardwood floor. "Hey, boy," Sam managed in a civil tone, scratching the mutt's ears as they moved into the spacious kitchen.

"Sure you don't want a hit?" Jayce asked as he moved toward the coffee maker.

"Pass, but thanks." Sam glanced at his watch. "Need to pick Harper up in a half hour."

"I'll make it quick," Jayce said as he poured strong-smelling java and signaled Brewster to lie down.

Brewster curled on a braided rug.

Jayce leaned back against the counter.

Sam stood in the middle of the kitchen, arms crossed, temper spiking. His famous patience two seconds from snapping.

"The Avenger," Jayce said. "Yesterday, I located his profile page, bypassed his privacy settings and poked around." He held up a hand, warding off questions. "Explaining my methods would take time. Just know I'm good at what I do. Once I determined his identity, gathering information was relatively easy. Did some digging, read a few reports, made some inquiries."

"What have you got?"

Jayce sipped coffee then cocked his head. "The Avenger is one Edward Wilson. The father of Harper's former fiancé. Andrew was an only son. A revered son. Smart as hell—an IT whiz. Edward's retired military, former officer, a by-the-books hard-ass who took great pride in his genius son's accomplishments. The boy could do no wrong in the old man's eyes, although Edward did frown on Andrew and Harper's whirlwind affair. Edward considered her a distraction for Andrew. A pretty face with no real substance."

Sam worked his jaw. "Go on."

"From the information I've gathered and accessed, Edward Wilson blames Harper for his son's death."

"That's warped and wrong. Wilson was suffering from post-traumatic stress syndrome. He snapped and—"

"I know. I read several accounts, reached out to a couple of people in Harper's old loop. Everything supports the version of the story Harper shared with you.

Right down to Andrew being the one who broke off their engagement. But remember what I said. Edward's a hard-ass and he had that boy on a pedestal. He twisted facts every which way until he came up with a scenario that made Andrew the victim and Harper the villain. In Edward's mind Harper seduced Andrew, clouding his mind with illusions of some fairy-tale marriage, distracting him from his job, his purpose, making it difficult for him to deal with the reality of a hostile environment. He came back traumatized, and instead of sticking with him when the going got tough, Harper deserted Andrew."

"Andrew broke things off, told her he needed space."

"According to Edward, if she had really loved his son, she would've pushed to help him. Instead, she buried her head in the sand, focusing on her work. If she would have stayed close, she could have headed off his meltdown."

"Intimating she failed him." Sam narrowed his eyes. "What do you mean 'according to Edward'? Did you speak with him?"

"Hacked and read some of Harper's old e-mails."

"You can do that?"

"Comes in handy when tracking down cyberbullies."

Sam blew out a breath. "So, what? Edward's been bullying her for three years now?"

"On and off from what I could find. Tapered off a year ago then flared up again recently."

"What the hell?"

"We're talking about a father's grief. A father who lost his only son. A guy with a chip on his shoulder and rage in his heart. He needs to blame someone and it's not going to be the military he thinks so highly of or the son he worshiped."

"So Harper's his whipping post."

"I dug a little, but it seems like Harper shut down emotionally after the incident. Didn't confide in friends and coworkers about what she was feeling or going through.

But I know Edward blasted her in public more than once. She escaped his in-the-face wrath by transferring to the American branch of that PR firm. Since he's still hassling her, I'm guessing he's part, if not all, of the reason she doesn't want to return to Canada."

Sam dragged both hands down his face. "Three frickin' years."

"Some people hold grudges for a lifetime. You've got a bitter, vengeful man on your hands, Sam. Wilson can't move on so he doesn't want Harper to move on, either."

"So he keeps reminding her, blaming her. He wants her to wallow in misery. Guilt. I'm sorry for the man's loss, Jayce, but this is bullshit." Sam glanced at his watch, anxious to get to Harper. "Can you get me some stats on Edward Wilson? Where he lives? Where he hangs out? His routine?"

Jayce—ever calm—caught Sam's troubled gaze. "Thinking of paying him a visit?"

"This has to stop."

"Agreed. You take Harper to Vegas. Do your thing with her and the Cupcake Lovers. I'll handle Edward."

"Why you?"

"Given my background in law enforcement, let's just say I'm experienced at making bad men see the error of their ways."

Sam raised a brow. "I appreciate the offer, Jayce, but when Edward posted that message to me, he opened the door for confrontation. I can't manage face-to-face right now, but I can make a call. If that doesn't do it, we'll take it from there."

Jayce nodded, took out his phone. "I'll forward Edward's cell number, but before you call, let me give you some pointers that'll add punch to your cease and desist."

"By the way," Sam asked, "how *did* Edward know about Harper and me? I haven't posted anything about us online. Neither has she."

"The old fox has been keeping tabs on her. I'm not the only PI in this state."

That would account for the feeling of "being watched." Sam envisioned a man staked out somewhere on Harper's property with a freaking pair of binoculars. Following them into town, maybe sitting two tables away when they'd had lunch at the Shack, chowing on apple pie and freaking *spying* on Harper and Sam then reporting back to Wilson.

Fury singed the last of Sam's patience.

"Before you blow a gasket, I already *reasoned* with the dick in question. He's out of the picture."

Sam dragged a hand through his hair, his blood pressure easing as he saved Edward's phone number to contacts. "Never knew you could be so scary, Bello."

Jayce just smiled.

THIRTY-ONE

Seven hours and forty-nine minutes after taking off from Starlight Airfield and making one pit stop in Kansas City, Nash and his copilot, Tripp, landed the charter jet at Henderson Executive, a small corporate airport just minutes from the Las Vegas Strip. The flight had been smooth and the attending Cupcake Lovers a delight.

Conversation, mimosas, and snacks had flowed. A delicious in-flight meal had been served. Their flight attendant, Bella, had been a doll. All in all, a fantastic experience for everyone involved, including Harper. She'd been anxiety-free all day and so far everything was going according to plan. She felt calm and in control with flashes of giddy excitement. She was getting married tonight and tomorrow the Cupcake Lovers would appear on *Brice and Kaylee— Live*! A personal milestone and a professional coup. Her mind kept spinning what ifs, but they were all good. Mostly all good. Which was a whole lot better than mostly bad.

She attributed part of her optimism to steeling her spine. Last night she'd broken her personal policy of not engaging with Edward Wilson. Engaging only fanned the flames of his vengeance. Distance and silence had long been Harper's defense of choice. It had worked for a while, but now that he was on the warpath again, she knew she had to change tactics. His taunts had to end. Maybe he couldn't forget or forgive but he had to leave Harper in peace. As much as she'd been fighting it, she'd fallen in love with Sam. A night of bowling with him and the kids had cinched her tender feelings. They'd stripped away the last layer of armor shielding her heart. She was vulnerable, but instead of feeling scared, she felt emboldened. She didn't want Edward's hatred tainting her and Sam's relationship. And she sure as hell didn't want his misery to touch Ben and Mina in any way.

She knew Edward wouldn't listen to reason if she called. He'd interrupt and manipulate the conversation.

She'd opted to write him a letter. It had taken two hours to compose a heartfelt but adamant e-mail. Two hours to put her feelings into words. Words that would have the desired impact.

I know how much you loved Andrew. I loved him, too.

She'd questioned the true depth of her feelings—egged on by Edward and her own guilt—for far too long. She'd fallen into an abyss of doubt, unable to grab hold of substantial memories. Good memories. She'd forgotten how special those first months with Andrew had been. Yes, there had been a whirlwind romance. Yes, she'd been over-the-moon obsessed with planning the perfect fairy-tale wedding for their perfect marriage. And yes, she'd been stunned by the negative transformation of Andrew, unbalanced by his rejection, at a loss for dealing with his somber mood and anger. She hadn't understood the exact nature of his suffering because he'd kept that suffering to himself. To protect her. Andrew never wanted to hurt her. He set her free because he loved her.

And she'd floundered because she loved him. True, genuine bone-deep love.

Sitting at her desk in her bedroom, glancing out the same window Mary Rothwell had dogged day after day, Harper suddenly felt a sense of closure that had eluded the heartbroken World War II bride. Unlike with Captain Joseph Rothwell, Harper knew for certain Andrew wouldn't be coming back. Turning back time wasn't within her power, but cherishing the love they'd shared and honoring that love by embracing the good in life was. In that moment, she swore she felt Andrew hug her. Or maybe it was Mary.

You can't punish me anymore, Edward, because I'm done punishing myself. Andrew will always hold a special place in my heart, but my heart is big enough to make room for more special. I deserve special. Andrew said so once. It just took me a while to remember and believe.

Her finger had hovered briefly over the send button. Had she made a sound and reasonable case? Did she believe what she'd written with her whole heart and soul?
Yes.
Teary-eyed and light-headed with serenity, Harper had sent the e-mail and slept through the night, dreaming first of Andrew and then of Sam. Sweet, hopeful dreams.
As of this morning, Edward had yet to reply to Harper's letter. If she was lucky, she'd never hear from him again. That thought had buoyed her all through the morning.
That, and the presence of Sam.
Harper hadn't told him about Edward or the letter. She was enormously proud that she'd handled that crisis on her own. She was determined to move on. Excited to move on.
With Sam McCloud.
The man was a rock, a calming force, and today he'd been especially attentive. He'd touched her endlessly—her hand, her elbow, her shoulder, the small of her back, her thigh, her knee. Not in a sexual way, but in a caring way. Letting her know he was there, that she was safe. Gentle touches and long glances, infusing her with hope and calm.

There would be no calamities, no snafus, no atrocities. They were flying to Vegas and they were going to have *fun*.

Daisy must have said so at least a dozen times.

Per Harper's prearrangements, a limousine was waiting, and soon after landing everyone, sans the crew, climbed into the stretch transport. Sam squeezed in next to Harper, casually draping his arm across the seat behind her, speaking amiably with the only other two men who'd come along—Vincent, Daisy's beau, and Helen's husband, Daniel. While they'd discussed the desert landscape and climate, Harper checked in with the production crew for *Brice and Kaylee*.

Minutes later they were sailing up the Las Vegas Strip and the senior Cupcake Lovers—Daisy, Helen, Ethel, and Judy—were gawking and oohing at the dazzling assortment of casinos and entertainment resorts. Some classic, some new. Some classy, some themed. A unique blend of opulence and cheese. So different from Norman Rockwell Sugar Creek.

"Vegas," Daisy said. "Viva Las Vegas. Gambling capital of the world. *Hellooooo*, Sin City!"

Harper smiled as the animated woman pumped her bony fist in the air. Her exuberance was contagious and her appearance endearing. She'd bleached her tight blue curls white, which would have looked natural for her age if not for the way those curls sparkled. She'd sprayed her hair with some sort of iridescent glitter. Harper wouldn't be surprised if she soon discovered colorful feather clip-ons or Day-Glo extensions. She was *that* adventurous. And at this moment, she was in her glory.

Harper tried to channel Daisy's wonder. She'd spent the last three years in the land of hard knocks and high hopes. Her experiences in Hollywood ranged from shocking to magical to absurd. Somewhere along the way she'd grown numb to it all—the glitz and the glam, the fanciful and fun. Right this minute Daisy and friends exuded mind-tripping glee. And all because of palm trees, dancing fountains, and casinos that resembled movie sets. A sphinx and a pyramid, a castle, the Big Apple, and the Eiffel Tower. At any other time Harper would have been oblivious, more interested in scrolling her phone apps—Twitter, TMZ— but today she focused on the Cupcake Lovers and the Strip. She tried very hard to see Sin City through Daisy's eyes. A blip of glee bubbled then welled. Rainbows and starshine ripped through three years of gloom.

Hellooooo, happy!

Harper felt the weight of Sam's stare, turned and noted a slight crook of his lips. "What?"

"Just enjoying that smile."

She beamed a little more. "Me, too."

Checking into the hotel would have gone faster if the senior Cupcake Lovers hadn't been distracted by the bells and whistles of their festive surroundings. Sam refrained from hurrying the ladies along, but damn, he was itching to get to his room. He needed to touch base with Jayce. In private.

"It's the largest permanent big top in the world," Daisy said as they cut through the main casino floor—the ringing, whirring, and blipping of various slot machines ramping the already chaotic noise level. "I looked it up on the computer."

"So did we," Helen said as she craned her head left and right and then up. "Daniel and I are looking forward to the featured circus acts!"

"Ethel and I have our hearts set on the penny slots," Judy said.

"If you get bored with that," Daisy said, "there's a midway with carnival games."

"And that's just in this one casino," Helen said as they passed several shops and restaurants. "The time change bought us three extra hours, still . . . so much to experience in two days' time."

"That's why you have me," said the young man who'd greeted them at the front entrance. "I'll get you every-where you want to go, just give me a list of the places you most want to see." His name was Sebastian. Harper had introduced him as a production assistant for *Brice and Kaylee.* He'd been assigned to act as liaison and tour guide. Sam was thankful for that, knowing the older ladies and gents would be in good hands while Sam and Harper stole away for the evening.

When they finally made it to the hotel lobby, Harper and Sebastian helped to expedite matters. Bellmen loaded luggage carts and led the way. Their rooms were in the newer tower. Harper had arranged for her and Sam to have adjoining rooms—for appearances' sake. Once inside their respective rooms, Sam tipped the doorman then opened the adjoining door on cue with Harper.

She flew into his arms. "I've been wanting to kiss you for nine hours."

Holding her close, Sam brushed his mouth over hers, and groaned when she took the kiss deeper. She tasted of coffee and cookies. She felt like a dream. Pulling away wasn't easy. "Helluva time to get me worked up, Slick. A limo's picking us up in ninety minutes and I've got errands to run."

She sighed. "That's okay. I want to take a shower, change my clothes. You kept the arrangements simple, right?"

"Per your request."

"It seems silly to do anything elaborate. It's just the two of us and, well, it is a business arrangement."

He smoothed her glossy waves off her gorgeous face and searched those sultry blue eyes. "Is it?"

"Isn't it?"

Her phone chimed and so did his.

"It's Tasha," she said. "Probably just arrived and—"

"Take it," Sam said. "I've got the kids here," he lied. It was Jayce.

Harper answered her phone and backed into her own room, smiling at Sam as she closed the door.

He closed his door, as well, moved toward the window and kept his voice low. "I got your text, Jayce, but I didn't see it until I landed. Are you positive Wilson booked a flight?"

"Figured I'd keep tabs on him over the next couple of weeks. Saw the booking listed on his credit card account."

"You can . . . ? Never mind. He booked the flight to Vegas after I spoke with him?"

"Before. Yesterday. Mind you, Harper tweeted and posted late Saturday regarding the Cupcake Lovers' television appearance. She made it clear she'd be with them in an official capacity." Jayce paused and Sam stewed. "Forgoing any delays with the Midwestern layover," Jayce continued, "Wilson will arrive in Vegas around midnight. Guess he didn't take your cease and desist seriously."

"Guess not." And Sam had been damned clear on the matter. "Wilson didn't apologize or back down. Said I should be grateful he'd warned me—one soldier to another—about Harper. I cut him off when he started listing her faults. The man's fixated."

"Obviously. So how did it end exactly?"

"With me listing some of the threats you suggested and him saying he heard me loud and clear."

"Hearing and listening," Jayce said. "Two different things."

"What the hell?"

"He doesn't want her to be happy, Sam. He sure as hell doesn't want her living happily ever after with another soldier while his son's dead in the ground."

"He'll get here too late to interfere with the ceremony."

"But not too late to make a scene. To reignite the story of his son's death, implicate Harper, stir up a shitstorm, get people talking and wondering and scrutinizing her character. Via national television."

Sam shoved a hand through his hair. "The talk show. It's live. Shit."

"I can catch a flight," Jayce said. "Be there tomorrow morning, before the show."

"No. I've got this."

"Sure?"

"Yeah."

"Sam. You need to give Harper a heads-up about Wilson."

"I know." He glanced at their adjoining doors, thought about her smiling face. "But not yet. She's been under a lot of stress, but not today. Today she's happy. I'd like to sustain that for the night at least."

"Considering your plans for the evening, I don't blame you. And, though you blindsided me with this eloping thing, let me be the first to say congratulations, Sam."

"Thanks. I don't expect everyone to be as accepting."

"Then you don't know your friends and family."

"There are extenuating circumstances."

"That may or may not come to light. I know. But I've seen you two together. It's not just about a green card."

Considering Sam hadn't specifically mentioned Harper's impending deportation . . . "Impressive deducing."

"Coupled with intuition. Wilson's a bully with a grudge," Jayce added. "You're going to have to make good on some of those threats, Sam."

"Trust me," Sam said. "That won't be a problem."

THIRTY-TWO

She didn't want special. She wanted simple. Special was fairy-tale and wishful thinking. Special was getting all excited and stupid about the perfect gown, the perfect flowers, the perfect venue. Harper had been down that road. Wanting to disconnect from the past, she'd left the details of this ceremony to Sam and she'd emphasized simple.

That had been before she'd written the letter to Edward. Before she'd found closure with Andrew. Now that she was less than a half hour away from taking her vows with Sam, Harper was having second thoughts. She wanted special. Not elaborate, just meaningful. She wished she had shopped for a new dress. Something specifically for this moment. Something specifically for Sam. If she had more time, she'd rush out now. Instead she devoted extra effort to her makeup and hair.

She applied smoky shadows to her eyes with an extra layer of ebony mascara. Instead of her signature red lipstick, she opted for rosy pink with a hint of gloss. She arranged her thick waves into a combination high bun and low-loose chignon. She thought about calling Daisy and asking if she could borrow her iridescent hair spray. But that would mean tipping Daisy off to the secret nuptials. Shimmery blush would have to do.

Wearing her blue chenille robe she padded to the closet where she'd hung the clothes she'd brought along. Her fingers skimmed three dresses, pausing on the lace and silk of a pale yellow shift, not fancy, but classy. The more elegant portion of her wardrobe was still at her apartment in L.A. A good number of Harper's possessions were still in L.A. She'd packed for a short getaway, intending to conquer her phobia in the seclusion of Sugar Creek, thinking she'd be back on the West Coast, back at the firm, in a matter of weeks.

Little had she known.

Her rent was paid through the first of August, but she'd have to go back before then to pack everything up. She'd sell the furniture, ship her personal belongings to Sugar Creek. It would involve time away from Sam and the kids. Time alone in L.A. where she'd possibly run into past clients and coworkers, where she'd have to face the crowds and chaos and potential violent outbursts that had sent her running in the first place. She felt a bite of anxiety and quickly chased it away. She'd worry about all that later. Now, this blessed, magical minute, she had a wedding to prepare for.

Just as she reached for the yellow dress, Sam knocked on the adjoining door. He was a few minutes early, but she didn't care. She was anxious to see him. She hoped he liked her hair.

She opened the door and faltered back a step, her palm pressed to her pounding chest. "Wow."

"Wow, good? Or wow, what were you thinking?"

"Wow, good. Wow, gorgeous." Harper drank in the sight of Sam in a suit. The stylish charcoal-gray jacket and matching pants. The pristine shirt and perfectly knotted tie. "Holy hell, Rambo. You're smoking hot."

His mouth crooked into a sexy grin. "I was just thinking the same about you, Slick. I didn't believe it was possible for you to look more beautiful than you do on a daily basis. You're stunning."

Harper flushed, lifting one hand to her coiled hair and another to the lapel of her robe. "That's sweet. Thank you, Sam." She'd never felt more awkward. He looked every bit a groom, whereas she . . . "I just need to get dressed." *Damn, damn, damn.*

"About that." Sam produced a garment bag. "I hope you don't mind. I know you asked for simple. I know you're in a business frame of mind, but you're a bride tonight, Harper. My bride. I wanted you to have something unique."

Heart threatening to burst through her chest, Harper grabbed the garment bag and fell back into her room. She hooked the hanger over the bathroom door, whizzed down the zipper, and fought back tears as she revealed a beautiful white dress. A strapless, shapely confection of gentle folds and sheer organza and iridescent lace. A simple yet elegant dress that would fall mid-shin. Stylish and lovely.

And worthy of a bride.

"Oh, Sam." She stared at the dress, enchanted by its beauty, stunned by his thoughtfulness.

"I hope I did okay. I ordered ahead of time online from a boutique here in Vegas. I raided your closet at home to pinpoint your dress and shoe size."

"Shoes?"

Harper turned and saw Sam holding up a pair of four-inch peekaboo pumps. "The sales attendant advised beige over white. All I know is that they're sexy and I'd love to see you in them."

Scarcely able to breathe Harper rushed forward and snatched the heels from Sam's hands. "You have to leave while I dress," she squeaked out.

"Hell, honey," he said with an ornery sparkle in his eyes. "I was looking forward to watching."

"But if you stay, you'll say or do something else that will push me over the edge."

His shoulders tensed.

"I don't want to cry, Sam." She fanned her face and blinked her burning eyes. "The dress, the shoes, you. It's all so . . . *special*."

He smiled then and backed into his room. "You've got ten minutes, Slick. Let me know if you need any help with that zipper."

Daisy had experienced some spine-tingling thrills in her lifetime, especially over these last few years, after vowing to live life to the fullest.

Taking Rocky's snowmobile for a joyride had been a thrill—until she'd crashed.

Zooming down a steep hill on a borrowed bicycle had been a thrill—until she'd crashed.

Speeding down the highway in her Caddy with the top down, while encouraging Chloe to act out in sort of a Thelma and Louise moment had been a thrill—until they'd gotten busted by a pinhead cop.

Starting her own business, tubing down the creek, moving in with her man friend, dyeing her hair crazy colors—all thrilling.

But nothing matched the adrenaline-charged feeling of walking toward the Graceland Wedding Chapel alongside the man who made her feel like a princess. Vincent had booked a limo to drive them from hotel to chapel—her second limo ride in one day. He'd bought her a pretty bouquet, too—daisies and petunias. He'd even ditched his plaid shirt and suspenders in favor of a white shirt and red bow tie. Vincent didn't imbibe, but champagne came with the limo so he'd shared a glass with Daisy to toast their Vegas adventure. She'd given him such short notice and yet he'd taken care of everything—the marriage license, the wedding package, the rings.

Now they were entering the little white chapel with the cobblestoned steeple and Daisy felt like she'd grabbed onto a live wire. Every particle of her old body sizzled and tingled, and since Vincent was that live wire, she held on all the tighter.

Bring it on!

He paused at the door. "Are you sure about this, Petunia?"

"I'm sure, Speedy."

"I'm sorry your daughter's out of town. Of all the rotten timing."

Daisy had swallowed her pride and called Kelly as soon as she'd settled into her hotel room. She thought they could at least meet for lunch. Vincent had encouraged Daisy to invite Kelly to the ceremony, saying maybe it would help to mend their broken bridge. Daisy doubted that but she *was* hoping for lunch. But instead of Kelly, a roommate had answered the phone, telling Daisy that Kelly was on a southwestern road trip with friends. Daisy had been disappointed, but not crushed. She hadn't been on easy terms with her daughter for years. Daisy was determined to fix that. Someday.

"Are you sure you don't want to invite Nash? He could walk you down the aisle."

"I've got Elvis for that and besides Nash is in his gambling glory. Some sort of poker tournament."

"There's still time to call your friends. I'm sure if you invited them—"

"Normally I enjoy big shindigs and I know that's what's on your mind. Awfully sweet of you, Vincent, but I'd like this to be our special moment. We can celebrate with the girls later after we join them for that magic show."

Vincent's bushy beard split with a humongous smile. "I was hoping you'd say that."

Daisy gave his chunky arm a squeeze. "I can't remember the last time I was this ecstatic and it's not just because Elvis is in the building. It's because I'm marrying you."

Vincent framed her face and planted a mushy kiss on her lips.

Since he normally didn't show affection in public, Daisy realized that his excitement matched hers. For the life of her, she didn't know why her cheeks felt hot. She stifled a giggle. "You got sparkles on your lips." She had applied a glittery lipstick to match her sparkly hair.

"I'll wipe them off after," he said. "I felt a little plain next to you and your snazzy silver jumpsuit. Now I don't."

Her faulty heart fluttered, and after a few preliminary whatcha-ma-whos, they moved into the interior chapel and the show began.

Daisy squealed a little as Elvis introduced himself and then complimented her jumpsuit, which wasn't nearly as razzly-dazzly as his. Music kicked in and the King sang "Viva Las Vegas" as he escorted Daisy down the aisle. She swiveled her hips a little—like Elvis—ignoring the ache in her joints and adding a jig. Glancing over her shoulder she saw Vincent swiveling and jigging right behind.

Upon reaching the altar, Elvis handed her over to Vincent and then serenaded them with two songs. At one point, Daisy wasn't sure she could stand it—all the hip swivels and sexy lip twitches—Vincent's, not Elvis's. Before she knew it they were exchanging vows, and since they'd requested the Elvis vows, it made her grin ear to ear.

"You'll never know 'Heartbreak Hotel,'" Vincent said.

"I'll never step on your 'Blue Suede Shoes,'" Daisy said.

"I'm your 'Hunk of Burnin' Love,'" Vincent growled, followed by his best lip twitch yet.

They were pronounced man and wife and Daisy got another one of those public smooches.

Because Vincent was such a quiet, grounded man, she marveled that he'd not only indulged her wish to be married by Elvis, he'd been better than a good sport, playing along to the max. Unlike her first wedding, *this* wedding had been *fun*. *Vincent* was *fun*.

"I'm the happiest woman in the world," she said.

"I'm the luckiest man in the world." His old eyes sparkled. "Let's go celebrate, Mrs. Daisy Petunia Redding."

"I now pronounce you man and wife." The minster smiled. "You may now kiss the bride."

Harper's breath stalled as Sam gently cupped her cheeks and graced her with the most memorable kiss of her life. Sweet and spicy and infused with love. It shot through her body like wildfire, igniting every nerve, revving all her senses. She gazed up into his eyes, heart in throat. She wanted to say, *I love you, Sam*. But her brain cells had melted along with her knees and she couldn't seem to form a coherent sentence.

Sam just smiled.

She was glad he didn't prompt her by saying the words first because that might have caused her to blurt, *I love you, too*. She didn't want it to sound like an automatic or courteous response. She wanted to say it first. Why wouldn't the words come?

Sam kissed the back of her hand and turned to thank the minister.

Gripping her lovely bouquet, Harper took in the beautiful surroundings one last time. She memorized every detail. The stone chapel with the stained-glass windows. Every plank of the two-story-high wooden terrace. The ceremony had taken place outside under an old-fashioned white gazebo decorated with twinkly white lights. Palm trees swayed in the soft, hot breeze. Early evening and the sky was a brilliant blue, the sun still shining, cheering Harper's already beaming mood.

The chapel had provided witnesses. The music had been traditional, appealing to Harper's fairy-tale sensibilities.

The minister had been warm and jovial and had kept the service brief but meaningful.

Harper admired her platinum wedding band embedded with four small diamonds. Understated elegance. This marriage was supposed to be a business arrangement and yet Sam had approached every detail as though it were a labor of love.

She could scarcely breathe.

She wanted to keep her beautiful rose bouquet forever and she secretly rejoiced when they took a few photos. She would have thought Sam camera shy. If he was, he sucked it up for her. He did everything he could to make their simple wedding special.

She'd never been so touched or felt so cherished.

Sam moved in beside her and handed her a flute of champagne. "Part of the package," he said with a teasing roll of the eyes. "We get to keep the glasses."

Harper grinned and clinked her flute to his. Again the words stuck.

"To us," he said. "To happy." Simple. *Special*. They sipped and then Sam asked, "How do you feel?"

Words bumped past the lump in her throat. "On top of the world."

"Funny you should say that."

Sam didn't think of himself as a romantic man, but there was something about Harper—the Harper he'd come to know—that inspired romantic gestures. Interesting, considering their relationship had started out as a purely sexual affair—emphasis on fast and dirty.

She'd kept him thinking and guessing and fascinated every step of the way. She twisted him up, tried his patience, mangled his perceptions.

Everything had come naturally with Paula.

Nothing came easily with Harper.

It was different territory and, God help him, Sam liked

a challenge. Looking beyond, looking deeper, he was determined to make Harper happy. Therein lay the path to his own joy.

He'd reflected on everything she'd ever shared and everything he'd had to surmise. He surmised that, deep down, even though she didn't think she deserved it, Harper yearned for a traditional wedding. The kind of wedding most girls dream of. The hearts-and-flowers wedding he'd shared with Paula. The fairy-tale event Harper had planned but never shared with Andrew.

So Sam had improvised.

The dress, the shoes, the flowers, the venue.

He wanted to make her smile. He wanted to gift her with a hearts-and-flowers memory. This moment would be the launching point of their life together and, even if they didn't make it past the two-year green card mark, Sam wanted this to be a day she'd never forget.

He knew she'd been overwhelmed and touched and he'd sworn she'd been on the verge of telling him that she loved him. Something held her back and that was okay, because he felt it, but Christ, it would be nice to hear. He would have declared his own feelings, but he sensed she wasn't ready to hear them, so he'd pulled back. *No rush*, he'd told her. *No pressure. No expectations.* He'd promised to take it slow.

Slow, he'd thought as they'd kissed under the gazebo, just might kill him.

Beyond the romantic ceremony, he'd made reservations for dinner at the Top of the World, a restaurant suspended eight hundred feet above Las Vegas, an award-winning restaurant with unparalleled views of the city. The ambience, the food, the wine—all top-notch. The only thing missing was Harper's smile.

"Where did I go wrong?" Sam asked as he sliced into his sizzling center-cut filet mignon.

Harper looked up from her Mediterranean sea bass. "What do you mean?"

"You're awfully somber. Would you have preferred to join the gang for dinner and a show? I know how committed you are to your job and—"

"Oh, no, Sam. It's not that at all. The CLs are in good hands with Sebastian." She smiled a little, reached over and touched his hand. "I'm exactly where I want to be tonight. With you. It's just . . . There's something I need to tell you."

Sam set aside his knife. There was something he needed to tell her, too, and he'd been wrestling all evening with the when and where. Some time after dinner, he'd thought, not during, but she'd opened the door for some sort of serious conversation, so he'd see where she led this and take it from there.

She leaned back in her chair, focused back on her plate and sighed. "This is horrible timing on my part. I don't want to ruin dinner. I don't want to ruin today." She met his gaze, spearing his heart with affection. "Everything's so perfect."

"The only way you could ruin today, honey, is by holding back whatever's bothering you. Just say it so we can fix it."

"*We*. That sounds nice."

"Yes, it does."

Blowing out a breath, she gestured to him to continue eating then picked up her own fork. "It's not a bad thing. It was, but I fixed it. I think I fixed it anyway. I wasn't going to tell you because I didn't want to worry you, and then you made today so incredible, so perfect, except while riding up in the elevator I realized it isn't perfect because I'm withholding something from you and that isn't fair because, although I think I fixed it, maybe I didn't. And what if it pops up in the future, what if it gets worse, what if . . ."

"Harper." Now Sam reached across the table and touched her. "Breathe."

"Right." She nodded, tasted her sea bass, smiled. "It's

delicious," she said, then sipped her Chablis. She rolled back her beautiful bare shoulders and breathed. "There's a man. Edward Wilson. Andrew's father."

Sam met her gaze and she paused.

"What?" she asked.

"I know about Edward."

She blinked and Sam decided to cut to the chase. "I was going to broach the subject later tonight, but what the hell. Let's address the bullshit so we can get back to perfect."

As calmly and as succinctly as possible, Sam shared how he'd learned about Edward's taunting post two days prior from Rocky and Rae, the message he himself had received from the bastard, and how Sam had handled it from there. To her credit, Harper didn't freak out or lash out nor did she interrupt until he got to the part where Sam told her Jayce provided him with Edward's cell number.

"Wait a minute," she said. "Don't tell me you called Edward."

"Spoke with him this morning."

Wide-eyed, she palmed her forehead. "I . . . What did you say? What did he say?"

Sam gave her the rundown of the discussion, watching her every expression. "I can't tell if you're angry or relieved that I addressed the situation. I took the lead without asking for your input. I'm sorry about that, Harper, but the way it all went down . . ."

"It's okay. To be honest I don't know how I feel exactly. I'm a little flattered that you played the knight in shining armor and a little disturbed that you considered me a damsel in distress. I know I've been unreliable lately, shaky, but I need you to know that I'm capable of fighting my own battles."

She told him about the letter she'd written and e-mailed. "When I hit the send button," she said, "I felt an exhilarating sense of closure. I put the past in perspective and took control of my future. I haven't heard back from Edward. I'm hoping I finally got through to him. Knowing you spoke with him as well . . ." She smiled now, that happy smile that jerked Sam's heart every which way. "Surely he wouldn't mess with Rambo and now that I'm Mrs. Rambo . . ." Her smile faltered. "What?"

"This is where it gets tricky."

THIRTY-THREE

Something clicked inside of Harper when Sam told her Edward was en route to Vegas. It wasn't panic. It wasn't fury. More like a dangerous calm. It hummed along her veins, kicking her crisis-solving mentality into gear, igniting her penchant for saving the day. That click would be Edward Wilson's downfall.

"Are you all right?" Sam asked when he finished laying out everything he knew and everything he and Jayce had projected.

"I'm fine." She sipped her wine then reached for her purse. "I'm going to step into the foyer. I need to make a phone call."

"I'll come with you." Sam motioned to their waiter, asking him to keep their food warm, then he escorted Harper out of the main restaurant.

She didn't protest. In fact, she reconsidered her strategy, deciding to share her plan with Sam before putting it into action. After all, now they were a *we*.

The foyer was crowded with tourists waiting for their chance to move inside and dine. Several people noted Harper's and Sam's attire, his boutonniere, and offered their congratulations. Harper flashed her practiced PR smile as she thanked them. Not that she wasn't thrilled to be Mrs. Sam McCloud, but right now she was fixated on a menace named Wilson.

Finding privacy was an effort but Sam located a space and Harper talked fast and just a notch above a whisper.

"Obviously, Edward wants to crush me. He wants to ruin my relationship with you. He wants to damage my professional reputation. He wants me to return to Canada with my tail tucked between my legs so he can continue to beat me up as a way of making himself feel better. None of that is going to happen."

Sam slid his hands in his pockets. "Go on."

"I agree with you and Jayce. I think Edward means to make a scene during the show. Mind you, you can't attend without a ticket and seating is limited."

"Maybe he snagged one," Sam said. "Or maybe he plans on crashing. You said the show is shooting from a different casino every day this week, right? And that tomorrow's shoot, the one taking place here, will be poolside. Outdoors. We're talking an open environment as opposed to a controlled showroom. Easier to slip past security."

Harper nodded. "Knowing Edward, I'm sure he has a plan. Let's assume he gets in, gets close. If he wants to hurt me, what better way to stir up gossip and speculation regarding my character than by accusing me of ruining his son's life, a traumatized solider, no less, on national television. Brice and Kaylee always take questions from the audience. Someone screens those questions ahead of time. Since the Cupcake Lovers' mission is to support soldiers, all Edward has to do is mention his military background along with his son's, following up with some bogus harmless question for the club. That's gold. I'm pretty sure he'd be selected and given his few seconds of fame. If not, he could always rush the stage during the cupcake segment and shoot his verbal bullets as rapidly as possible before security whisked him away. If the show were taped instead of live, we'd have more options. But it is what it is, so here's what we're going to do.

"I'm going to call Val, right now, and alert her of the potential threat. I'm going to advise that we alert hotel security and that they monitor incoming guests. Head Edward off before he gets poolside, before he takes his seat or slithers into the wings waiting for his chance. Whatever his plan is—preempt it, and detain him until after the show is over."

"A proactive and wise plan," Sam said.

"We can provide the security officers with a photo of Edward for easier verification," Harper said. "And I'll print out some of his past taunting e-mails so Val has proof that a true threat exists. I'll make it clear that it's a personal vendetta against me. That Edward's been stalking me, and that the private detective I hired to keep tabs on him—a slight spin on the truth—alerted me that Edward's en route to Vegas. They can check the passenger manifest to verify. Val won't want to risk an outburst."

"Not even for spiked ratings?"

"Not even. Because, like me, she'll spin scenarios. What if Edward sought revenge in another way? A more violent way? What if he pulled a gun in a public venue, holding everyone hostage as he made his speech to the cameras? What if he threatened the Cupcake Lovers, *you*, to get to me? What if he lost it and fired that gun? Val won't risk any of that. She won't risk lives. Not even for a media boost."

Harper placed a hand to her heart, surprised by her calm. A week ago and that string of what ifs would have sparked a panic attack. Instead she was intent on waylaying a personal crisis with the same focused determination she'd apply to any one of her clients.

She felt another click, a shift in her makeup. She'd been sabotaging her own happiness for more than three years, shoving down her needs, her desires, putting everyone else's well-being and contentment ahead of her own. If there was a time to pull a Daisy, to come out of her shell and to live life on her own terms, that moment was now.

Sam touched her waist, urged her closer. He searched her eyes and he smiled. "You're right. You can fight your own battles. That makes me enormously happy. But I have a favor to ask. Let me handle Edward on my own."

His request knocked her off balance. "But—"

"Hear me out. I had thoughts similar to yours about alerting security, but why drag Val into it?"

"Professional courtesy plus I feel it would be safer for all concerned."

"Understood, but surely she'd inform other members of the production crew. Maybe even the cast. What if it leaked to Daisy and the other seniors? Why put everyone on pins and needles? Why tempt hysteria? Here's another angle to consider. What if Val eliminates the risk completely by canceling the Cupcake Lovers and pulling in a last-minute substitute? Personally, I don't care, but the ladies would."

Harper frowned. "I don't think Val would do that."

"But she might."

Harper pondered and nodded. "She might."

"Let me handle it."

Harper wet her lips, shifted her weight. The thought of Sam in some sort of personal scuffle with Edward made her uneasy.

"If it will make you feel better, Jayce offered to fly out. He can be here in the morning, before the show."

Jayce was former NYPD. Jayce had a dual golden boy/ tough guy reputation. Between him and Sam, a former marine and tough guy in his own right, Harper could easily see them defusing the situation. "Not that I don't have faith in your bad boy abilities, Rambo, but yes, that would make me feel better."

Sam nabbed his phone, sent a quick text, then pulled

Harper against his strong and oh-so-capable body. He nuzzled her ear. "It'll be all right, Slick."

"Absolutely." She envisioned a positive outcome and played it over and over in her mind. "Giving up control isn't easy, but I trust you, Sam."

"I'm glad." He dropped his forehead to hers. "Now. How do we get back to perfect?"

Sam was impressed by the way Harper had handled the news about Edward. The way she'd devised a sound and wise plan—even though he'd asked her to revise it. He was touched that she trusted him to handle the situation and that she'd directed all her energy to a positive outcome. Her calm demeanor overall had been a surprise and his heart had swelled when she suggested they return to the restaurant to finish their meal. She'd even been game for dessert.

It was as if she'd put the situation with Edward into perspective, knowing there was nothing more to be done about it tonight. Knowing there was no advantage to discussing it to death.

She directed the conversation toward the kids, how and when they should break the news about the marriage, how and when to handle the move from his house to hers. They talked about the Cupcake Lovers, and Harper told Sam about the first time she'd heard the sad tale of Mary Rothwell and how she sometimes felt Mary's spirit and that she thought she was happier these days, less lonely. Sam liked to believe that was true even though he didn't actually believe Mary's spirit lingered. He told Harper about the upgrades he'd researched for his furniture-making Web site and they discussed Harper's work on Rae's behalf, promoting children's programs and charities, and how she'd like to throw more muscle behind those efforts.

Conversation flowed along with great food, one bottle

of very expensive wine, and a panoramic view of the vibrant sunset and glittering vista. Sam marveled how quickly and expertly Harper finessed their evening back to perfect. For the first time, he seriously considered the work she'd done for her past clients. He knew without a doubt that she'd been amazing. He couldn't fathom how the firm could so easily cut her loose, but he was morbidly happy that they had because now Harper was his to cherish. Ben and Mina, the Cupcake Lovers, and Rae's charities would benefit from her warm and vibrant spirit. Hollywood's loss was Sugar Creek's gain.

Sam signaled the waiter for their check and Harper excused herself to go to the ladies' room. Sam watched her go, admiring her beautiful body, her confident, sexy stride. As soon as she was out of sight, his mind skipped ahead. He'd only planned up through dinner. Should he take her dancing, to a late-night show, drinks on the observation deck?

His phone blipped.

A text from Harper. NEED U NAKED.

HOW FAST?

FAST.

Sam grinned, typing, MEET ME @ ELEVATOR.

Hallelujah.

Harper had ideas of her own.

Harper contained herself until they were within the backseat of a taxicab. Then she practically crawled onto Sam's lap. She was an energized ball of tangled emotions. Sam's calm was a turn-on. His kindness was a turn-on. His let-me-handle-it confidence a massive turn-on. The latter felt a little shallow. A little too Hollywood. But she was blinded by love, so everything, every thought, every feeling, every desire, felt right.

She clutched his lapels and yanked him close for a kiss. A ravishing kiss. A hot and heavy, brain-frying kiss.

IN THE MOOD FOR LOVE 269

"Newlyweds," she heard the driver say.

She tightened her hold, deepened the kiss. Sam's tongue danced with hers, a crazy tango with him leading. He finessed her fully onto his lap, cupping her face, fanning the fire.

Harper had never climaxed while kissing, just kissing, but she swore it was possible because she was close, *so close*.

The cab stopped, and in order to pay the driver, Sam shifted, breaking the kiss, but not the heat. Harper wasn't thinking very straight but straight enough to grab her lovely bouquet and her purse that contained their souvenir flutes.

Sam whisked her from the cab and escorted her into the building. She didn't feel like she was walking as much as floating or flying. She was high on that kiss, on Sam, and on the future they'd discussed.

"If we pass any of the Cupcake Lovers along the way," Sam said as he guided her through the bustling casino, "we'll have to explain our fancy duds and the flowers."

"The magic show just started at seven-thirty and it runs two hours," Harper said. "Then Sebastian's treating them to after-dinner drinks and the Fountains of Bellagio. And I think Ethel and Judy wanted to play slots. We're fine. I'm sure we're fine." Why did her voice sound so gravelly? Why was her vision a little hazy?

Sam pulled her into an elevator, an empty elevator, where they kissed again. Seconds or a lifetime later, he finessed her down the hall then swept her into his arms, into his room. Had he just carried her over the threshold?

The door clicked shut and Sam lowered her to her feet. "I don't know what to do with you first," he said.

"Anything that involves naked would be great." She pushed his jacket off his shoulders, loosened his tie and whipped it from his neck a little too fast to be seductive. She told herself to slow down. She knew how to tease. She knew how to tempt. Right now she felt as clumsy as a virgin.

He lowered the zipper at the back of her dress, his fingers skimming her skin, igniting her senses.

She fumbled with the buttons of his shirt. She'd never fumbled before. She felt Sam smiling against her neck, kissing down her neck, over her bare shoulder. She wanted to do the same to him. Frustration welled as she struggled with the last button. Meanwhile Sam had expertly slid her dress to her hips. She yanked his shirt apart and that damned button popped.

Well, hell.

Sort of mortifying. Sort of sexy.

"Wanna know what I think?" Sam asked as she peeled his shirt off his broad shoulders and down his muscled arms.

"Sure," she said, trailing her lips over his chest while wiggling out of her dress.

"I like the heels. Keep the heels."

Sam unclasped her strapless bra and Harper nixed her thong. She kept the heels.

"I want you flat on your back," Sam said as he seductively nudged her toward his king-sized bed. "I want to lick every inch of your body, concentrating my energy in one delicious place. I want you to come for me again and again and again. When you're weak and whimpering I'll bury myself inside you and make you beg for more."

Her heart hammered as he yanked back the satiny comforter. "I don't beg easily," she warned as she fell back on the pillow-soft mattress.

"Good." He crawled onto the bed—all panther like and predatory—parted her legs, and lowered his head.

His mouth claimed her heat and within seconds Harper was whimpering, drowning in euphoric sensations. She exploded with a climax. So fast, so intense. Her body quivered and ached for more. *Take me,* her mind whispered. But she refused to beg. She wanted to pleasure Sam with her hands and mouth. To make him crazy with lust. But she hesitated a second too long. He was kissing his way up her body, making her shiver and burn with every flick of his tongue. Her body pulsed with renewed need— building, intensifying. She gripped his shoulders, pulling him closer. She wiggled against his erection—yearning, needing.

"I want to feel you," she whispered, her heart pounding in her ears.

"You can't feel this?" Sam asked. He suckled her breast while touching her heat, his fingers stroking, working her up, working her over.

She tensed and came . . . again and again. "Want you inside me," she said, voice weak, mind spinning. "Please."

Sam stilled then shifted, his amazing body hovering over hers, his gorgeous face looking down at her with such intensity, her heart ceased to beat.

She was grateful he didn't prolong her misery, sighed when he slid inside—so hard, so thick—filling her, pleasing her. She reveled in the friction, the rocking, and pulsing. She should do more, take control, but Sam's dominance pushed all the right buttons, making her crazy with lust . . . and love. "Oh, God."

She buried her hands in his hair—*kissing, kissing, kissing*.

He changed his rhythm, the intensity. His body tensed as he broke the kiss to gaze deeply into her eyes, her soul. "Come for me, wife."

Wife.

Harper broke and shattered and soared and shattered some more.

Sam peaked, matching her fervor.

They held each other tight, continued to hold tight.

The words danced through her mind, tingled on her lips. *I love you. I love you I love you.*

Her eyes burned with the beauty of this day, this moment, and with her inability to declare her feelings.

Sam rolled to his side and pulled her against his body. He smoothed her hair from her face.

She saw it in his eyes, sensed what he was feeling, what he was about to say. She gently touched her fingers to his mouth. "Don't say it." She needed to say it first. Wanted to say it first. And yet the words froze.

"Okay," he said after a long second. "But know what I feel." He clasped her hand then pressed it to his chest.

Overwhelmed, Harper took his other hand and held it close to her breastbone. Their hearts beat hard and fast in tandem and she smiled a little as she repeated the toast she'd remember all her life. "To us. To happy."

THIRTY-FOUR

Adam was up before the butt-crack of dawn. Restful sleep had eluded him for yet another night this week. His mind wouldn't shut down. He was trying not to obsess on Peppy. On how great the sex had been with Peppy. How cute she was and how funny she could be when she wasn't in a pissy mood. Her moods changed with the wind. He chalked it up to her artistic nature. Artists—musicians, actors, painters—tended to be eccentric, right?

Adam swung his legs over the side of his bed, scrubbed a hand over his stubbled jaw, dragged his fingers through his rumpled hair. He glanced toward his window. Still dark outside. He didn't mind running in the dark and dawn would be on his heels. He needed to burn off this edginess. In addition to work, he had an important meeting this morning. He needed to be focused and sharp, not daydreaming about a pixie half-pint who possessed some wicked moves in bed. A woman who'd named her hoo-haw Lucy.

Oh, yeah. Lucy and George got along fine. Better than fine. Better than Peppy and Adam.

After their morning romp, they'd taken a morning run. Peppy had bitched throughout most of the jog, she hated running, but she was determined to transform her body. Adam didn't have a problem with Peppy's body, but Peppy did. She'd gone off on a tangent about the Ivy Vines in the world getting all the big breaks and how talent rated second to sex appeal. Adam wasn't in the business. He wasn't keen on the ins and outs of entertainment, but he knew what he heard and saw and what he liked when it came to music. Or movies, for that matter. And, yeah, okay, sometimes sex and beauty trumped impressive talent.

Peppy had talent.

He'd recognized it when he'd heard her rocking that electric guitar with Mountain Fever. He heard it here at home when she picked and strummed that fat-bodied acoustic.

Last night she'd locked herself in her bedroom, working on a new song. She was a songwriter, she'd informed him. And one of these days she'd hook a major recording artist with her original compositions. She'd been sending out demos.

"All it takes is one break," she said, flouncing toward her room with a cocky wave to Adam, saying, "Inspiration calls."

He'd thought maybe she'd emerge an hour or two later. Thought maybe they'd watch another movie. Thought maybe they'd fool around. But she'd remained behind closed doors, working on that new composition for the rest of the night. Because the walls were thin, because he'd turned down the TV, because he was curious, Adam had listened as she'd gone through the process. Different chords, different arrangements. He'd listened to a song take shape and he'd known when she'd gotten it just right. He'd gotten a weird rush.

And then there'd been silence.

Sort of like now.

Adam pulled on his running shorts, yanked a wrinkled tee over his head. He padded out of his room barefooted, needing to pee. Peppy's bedroom door was closed but he heard movement in the living room. He spied her silhouette, fully clothed and juggling two suitcases and an amplifier. She was creeping toward the front door. *What the hell?*

Adam hit the nearest lamp, flooding the room with light. "Going somewhere?"

She gasped and turned. "Scared the daylights out of me, Adam. Jeez!"

"Sorry about that."

Her face turned beet red. Her gaze bounced around the room.

He leaned against the wall, crossed his arms, and waited.

"I have to leave," she finally said. "I got a gig. A gig with a band that opens for headliners. You wouldn't know them. *Yet.* But you will. They're based in Nashville and, well, this is the break I've been waiting for. I got the call late last night. Thought I'd get an early start."

An ember of anger glowed in Adam's gut. "Without saying good-bye?"

"I left you a note. It's on the kitchen table. I'm not good at good-byes," she added when he raised a brow. She shifted, her arms no doubt cramping from the weight of her gear. "I should go."

"Hold up. I'll write you a check."

"For what?"

"A refund for your month's rent," he said while moving toward the computer desk wedged in the corner.

"I don't want a refund. That's not fair to you."

"I'll write a refund minus three days." That's how long she'd lasted.

Luke had warned him.

That girl's got wanderlust. You'll be lucky if she lasts a month.

Ha. Try three frickin' days.

"I don't want it," Peppy said, sounding angry now as he stuffed the check in her rear pocket.

The woman was broke and she was driving a clunker. How did she think she was going to make it all the way to

Nashville? Unless . . . maybe she'd borrowed some cash from her dad. *Not my problem,* Adam told himself.

"Think of it as my contribution toward your career," he said. "I heard that song last night, Peppy. You deserve your break." He relieved her of the amp and one of the suitcases. "Your guitars—"

"Already loaded in my car."

So he'd slept heavier than he'd first thought. And she'd crept around like a thief in the night, intending to skip out because, why? Oh, yeah. She sucked at good-byes. How many other people had she skipped out on in her short lifetime? He shouldn't care, but he did. He'd just been another stopping point on Peppy's journey to the top.

Temper burning, Adam opened the door, motioned her ahead. The first rays of dawn barely breached the horizon. He imagined Peppy driving all those miles . . . Imagined her clunker of a car breaking down or running out of gas. He wanted to say, *Call me when you get there,* but he didn't. He felt betrayed. It was crazy. He knew it was crazy. But he'd sworn they'd connected . . . and now this.

"Thanks," she grumbled when Adam loaded her stuff in the trunk.

"Don't forget Daisy and the Cupcake Lovers are going to be on television today," Adam said, because what the hell else was there to say? "Considering your grandpa's with her, he'd probably be pleased if you watched."

"The show airs at three our time, right? Thought I'd stop at a bar or diner. Sweet-talk the management into tuning it in."

Sweet-talk wasn't in Peppy's repertoire, not that Adam had seen anyway, but he kept that thought to himself.

She climbed behind the wheel and shut the door. She rolled down the window, which stuck halfway.

Adam rocked back on his bare heels, his mood worsening by the minute. "Drive safe and good luck."

"Break a leg."

"What?"

She shoved her shaggy bangs out of her eyes and turned the engine over. "In show biz, telling someone good luck is bad luck. You're supposed to say *break a leg*."

Adam didn't bite because he imagined her doing just that . . . after her clunker ran out of gas and she had to walk a mile, after she tripped and fell down a steep mountain shoulder. He told himself to stop worrying. She wasn't his to worry about. She was a grown woman. Impetuous, but grown, and sure as hell independent.

Peppy cleared her throat, gave Adam one of those cocky salutes then peeled out of his drive.

Her car backfired as she drove away.

George bemoaned the loss of Lucy.

Adam glared down at his crotch. "Shut up."

He stood there a moment, mystified by the intensity of the knot in his gut and the freaking ache in his chest. He barely knew Peppy but he'd felt a deep connection.

She's the one.

Yet he'd allowed her to blow out of his life without a fight. He'd done the same thing with Rocky. Stepped aside, snuffed his affections. Considering the circumstances, it had been the right thing to do. This—allowing Peppy to leave without acknowledging she'd touched his heart, without exploring the chance of something more—felt wrong.

He could call her later, but life was freaking short. He turned for the house—he'd grab his keys, chase her down—but then a series of short beeps rent the air, causing him to look back toward the road. Peppy had done a one-eighty and was headed back his way.

Heart pounding, he jogged to the end of the drive.

She pulled to a stop, staring straight ahead, both hands locked on the wheel. She looked angry and lost.

And *sweet*.

Adam braced his hands on the car-top and peered

through the partially open window. He feigned nonchalance. "Forget something?"

"Yeah." She shoved open the door, nearly knocking Adam on his ass. But then she was in his arms. Kissing him hard. Her arms locked around his neck.

His thoughts blurred. His heart sang. He kissed her back, held her tight. He had no intention of letting go.

When she eased back, he stuck close, leaning in as she fell back against the car. She palmed her forehead, looking all kinds of miserable. "Why did you have to happen now, Brody?"

"My timing's been off since the moment I met you," he said with a grin.

"I have to follow through with this Nashville gig."

"I know."

"This is my big break and, cripes . . ." She blew out a frustrated breath. "I'm nervous."

He imagined that confession dinged her pride plenty. "I've got something big brewing myself. Reaching for a dream is scary stuff."

She nodded. "I know you have a job—meeting and commitments—and this is short notice. Really short notice and crazy besides, but . . . How would you feel about a road trip?"

Adam swallowed. "You want me to come with you to Nashville?"

"Just for the drive, and maybe to help me get settled and to, you know, lend a little moral support when I audition live with the band."

"I thought this was a firm offer."

"That doesn't mean it won't backfire."

Adam wondered if anyone, including her father, had ever gone out of their way to support Peppy's dream. It wasn't her style to reach out, to admit insecurities, to ask for help. Yet here she was reaching out to Adam.

Oh, boy.

"I have an important meeting at nine. Should last an hour at most," he said. "After that I'm yours."

She didn't ask for how long and he didn't offer a time frame. He figured they'd feel their way. All he knew was that this, Peppy, felt right.

Her eyes filled with tears and his chest swelled. He blotted out everything that could go wrong and focused on what could swing around to being the best thing that ever happened to him. He hooked his arm around Peppy's waist and guided her back to the house. "Come inside. Have some coffee and a cupcake while I juggle arrangements."

Her eyebrows shot up under her bangs. "You have cupcakes?"

"Stopped by Moose-a-lotta late yesterday. Thought you might like—"

"You bought cupcakes for *me*?"

"Not a big deal," he lied while sweeping her over his threshold.

"Maybe not," she said. "But this road trip . . . I'll probably get on your nerves after the first hundred miles."

"Doubt it will take that long."

She snorted, then swiveled in front of him, planting a hand to his chest. How the hell did she manage to look vulnerable and headstrong at the same time? "I'm thinking this will be a short-lived, hot and heavy affair."

"Hot and heavy, yes. Short-lived?" He palmed her hand and squeezed. "Maybe. Maybe not."

She narrowed her eyes. "Lucy's intrigued."

"George is intrigued, too." Adam brushed a thumb over Peppy's blushing cheek. "What about you?"

She leaned into his touch, her eyes sparking with an intoxicating mix of mischief, wariness, and affection. "Definitely intrigued."

THIRTY-FIVE

Sam woke up long before dawn. His body clock was off, three hours ahead of Pacific time. Not wanting to wake Harper, he moved to a corner club chair, melting into the dark while checking e-mails and social sites on his phone.

No messages from Edward Wilson, but a new text from Jayce. Wilson had checked into a cheap hotel on the south end of town. His return flight was later tonight. Obviously he hadn't come for the sights and sounds. No R & R. In and out. One day. Just long enough to humiliate Harper, just long enough to screw with her head and career.

Sam still had trouble comprehending why the man would go to such lengths, why he'd hold a grudge for so long. Jayce hadn't uncovered anything that led him or Sam to believe that Edward would employ violence. Neither of them anticipated a mass shooting. He wasn't coming to take the lives of innocent bystanders or to forfeit his own. He was coming to tarnish Harper's.

Regardless, in a bid to cover all bases, Jayce had connected with an old friend, a former member of the NYPD who'd transferred to Vegas. Ian had agreed to conduct some off-duty surveillance. He'd be on Wilson's ass as soon as he left the hotel, tailing him and advising Jayce and Sam with his exact location. Sam had also reached out to Nash and his copilot, Tripp. Wilson wouldn't make it within ten feet of that shoot. A cop, a PI, two badass pilots, and a marine would make sure of it. Sam wasn't an arrogant man, but he was confident. And Edward had misjudged if he thought Sam wouldn't carry through on his threats. He was actually looking forward to this face-to-face. There *would* be a positive outcome.

The sheets stirred and Sam's heart jerked as he glanced toward the woman sleeping in his bed. They'd gone a couple of rounds last night. The first time had been hot and romantic. The second, hot with a dash of kink. Both times had ended in a tender embrace almost, but not quite, leading to spoken words of affection. Harper had yet to declare her feelings out loud and she'd stopped Sam short of voicing his love. He didn't know what that was about, but he let it slide, Rae's voice ringing in his ears. *"You can't force love."*

As if she sensed Sam was watching her, Harper stirred then flicked on the nightstand lamp. She blinked across the room looking rumpled, and sexy, and slightly disoriented. "What time is it?" she asked in a croaky voice.

"A little after four."

"In the morning?" She checked the bedside clock then rubbed her eyes. "Why are you up so early?"

"It's after seven in Vermont, hon."

"Oh, right. The time change. I've flown coast to coast so many times, it doesn't throw me anymore."

She bunched her pillow and pushed up a little, pulling the sheets with her to cover her bare breasts. Now that was disappointing. He would have enjoyed the show.

"I'm surprised the Cupcake Lovers stayed out so late," she went on. "When Daisy sent us that text to join them down in the bar it was, what? Eleven?"

"Almost."

"Two in the morning Vermont time. I can't believe they were still awake."

"Making the most of their two days in Sin City," Sam said. "Besides, you know Daisy. Not one to pass up a thrill."

Harper's lip twitched. "I really like that about her. So what do you think her surprise is?"

Sam set aside his phone, shrugged. "Maybe she got a tattoo."

"She wouldn't."

Sam raised a brow.

"You're right. She would. But wait. The text read: VINCENT AND I HAVE SURPRISE." She furrowed her brow. "Matching tattoos? Wouldn't that be a scream? If Daisy got inked, I wonder where and what . . . Oh, God. You don't think she'd try to show it off on live TV, do you? "

"Maybe it's something else," Sam said. "Maybe they eloped."

A slow smile spread over Harper's gorgeous face. "Wouldn't that be something? Speaking of . . ." She admired her left hand. "I don't want to take off my ring, Sam."

His pulse tripped. "I'm glad."

"When the CLs see it . . . they'll ask questions. I know we agreed to tell them after the show, but . . ."

"We'll tell them at breakfast."

"I don't want to overshadow Daisy and Vincent's surprise—whatever it is."

"We'll wait for the right moment."

"Today's a big day on so many levels."

Sam saw a spark of anxiety though she quickly doused it. "A good day," he said.

"A very good day." She smiled then, raked her gaze over his naked torso. "Why are you sitting so far away?"

"I'm wondering the same thing."

"We've got an hour or so to kill," she said, shifting so the sheet fell away. "Got any ideas?"

"A few." Sam devoured the sight of her naked flesh, shedding his boxers and freeing the erection he'd been sporting for the last five minutes. "How about we play doctor?"

"Lucky you," she said, grazing her fingers along long, hard Johnson. "I've got a cure for your condition."

Dressed and prepared for the day, Harper and Sam made their way to the elevator and down to the main floor a half hour before their scheduled breakfast with the senior CLs and Tasha. Sam wanted to do a preliminary walk around the pool. He wanted to know the lay of the land. He'd make an excellent bodyguard for celebrities, Harper thought, even though he didn't swing that way. Sam was low profile. She liked that about him. His grounded calm was a gift for everyone around him. Harper was determined to cultivate and hone that quality for herself. It would make her a better publicist. A better wife and mother. Calm, she imagined, would prove advantageous in the future whenever things got dicey with Ben and Mina. And surely there would be bumps in the road with her and Sam. It wouldn't always be like this between them—this honeymoon high.

Holding hands, they made their way outside. The sun was bright, the air dry and warm and hinting toward sizzling. Harper and Sam slid on their sunglasses in tandem as they moved toward the glittering aqua pool. Her gaze immediately flew to the makeshift stage. A brightly striped canopy offered a patch of shade and protection from the heat. The set was modest. Yellow and red club chairs with a matching sofa, a couple of tables, a potted palm. A little to the left a portable bar and on either side large television screens that would feature B-roll. Tech crews were busy setting and wiring visual and audio gear—sound boards, lighting, monitors, computers, cameras.

Harper was familiar with the drill and felt confident and serene as she took in what she knew would be overwhelming for the Cupcake Lovers—except maybe Sam who never got rattled. She glanced over and saw him scoping the perimeter. Harper did the same, trying to take in the scene through his eyes. She assumed he was noting every point of entry. The distance from the small audience seating to the stage.

The pool area was dotted with tables, striped umbrellas, chaise lounges, and the occasional desert palm. A wide-open area. Nowhere to hide except within the crush of spectators. Security guards would be stationed and circulating. There would be crowd control. There would be order and procedure. Now that she was on site, Harper had no doubt that Sam and Jayce and friends would easily locate Edward. She was starting to feel irritated more than fearful regarding the man's intrusion.

"What are you going to do with Edward once you find him?" Harper asked.

"We'll steer him away from the scene and lay down the law, so to speak."

"What if he won't go quietly?"

"Ian's badge will come in handy in that regard. Jayce is scary persuasive and I'm particularly motivated to end this bullshit."

"Don't hurt him."

Sam shifted, looking down at her over the rims of his Ray-Bans. "What?"

"If he insults me or threatens me or you, if he's looking for a fight—"

"I won't give him one. Not with my fists anyway." Sam touched her arm. "I know how you feel about violence, hon. And I know some part of you feels sorry for Edward. Nash said he can work magic and get Wilson on the first flight back to Canada. Jayce and Ian will make sure he gets on that flight, since I have to stay here for the show. You won't have to deal with any of this. You won't have to see him." He angled his head. "Unless you want to."

Harper wondered what she would even say and instantly knew she'd said everything in her letter. She'd found her closure. By not seeing Edward now she wasn't running away, she was moving forward. "I don't need to see him."

Sam pressed his lips to her forehead and Harper absorbed the affection and calm.

She caught sight of movement and a wave and saw Val coming their way. "Come on, Rambo," Harper teased, "Val wants to meet her eye candy."

Daisy figured if her old heart gave out, if she keeled over face-first in her oatmeal, or bit the dust while dishing cupcakes with Brice and Kaylee, she'd die the happiest woman on this planet.

Last night she'd married a man who put a spring in her step and a zing in her ticker. A man who could lip-twitch better than Elvis, although, of course, the jumpsuited singer who'd rocked their blue suede shoes hadn't been the real Elvis. Still, that impersonator probably practiced his twitches and swivels in the mirror and she was pretty sure Vincent had never practiced.

After leaving the chapel they'd met up with the rest of their gang minus Sam and Harper. Daisy thought it was sweet that the younger couple had stolen away on their own. She secretly hoped they were doing some mattress dancing in addition to sightseeing. The more she saw those two together, the more she knew they were meant to be. She hoped things were going as well between Adam and Peppy.

As for Daisy and Vincent, they'd floated through dinner and the magic show on a cloud of love. They danced under the stars while watching an amazing fountain show. At the end of the night, after breaking the news of their marriage to their friends, they'd boogied in the hotel lounge until midnight. After that they'd gone back to their room for some private cuddly time.

Daisy went to sleep happy and woke up happy. Now

they'd gathered with the CLs for a breakfast buffet, and with every passing second, happy climbed a notch. To her surprise Jayce had flown in to watch them live and in person on stage, plus he had some business, he said. And Nash rolled out of bed early (early for him) to join them all for breakfast. So exciting to be joined by more family! By the time they stepped on stage with Brice and Kaylee, Daisy imagined she'd be downright giddy!

She looked up from her Spanish omelet and squealed. "Here they come!"

"Such a striking couple," Judy said.

"Too bad they missed out on the festivities last night," Helen said.

"Can you believe they went to bed so early? Where's their sense of fun?" Ethel asked.

Daisy snickered. "Who says they weren't having fun?"

"Who says they were sleeping?" Vincent asked while pouring syrup on his waffles.

Daisy snickered some more.

"Sorry we're late," Harper said as she and Sam neared the table. "Got tied up with a short preshow chat with Val."

"Everything still on track?" Daisy asked.

"We're good to go," Harper said.

"Should be fun," Sam said, even though Daisy knew he wasn't thrilled about being on television. She knew he was here to support the club and probably as a favor to Harper. Sam was a good man, and if Daisy wasn't mistaken, he looked awfully content.

"Did you get the good-luck texts from everyone?" Daisy asked. "Rocky, Chloe, Dev, Monica, Rae and Luke—"

"My phone's been pinging all morning," Sam said with a slight smile.

"Mine, too," Harper said, sweeping her gaze around the long and crowded table. "Where's Tasha?"

"Tasha's having breakfast in her room with her husband," Daisy said. "Apparently she doesn't do buffets," she added with a snort.

"But Jayce and Nash are here," Helen said. "Such a nice surprise."

"They're over there," Ethel said, "grabbing something from the buffet."

"You two go fill your plates. When you're all seated, Vincent and I will share our news."

"Can't wait," Harper said.

"We'll hurry," Sam said.

Daisy leaned into Vincent as they walked away—hand in hand. "They look happy."

"Very happy," Vincent said. "Looks like you were right about Sam and Harper, Petunia. And you might be two for two."

"What do you mean?"

"When Nash first came in he told me he spoke with Adam this morning. Peppy got a job with a band in Nashville."

"What?"

"She hit the road at dawn." He raised a brow. "Adam went with her."

Daisy gawked. "For good?"

"For now."

"That sounds promising."

"Definitely interesting."

Daisy smiled. She couldn't predict the future, but she did trust her gut. "I foresee great happiness for that girl."

"Glad to hear it," Vincent said.

By the time Sam and Harper and Jayce and Nash were seated, Daisy had already ordered a round of mimosas for the table. "The seniors already know, but this will be news for you four." She squeezed Vincent's hand. "Speedy and I got hitched!"

There was a slight hesitation, a moment of surprise, then the younger set beamed and the well-wishing and hugs commenced. Daisy hoped they got the same cheerful reaction when she shared the news with her stick-up-the-butt son and his stick-up-the-butt eldest.

Nash offered a toast and they all drank to Daisy's and Vincent's health and happiness.

Sam cleared his throat. "As long as we're sharing good news . . ." He and Harper held up their left hands and everyone saw the rings and gasped. "I know it's unexpected—"

"Not by me," Daisy said with a yip. "I saw it in the stars!" She waved her napkin at a waitress while the others expressed their joy. "More mimosas!"

THIRTY-SIX

It was a beautiful day. Sunny. Hot but dry. Breezy, but not too breezy.

Hotel security was efficient and plentiful. The production and tech crew worked flawlessly. Brice and Kaylee were personable and professional and went out of their way to make all of their guests feel welcome, visiting them prior to the show in the makeshift tented green room located a few feet from the stage.

Daisy, Ethel, Helen, Judy, and Tasha were anxiously awaiting their moment to take the stage. Harper had worried they'd be overwhelmed by all the high-tech gear and general production atmosphere. They weren't. Daisy and her pals were especially excited about a chance to share stories regarding the history and mission of the club. After one face-to-face with Tasha, Harper had no doubt the beautiful woman would charm Brice's socks off and she'd definitely light up the stage with the sentimental story about her mom and grandmother, both former CLs. But Harper also recognized Tasha's deep need for attention, recognition, and probably respect. Harper knew her type all too well. Appearing on national TV and grabbing fifteen minutes of fame was probably a much bigger deal to Tasha than to any of the other CLs. She was a little snooty and a lot polished, but Harper didn't dislike Tasha Burke. She understood her and even felt a little sorry for her.

Meanwhile, Tasha's husband—also kind of snooty, but definitely in love with his wife—was seated in the VIP area along with Vincent, and Helen's husband, Daniel.

Sam . . . Sam was somewhere out there with Edward. He'd taken off with Jayce, Nash, Tripp, and Ian an hour before spectators started gathering. Even though they'd split up, they were in touch via their phones. The whole time they'd been prowling the premises for Edward, Harper had concentrated on doing her job while keeping one eye peeled for Edward herself.

What if he slips past them?

She'd nipped the negative what if in the bud, but remained alert all the same. Alert and on pins and needles. She'd busied herself putting the Cupcake Lovers at ease, reminding them they went on after Oksana, a Russian performer who dazzled audiences with acrobatic skills and hula hoops. She reminded them that Brice and Kaylee would take the lead, prompting them throughout the feature. They'd cover the history and mission of the club, stories related to baking and charity events. They'd talk soldiers and cupcakes, and the recipe book. There'd be a Q&A with the audience. As a bonus spectators would be gifted with their own copy of *Cupcake Lovers Delectable Delights: Making a Difference One Cupcake at a Time* on behalf of Brice and Kaylee.

Somewhere toward the end of her pep talk, Harper got a text from Sam. Her heart pounded as she read: GOT HIM. B WITH U IN A FEW.

She froze up with a mix of elation and dread. That meant Sam and his team had whisked Edward away. It meant that Sam and Edward were in the midst of a confrontation. She just wanted it to be over. She wanted Sam here beside her and Edward gone.

The Cupcake Lovers were scheduled to take the stage about twenty minutes into the show which was about five minutes from now. She refrained from texting, WHERE ARE YOU, and a heartbeat later she heard, "Here I am."

Sam hugged her from behind, spoke close to her ear. "It's all good."

So Sam had issued his threat of a harassment charge? A restraining order? The "I'll make your life hell" speech as dictated by Jayce who was privy to some not so legal computer tricks? So Edward had buckled and was now being escorted back to the airport by Jayce, Nash, Tripp, and Ian?

Before she could ask for details, Sebastian tapped Sam's shoulder. "We need to wire you with a mic, Sam."

The production assistant dragged Sam away and Harper grabbed hold of the back of a chair for stability. She felt dizzy with relief, blindsided by the anticlimactic moment. She realized suddenly that deep down she'd expected something horrible to happen.

Instead Sam and friends had saved the day—a peaceful takedown. Everything was fine. She let out a shaky breath, rubbed the ache in her chest until she felt a tiny blip of glee. A smile touched her lips as she glanced over and saw Sam huddled with the other CLs—all wired and ready to go. Everyone but Daisy.

"What the—"

Harper whirled and knocked into five feet of cocoa-brown fur.

Oh, no.

"Are my antlers straight?" she asked then used her paw to give Harper a playful nudge. "Don't look so horrified, Slick. I checked with Kaylee first and she said it would be a hoot!"

A twenty-minute feature flew by in a heartbeat. Harper had watched from the sidelines, tears filling her eyes as each and every member of the attending Cupcake Lovers shared sentimental memories and uplifting stories all revolving around cupcakes and their mission to bring joy to soldiers and their families. She never realized Judy had a dry sense of humor or that Ethel had lost her first husband in a foreign conflict. She learned that Helen could bake one hundred and twenty different cupcake recipes from memory. Daisy had been Daisy—except for when she was Millie Moose—and Tasha had dazzled. Sam had endured Kaylee's none-too-subtle flirtations, remaining quiet for the most part until he'd spoken as a former soldier, sharing his personal experiences when it came to receiving care packages while serving overseas.

The audience loved them. Brice and Kaylee praised them. And Harper knew, without a doubt, that recipe book sales as well as outright donations to charities supporting the military would spike and soar. It was her proudest moment as a publicist and she felt honored to call the Cupcake Lovers friends.

As for Sam, Harper loved him so much it hurt. She wanted to hug him and tell him as soon as he stepped offstage, but he whispered, "I need to borrow you. Can we duck out for a few minutes?"

Pulse skipping, she moved to Sebastian, telling him she'd be back and asking him to please keep an eye on the ladies who were settling back in the green room to watch the rest of the show while being treated to fruity cocktails.

Sam guided her quietly along the sidelines, away from the crowd, away from the pool. Once inside the building, he pulled Harper aside. He gently grasped her shoulders. "Edward wants a moment with you."

Her heart hammered. "What?"

"I was wrong about his reasons for being here, hon. Yes, when he originally booked the flight it was with foul intentions. But then he received your lengthy, heartfelt letter and my short, but heartfelt phone call. Maybe it's because it's been three years now, maybe it's because something you said finally got through to him, and I know, soldier to soldier, I gave him pause regarding his behavior." Sam squeezed her shoulder. "I need you to breathe, babe."

She nodded, unaware that she'd been holding her breath, grateful that Sam had a grip on her because she felt a little woozy.

"He decided not to cancel his reservation and instead to fly out here to close this chapter of your lives in person. He's just a few steps away, in the lounge with Jayce and the guys. Nash stepped up his return flight so time's an issue." Sam pulled her into his arms, held her tight and spoke close to her ear. "You don't have to see him, Harper. But I think you, and Mr. Wilson, would benefit if you did."

She held Sam tight, absorbed his calm, his words. She was speechless and she couldn't believe what he'd said, although she very much wanted to. She licked her lips and eased away. She nodded.

Sam took her hand and led her around the corner, into a quiet, dimly lit lounge. She saw Jayce and Nash first, and when they stood, Edward, who'd been sitting with his back to her, rose as well.

Harper approached the man and Jayce and friends jockeyed to the sidelines. Harper noted how much older Edward looked. Three years of bitterness and grief had been unkind to him. Still, his posture was ramrod straight, his gray hair buzzed. He wore creased trousers and a neatly tucked polo shirt. He didn't extend a hand in greeting and neither did she, but she did move closer.

Sam stayed near, but far enough away to suggest he was giving them privacy.

"Harper."

"Mr. Wilson."

He cleared his throat, bolstered his shoulders.

Harper clasped her hands in front of her, her thumb brushing her wedding ring. She relaxed a little, but she didn't smile.

"I'm sure Sam filled you in and I'm not comfortable articulating my feelings. Especially since I'm still wrestling with a few. So I'll make this brief. Your letter . . . I acknowledge your words and sentiments and I believe them. You won't be hearing from me again. I wish you and Sam well."

Harper squeezed her fingers together, still at a loss for words, not sure any were needed.

Edward reached down and pulled a large plastic bag from his over-the-shoulder briefcase. "These were among Andrew's belongings. They're some of the letters you wrote to him while he was overseas. There's also a journal." He cleared his throat again—a gruff staccato sound that bumped Harper's heart to her throat. "Andrew jotted down some of his experiences, his musings while he was away. The, uh, references to battle, they're rough. You may want to skip those. But the parts about you . . ." He passed her the bag, full of crinkled envelopes and a small brown book. "I thought you might want these."

As he backed away, Harper licked her lips, clutching her and Andrew's words to her aching stomach.

Edward picked up his briefcase, checked his watch. "I should be going."

Jayce, Nash, and Tripp moved out ahead of him, and the gentleman she didn't know—Ian, she assumed—took up the rear.

Edward nodded at Sam then at Harper as he passed.

She turned slowly, watching him go, her heart lightening with his every step. "Mr. Wilson. Thank you," she said, when he looked over his shoulder. "I wish you peace."

Her mind was whirling, but Harper didn't have time to slump into a seat and decompress. She had to get back to the Cupcake Lovers, to the show that would soon be wrapping. She had a job to do.

Sam touched her elbow. "You okay?"

She nodded, looked down at the bag clutched in her hands. "I'm not sure I want to read Andrew's journal."

"From what Edward said, I'm guessing there are several pages in there expressing Andrew's love for you."

"It's the pages referring to whatever horrors he saw, whatever he experienced, that broke him . . . I'm not sure I want to know."

"I doubt Andrew would want you to know those specifics. I know I wouldn't."

She held Sam's gaze. "My feelings for Andrew and what we shared are separate from what I feel and share with you."

"As are my feelings for Paula and my feelings for you. One relationship doesn't negate the other."

"So you don't mind if I keep the journal?"

"I don't mind."

"Although I may never read it."

"I understand."

She blew out a breath, feeling the weight of the world lift away. "I need to get back."

"I know."

Holding her past in her hands, she turned to leave then abruptly swiveled and rushed into the arms of her present and future. "I love you, Sam."

His body molded to hers, their hearts beating in tandem—hard and fast—as he cupped her face, looked into her eyes and hugged her soul. "I love you, Harper."

He kissed her and the world sparkled. *This*, she thought, *is happy.*

"I could tack on a couple of days," Sam said, "treat you to a fairy-tale honeymoon."

She thought about that, and though it appealed, something else called to her more. "Would you mind if we went back tomorrow as planned?"

He raised a brow.

"Remember when you said, home is where the heart is?" She smiled up into his eyes. "My heart is in Sugar Creek with you and the children. Bowling and burgers? Miss Kitty fashion shows and superhero movies? Snuggling with you in our own bed? I couldn't spin a better honeymoon."

EPILOGUE

Seven months later
Sugar Creek, VT

Harper typed fast and furious, trying to bullet-point her publicity agenda for the Cupcake Lovers' latest charity project before the ideas flew out of her head. She'd been finding it harder and harder to concentrate on business. She was preoccupied with family.

Never more so than today.

Summer with Sam and the kids had been a delight, giving new meaning to the cliché: honeymoon phase. Monica and Leo had welcomed twin boys into the world, and soon after Rae and Luke had welcomed Jillian—the cutest baby girl in Sugar Creek with the exception of her slightly older cousin Lily. There'd been several family celebrations—big and small. And of course there were the traditional Sunday dinners at Rocky and Jayce's house. With the exception of Daisy and Vincent, not everyone made every dinner, but they all caught up with each other at some point during the week. The Monroes and their extended clan were tightknit and ever growing. Harper finally had what she'd always dreamed of.

A family.

It was more challenging and vastly more wonderful than she'd ever imagined. And it was about to get better.

Maybe.

Ignoring a fluttery feeling in her stomach, Harper focused hard on her computer screen. The sooner she finished this publicity plan, the sooner she could join Sam and the kids downstairs. Ben and Mina had decided the Christmas tree they'd trimmed just after Thanksgiving was in dire need of more decorations. There was scarcely a spare needle on the massively tall spruce, but who was she to argue? Day by day, as a family, they'd infused this house with joy and warmth, and dozens of beautiful memories. Either Mary's spirit had at last crossed over to join her beloved Joseph or she was simply too happy to be sad. The house fairly burst with vibrant, loving energy.

Speaking of . . .

"Mom-*eee!*"

Harper turned just as Mina skidded into the room. She'd traded her signature tiara for an elf's cap—albeit a pink elf's cap—and sported a brown moustache—compliments of hot cocoa. Harper's chest swelled with love. "What's up, baby?"

The animated imp, who'd just recently turned six, thrust a smartphone at Harper. "Daddy said you forgot this."

No longer plugged in twenty-four/seven, Harper had been forgetting her phone a lot. She was too busy living her own life and managing the needs of family as opposed to the needs of virtual strangers. She skimmed new messages, noting a text from Daisy regarding the annual Cupcake Lovers' holiday party. It would be Harper's first. She couldn't wait.

"Are you coming down soon, Mommy?"

"Very soon."

"Ben made popcorn and now we're sticking a needle and thread through it. Only I stuck myself." She held up her tiny index finger. "See?"

Sam had already applied a princess adhesive strip, and

Harper was sure it was nothing. All the same, Mina sniffed back crocodile tears. Luckily Harper had a lot of practice with drama queens. "Stupid needle," she said, then kissed the tip of Mina's finger. "Better?"

"Mommy magic!" Beaming, she skipped from the room.

Harper stemmed her own tears—joyful tears—and focused back on work. Even if she only hit the highlights . . .

Her phone blipped with a new text.

Sam.

MISS YOU.

More warm fuzzies. Harper glanced at the time, then her barely-there agenda. Had she really been at it for an hour? "Screw it."

She powered off and hurried downstairs. She heard Christmas music and laughter. Smelled pine needles and freshly baked peppermint cupcakes. Sam was mending a nutcracker's broken leg. Mina was dancing with a stuffed reindeer. And Ben was hard at work on his popcorn garland.

Harper moved in behind her creative son and squeezed his shoulder. He'd taken his time, placing every ornament and tinsel strand just so. "The perfect touch for the most beautiful tree in Sugar Creek."

Ben didn't look up, but she caught his crooked smile and the shy affection in his voice. "Thanks, Mom."

Mom. The most special word in the world, she'd decided, alongside love.

Sam caught Harper's gaze and winked, causing her heart to dance along with Mina and her furry reindeer.

Harper battled emotional tears while counting her lucky stars. She thanked Mary for pulling her to Sugar Creek and Sugar Creek for introducing her to the Cupcake Lovers. She blessed each and every member for inspiring her to be a better person and for exposing her to the love of her life. She'd fought hard against the fall, but, looking back, she'd been a goner from their adrenaline-charged first meeting. She'd agreed to marry Sam in order to obtain a green card. She'd been prepared for a business arrangement and instead had been gifted with a passionate, caring husband and two amazing children.

Perfect.

How many times in the last few months had Sam declared their lives perfect? She glanced at her wedding band. Four diamonds winked back. Diamonds that represented their family—only now they didn't.

Assaulted by stomach jitters, Harper nodded toward three empty mugs and a plate of cupcake crumbs. "Who's up for eggnog and Christmas cookies?"

A unanimous "me" had Harper scrambling toward the kitchen. "Get it together," she told herself. She'd only been living with this secret since morning. She'd feel better once she told Sam.

Maybe.

What if he wasn't happy about her rocking their perfect boat? What if Ben and Mina resented the change? What if—

"Need some help, Slick?"

Harper started at the sound of her husband's voice. "No, I'm good. Thanks," she added without making eye contact. She willed her hands and mind steady as she poured four servings of alcohol-free eggnog.

Sam moved in, turned, and lazed back against the counter. "Learned some family gossip today. You'll get the dirt tomorrow at dinner, but if you want the early scoop—"

"Always." She sprinkled nutmeg on their tasty treats, all too aware of the tasty treat standing beside her. Sam's presence was unnerving and exhilarating. God, she loved this man.

"After months of maintaining a long-distance relationship, Peppy's moving home to be with Adam."

"She's quitting that band?"

"In order to focus more on her true passions. Songwriting and Adam."

Harper smiled. "That's nice."

"That resort he bought is thriving under his management. The pub is small but perfect if Peppy gets the itch to perform her tunes."

"Bonus." Harper liked Adam. Everyone liked Adam. His happily-ever-after had been long in the making. "Daisy and Vincent must be thrilled." A good grounded man for Vincent's impetuous, artistic granddaughter.

"There's more," Sam said, while helping Harper to reach the cookie tin stashed on top of the fridge. "Between his poker winnings and several smart investments, Nash is buying Starlight Airfield."

"Wow."

"And he's hiring Joey to manage it."

The goth-girl Cupcake Lover with super-smart business skills. "I wonder if Daisy had a hand in that?" Harper asked as she arranged colorful cookies on a festive Santa plate.

"Why would she?"

"Nash is on her family bucket list."

"Oh, right."

"Joey has a huge crush on Nash and Daisy knows it. Most everyone knows." She snorted. "Except Nash."

"Should be interesting," Sam said, clearly amused. "There's more."

"Aren't you the gossip monger?"

"Jayce and Rocky adopted another dog."

"That makes three. Geez. You know, Ben's been asking for a puppy for Christmas—"

"We're having a baby."

Harper froze.

"You seemed to be wrestling with breaking the news to me, so I thought I'd help out."

She stared at the eggnog and cookies, too anxious to meet his gaze. "How—"

"When I took out the trash I spied—"

"The home pregnancy test box."

Sam finessed her into his arms and bade her gaze. "Did you think I wouldn't be happy?"

"Are you?"

"Aren't you?"

"It's just we never talked about this. I was on birth control, only I guess I screwed up."

"Lucky us."

"Really?" Oh, God. Her voice squeaked and a honking fat tear rolled down her cheek. "What about Ben and Mina?"

"A baby brother or sister? Come on." He thumbed her cheek dry. "Better than a puppy."

Harper raised a brow.

Sam grinned. "Okay. We'll get the puppy, too."

Heart bursting, Harper pulled her husband down for a passionate kiss. Lost in the magic, she barely heard the kitchen door swing open.

"Oh, gee," Mina said. "They're at it again."

"You're the one who told them to watch that stupid, mushy *Twilight* movie," Ben said.

"Except Daddy's not all sparkly."

Sam nuzzled Harper's ear. "Only on the inside." Then he made her head swim with another brief, but hot kiss.

The kids groaned, then raced forward.

Mina took the cookie plate. "We picked out a Christmas movie."

"Kind of sappy, but not mushy," Ben said, while nabbing the tray of eggnog.

Sam smiled at the kids, "We'll be right there," while palming Harper's belly and enchanting her soul.

"Take your time," Ben said, with a teasing snort.

Mina made smooching noises, then giggled.

Weak-kneed and heart full, Harper absorbed the love in the room, knowing their happily-ever-after had only just begun.

HONORARY CUPCAKE LOVERS

Submitted Recipes from On-Line Members

RECIPE 1

GINGERBREAD CUPCAKES
(submitted by Gina Husta of New Jersey)

Ingredients
2 cups flour
1 cup brown sugar
1 ¼ tsp. baking soda
2 tsp. ground ginger
1 ½ tsp. cinnamon
¼ tsp. ground allspice
½ tsp. plus an extra pinch salt
½ cup plus 2 tbsp. molasses
¾ cup water
¾ cup butter
2 eggs, slightly beaten

Directions
- Preheat over to 350 degrees F
- In a large bowl, combine flour, brown sugar, baking soda, ginger, cinnamon, allspice, and salt.

- In sauce pan over low heat, combine molasses, water and butter. Stir constantly until it simmers–immediately remove from heat.
- Gently whisk hot mixture into dry ingredients. Mix until thoroughly blended. Add slightly beaten eggs. Mix well.
- Fill the cupcake liners about 2/3 full with batter.
- Bake for about 15 to 20 minutes. Ovens may vary. When a toothpick comes out clean when inserted into middle of cupcake, they are done.
- Let cool.

For frosting
- 6 ounces cream cheese, softened
- 2 tbs. butter softened
- ½ tsp. vanilla extract
- 2 cups confectioners' sugar

Gradually beat cream cheese with butter until light and fluffy, add vanilla extract. Slowly add 2 cups of confectioners' sugar, beat for about 3 minutes. If desired, add a sprinkle of crystallized ginger on top of each frosted cupcake.

◇◇

RECIPE 2

KEY LIME CUPCAKES WITH COCONUT BUTTERCREAM FROSTING
(submitted by Mary Stella of Florida)

Makes 24 cupcakes.

The most successful batches of cupcakes from this

recipe are the ones where the batter is not overbeaten. It's also best if you're fortunate enough to have access to actual key limes, rather than key lime juice from a bottle.

Use quality ingredients instead of bargain brands of all-purpose flour, sugar, butter, and milk. Have all ingredients at room temperature.

Ingredients for Cupcakes
3 cups of all-purpose white flour
2 tsps. baking powder
½ tsp. salt
1 cup whole milk
2 tsps. pure vanilla extract
3 tbsp. key lime juice
1 tbsp. key lime zest
1 cup (2 sticks) unsalted butter
2 cups granulated sugar
2 large eggs
4 large egg whites (whisked to frothy but not whipped to peaks)

Directions
- In separate bowl, sift together flour, baking powder and salt. Whisk to thoroughly combine.
- In small bowl, mix together milk, vanilla, key lime juice and key lime zest
- In mixing bowl, cream butter until pale, light and fluffy. Slowly add sugar, beating until incorporated in butter and fluffy.
- Slowly add eggs and egg whites until just mixed into sugar and butter. Don't overbeat.
- Alternate adding the flour/baking powder/salt mix-

ture with the milk/vanilla/key lime mixture–approximately half of each at a time. Mix together each time at low speed and don't overbeat. Stop mixer periodically to make sure all ingredients are incorporated.

- Line cupcake pans with liners. Use an ice cream scoop or a quarter cup measuring cup to distribute batter evenly in each liner. Start with conservative scoops. You can "top them off" later. Do not over fill.
- Bake in preheated 350 degree oven for approximately 23 minutes. Check doneness with toothpick. When inserted, toothpick should come out clean. Cool pans on a wire rack before frosting.

Coconut Buttercream Frosting
4 cups powdered confectioners' sugar
2 tsps vanilla
½ cup (one stick) unsalted butter, softened
1–1 ½ tbsp. of coconut oil
Splash of coconut water (optional)
Approx. 1–3 tbsp. of whole milk (Amount depends on if you use coconut water)

Directions
- In a mixer on low speed, mix together all of the ingredients except the milk. Check the thickness and consistency. It should be slightly thick. Gradually add in a little bit of milk at a time, mix, and check again. If you need more milk to achieve desired consistency, do so. If you've added too much milk, mix in a little bit more powdered sugar.
- Once cupcakes are cool, you can either frost them evenly with the coconut frosting, or fill a bag and pipe on frosting as desired. Sprinkle with slivers of

slightly toasted coconut, candy pearls, or the other edible decoration of your choice.

◇◇◇

RECIPE 3

QUICK AND EASY CHOCOLATE CUPCAKES WITH CARAMEL FILLING
(submitted by JoAnn Schailey of Pennsylvania)

Ingredients
Devil's Food cake mix (moist)
Classic Caramel Sundae Syrup (Can be found near the ice cream section of most food stores.)
1 can of milk chocolate icing or vanilla icing (Do not use low sugar or whipped varieties.)

Directions
- Bake Devil's Food Cupcakes according to the directions on the package. Don't forget to put cupcake liners in the cupcake pans.
- Use an apple corer or knife to cut a plug about 1/3 the depth of the cupcake. Remove the plug and trim off the excess to 1/8 inch, keeping the top of the plug intact. Squeeze Caramel Sundae Syrup into cupcake opening until almost full. Replace plug. Refrigerate for at least 10 minutes.
- Microwave icing on 50% power for 10 seconds. The icing will be very thin. Frost cupcakes. The cupcakes will have a shine. Cool in the refrigerator. You can add a small amount of vanilla Easy Frost (no fuss frosting) to the top of the chocolate cupcakes.

RECIPE 4

CHOCOLATE STILETTO CUPCAKES
(submitted by JoAnn Schailey of Pennsylvania)

Ingredients
Devil's Food Cake Mix (moist)
Milk Chocolate chips
Pepperidge Farm Milano Milk Chocolate Cookies (or a similar substitute)
Pepperidge Farm Pirouette Crème Filled Wafers (or a similar substitute) (Chocolate Hazelnut or any other filling)
Can of Milk Chocolate Icing

Directions
- The Pirouette Wafer will be used as the stiletto. The Milano Cookie will be the sole of the high heel. The cupcake will be the front of the high heel. Now it's time to play with your food.
- Bake cupcakes as directed on package. You can use a mini cupcake pan or a regular cupcake pan. Melt chocolate chips in the microwave using 50% power for 1 minute or less depending on the amount of chips used. Stir melted chocolate. Cut an opening on the angle a ½ inch from the side of the cupcake. Put chocolate on one end of the Milano cookie and insert into the angled opening.
- Each Pirouette Wafer can make 2 stilettos. Cut the Pirouette Wafer on a slant and dip one end in the melted chocolate. Use the melted chocolate to affix the "stiletto" to the Milano cookie which you

hold on an angle (The stiletto should be close to the edge of the cookie.) Remove the cupcake paper and trim a small amount off the bottom of the cupcake so that the cupcake will be in proportion to the high heel and stiletto. Refrigerate the cupcake, Milan cookie, and Pirouette wafer until the combination holds together. If you used a regular size cupcake pan, trim the excess cupcake so that it looks like the front of the high heel. The mini cupcake pan will be closer to the size you want.

- Microwave the icing on 50% or 10 seconds. Use a spoon to coat the cupcake. You don't need to coat the cookies. Enjoy!

<><><><><><><><><><><><><><><><><><><><><><><><><><><><>

RECIPE 5

Moody Blue Cupcakes
(submitted by Dawn Jones of New Jersey)

All Ingredients
1 box Signature French Vanilla Cake Mix
½ cup of fresh blueberries
1 can vanilla frosting
1 jar of blue sugar (any brand)

Cake Directions
- Preheat oven according to cake mix.
- Line a muffin pan with paper liners.
- Follow directions on box.
- Add the fresh blueberries to the batter and stir lightly
- Pour or spoon batter into the prepared liners.

- Bake according to cake mix, Cake is done when it springs back to the touch or when a cake tester or toothpick inserted in center comes out clean.
- After you frost the cupcakes sprinkle with the blue sugar.

Makes about 24 cupcakes, depending on the cake mix